Helen and Frida by Anne Finger

A young girl imagines an encounter between Helen Keller and
Frida Kahlo—two women with
very different approaches to their disabilities.

Hearing the Sunrise by Nancy Scott

Re-imagining sight, this eloquent poem sings to the reader, as the
rising sun serenades its author.

Her Sense of Timing by Stanley Elkin

An old curmudgeon living by the "cripple code" struggles to fend
for himself after his wife of 36 years leaves him.

Pony Party by Lucy Grealy

Adolescent memories of pony parties and the stares of
laughing children help a cancer patient explore herself
and her place in the world.

Heart Ear by Edward Nobles

A moving ballad about hearing loss exposes a world of
hidden disabilities.

*P.H.*reaks* adapted by Doris Baizley and Victoria Ann-Lewis

An enlightening portrait that challenges us to look at the
disabilities of Franklin Roosevelt and Henri Matisse in a new way.

STARING BACK

The Disability Experience
from the Inside Out

KENNY FRIES is known for his teachi[ ] [in the]
area of disability rights. The winner o[ ]
for AIDS Writing, and the recipient [ ]
The MacDowell Colony, he is the au[thor of]
Night After Night and *Anesthesia*, as wel[ ]
(Dutton). He lives in Northampton, Massachusetts, and teaches in
the MFA in Writing Program at Goddard College in Vermont.

STARING BACK

The Disability Experience
from the Inside Out

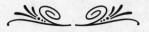

EDITED BY

Kenny Fries

A PLUME BOOK

PLUME
Published by the Penguin Group
Penguin Putnam Inc., 375 Hudson Street,
New York, New York 10014, U.S.A.
Penguin Books Ltd, 27 Wrights Lane,
London W8 5TZ, England
Penguin Books Australia Ltd, Ringwood,
Victoria, Australia
Penguin Books Canada Ltd, 10 Alcorn Avenue,
Toronto, Ontario, Canada M4V 3B2
Penguin Books (N.Z.) Ltd, 182–190 Wairau Road,
Auckland 10, New Zealand

Penguin Books Ltd, Registered Offices:
Harmondsworth, Middlesex, England

First published by Plume, an imprint of Dutton Signet,
a member of Penguin Putnam Inc.

First Printing, October, 1997
10 9 8 7 6 5 4 3 2 1

Pages 411–414 constitute an extension of this copyright page.

  REGISTERED TRADEMARK—MARCA REGISTRADA

LIBRARY OF CONGRESS CATALOGING-IN-PUBLICATION DATA:

Staring back : the disability experience from the inside out / edited
    by Kenny Fries.
        p.   cm.
    ISBN 0-452-27913-5
    1. Physically handicapped, Writings of the, American.
    2. Physically handicapped—United States—Literary collections.
    3. American literature—20th century.   I. Fries, Kenny.
PS508.P56S73   1997
810.8'0920816—DC21   97-15209
                                                                                CIP

Printed in the United States of America
Set in New Baskerville
Designed by Leonard Telesca

PUBLISHER'S NOTE
Some of these selections are works of fiction. Names, characters, places, and incidents
either are the products of the authors' imagination or are used fictitiously, and any
resemblance to actual persons, living or dead, events, or locales is entirely coincidental.

for
Marilyn Golden and Anne Finger,
distinguished disability rights activitists,
whose combination of love and wisdom
has graced so many lives

and to all those with disabilities
who have not yet been given the opportunity
to be heard

Contents

FICTION

THEATER

It is hereby prohibited for any person who is diseased, maimed, mutilated, or deformed in any way so as to be an unsightly or disgusting object to expose himself to public view.

—1911 City of Chicago Ordinance

Introduction

~⊱ ⊰~

KENNY FRIES

I — *"You would have been better off dead."*

We've been shadow spirits lost between our nondisabled (for most of us) upbringing and our Disability lessons in life.
—Carol Gill, Ph.D.

Throughout history, people with disabilities have been stared at. Now, here in these pages—in literature of inventive form, at times harrowingly funny, at times provocatively wise—writers with disabilities affirm our lives by putting the world on notice that we are staring back.

Throughout history, those who live with disabilities have been defined by the gaze and the needs of the nondisabled world. Many times, those who live with disabilities have been isolated in institutions, experimented upon, exterminated. We who live with disabilities have been silenced by those who did not want to hear what we have to say. We have also been silenced by our own fear, the fear that if we told our stories people would say: "See, it isn't worth it. You would be better off dead."

Seven years ago, I began searching for the words with which to begin speaking about my own experience living with a congenital physical disability, a disability I was born with for no known scientific reason, a disability with no medical name except the generic "congenital deformities of the lower extremities"—one way of saying I was missing bones in both legs. In the summer of 1989, I took the initial steps of finding the language, unearthing the images, shaping the forms with which I could express an experience I had never read about before, so that my experience as a person with a disability could become meaningful to others.

What I remember most about that summer is wanting to throw all those drafts away, not thinking them poems. Not having a role model in whose steps I could follow, unsure of my own identity as both a writer and a person who lives with a disability, I felt like one of those "shadow spirits" Carol Gill writes about, unable to successfully meld on the page the nondisabled world I lived in with my experience of being disabled in that world.

I also felt afraid. I felt a fear that Anne Finger was writing about at almost the same time in *Past Due: A Story of Disability, Pregnancy and Birth*. In *Past Due* Finger recounts her experience at a feminist conference when she talked about her inhumane treatment as a child in the hospital because of complications from polio. After Finger publicly shares her story, a colleague says: "If you had been my child, I would have killed you before I let that happen. I would have killed myself, too." Finger reacts:

> *My heart stops. She is telling me I should not be alive. It is my old fear come true: That if you talk about the pain, people will say, "See, it isn't worth it. You would be better off dead."*

If this was a friend's response to Finger's experience, how would my friends, not to mention those who did not know me, react to what I had to say? And, after knowing what I had gone through how could they believe there was so much more to living with my disability than pain?

All the work in *Staring Back* speaks of the disability experience from the inside out. At Gallaudet College, when the hearing majority on its board rejected two qualified deaf educators for president to select yet another hearing candidate, student-government president Greg Hilbok asked, "Who has decided what the qualifications for president should be?" And historian Paul K. Longmore similarly asks: "Who should have the power to define the identities of people with disabilities and to determine what it is they *really* need?"

The work in *Staring Back* not only shows that pain is but a small part of living life as a person with a disability. It also challenges us to look anew at the disabilities of FDR and Matisse (Doris Baizley and Victoria Ann-Lewis's "P.H.*reaks"), the lives of Helen Keller and

Frida Kahlo (Anne Finger's "Helen and Frida"), and the work of Stephen Hawking (Mark O'Brien's "The Unification of Stephen Hawking"); to redefine what is meant by cure (Marilyn Hacker's "Cancer Winter"); to understand hidden disabilities (Edward Nobles's "Heart Ear"); to expand definitions of cross-cultural identities (Nancy Mairs's "Carnal Acts," Lynn Manning's "The Magic Wand," David Manuel Hernández's "Back Problems," Johnson Cheu's "Banana Stealing"); to reimagine the reality and symbol of a wheelchair (Katinka Neuhof's "Blue Baby"); to become familiarized with other ways to speak (Elizabeth Clare's "Learning to Speak"); to hear (Raymond Luczak's "Ten Reasons Why Michael and Geoff Never Got It On," Terry Galloway's "The Engines Are Roaring"); to see (Nancy Scott's "Hearing the Sunrise"); and to read (Stephen Kuusisto's "Learning Braille at 39," Ved Mehta's "Bells"); to realize we are all part of one world (selections from John Hockenberry's "Walking with the Kurds," Adrienne Rich's "Contradictions: Tracking Poems"), not as separate and disparate as we might think.

If asked what, besides the fact that all the work in *Staring Back* has been written by a writer who lives with a disability and that I chose each piece first and foremost for its literary merit, binds together this work, I must reply it is the theme of human connection—connection with the past, connection with one another, connection with our bodies, connection with our selves.

II — "... lost to the crip world, like Mayan dialects and Incan shopping lists."

Disabled characters shaped by the old moral and medical models of representation have filled the stage for generations. . . . Consider the ease of signaling Good vs. Evil by the addition of a hook, peg leg, or eye patch. Introductory guides to screenwriting actually counsel fledgling authors to give their villain a limp or an amputated limb. The seductive plot possibilities of the medical model with its emphasis on overcoming and cures are irresistible in creating conventional dramatic structure. . . . The medical model also serves as terrific PR for one of the most powerful American myths: the rugged individual who pulls himself up by his own bootstraps. . . . We Americans want our characters to exist outside the forces of history and economics, making it easier to fix things and achieve a happy ending, which, in the case

*of disabled depiction, translates into the cheerful cripple who over-
comes all obstacles by sheer willpower.*

—Victoria Ann-Lewis

Jessica Hagedorn, editor of *Charlie Chan Is Dead*, an anthology of
contemporary Asian-American fiction, lists "the demeaning legacy
of stereotypes" that is ingrained in American popular culture. She
lists Fu Manchu, Stepin Fetchit, Sambo, Aunt Jemima, Amos 'n
Andy, Speedy Gonzalez, Tonto, and Little Brown Brother. She dis-
cusses how the stereotypical images of Asian-Americans have now
evolved into subtler stereotypes such as "the greedy, clever, Japanese
businessman, and the Ultimate Nerd, the model Asian-American
student, obsessed with work, excelling in math and computer science."

Those of us who live with disabilities have seen ourselves represented in a similar fashion. As Leonard Kriegel points out in his
essay "The Wolf in the Pit of the Zoo," "images of disability have
always been important in Western myth and literature. Probably all
cultures link physical handicap to moral culpability. Stigmatization,
one suspects, is prehistorical." For Kriegel, "the classical world saw
the cripple as the man defined by others (Hephaestus) and the man
defined by his own excess (Oedipus). They balanced the cripple as
cuckold with the cripple who goes beyond the boundaries acceptable to the 'normal.' "

In a statement remarkably similar to that of Hagedorn, Kriegel
writes: "For generations, blacks were asked to see their lives in the
comic obsequiousness of Butterfly McQueen and Stepin Fetchit. An
image can become so pervasive that its consequences are swallowed
up by the welter of moralistic judgments it calls forth."

And so it has been for the representation of people with disabilities in literature. The "Demonic Cripple" (Shakespeare's Rich-
ard III, Melville's Ahab, Mary Shelley's Frankenstein, the villains
in James Bond films) is "not merely physically crippled. . . . He is
crippled in the deepest spiritual sense. His injury subsumes his
selfhood." David Hevey, the British disabled photographer and disability theorist, points out, "As these stories unfold, the antihero's
limited and semi-human consciousness glimpses their tragic existence through the cracked mirror of their hatred for themselves.
They all live bitterly, with the festering sores of their loss, until their
self-destructive rage explodes on to the world."

The Demonic Cripple inspires fear. Whereas the Demonic Cripple's spiritual opposite, the "Charity Cripple" (Dickens's Tiny Tim, Melville's Black Guineau), according to Kriegel, functions "to perpetuate in his audience the illusion of its own goodness." These characters "charm because they relieve guilt. The Charity Cripple, ever evident on telethons, inspires pity." Kriegel points out that both the Demonic Cripple and the Charity Cripple define the disabled person from outside their existence, "one image reflecting the culture's fears and taboos, the other its sentimentality and aspirations."

The onset of the Civil War and society's increasing industrialization, with its demands made by the more rapid pace of machines and production lines geared to nondisabled norms, both gave rise to an increase in the population of those who live with disabilities. In fact, Victor Finkelstein, the first disabled social scientist to put forth a theory that shifts the discussion of disability away from the personal tragedy and medical view of disability, persuasively argues that it is with industrialization that the disabled for the first time began to be segregated out into the class of "deserving poor," as opposed to the "undeserving poor" (those who were physically able but did not work). This segregation was often literal, as asylums, hospitals, and segregated schools were created to deal with the disabled who were excluded from what Hevey calls the "time-as-money norm."

Both Finkelstein and Hevey point out that it was during this phase that the relationship between the disabled and society becomes a paradox of mutual dependency—the disabled dependent upon the "impairment specialists workers" or "the disability professions" that were geared to either care or cure; and the institutions and their employees now capitally dependent on those who depend on them.

But after industrialization, even with the advent of the Realist novelists such as William Dean Howells, those in the United States were still not forced by their literature to look at the actual lives of those who were disabled. Nor were these new social relationships dealt with in our novels and on our stages as the nineteenth century expired.

It is not until the 1930s and 1940s that we see a change in the attitude of American writers. But once again, as Kriegel points out, instead of the actual lives of the disabled being examined and portrayed, in work by writers such as Nathanael West, Dalton Trumbo, Nelson Algren, and Carson McCullers, we see depictions of the disabled, though still horrific, "come increasingly to reflect the values of being an outsider for writers who have growing doubts about the society spawned by insiders." In other words, the reality of living with a disability is not depicted, but disability becomes a stand-in, a metaphor, for the social outcast, who is marginalized, misunderstood.

Kriegel ends "The Wolf in the Pit of the Zoo" with a look at the "by no means central character" of William Einhorn in Saul Bellow's *The Adventures of Augie March.* In Einhorn, Kriegel identifies another literary classification of the disabled: the Survivor Cripple, "who is stronger than those on whom he is dependent." Bellow writes: "He wouldn't stay a cripple, Einhorn; he couldn't hold his soul in it."

Looming behind the Survivor Cripple is the image of Franklin Delano Roosevelt, who has arguably done more than anyone else to put forth the image of the disabled person who succeeds despite his disability, by overcoming it. With this image of FDR we are firmly rooted in the medical model of disability. According to this model, disability is defined by the impairment and how an individual deals with the impairment, as opposed to the more current notion that disability be seen as a category defined by a social structure that does not allow full participation of the disabled in the life of the culture.

To most, FDR is viewed as overcoming his disability because he went to great lengths to keep the true nature of his disability hidden. But to John Hockenberry, a fellow wheelchair user, FDR "was the champion self-loather who was never photographed in a chair during his lifetime and made a deal with the press corps that he was never to be even seen in crutches."

Hockenberry points out that if "FDR had done wheelies or had worked out advanced transferring techniques on the White House furniture, that information is lost to the crip world, like Mayan dialects or Incan shopping lists." To this day, as evident in the decision not to show FDR in his wheelchair in the original design for the memorial currently being built on The Mall in Washington, D.C., details of history have been, "put out with the trash," suppressed to disabled and nondisabled alike.

The damage done by this medical model of disability has been considerable. If an individual is defined by his or her ability to overcome a disability, he or she is viewed as a failure if unable to do so. Instead of seeing the forces outside the body, outside the impairment, outside the self, as essential to a disabled person's successful negotiation with an often hostile society (whether the barriers be financial, physical, or discriminatory), this view of disability, where cure and eradication of difference are the paramount goals, puts the blame squarely on the individual when a physical impairment cannot be overcome.

Historian Longmore, echoing Finkelstein, points out that this medical model also provides for great economic benefit to those interests which include "vendors of over-priced products and services; practitioners who drill disabled people in imitating the 'able-bodied' and deaf people in mimicking the hearing; a nursing-home industry that reaps enormous revenues from incarcerating people with disabilities." This model creates a class of "incurable" persons with disabilities who are "confined within a segregated economic and social system and to a socioeconomic condition of childlike dependency."

But that's not all. The defining of the disabled individual by what he or she can and cannot physically achieve, how productive he or she might or might not be, comes with great psychic cost. When the only choices deemed viable—kill it or cure it—are choices that would erase the disability, what does this say about how society disvalues disabled lives?

As we move away from viewing disability within the confines of the moral and medical models, we are moving toward a social definition of disability. As Finkelstein so concisely states, whereas in the medical model the "focus of attention is firmly on the physically impaired individual," now it shifts to where "the focus is the nature of society which disables physically impaired people."

That the disability experience is not solely rooted in bodily impairment is evidenced by how the definition of disability changes from society to society. What is considered a disability in some societies, for example club- or flatfeet, is not considered a disability in others. And what was considered a disability in our culture years ago would no longer be considered a disability today. Consider poor eyesight before eyeglasses. For example, in a preliterate, agrarian society, visual acuity, the need to read print or traffic signs, was not necessary or could be compensated for.

Viewed from this perspective, it is clear that it is the barriers, both physical and attitudinal, that need to be changed, not the impairments or the bodies with which we live. I have asked many disabled persons what causes them more difficulty, the disability itself or the discriminatory barriers put in their way. The answer is overwhelmingly the latter.

The experiences of those with disabilities prove there are countless different and effective ways of moving through the world. But old models die hard. Literature, which reflects the richness of the different ways we conceptualize how we live within the world and the ways the world lives within us, thankfully does not, and should not, conform to the dictates of current political or social discourse. In *Staring Back*, along with the literature that clearly espouses the social model of looking at disability, can be found vestiges of the moral and medical models of disability that have been internalized. We come up against these habits of thinking in ourselves as much as we actually come up against them in our daily lives.

However, what distinguishes the creative nonfiction, poetry, fiction, and drama in *Staring Back* is that each work chosen is the product of a disabled writer's encounter with his or her disability experience. Whether it be reflected in the poems of Larry Eigner, whose disability profoundly affected the work's actual composition, or the fiction of Marcia Clay, whose experience as a young woman with cerebral palsy is strikingly rendered in "Wolf," at the center of each work is an experience told from the perspective of a writer who lives with a disability. (This is so even when the work's central focus is not disability or a disabled character, as in Andre Dubus's luminous "Dancing After Hours.")

What differentiates the oppression and discrimination of the disabled from other traditionally marginalized groups is that in one quick instant—a slip in the bathtub, a virus-borne disease—anyone can join us, the disabled (currently estimated at 49 million in the United States). In fact, at some point in our lives, each and every one of us, sooner or later, will be, whether for short term or long, in some way disabled. Because of this fact, those of us who live with disabilities are viewed with a fear, though irrational, that is perhaps too easy to understand. (And if there's one thing those who live with disabilities understand it is change; e.g. Barbara Rosenblum's "Living in an Unstable Body.") Ultimately, those of us who live with disabilities are too often treated as unwelcome reminders of the mortality that is the fate of us all.

III — *"The task is to explore or create a disability culture"*

Beyond proclamations of pride, deaf and disabled people have been
uncovering or formulating sets of alternative values derived from
within the deaf and disabled experience. . . . They declare that they
prize not self-sufficiency but self-determination, not independence but
interdependence, not functional separateness but personal connection,
not physical autonomy but human community.

—Paul K. Longmore

A lot has happened during the seven years since I first began to write about my experiences living with a disability. In 1990, the process, which began in 1968 with the Architectural Barriers Act and sections 504 and P.L. 94–162 of the Rehabilitation Act of 1973, culminated in the passage and signing into law of the Americans with Disabilities Act, called the most far-reaching civil rights legislation since the Civil Rights Act of 1964. As historian Longmore points out, with the ADA's passage, even as the "quest for civil rights, for equal access and equal opportunity, for inclusion" continues, we have moved on to a second phase, which he defines as "a quest for collective identity" in which "the task is to explore or to create a disability culture."

In many ways, *Staring Back* mirrors this very quest. In 1994, I was invited to and participated in the historic "A Contemporary Chautauqua: Disability and Performance," organized by Victoria Ann-Lewis, director of Other Voices, at the Mark Taper Forum in Los Angeles. That April weekend, prominent artists with disabilities gathered from all across the United States to perform, read, teach, learn, talk, and get to know one another. That we had something valuable to offer was evidenced not only by an audience hungry to share our work, not only by the overcrowded classes, the sold-out performances, the TV camera crews from CNN and WNET, but also by the lasting nurturing relationships forged by many of the participant artists.

When leaving Los Angeles, I did not know the writing I was exposed to that weekend would eventually form the core of this anthology. But returning home, I knew I was not alone in my struggle to give voice to the disability experience, an experience which throughout history has been marginalized or coopted, if not ignored. It is my hope that *Staring Back* is just one step in an ongoing effort to bring the lives of those of us who live with disabilities closer to the center where a truer understanding of the richness of our lives can be forged.

Kenny Fries
Northampton, Massachusetts
January 1997

I am grateful to acknowledge the following texts, from which I have quoted and read before writing the introduction to *Staring Back*:

Ann-Lewis, Victoria, "The Secret Community: Disability and the American Theater," in *The Disability Rag and Resource*, September/October 1995.

Finger, Anne, *Past Due: A Story of Disability, Pregnancy and Birth.* (Seattle: The Seal Press, 1990).

Finkelstein, Victor, *Attitudes and Disabled People.* (New York: World Rehabilitation Fund, 1980).

Gallagher, Hugh Gregory, *FDR's Splendid Deception.* (New York: Dodd, Mead and Company, 1985).

Gill, Carol, quote taken from *The Disability Rag and Resource*, September/October 1995, p. 5.

Hagedorn, Jessica, introduction to *Charlie Chan Is Dead: An Anthology of Contemporary Asian-American Fiction.* (New York: Viking, 1993).

Hevey, David, *The Creatures Time Forgot: Photography and Disability Imagery.* (London: Routledge, 1994).

Hockenberry, John, *Moving Violations: War Zones, Wheelchairs, and Declarations of Independence.* (New York: Hyperion, 1995).

Kriegel, Leonard, "The Wolf in the Pit in the Zoo," in *Falling into life* (San Francisco, North Point Press, 1991).

Longmore, Paul K., "The Second Phase: From Disability Rights to Disability Culture," in *The Disability Rag and Resource*, September/October, 1995.

NONFICTION

Pony Party

LUCY GREALY

My friend Stephen and I used to do pony parties together. The festivities took place on the well-tended lawns of the vast suburban communities that had sprung up around Diamond D Stables in the rural acres of Rockland County. Mrs. Daniels, the owner of Diamond D, took advantage of the opportunity and readily dispatched a couple of ponies for birthday parties. In the early years Mrs. Daniels used to attend the parties with us, something Stephen and I dreaded. She fancied herself a sort of Mrs. Roy Rogers and dressed in embarrassing accordance: fringed shirts, oversized belt buckles, ramshackle hats. I'd stand there holding a pony, cringing inwardly with mortification as if she were my own mother. But as we got older and Stephen got his driver's license, and as Diamond D itself slowly sank into a somewhat surreal, muddy, and orphaned state of anarchy, we worked the parties by ourselves, which I relished.

We were invariably late for the birthday party, a result of loading the ponies at the last minute, combined with our truly remarkable propensity for getting lost. I never really minded, though. I enjoyed the drive through those precisely planned streets as the summer air swirled through the cab of the pickup, rustling the crepe-paper ribbons temporarily draped over the rear-view mirror. When we finally found our destination, we'd clip the ribbons into the ponies' manes and tails in a rather sad attempt to imbue a festive air. The neighborhoods were varied, from close, tree-laden streets crammed with ranch-style houses to more spacious boulevards dotted with outsized Tudors. Still, all the communities seemed to share a certain carbon-copy quality: house after house looked exactly like the one next to it, save for the occasional cement deer or sculpted shrub. A dog would always appear and chase the trailer for a set number of lawns—some mysterious canine demarcation of territory—before suddenly dropping away, to be replaced by another dog running and barking behind us a few lawns later.

I liked those dogs, liked their sense of purpose and enjoyment and responsibility. I especially liked being lost, tooling through strange neighborhoods with Stephen. As we drove by the houses, I gazed into the windows, imagining what the families inside were like. My ideas were loosely based on what I had learned from TV and films. I pictured a father in a reclining chair next to a lamp, its shade trimmed with small white tassels. Somewhere nearby a wife in a coordinated outfit chatted on the phone with friends while their children set the dinner table. As they ate their home-cooked food, passing assorted white serving dishes, they'd casually ask each other about the day. Perhaps someone would mention the unusual sight of a horse trailer going past the house that day. Certain that these families were nothing like my own, a certainty wrought with a sense of vague superiority and even vaguer longing, I took pride and plea-sure in knowing that I was the person in that strangely surreal trailer with the kicking ponies and angry muffler, that I had driven by their house that day, that I had brushed against their lives, and past them, like that.

Once we reached the party, there was a great rush of excitement. The children, realizing that the ponies had arrived, would come running from the backyard in their silly hats; their now forgotten balloons, bobbing colorfully behind them, would fly off in search of some tree or telephone wire. The ponies, reacting to the excitement of new sounds and smells, would promptly take a crap in the drive-way, to a chorus of disgusted groans.

My pleasure at the sight of the children didn't last long, however. I knew what was coming. As soon as they got over the thrill of being near the ponies, they'd notice me. Half my jaw was missing, which gave my face a strange triangular shape, accentuated by the fact that I was unable to keep my mouth completely closed. When I first started doing pony parties, my hair was still short and wispy, still growing in from the chemo. But as it grew I made things worse by continuously bowing my head and hiding behind the curtain of hair, furtively peering out at the world like some nervous actor. Unlike the actor, though, I didn't secretly relish my audience, and if it were possible I would have stood behind that curtain forever, my head bent in an eternal act of deference. I was, however, dependent upon my audience. Their approval or disapproval defined everything for me, and I believed with every cell in my body that approval wasn't written into my particular script. I was fourteen years old.

"I *hate* this, why am I doing this?" I'd ask myself each time, but I had no choice if I wanted to keep my job at the stable. Everyone who worked at Diamond D had to do pony parties—no exceptions. Years later a friend remarked how odd it was that an adult would even think to send a disfigured child to work at a kid's party, but at the time it was never an issue. If my presence in these backyards was something of an anomaly, it wasn't just because of my face. In fact, my physical oddness seemed somehow to fit in with the general oddness and failings of Diamond D.

The stable was a small place near the bottom of a gently sloping hill. Each spring the melting snow left behind ankle-deep mud that wouldn't dry up completely until midsummer. Mrs. Daniels possessed a number of peculiar traits that made life at Diamond D unpredictable. When she wasn't trying to save our souls, or treating Stephen's rumored homosexuality by unexpectedly exposing her breasts to him, she was taking us on shoplifting sprees, dropping criminal hints like some Artful Dodger.

No one at Diamond D knew how to properly care for horses. Most of the animals were kept outside in three small, grassless corrals. The barn was on the verge of collapse; our every entry was accompanied by the fluttering sounds of startled rats. The "staff" consisted of a bunch of junior high and high school kids willing to work in exchange for riding privileges. And the main source of income, apart from pony parties, was hacking—renting out the horses for ten dollars an hour to anyone willing to pay. Mrs. Daniels bought the horses at an auction whose main customer was the meat dealer for a dog-food company; Diamond D, more often than not, was merely a way station. The general air of neglect surrounding the stable was the result more of ignorance than of apathy. It's not as if we didn't care about the horses—we simply didn't know any better. And for most of us, especially me, Diamond D was a haven. Though I had to suffer through the pony parties, I was more willing to do so to spend time alone with the horses. I considered animals bearers of higher truth, and I wanted to align myself with their knowledge. I thought animals were the only beings capable of understanding me.

I had finished chemotherapy only a few months before I started looking in the Yellow Pages for stables where I might work. Just fourteen and still unclear about the exact details of my surgery, I made my way down the listings. It was the July Fourth weekend, and Mrs. Daniels, typically overbooked, said I had called at exactly the right moment. Overjoyed, I went into the kitchen to tell my mother I had a job at a stable. She looked at me dubiously.

"Did you tell them about yourself?"

I hesitated, and lied. "Yes, of course I did."

"Are you sure they know you were sick? Will you be up for this?"

"Of *course* I am," I replied in my most petulant adolescent tone.

In actuality it hadn't even occurred to me to mention cancer, or my face, to Mrs. Daniels. I was still blissfully unaware, somehow believing that the only reason people stared at me was because my hair was still growing in. So my mother obligingly drove all sixty-odd pounds of me down to Diamond D, where my pale and misshapen face seemed to surprise all of us. They let me water a few horses, imagining I wouldn't last more than a day. I stayed for four years.

That first day I walked a small pinto in circle after circle, practically drunk with the aroma of the horses. But with each circle, each new child lifted into the tiny saddle, I became more and more uncomfortable, and with each circuit my head dropped just a little bit further in shame. With time I became adept at handling the horses, and even more adept at avoiding the direct stares of the children.

When our trailer pulled into the driveway for a pony party, I would briefly remember my own excitement at being around ponies for the first time. But I also knew that these children lived apart from me. Through them I learned the language of paranoia: every whisper I heard was a comment about the way I looked, every laugh a joke at my expense.

Partly I was honing my self-consciousness into a torture device, sharp and efficient enough to last me the rest of my life. Partly I was right: they *were* staring at me, laughing at me. The cruelty of children is immense, almost startling in its precision. The kids at the parties were fairly young and, surrounded by adults, they rarely made cruel remarks outright. But their open, uncensored stares were more painful than the deliberate taunts of my peers at school,

where insecurities drove everything and everyone like some looming, evil presence in a haunted machine. But in those backyards,
where the grass was mown so short and sharp it would have hurt to
walk on it, there was only the fact of me, my face, my ugliness.

This singularity of meaning—I *was* my face, I *was* ugliness—
though sometimes unbearable, also offered a possible point of escape. It became the launching pad from which to lift off, the one
immediately recognizable place to point to when asked what was
wrong with my life. Everything led to it, everything receded from
it—my face as personal vanishing point. The pain these children
brought with their stares engulfed every other pain in my life. Yet
occasionally, just as that vast ocean threatened to swallow me whole,
some greater force would lift me out and enable me to walk among
them easily and carelessly, as alien as the pony that trotted beside
me, his tail held high in excitement, his nostrils wide in anticipation
of a brief encounter with a world beyond his comprehension.

The parents would trail behind the kids, iced drinks clinking,
making their own, more practical comments about the fresh horse
manure in their driveway. If Stephen and I liked their looks (all our
judgments were instantaneous), we'd shovel it up; if not, we'd tell
them cleanup wasn't included in the fee. Stephen came from a
large, all-American family, but for me these grownups provided a
secret fascination. The mothers had frosted lipstick and long bright
fingernails; the fathers sported gold watches and smelled of too
much aftershave.

This was the late seventies, and a number of corporate head-
quarters had sprung up across the border in New Jersey. Complete
with duck ponds and fountains, these "industrial parks" looked
more like fancy hotels than office buildings. The newly planted suburban lawns I found myself parading ponies on were a direct result
of their proliferation.

My feelings of being an outsider were strengthened by the reminder of what my own family didn't have: money. We *should* have
had money: this was true in practical terms, for my father was a
successful journalist, and it was also true within my family mythology,
which conjured up images of Fallen Aristocracy. We were displaced
foreigners, Europeans newly arrived in an alien landscape. If we had
had the money we felt entitled to, we would never have spent it on
anything as mundane as a house in Spring Valley or as silly and
trivial as a pony party.

Unfortunately, the mythologically endowed money didn't materialize. Despite my father's good job with a major television network, we were barraged by collection agencies, and our house was falling apart around us. Either unwilling or unable, I'm not sure which, to spend money on plumbers and electricians and general handymen, my father kept our house barely together by a complex system of odd bits of wire, duct tape, and putty, which he applied rather haphazardly and good-naturedly on weekend afternoons. He sang when he worked. Bits of opera, slapped together jauntily with the current top forty and ancient ditties from his childhood, were periodically interrupted as he patiently explained his work to the dog, who always listened attentively.

Anything my father fixed usually did not stay fixed for more than a few months. Flushing our toilets when it rained required coaxing with a Zenlike ritual of jiggles to avoid spilling the entire contents of the septic tank onto the basement floor. One walked by the oven door with a sense of near reverence, lest it fall open with an operatic crash. Pantheism ruled.

Similarly, when dealing with my mother, one always had to act in a delicate and prescribed way, though the exact rules of protocol seemed to shift frequently and without advance notice. One day, running out of milk was a problem easily dealt with, but on the next it was a symbol of her children's selfishness, our father's failure, and her tragic, wasted life. Lack of money, it was driven into us, was the root of all our unhappiness. So as Stephen and I drove through those "bourgeois" suburbs (my radical older brothers had taught me to identify them as such), I genuinely believed that if our family were as well-off as those families, the extra carton of milk would not have been an issue, and my mother would have been more than delighted to buy gallon after gallon until the house fairly spilled over with fresh milk.

Though our whole family shared the burden of my mother's anger, in my heart I suspected that part of it was my fault and my fault alone. Cancer is an obscenely expensive illness; I saw the bills, I heard their fights. There was no doubt that I was personally responsible for a great deal of my family's money problems: ergo, I was responsible for my mother's unhappy life. During my parents' many fights over money, I would sit in the kitchen in silence, unable to move even after my brothers and sisters had fled to their bedrooms. I sat listening as some kind of penance.

The parents who presided over the pony parties never fought, or at least not about anything significant, of this I felt sure. Resentment made me scorn them, their gauche houses, their spoiled children. These feelings might have been purely political, like those of my left-wing brothers (whose philosophies I understood very little of), if it weren't for the painfully personal detail of my face.

"What's wrong with her face?"

The mothers bent down to hear this question and, still bent over, they'd look over at me, their glances refracting away as quickly and predictably as light through a prism. I couldn't always hear their response, but I knew from experience that vague pleas for politeness would hardly satisfy a child's curiosity.

While the eyes of these perfectly formed children swiftly and deftly bored into the deepest part of me, the glances from their parents provided me with an exotic sense of power as I watched them inexpertly pretend not to notice me. After I passed the swing sets and looped around to pick up the next child waiting near the picnic table littered with cake plates, juice bottles, and party favors, I'd pause confrontationally, like some Dickensian ghost, imagining that my presence served as an uneasy reminder of what might be. What had happened to me was any parent's nightmare, and I allowed myself to believe that I was dangerous to them. The parents obliged me in this: they brushed past me, around me, sometimes even smiled at me. But not once in the three or so years that I worked pony parties did anyone ask me directly what had happened.

They were uncomfortable because of my face. I ignored the deep hurt by allowing the side of me that was desperate for any kind of definition to staunchly act out, if not exactly relish, this macabre status.

Zoom lenses, fancy flash systems, perfect focus—these cameras probably were worth more than the ponies instigating the pictures. A physical sense of dread came over me as soon as I spotted the thickly padded case, heard the sound of the zipper, noted the ridiculous, almost surgical protection provided by the fitted foam compartment. I'd automatically hold the pony's halter, careful to keep his head tight and high in case he suddenly decided to pull down for a bite of lawn. I'd expertly turn my own head away, pretending I was only just then aware of something more important off to the side. I'd tilt away at exactly the same angle each time, my hair falling in a perfect sheet of camouflage between me and the camera.

I stood there perfectly still, just as I had sat for countless medical photographs: full face, turn to the left, the right, now a three-quarter shot to the left. I took a certain pride in knowing the routine so well. I've even seen some of these medical photographs in publications. Curiously, those sterile, bright photos are easy for me to look at. For one thing, I know that only doctors look at them, and perhaps I'm even slightly proud that I'm such an interesting case, worthy of documentation. Or maybe I do not really think it is me sitting there, *Case 3, figure 6-A.*

Once, when my doctor left me waiting too long in his examining room, I leafed through my file, which I knew was strictly off-limits. I was thrilled to find a whole section of slides housed in a clear plastic folder. Removing one, I lifted it up to the fluorescent light, stared for a moment, then carefully, calmly replaced it. It was a photograph taken of me on the operating table. Most of the skin of the right side of my face had been pulled over and back, exposing something with the general shape of a face and neck but with the color and consistency of raw steak. A clamp gleamed off to the side, holding something unidentifiable in place. I wasn't particularly bothered; I've always had a fascination with gore, and had it been someone else I'd have stared endlessly. But I simply put the slide in its slot and made a mental note not to look at slides from my file again, ever.

With the same numbed yet cavalier stance, I waited for a father to click the shutter. At least these were photographs I'd never have to see, though to this day I fantasize about meeting someone who eventually shows me their photo album and there, inexplicably, in the middle of a page, is me holding a pony. I have seen one pony party photo of me. In it I'm holding on to a small dark bay pony whose name I don't remember. I look frail and thin and certainly peculiar, but I don't look anywhere near as repulsive as I then believed I did. There's a gaggle of children around me, waiting for their turn on the pony. My stomach was always in knots then, surrounded by so many children, but I can tell by my expression that I'm convincing myself I don't care as I point to the back of the line. The children look older than most of the kids at the backyard parties: some of them are even older than nine, the age I was when I got sick. I'm probably thinking about this, too, as I order them into line.

I can still hear the rubbery, metallic thud of hooves on the trailer's ramp as we loaded the ponies back into the hot and smelly box for the ride back to Diamond D. Fifteen years later, when I see that photo, I am filled with questions I rarely allow myself, such as, how do we go about turning into the people we are meant to be? What relation do the human beings in that picture have to the people they are now? How is it that all of us were caught together in that brief moment of time, me standing there pretending I wasn't hurt by a single thing in this world while they lined up for their turn on the pony, some of them excited and some of them scared, but all of them neatly, at my insistence, one in front of the other, like all the days ahead.

Walking with the Kurds

JOHN HOCKENBERRY

There were legs below. Stilts of bone and fur picking around mud and easing up the side of a mountain near the Turkish border with Iraq. Two other legs slapped the sides of the donkey at each step like denim-lined saddlebags. They contained my own leg and hip bones, long the passengers of my body's journeys, and for just as long a theme of my mind's wanderings.

I was on the back of a donkey plodding through the slow, stunned bleed of the Gulf War's grand mal violence. The war was over. It remained only for Desert Storm's aftermath to mop up the historical details wrung out of Iraq. The Kurds were one such detail. It had taken another war, Desert Storm, for the Kurds to unexpectedly emerge from the obscurity they had received as a reward for helping the Allies during the First World War, nearly eight decades before. The Kurds had helped the Allies again this time, but this was just another detail.

In the calculus of victory and defeat echoing through world capitals and in global headlines, in the first moments of Iraq's surrender there were few details, and fewer human faces. The first pictures of the war were taken by weapons; Baghdad, a city of five million, rendered in fuzzy, gun-camera gray. Snapshots of hangars, bridges, roads, and buildings. No people.

We had won. They had lost.

The winners were well known: they were the faces on billboards. The smiling, enticing face of the West, its prosperity and its busy president, Bush, were known to the youngest schoolchild in the Middle East. In the West only one Middle Eastern face was as prominent, the face of the demon who became the vanquished, the singular, ever-present Saddam Hussein. The other losers were invisible. As time went on the war began to bleed the faces of its true victims.

Here on the Turkish border it was an open artery of Kurdish faces, streaming out of Iraq and down mountainsides in Turkey and Iran as the world's latest refugee population. Under cover of surrender and Western backslapping, Saddam Hussein had uprooted the mutinous Kurds and sent them packing under helicopter gunship fire north and east into nations that are neighbors only on the most recent of maps. To the Kurds, the region from northern Iraq to eastern Syria, southeastern Turkey, and western Iran is all one land: Kurdistan. It has been this way for more than one thousand years of warfare and map drawing. So for these Kurdish refugees, border checkpoint traffic jams were just old insults lost in the latest slaughter.

My fists held tight to the saddle and up we went toward the final ridge on the edge of Iraqi Kurdistan. A village called Üzümlü on the Turkish side was the destination. It lay three or more valleys beyond. There, the horizon contained the spilled wreckage of the refugee exodus from inside northern Iraq. Here it was just mountains against the brisk, gray, clouded sky punched through with brilliant patches of blue. Deep below in the valley roared the Zab River, muddy with the melting snowpack's promise of spring.

In March of 1991 the spectacular sky and the brisk air rimmed with intermittent hot alpine sun was a welcome escape from the visa lines and news briefings, SCUD missile attacks and second guessing of Saddam, Bush, and Schwarzkopf that so dominated the business of covering Desert Storm. I watched the sky while everyone else stared at their own feet. Ahead and behind, Kurdish men in black slacks walked with enormous sacks of bread on their backs. Like a line of migrating ants, a parade of white bundles snaked up the mountain on black legs.

Neither the heroic foot-borne relief efforts, anticipation of the horrors ahead, nor the brilliance of the scenery around me struck home as much as the rhythm of the donkey's forelegs beneath my hips. It was walking, that feeling of groping and climbing and floating on stilts that I had not felt for fifteen years. It was a feeling no wheelchair could convey. I had long ago grown to love my own wheels and their special physical grace, and so this clumsy leg walk was not something I missed until the sensation came rushing back through my body from the shoulders of a donkey. Mehmet, a local

Kurd and the owner of the donkey, walked ahead holding a harness. I had rented the donkey for the day. I insisted that Mehmet give me a receipt. He was glad to oblige. I submitted it in my expense report to National Public Radio. The first steps I had taken since February 28, 1976, cost thirty American dollars.

It was a personal headline lost in the swirl of news and refugees. I had been in such places before. In my wheelchair I have piled onto trucks and jeeps, hauled myself up and down steps and steep hillsides to use good and bad telephones, to observe riots, a volcano, street fighting in Romania, to interview Yasir Arafat, to spend the night in walk-up apartments on every floor from one to five, to wait out curfews with civilian families, to explore New York's subway, to learn about the first temple of the Israelites, to observe the shelling of Kabul, Afghanistan, to witness the dying children of Somalia. For more than a decade I have experienced harrowing moments of physical intensity in pursuit of a deadline, always keeping pace with the rest of the press corps despite being unable to walk. It is the rule of this particular game that it be conducted without a word of acknowledgment on my part. To call attention to the wheelchair now by writing about it violates that rule. My mind and soul fight any effort to comment or complain, even now, years after the events I write about.

This quiet, slow donkey ride was easily the farthest I had gone, out onto a ledge that was never far from my mind during the fifteen years I had used a wheelchair. It was a frightening edge where physical risks loomed like the echoes of loose stones falling into a bottomless canyon, and the place where I discovered how completely I had lost all memory of the sensation, the rhythm, even the possibility of walking. I held on to the saddle or the donkey's neck. The locking of donkey knees and the heavily damped strokes of each donkey leg finding a cushioned foothold in the cold, soft mud of the Iraqi hillside rippled up my hanging limbs and drove into the bones of my arms. My arms were the sentries holding me in place, doing the job of arms and legs once again, as they had for a decade and a half. Though this was the closest to walking that I had felt in all of that time, the job of my arms could not change. FIRST STEPS IN FIFTEEN YEARS. It was a headline composed and discarded, footnote without essay, ridiculous, like the young blond man on the donkey on the mountain. And it was all perfectly true.

In March 1991 I found myself climbing a hillside where civilization was bulldozing a whole people up onto the mud and snow of a place called "no-man's-land" on maps. It was the end of a very long journey; I had arrived in a place that I could not have imagined. In this soupy outpost, the trucks seemed to have arrived long before the roads. As I watched out taxi windows, I could see that there would come a point where the wheelchair would have to be left behind if I was to make it to the place where early reports said hundreds of thousands of civilians were fleeing Saddam Hussein's terror. Wheels of any kind were out in this terrain. Saddam Hussein had chased the Kurds to the edge of pavement and well beyond. In the pockets of snow, starvation, rock and mud, only legs could travel.

The story of the Kurds had drawn me from a hotel room in Ankara, onto a plane to Istanbul, then on a charter flight to Van, an old Kurdish city once part of the Armenian empire, on a long, boring drive to the village of Hakkari and then a plunge through the boulder strewn mountain trails to the border town of Çukurca. I left my wheelchair with the driver from Van beside the road to Çukurca and climbed onto a tawny-colored, medium-size donkey who accepted without a sound what was a more than ample load. Before we began the steep ascent, I had only the time it took to cross a rope and plank bridge in a perilous state of disrepair to figure out how to keep my mostly paralyzed body on the animal's back. We crossed over the raging waters of the Zab River in the first weeks of the spring thaw and began the slow, steep climb toward Üzümlü.

The bare facts of what had happened in Iraq and Kuwait in the initial aftermath of Desert Storm read like a random shooting in America: "World outraged as crazed father attacks neighbor then turns guns on family and self." The truth was not as simple. For one thing, Saddam took great pains to make sure that he would not get hurt. Others were neither so lucky, nor did they have much in the way of control over their destiny. The civilians in Baghdad, the Shia of southern Iraq, and the Kurds of the north were all innocent bystanders, caught in the forty day drive-by shooting that was Desert Storm. Unlike the Kurds, I had some control over my destiny, but in pursuit of this slice of Saddam's long, brutal story I took none of his pains to avoid harm. I would get into northern Iraq any way possible. Whatever difficulties I might encounter in being separated from my wheelchair in the open mountainous country across the border, I would deal with then. I had made this calculation many times before in covering the Middle East, or in deciding to do anything out in a world not known for its wheelchair-friendly terrain.

I had often thought of riding a donkey in the mountains of western America as recreation but had never found the time to orchestrate such a break in space and time. As a vacation it had seemed like a lot of bother, but here, for the sake of a story, the impulse to toss my own wheelchair to the wind was as natural as carrying a notebook is to other journalists. Still, that I would find myself here, holding on for dear life, with no sense of what lay ahead and certainly no way to control events from the top of a donkey, was unsettling. Was I supposed to be here, or was I in the way? To Mehmet the donkey man, I was just another paying customer.

Feeling out of place was an old sensation, almost as old as the paralysis in my legs. It was a feeling I had among friends, among strangers, and just as often when completely alone. I worried when I held up a check-out line at the supermarket. I smiled sheepishly at restaurant patrons as I made my way through the narrow spaces between the tables to my own place. My anonymity torn from me, I interrupted conversations, intruding on peaceful diners. Was it their eyes or mine that said I was in the way until proven otherwise? I could go away or push ahead. Where wheelchairs could not venture, people working together inevitably could. Still, the choice of pushing ahead through the obstacles or just going away was always a matter of selecting the lesser of two evils. Going away was always a defeat. Pushing ahead was never a victory, and asking for help always reduced the score.

The staring began with the trickle of refugees near the village. They walked slowly, mostly downhill now, toward Turkey. They looked up from their feet at the passenger on the donkey. The incongruity suggested neither disability nor pity. The first refugees we met were the least affected by their week-long trek and a harrowing three days in the mud and snowy cold of the mountainous border region. They carried sacks and misshapen crates of clothing and provisions looted from their own hastily departed neighborhoods in Mosul, Sulaimaniya, Zakho, Kirkuk, and Erbil. Some of the women raised their eyes, wondering why a perfectly good donkey should be wasted on a blond Westerner who seemed to be so well-fed. One man suggested to the guide that the donkey would be better suited to carrying a sack of bread, or perhaps a dead or sick person. In Arabic and Kurdish, Mehmet told them that I was a reporter come to see Üzümlü, and that I was unable to walk.

I had been anonymous for a moment; now I was unmasked. The faces of these Kurdish refugees became faces of familiar worry and pity, faces that I had spent so much time thanking. Their concern was appreciated, I told them, but misguided in my case. The men and women gathered around and started to warn me of the dangers ahead. "If you cannot walk, why are you here?" they asked. "There is only death here. People are dying everywhere in Üzümlü. Saddam is killing everyone. Why did America not help us?" they asked. "There is no food. You could die."

I responded just as I did when people wanted to push my chair, or hold a door, or hand me something they thought I was looking at on a supermarket shelf. With a workable, relaxed face of self-assured confidence I could dismiss all of these people politely or rudely, but dismiss them I did. "No need to be concerned," I said. "I've got the door. I am fine. I can make it across the street. No problem. I'm not sick. I don't need a push. I'm not with anyone, no." It was habit, not arrogance that caused me to insist: "I'm just fine here on the donkey in the middle of one hundred and fifty thousand starving, war-terrified refugees."

In Üzümlü, flimsy shelters made of sticks and plastic sheets covered people forced to sleep on crusted mud. A dirty graveyard contained the twenty to fifty people who died each night. The yellow, bloodless, milky-eyed corpse of a child lay next to a partially dug grave. Perhaps two hundred thousand people would pass through here on their way to official Turkish refugee camps. The first had come across minefields, and among the initial group to gather around me and Mehmet and the donkey were a man and the gray-skinned unconscious companion on his back. He had an ugly blackened bandage around his waist, and one of his legs was merely a stump. This man would not make it to the Zab River, let alone the medical facility in Hakkari three hours away by car and already overflowing with casualties. His back and leg had absorbed a mine explosion that had halved his brother. The man carrying him looked at me with authority, pointed at his wounded friend, and said: "There is danger here. He cannot walk . . . we have here many who cannot walk. We have enough," he said with muted anger. "Why are you here?"

I got down off the donkey, sat on the ground, and assembled my tape recorder and microphone. The Kurdish refugees wanted to know why I couldn't walk and if the Iraqis had shot me. Gradually they began to talk.

"The helicopters came and we had to leave. I am a teacher," said one. "I am an engineer," said another.

To an outsider, they were only the sick and the well. Otherwise they were differentiated by the time of day they had decided to flee for the border. Those who fled at night were wearing pajamas under overcoats. Those caught during the day had time to don what looked like their entire wardrobes, especially the children, who stood staring and bundled up like overstuffed cloth dolls. Occasionally someone would walk by in just a thin jacket and torn slacks. Such shivering people explained that they were caught away from home running errands when the gunships came.

Mostly they wanted to talk about "Bush." It was in the bitterest of terms that the leader of Desert Storm was evoked on those cold muddy hills. "Bush is liar. Why he not help us?" "We fight Saddam, but why Bush let Saddam fly helicopters?" They said the word "helicopter" with the accent on the third syllable, and spit it out like an expletive. I sat cross-legged beneath a circle of anger, aiming the microphone to catch the shouting voices.

At that moment, much of the world I knew was reveling in victory. Two days earlier in a conversation with someone from Washington I had learned of the stellar approval ratings for President Bush. Historic peaks in the nineties, enshrining in statistics the apparently unshakable kingship behind the second sacking of Baghdad in a thousand years. As the Kurds might have said, "The warlord Tamerlane did a better job the first time," in 1253. The wind picked up and rattled the plastic sheeting anchored to stubborn mountain shrubs. The plastic made blurry apparitions of the blank young and very old faces inside. A large man stepped up and grabbed my microphone and began to speak in a hoarse, exhausted voice.

"Why is Saddam alive and we are dead? What is for America democracy? Bush is speaking of freedom and here we are free? You see us. They send you to us. You, who cannot stand? You are American, what is America now? Why are you here?" His words echoed out from the hill and mixed with the sobs and squeals of the refugees. To him my presence was an unsightly metaphor of America itself: able to arrive but unable to stand. I could not escape his metaphor any more than I could get off that mountain by myself. These were the questions. And so they remain.

The day was beginning to fade. It was a four-hour ride back down the mountain and at least another hour to file stories to Washington. It was time to go. Mehmet and I hoisted me up onto the donkey and we started our descent. The Turkish army had begun to airlift soldiers by helicopter to the mountaintop to urge the refugees down from Üzümlü and into a camp at a lower elevation. Later the Kurds would discover that this new camp was actually inside Iraq by a couple of hundred yards, a fact Secretary of State James Baker would learn in a photo op visit to the camp three days later. With its own far less headline-grabbing program of Kurdish oppression in southeastern Turkey, the Turkish government made it clear that it did not want the Iraqi Kurds.

Until the biblical scale of the catastrophe was apparent, the U.S. government was inclined to agree with Turkey. James Baker and George Bush spoke of territorial integrity in regards to the Kurdish issue. There would be no partitioning of Iraq, they said. The Kurds would have to move . . . again. The Turkish soldiers on the mountain pass fired their automatic weapons into the air, herding people like cattle. The narrow trail down to a spit of Iraqi border territory near the Turkish town of Çukurca was soon clogged with Kurds.

Donkey riding was a slow business. Without any abdominal muscles, my spine twisted and folded with each step. To sit up straight was to get a brief respite from the sharp back pains, but it could only be sustained for a few moments. I held the entire weight of my upper body in my wrists, rubbery and cramped from hours of gripping. They collapsed with each stumble and downward slide of the donkey, pressing my face helplessly into the mane of my tireless friend.

I hadn't figured that the trip down the mountain would be so much harder than the trip-up. With the donkey angled upward during the ascent, my weight was pulled back, and holding on had been a simple clinging maneuver. With the donkey descending and angled downward in something of a controlled slide, I had to maintain my weight on my hands, balancing my shifting hips with sheer arm and wrist muscle. The alternative was to tumble down onto the rocks or into one of the many ravines. The crush of refugees narrowed the options for my sure-footed companion and had the effect of periodically spooking him. Mehmet had begun to tire of the earlier novel challenge of escorting the paraplegic on the donkey, and was dragging on the harness. He was also aware that the trail was in considerable danger of jamming into a pedestrian gridlock of desperate refugees.

The sounds of Turkish gunfire caused the donkey to lurch, and me to hold tighter. The rhythm of the donkey's forelegs was intoxicating; it vibrated mechanically up my arms. My whole frame was suspended like a scarecrow on two sticks locked at the elbows. Beneath me walked people clutching their belongings and hurrying to get to shelter before the sun set. Their heads wound along the trail stretching to the horizon.

All around me children stopped to relieve themselves in an agony of diarrhea. In the very same soil, the muddy foot tracks of people and animals filled with snowmelt and rainwater, and children stooped to drink from the puddles. They stood up, and their lips were ringed with brown mud like the remains of a chocolate milk shake. I had drunk nothing all day and had eaten nothing either.

If I was different from other reporters it was in the hydrogen peroxide I carried along with microphones, notebooks, audio tapes, cassette recorders, and cash. Peroxide was the most important item, especially here. In this remote area soaked in mud and surrounded by human waste, there were limits to sanitation. While the closest most reporters came to contaminating their own bodies was by eating a piece of local bread with unwashed hands, for me it was quite different. I use a catheter. Every four hours, every day, for the past fifteen years I have had to insert a tube to empty my bladder. It is a detail which can remain fairly discreetly hidden in most situations. While the processes demanding filling and emptying remained just as urgent here, this environment was hardly optimal for maintaining the near-sterile conditions necessary for using a catheter safely. To expose the catheter to the elements for even a few seconds was to risk infection as definitively as using a contaminated hypodermic syringe risked introducing hepatitis, or worse, into the blood.

After two days my hands had become utterly filthy, and my tattered gloves were soaked through with every local soil. At a certain point one can feel the collective momentum of a human tragedy. With overwhelming power, biological forces penetrate skin, culture, geography, careers, and deadlines. The Kurdish refugees clawed through the mountain foliage, plowing up a rich loam of conquered humanity. I did not want to become fertilizer.

It was not the first time I had encountered potentially lethal mud in the course of covering a story. To prevent infections in such situations, I adopted a simple if crude strategy of self-denial that had served me well in the past. I would go into something of an emergency-induced body shutdown. Nothing in; nothing out. No food meant no waste. No water meant no parasites and therefore no infection.

In an environment without anything resembling a toilet, the inability to stand, squat, or balance above the ground meant that the simplest of bodily functions was impossible to perform without making a mess well outside the specifications of a person's normal notions of human dignity. In this place, human dignity was hard to fathom and beside the point.

But to lose control meant certain contamination. Aside from preventive deprivation, I could ration the peroxide carefully, avoid food and water, and pop vitamin C tablets to keep the acid content and therefore the antibacterial chemistry of my urine high. There was no room for error out here. The weakness that came with intense thirst and having starved for three days, along with being an equal number of travel days from any kind of hospital, would give infection an absolutely lethal head start.

So whatever my face conveyed to the concerned refugees coming down the mountain, I was no more fine than they were, and I was about as confused as to why I was here in this barely inhabitable edge of two warring nations. The accumulated delirium of the war, the Kurdish refugees, and my own deprivation made a dirgelike dream of the donkey ride. From this perch I was again as tall as I used to be. I could see the tops of heads and the shoulders all around me laden with leather straps tied to overstuffed suitcases. In this position my knees seemed farther away from my face. My feet were fully out of view. I had to strain to see them below the flanks of Mehmet's donkey. My abdomen was stretched by my extended and hanging leg bones. It gave me the impression that my lungs had grown larger. None of these details would have mattered to anyone else sitting on a donkey. To me they were a richly hued garment of memory and sensation long lost. In this wondrous garment I was invisible.

The joy of these sensations stood out in surroundings overrun with terror and death. I was unknown and unseen here. There were no presumptions about my body. All that people could tell, unless they were told otherwise, was that I was well-fed and blond. Beyond this, nothing was given away. As time went on I ceased even to look like an American journalist. Anonymity intensified the feeling of who I was, where I had come from, and how my own body worked, or didn't. As an American I had no right to be afraid here, I thought. I was safe and distinct from this horror. As a human being I had no way to separate myself from the river of Kurdish flesh making its way toward the valley. In my own invisible way, I was as close to death as they were. As a paraplegic, I was inside a membrane of unspoken physical adversity. There was no reason to expect bodies to function in such conditions, and each additional moment of life required a precise physical calculation. Durability of flesh pitted against the external elements. Each transaction final. The limits fully real. There was no room for mistakes.

I was not alone in contemplating those limits. Each dying person knew who he or she was. Each struggling refugee could see how much they had left to wager. The chill of circumstance made the crowd and myself quiet. Energy was conserved. The well-fed Turkish conscripts ahead and behind swaggered and fired their weapons, breaking the collective silence of one hundred thousand people.

Why was I there? It is an imperative of journalists to get the story. It was an imperative of those civilians to make their way off the mountain. There were others. The global imperatives of America to confront Saddam. The imperative of America to go home and beat the drum or lick its wounds. In victory, the United States lifted off from Iraq just as it did from the embassy roof in Saigon in 1975 following defeat in Vietnam. Some Vietnamese clung to the chopper back then. They imagined that despite the circumstances of defeat, the promises of America might be honored elsewhere.

In 1991 those promises seemed hollow and frozen, archived for unborn historians. The Kurds wondered why in victory the Americans would leave them to the wolves more swiftly and surely than the Cambodians and South Vietnamese were abandoned following America's humiliating defeat in Indochina. Aside from the few colorless platitudes thrown their way from Washington, the Kurds had little to do with the business at hand for a triumphant president and his new world. In the anger of the Kurds there was no expectation that America would find their cause worthy, no expectation that their cries would be heard. They had given up on this America without a message and no interest in moving hearts and minds in Iraq. This time when the American chopper lifted off, no one would bother to hold on. Walking in the mud seemed the surer course now.

Fifteen years after lying in an intensive care unit in Pennsylvania I was near the summit of a mountain on the Iraqi border. If this was another event in the struggle for independence and triumph over physical adversity, what about the people who were dying all around me? Was I here to do something for them, or was it for me?

On a donkey among the Kurds at the end of a dreadful back-lot surgical abortion of a war, the paths of truth and physical independence seemed to diverge. I had no good answer for the Kurdish man who insisted that there were already too many people who could not walk in Üzümlü. Why I had gone to Kurdistan was as complicated a question as why George Bush's army did not in the first weeks after the war. What seemed an unquestionable virtue had become an excuse for doing something in my case, nothing in the president's.

During the Gulf War, President Bush spoke a lot about how America could regain its sense of mission, its confidence as a world leader, and declare independence from a burden of history. But in a war against historical burdens, the wider battlefield is blocked from view. There is no place for the identity of the people who are simply fighting to save their own miserable lives, the lives that never made it onto the American gun-camera videos, the lives of those we called the enemy, or the Kurdish friends in Iraq we never even knew we had until many thousands of them were dead.

I was fighting my own burdens. Holding on to the flimsy saddle and feeling each donkey step in my back and in my cramped and throbbing fingers, I could see that my entire existence had become a mission of never saying no to the physical challenges the world presented to a wheelchair. It was this that had gotten me through a fiery accident and would provide me with a mission upon which I could hang the rest of my life. I had made the decision to get on that donkey when I had gotten out of a hospital bed years before and vowed never to allow the world to push me. I would pull it instead. In Kurdistan I discovered that the world is a much larger place than can be filled by the mission of one man and his wheelchair.

If the Kurds had truly left me alone and gone about the business of only saving themselves, I would just have died right there, holding my tape recorder. They did not. "I'm fine," I said. There on the mountains between Turkey and Iraq, I had lost my way. It was up to Mehmet, the donkey, and me to find my way back.

In the last valley before the river, the steep trail was teeming with refugees. Just eight hours before it had been deserted and tinged with early spring grass; now each bend had been churned into slippery mud. The donkey was having trouble keeping its footing; Mehmet pulled on the harness as the beast locked knees next to a family pushing a wheelbarrow piled with clothes, utensils, a cassette player, and some toys. The animal would not budge, and Mehmet angrily shoved it and yanked on its tail. The donkey made a spitting noise, moaned, and bolted down a steep slope toward the grass. I held on and twisted as the animal half-tumbled off the trail.

Trail was a generous description for the steep, narrow switchback that folded three times along the gravelly slope. With tens of thousands of refugees clogging the trail, the hillside began to look like a rickety shelf of old books shaking in an earthquake. Every few minutes rocks from the upper trail would be dislodged by someone's feet and tumble down on people one and two tiers below. Shouts and screams would greet the stones. A shower of debris was kicked up by the feet of my fleeing donkey. He landed in a hillock of grass at the river's bank and began to munch and graze with a resolve that suggested that his paraplegic reporter carrying duties had ended.

I had slipped off the donkey's back farther up the hill. With an exhausted smile, I rolled onto my back, clutched my bag of equipment, and stared up at the sky. The refugees made a moving silhouette against the fiery dusk sky, and the rope bridge over the river was now in darkness. The only sounds were the roar of the river and the shouts of refugees who argued with Turkish soldiers attempting to control access to the bridge.

The crowd was trying to storm a flimsy bridge that could withstand perhaps twenty people at a time without collapsing. The sound of Turkish weapons fired into the air peppered the din. My arms and cramped fingers ached. It felt good to lie down in the cold, wet grass. But I needed to cross that bridge to have any chance at all of filing a story. Without a donkey there seemed to be no way to even approach it from my repose on the river's bank. I turned my head and saw the muddy water raging in frosty darkness. There was no chance of swimming the Zab. The water churned its way around the canyon toward the Tigris, Baghdad, and the Persian Gulf hundreds of miles away. The opposite bank was a traffic jam of relief trucks and makeshift camps, as flimsy shelters from Üzümlü were erected once again along the road to Çukurca. Flickering fires and headlights made shadows on the rocks. Prone and unable to walk on the bank of an unswimmable river with a runaway donkey lost in a crowd of one hundred thousand refugees seemed to be as good an excuse as any for missing a deadline.

Mehmet was taking my predicament much more seriously than I was. He had brought back three men, and insisted on carrying me up to the bridge on a blanket. On the boggy riverbank the blanket quickly became saturated, making it difficult to hold with a body inside. They dropped me half a dozen times and eventually gave up. I laughed. Mehmet's crew went back to attend to their own places in the line to cross the bridge.

I lay there reveling in being invisible. My sore arms were stiff. There was a certain joy in just lying quietly in the grass while the river and the people swirled around me. For two years, more or less, I had been a correspondent in the Middle East. For all that time I had stood out as an American or as a journalist with a microphone; for fifteen years I had been scrutinized continuously because of my wheelchair. But for that moment in Kurdistan surrounded by thousands of refugees, covered with mud, without a chair, and lying in the grass, I was utterly, completely anonymous.

Mehmet's attempts to move me had brought us closer to the bridge, and the confusion of the mob was almost overhead. Sheep grazed near my head in the growing darkness. Up on the bridge some members of the international press corps had arrived and were shooting pictures. I recognized two faces, though I couldn't remember which newspaper they worked for. But they looked at the man with the backpack and after a moment recognized me. They must have recalled that I used a wheelchair. They looked around with some alarm. No wheelchair to be seen. I shrugged my shoulders at them. I mouthed the words "I'm fine." I chuckled out loud, and said, "I could use a donkey right about now." Like the slow movement of the moon over the sun during an eclipse, my moment of anonymity was passing.

In the end, Mehmet himself, a cigarette in his mouth, carried me on his back up the slope to the bridge. After a screaming argument with the Turkish officer, he carried me across and put me down next to a family with their belongings spread out by the road.

"I am American," I said when asked by a young Kurdish boy.

"Do you know Chicago?" he asked. "I have a brother in Chicago."

I nodded and tried out some broken Arabic on him to pass the time. As darkness fell, the Kurdish taxi driver from Van who had been taking care of my chair for twelve hours found me in the crowd and joyfully hugged me. He had watched the exodus of his Kurdish compatriots with tears in his eyes, and with alarm had watched all day for me to appear in the crowd. He brought my wheelchair over and I hoisted myself into it: it felt so good to move and to feel its support beneath my sore shoulders. There were my feet, just below my knees and my lap, right there below my face. Creased since 1976, my six-foot frame folded itself back into a sitting position once again. After only a day I had forgotten what it felt and looked like.

I took a breath and paused for a moment before I rolled toward where the driver had parked his cab. I looked around. There around me, the noise of the refugees quieted. I saw all eyes watching. In their staring gazes I was home. I waved good-bye. I made the deadline.

Falling into life

LEONARD KRIEGEL

It is not the actual death a man is doomed to die but the deaths his imagination anticipates that claim attention as he grows older. We are constantly being reminded that the prospect of death forcefully concentrates the mind. While that may be so, it is not a prospect that does very much else for the imagination—other than to make us aware of its limitations and imbalances.

Over the past five years, as I have moved into the solidity of middle age, my own most formidable imaginative limitation has turned out to be a surprising need for symmetry. I am possessed by a peculiar passion: I want to believe that my life has been balanced out. And because I once had to learn to fall in order to keep that life mine, I now seem to have convinced myself that I must also learn to fall into death.

Falling into life wasn't easy, and I suspect that is why I hunger for such awkward symmetry today. Having lost the use of my legs during the polio epidemic that swept across the eastern United States during the summer of 1944, I was soon immersed in a process of rehabilitation that was, at least when looked at in retrospect, as much spiritual as physical.

That was a full decade before the discovery of the Salk vaccine ended polio's reign as the disease most dreaded by America's parents and their children. Treatment of the disease had been standardized by 1944: following the initial onslaught of the virus, patients were kept in isolation for a period of ten days to two weeks. Following that, orthodox medical opinion was content to subject patients to as much heat as they could stand. Stiff, paralyzed limbs were swathed in heated, coarse woolen towels known as "hot packs." (The towels were the same greenish brown as the blankets issued to American GIs, and they reinforced a boy's sense of being at war.) As soon as the hot packs had baked enough pain and stiffness out of a patient's body that he could be moved on and off a stretcher, the treatment was ended, and the patient faced a series of daily immersions in a heated pool.

I was ultimately to spend two full years at the appropriately named New York State Reconstruction Home in West Haverstraw. But what I remember most vividly about my stay there was, in the first three months, being submerged in a hot pool six times a day for periods of between fifteen and twenty minutes. I would lie on a stainless steel slab, only my face out of the water, while the wet heat rolled against my dead legs and the physical therapist at my side worked at a series of manipulations intended to bring my useless muscles back to health.

Each immersion was a baptism by fire in the water. While my mind pitched and reeled with memories of the "normal" boy I had been a few weeks earlier, I would close my eyes and focus not, as my therapist urged, on bringing dead legs back to life but on my strange fall from the childhood grace of the physical. Like all eleven-year-old boys, I had a spent a good deal of time thinking about my body. Before the attack of the virus, however, I thought about it only in connection with my own lunge toward adolescence. Never before had my body seemed an object in itself. Now it was. And like the twenty-one other boys in the ward—all of us between the ages of nine and twelve—I sensed I would never move beyond that fall from grace, even as I played with memories of the way I once had been.

Each time I was removed from the hot water and placed on a stretcher by the side of the pool, there to await the next immersion, I was fed salt tablets. These were simply intended to make up for the sweat we lost, but salt tablets seemed to me the cruelest confirmation of my new status as spiritual debtor. Even today, more than four decades later, I still shiver at the mere thought of those salt tablets. Sometimes the hospital orderly would literally have to pry my mouth open to force me to swallow them. I dreaded the nausea the taste of salt inspired in me. Each time I was resubmerged in the hot pool, I would grit my teeth—not from the flush of heat sweeping over my body but from the thought of what I would have to face when I would again be taken out of the water. To be an eater of salt was far more humiliating than to endure pain. Nor was I alone in feeling this way. After lights-out had quieted the ward, we boys would furtively whisper from cubicle to cubicle of how we dreaded being forced to swallow salt tablets. It was that, rather than the pain we endured, that anchored our sense of loss and dread.

Any recovery of muscle use in a polio patient usually took place within three months of the disease's onset. We all knew that. But as time passed, every boy in the ward learned to recite stories of those who, like Lazarus, had witnessed their own bodily resurrection. Having fallen from physical grace, we also chose to fall away from the reality in front of us. Our therapists were skilled and dedicated, but they weren't wonder-working saints. Paralyzed legs and arms rarely responded to their manipulations. We could not admit to ourselves, or to them, that we were permanently crippled. But each of us knew without knowing that his future was tied to the body that floated on the stainless steel slab.

We sweated out the hot pool and we choked on the salt tablets, and through it all we looked forward to the promise of rehabilitation. For, once the stiffness and pain had been baked and boiled out of us, we would no longer be eaters of salt. We would not be what we once had been, but at least we would be candidates for reentry into the world, admittedly made over to face its demands encased in leather and steel.

I suppose we might have been told that our fall from grace was permanent. But I am still grateful that no one—neither doctors nor nurses nor therapists, not even that sadistic orderly, himself a former polio patient, who limped through our lives and through our pain like some vengeful presence—told me that my chances of regaining the use of my legs were nonexistent. Like every other boy in the ward, I organized my needs around whatever illusions were available. And the illusion I needed above any other was that one morning I would simply wake up and rediscover the "normal" boy of memory, once again playing baseball in French Charley's Field in Bronx Park rather than roaming the fields of his own imagination. At the age of eleven, I needed to weather reality, not face it. And to this very day I silently thank those who were concerned enough about me, or indifferent enough to my fate, not to tell me what they knew.

Like most boys, sick or well, I was an adaptable creature—and rehabilitation demanded adaptability. The fall from bodily grace transformed each of us into an acolyte of the possible, a pragmatic American for whom survival was method and strategy. We would learn, during our days in the New York State Reconstruction Home, to confront the world that was. We would learn to survive the way we were, with whatever the virus had left intact.

I had fallen away from the body's prowess, but I was being led toward a life measured by different standards. Even as I fantasized about the past, it disappeared. Rehabilitation, I was to learn, was ahistorical, a future devoid of any significant claim on the past. Rehabilitation was a thief's primer of compensation and deception: its purpose was to teach one how to steal a touch of the normal from an existence that would be striking in its abnormality.

When I think back to those two years in the ward, the boy who made his rehabilitation most memorable was Joey Tomashevski. Joey was the son of an upstate dairy farmer, a Polish immigrant who had come to America before the Depression and whose English was even poorer than the English of my own *shtetl*-bred father. The virus had left both of Joey's arms so lifeless and atrophied that with pinky and thumb I could circle where his biceps should have been and still stick the forefinger of my other hand through. And yet Joey assumed that he would make do with whatever had been left him. He accepted without question the task of making his toes and feet into fingers and hands. With lifeless arms encased in a canvas sling that looked like the breadbasket a European peasant might carry to market, Joey would sit up in bed and demonstrate how he could maneuver fork and spoon with his toes.

I would never have dreamed of placing such confidence in my fingers, let alone my toes. I found, as most of the other boys in the ward did, Joey's unabashed pride in the flexibility and control with which he could maneuver a forkful of mashed potatoes into his mouth a continuous indictment of my sense of the world's natural order. We boys with dead legs would gather round his bed in our wheelchairs and silently watch Joey display his dexterity with a vanity so open and naked that it seemed an invitation to being struck down yet again. But Joey's was a vanity already tested by experience. For he was more than willing to accept whatever challenges the virus threw his way. For the sake of demonstrating his skill to us, he kicked a basketball from the auditorium stage through the hoop attached to a balcony some fifty feet away. When one of our number derisively called him "lucky," he proceeded to kick five of seven more balls through that same hoop.

I suspect that Joey's pride in his ability to compensate for what had been taken away from him irritated me because I knew that, before I could pursue my own rehabilitation with such singular passion, I had to surrender myself to what was being demanded of me. And that meant I had to learn to fall. It meant that I had to learn, as Joey Tomashevski had already learned, how to transform absence into opportunity. Even though I still lacked Joey's instinctive willingness to live with the legacy of the virus, I found myself being overhauled, re-created in much the same way as a car engine is rebuilt. Nine months after I arrived in the ward, a few weeks before my twelfth birthday, I was fitted for double long-legged braces bound together by a steel pelvic band circling my waist. Lifeless or not, my legs were precisely measured, the steel carefully molded to form, screws and locks and leather joined to one another for my customized benefit. It was technology that would hold me up— another offering on the altar of compensation. "You get what you give," said Jackie Lyons, my closest friend in the ward. For he, too, was now a novitiate of the possible. He, too, now had to learn how to choose the road back.

Falling into life was not a metaphor; it was real, a process learned only through doing, the way a baby learns to crawl, to stand, and then to walk. After the steel bands around calves and thighs and pelvis had been covered over by the rich-smelling leather, after the braces had been precisely fitted to allow my fear-ridden imagination the surety of their holding presence, I was pulled to my feet. For the first time in ten months, I stood. Two middle-aged craftsmen, the hospital bracemakers who worked in a machine shop deep in the basement, held me in place as my therapist wedged two wooden crutches beneath my shoulders.

They stepped back, first making certain that my grip on the crutches was firm. Filled with pride in their technological prowess, the three of them stood in front of me, admiring their skill. Had I been created in the laboratory of Mary Shelley's Dr. Frankenstein, I could not have felt myself any more the creature of scientific pride. I stood on the braces, crutches beneath my shoulders slanting outward like twin towers of Pisa. I flushed, swallowed hard, struggled to keep from crying, struggled not to be overwhelmed by my fear of falling.

My future had arrived. The leather had been fitted, the screws had been turned to the precise millimeter, the locks at the knees and the bushings at the ankles had been properly tested and re-tested. That very afternoon I was taken for the first time to a cavernous room filled with barbells and Indian clubs and crutches and walkers. I would spend an hour each day there for the next six months. In the rehab room I would learn how to mount two large wooden steps made to the exact measure of a New York City bus's. I would swing on parallel bars from one side to the other, my arms learning how they would have to hurl me through the world. I balanced Indian clubs like a circus juggler because my therapist insisted it would help my coordination. And I was expected to learn to fall.

I was a dutiful patient. I did as I was told, because I could see no advantage to doing anything else. I hungered for the approval of those in authority—doctors, nurses, therapists, the two bracemakers. Again and again, my therapist demonstrated how I was to throw my legs from the hip. Again and again, I did as I was told. Grabbing the banister with my left hand, I threw my leg from the hip while pushing off my right crutch. Like some baby elephant (despite the sweat lost in the heated pool, the months of inactivity in bed had fattened me up considerably), I dangled from side to side on the parallel bars. Grunting with effort, I did everything demanded of me. I did it with an unabashed eagerness to please those who had power over my life. I wanted to put myself at risk. I wanted to do whatever was supposed to be "good" for me. I believed as absolutely as I have ever believed in anything that rehabilitation would finally placate the hunger of the virus.

But when my therapist commanded me to fall, I cringed. The prospect of falling terrified me. Every afternoon, as I worked through my prescribed activities, I prayed that I would be able to fall when the session ended. Falling was the most essential "good" of all the "goods" held out for my consideration by my therapist. I believed that. I believed it so intensely that the belief itself was painful. Everything else asked of me was given, and given gladly. I mounted the bus stairs, pushed across the parallel bars until my arms ached with the effort, allowed the medicine ball to pummel me, flailed away at the empty air with my fists because my therapist wanted me to rid myself of the tension within. The slightest sign of approval from those in authority was enough to make me puff with pleasure. Other boys in the ward might not have taken rehabilitation seriously, but I was an eager servant cringing before the promise of approval.

Only I couldn't fall. As each session ended, I would be led to the mats that took up a full third of the huge room. "It's time," the therapist would say. Dutifully, I would follow her, step after step. Just as dutifully, I would stand on the edge of those two-inch-thick mats, staring down at them until I could feel my body quiver. "All you have to do is let go," my therapist assured me. "The other boys do it. Just let go and fall."

But the prospect of letting go was precisely what terrified me. That the other boys in the ward had no trouble in falling added to my shame and terror. I didn't need my therapist to tell me the two-inch-thick mats would keep me from hurting myself. I knew there was virtually no chance of injury when I fell, but that knowledge simply made me more ashamed of a cowardice that was as monumental as it was unexplainable. Had it been able to rid me of my sense of my own cowardice, I would happily have settled for bodily harm. But I was being asked to surrender myself to the emptiness of space, to let go and crash down to the mats below, to feel myself suspended in air when nothing stood between me and the vacuum of the world. *That* was the prospect that overwhelmed me. *That* was what left me sweating with rage and humiliation. The contempt I felt was for my own weakness.

I tried to justify what I sensed could never be justified. Why should I be expected to throw myself into emptiness? Was this sullen terror the price of compensation, the badge of normality? Maybe my refusal to fall embodied some deeper thrust than I could then understand. Maybe I had unconsciously seized upon some fundamental resistance to the forces that threatened to overwhelm me. What did it matter that the ground was covered with the thick mats? The tremors I feared were in my heart and soul.

Shame plagued me—and shame is the older brother to disease. Flushing with shame, I would stare down at the mats. I could feel myself wanting to cry out. But I shriveled at the thought of calling more attention to my cowardice. I would finally hear myself whimper, "I'm sorry. But I can't. I can't let go."

Formless emptiness. A rush of air through which I would plummet toward obliteration. As my "normal" past grew more and more distant, I reached for it more and more desperately, recalling it like some movie whose plot has long since been forgotten but whose scenes continue to comfort through images disconnected from anything but themselves. I remembered that there had been a time when the prospect of falling evoked not terror but joy: football games on the rain-softened autumn turf of Mosholu Parkway, belly-flopping on an American Flyer down its snow-covered slopes in winter, rolling with a pack of friends down one of the steep hills in Bronx Park. Free-falls from the past, testifying not to a loss of the self but to an absence of barriers.

My therapist pleaded, ridiculed, cajoled, threatened, bullied. I was sighed over and railed at. But I couldn't let go and fall. I couldn't sell my terror off so cheaply. Ashamed as I was, I wouldn't allow myself to be bullied out of terror.

A month passed—a month of struggle between me and my therapist. Daily excursions to the rehab room, daily practice runs through the future that was awaiting me. The daily humiliation of discovering that one's own fear had been transformed into a public issue, a subject of discussion among the other boys in the ward, seemed unending.

And then terror simply evaporated. It was as if I had served enough time in that prison. I was ready to move on. One Tuesday afternoon, as my session ended, the therapist walked resignedly alongside me toward the mats. "All right, Leonard. It's time again. All you have to do is let go and fall." Again I stood above the mats. Only this time it was as if something beyond my control or understanding had decided to let my body's fall from grace take me down for good. I was not seized by the usual paroxysm of fear. I didn't feel myself break out in a terrified sweat. It was over.

I don't mean that I suddenly felt myself spring into courage. That wasn't what happened at all. The truth was I had simply been worn down into letting go, like a boxer in whose eyes one recognizes not the flicker of defeat—that issue never having been in doubt—but the acceptance of defeat. Letting go no longer held my imagination captive. I found myself quite suddenly faced with a necessary fall— a fall into life.

So it was that I stood above the mat and heard myself sigh and then felt myself let go, dropping through the quiet air, crutches slipping off to the sides. What I didn't feel this time was the threat of my body slipping into emptiness, so mummified by the terror before it that the touch of air preempted even death. I dropped. I did not crash. I dropped. I did not collapse. I dropped. I did not plummet. I felt myself enveloped by a curiously gentle moment in my life. In that sliver of time before I hit the mat, I was kissed by space.

My body absorbed the slight shock and I rolled onto my back, braced legs swinging like unguided missiles into the free air, crutches dropping away to the sides. Even as I fell through the air, I could sense the shame and fear drain from my soul, and I knew that my sense of my own cowardice would soon follow. In falling, I had given myself a new start, a new life.

"That's it!" my therapist shouted triumphantly. "You let go! And there it is!"

You let go! And there it is! Yes, and you discover not terror but the only self you are going to be allowed to claim anyhow. You fall free, and then you learn that those padded mats hold not courage but the unclaimed self. And if it turned out to be not the most difficult of tasks, did that make my sense of jubilation any less?

From that moment, I gloried in my ability to fall. Falling became an end in itself. I lost sight of what my therapist had desperately been trying to demonstrate for me—that there was a purpose in learning how to fall. She wanted to teach me through the fall what I would have to face in the future. She wanted to give me a wholeness I could not give myself. For she knew that mine would be a future so different from what confronts the "normal" that I had to learn to fall into life in order not to be overwhelmed.

From that day, she urged me to practice falling as if I were a religious disciple being urged by a master to practice spiritual discipline. Letting go meant allowing my body to float into space, to turn at the direction of the fall and follow the urgings of emptiness. For her, learning to fall was learning that most essential of American lessons: How to turn incapacity into capacity.

"You were afraid of hurting yourself," she explained to me. "But that's the beauty of it. When you let go, you can't hurt yourself."

An echo of the streets and playgrounds I called home until I met the virus. American slogans: Go with the flow, roll with the punch, slide with the threat until it is no longer a threat. They were simple slogans, and they were all intended to create strength from weakness, a veritable world's fair of compensation.

I returned to the city a year later. By that time I was a willing convert, one who now secretly enjoyed demonstrating his ability to fall. I enjoyed the surprise that would greet me as I got to my feet, unscathed. However perverse it may seem, I felt a certain pleasure when, as I walked with a friend, I felt a crutch slip out of my grasp. Watching the thrust of concern darken his features, I felt myself in control of my own capacity. For falling had become the way my body sought out its proper home. It was an earthbound body, and mine would be an earthbound life. My quest would be for the solid ground beneath me. Falling with confidence, I fell away from terror and fear.

Of course, some falls took me unawares, and I found myself letting go too late or too early. Bruised in ego and sometimes in body, I would pull myself to my feet to consider what had gone wrong. Yet I was essentially untroubled. Such defeats were part of the game, even when they confined me to bed for a day or two afterward. I was an accountant of pain, and sometimes heavier payment was demanded. In my mid-thirties, I walked my two-year-old son's babysitter home, tripped on the curbstone, and broke my wrist. At forty-eight, an awkward fall triggered by a carelessly unlocked brace sent me smashing against the bathtub and into surgery for a broken femur. It took four months for me to learn to walk with the crutches all over again. But I learned. I already knew how to fall.

I knew such accidents could be handled. After all, pain was not synonymous with mortality. In fact, pain was insurance against an excessive consciousness of mortality. Pain might validate the specific moment in time, but it didn't have much to do with the future. I did not yet believe that falling into life had anything to do with falling into death. It was simply a way for me to exercise control over my own existence.

It seems to me today that when I first let my body fall to those mats, I was somehow giving myself the endurance I would need to survive in this world. In a curious way, falling became a way of celebrating what I had lost. My legs were lifeless, useless, but their loss had created a dancing image in whose shadowy gyrations I recognized a strange but potentially interesting new self. I would survive. I knew that now. I could let go, I could fall, and, best of all, I could get up.

To create an independent self, a man had to rid himself both of the myths that nurtured him and the myths that held him back. Learning to fall had been the first lesson in how I yet might live successfully as a cripple. Even disease had its inviolate principles. I understood that the most dangerous threat to the sense of self I needed was an inflated belief in my own capacity. Falling rid a man of excess baggage; it taught him how each of us is dependent on balance.

But what really gave falling legitimacy was the knowledge that I could get to my feet again. That was what made letting go a fall into life. That was what taught me the rules of survival. As long as I could pick myself up and stand on my own two feet, bracebound and crutch-propped as I was, the fall testified to my ability to live in the here and now, to stake my claim as an American who had turned incapacity into capacity. For such a man, falling might well be considered the language of everyday achievement.

But the day came, as I knew it must come, when I could no longer pick myself up. It was then that my passion for symmetry in endings began. On that day, spurred on by another fall, I found myself spinning into the inevitable future.

The day was actually a rainy night in November of 1983. I had just finished teaching at the City College Center for Worker Education, an off-campus degree program for working adults, and had joined some friends for dinner. All of us, I remember, were in a jovial, celebratory mood, although I no longer remember what it was we were celebrating. Perhaps it was simply the satisfaction of being good friends and colleagues at dinner together.

We ate in a Spanish restaurant on 14th Street in Manhattan. It was a dinner that took on, for me at least, the intensity of a time that would assume greater and greater significance as I grew older, one of those watershed moments writers are so fond of. In the dark, rainswept New York night, change and possibility seemed to drift like a thick fog all around us.

Our mood was still convivial when we left the restaurant around eleven o'clock. The rain had slackened off to a soft drizzle and the streetlights glistened on the wet black creosote. At night, rain in the city has a way of transforming proportion into optimism. The five of us stood around on the slicked-down sidewalk, none of us willing to be the first to break the richness of the mood by leaving.

Suddenly the crutch in my left hand began to slip out from under me, slowly, almost deliberately, as if the crutch had a mind of its own and had not yet made the commitment that would send me down. I had apparently hit a slick patch of city sidewalk, some nub of concrete worn smooth as medieval stone by thousands of shoppers and panhandlers and tourists and students who daily pounded the bargain hustlings of 14th Street.

Instinctively, I at first tried to fight the fall, to seek for balance by pushing off from the crutch in my right hand. But as I recognized that the fall was inevitable, I simply went slack—and for the thousandth time my body sought vindication in its ability to let go and drop. These good friends had seen me fall before. They knew my childish vanities, understood that I still thought of falling as a way to demonstrate my control of the traps and uncertainties that lay in wait for us all.

Thirty-eight years earlier, I had discovered that I could fall into life simply by letting go. Now I made a different discovery—that I could no longer get to my feet by myself. I hit the wet ground and quickly turned over and pushed up, trying to use one of the crutches as a prop to boost myself to my feet, as I had been taught to do as a boy of twelve.

But try as hard as I could, I couldn't get to my feet. It wasn't that I lacked physical strength. I knew that my arms were as powerful as ever as I pushed down on the wet concrete. It had nothing to do with the fact that the street was wet, as my friends insisted later. No, it had to do with a subtle, mysterious change in my own sense of rhythm and balance. My body had decided—*and decided on its own, autonomously*—that the moment had come for me to face the question of endings. It was the body that chose its time of recognition.

It was, it seems to me now, a distinctively American moment. It left me pondering limitations and endings and summations. It left me with the curiously buoyant sense that mortality had quite suddenly made itself a felt presence rather than the rhetorical strategy used by the poets and novelists I taught to my students. This was what writers had in mind when they spoke of the truly common fate, this sense of ending coming to one unbidden. This had brought with it my impassioned quest for symmetry. As I lay on the wet ground—no more than a minute or two—all I could think of was how much I wanted my life to balance out. It was as if I were staring into a future in which time itself had evaporated.

Here was a clear, simple perception, and there was nothing mystical about it. There are limitations we recognize and those that recognize us. My friends, who had been standing around nervously while I tried to get to my feet, finally asked if they could help me up. "You'll have to," I said. "I can't get up any other way."

Two of them pulled me to my feet while another jammed the crutches beneath my arms, as the therapist and the two bracemakers had done almost four decades earlier. When I was standing, they proceeded to joke about my sudden incapacity in that age-old way men of all ages have, as if words might codify loss and change and time's betrayal. I joined in the joking. But what I really wanted was to go home and contemplate this latest fall, in the privacy of my apartment. The implications were clear: I would never again be an eater of salt; I would also never again get to my feet on my own. A part of my life had ended. But that didn't depress me. In fact, I felt almost as exhilarated as I had thirty-eight years earlier, when my body surrendered to the need to let go and I fell into life.

Almost four years have passed since I fell on the wet sidewalk of 14th Street. I suppose it wasn't a particularly memorable fall. It wasn't even particularly significant to anyone who had not once fallen into life. But it was inevitable, the first time I had let go into a time when it would no longer even be necessary to let go.

It was a fall that left me with the knowledge that I could no longer pick myself up. That meant I now needed the help of others as I had not needed their help before. It was a fall that left me burning with this strange passion for symmetry, this desire to balance my existence out. When the day comes, I want to be able to fall into my death as nakedly as I once had to fall into my life.

Do not misunderstand me. I am not seeking a way out of mortality, for I believe in nothing more strongly than I believe in the permanency of endings. I am not looking for a way out of this life, a life I continue to find immensely enjoyable—even if I can no longer pull myself to my own two feet. Of course, a good deal in my life has changed. For one thing, I am increasingly impatient with those who claim to have no use for endings of any sort. I am also increasingly embarrassed by the thought of the harshly critical adolescent I was, self-righteously convinced that the only way for a man to go to his end was kicking and screaming.

But these are, I suppose, the kinds of changes any man or woman of forty or fifty would feel. Middle-aged skepticism is as natural as adolescent acne. In my clearer, less passionate moments I can even laugh at my need for symmetry in beginnings and endings as well as my desire to see my own eventual death as a line running parallel to my life. Even in mathematics, let alone life, symmetry is sometimes too neat, too closed off from the way things actually work. After all, it took me a full month before I could bring myself to let go and fall into life.

I no longer talk about how to seize a doctrine of compensation from disease. I don't talk about it, but it still haunts me. In my heart, I believe it offers the only philosophy by which anyone can actually live. It is the only philosophy that strips away both spiritual mumbo jumbo and the procrustean weight of existential anxiety. In the final analysis, a man really is what he does.

Believing as I do, I wonder why I so often find myself trying to frame a perspective that will prove adequate to a proper sense of ending. Perhaps that is why I find myself sitting in a bar with a friend, trying to explain to him all I have learned from falling. "There must be a time," I hear myself tell him, "when a man has the right to stop thinking about falling."

"Sure," my friend laughs. "Four seconds before he dies."

Carnal Acts

NANCY MAIRS

Inviting me to speak at her small liberal-arts college during Women's Week, a young woman set me a task: "We would be pleased," she wrote, "if you could talk on how you cope with your M.S. disability, and also how you discovered your voice as a writer." Oh, Lord, I thought in dismay, how am I going to pull this one off? How can I yoke two such disparate subjects into a coherent presentation, without doing violence to one, or the other, or both, or myself? This is going to take some fancy footwork, and my feet scarcely carry out the basic steps, let alone anything elaborate.

To make matters worse, the assumption underlying each of her questions struck me as suspect. To ask *how* I cope with multiple sclerosis suggests that I *do* cope. Now, "to cope," *Webster's Third* tells me, is "to face or encounter and to find necessary expedients to overcome problems and difficulties." In these terms, I have to confess, I don't feel like much of a coper. I'm likely to deal with my problems and difficulties by squawking and flapping around like that hysterical chicken who was convinced the sky was falling. Never mind that in my case the sky really *is* falling. In response to a clonk on the head, regardless of its origin, one might comport oneself with a grace and courtesy I generally lack.

As for "finding" my voice, the implication is that it was at one time lost or missing. But I don't think it ever was. Ask my mother, who will tell you a little wearily that I was speaking full sentences by the time I was a year old and could never be silenced again. As for its being a writer's voice, it seems to have become one early on. Ask Mother again. At the age of eight I rewrote the Trojan War, she will

say, and what Nestor was about to do to Helen at the end doesn't
bear discussion in polite company.

Faced with these uncertainties, I took my own teacherly advice,
something, I must confess, I don't always do. "If an idea is giving
you trouble," I tell my writing students, "put it on the back burner
and let it simmer while you do something else. Go to the movies.
Reread a stack of old love letters. Sit in your history class and take
detailed notes on the Teapot Dome scandal. If you've got your idea
in mind, it will go on cooking at some level no matter what else
you're doing." "I've had an idea for my documented essay on the
back burner," one of my students once scribbled in her journal,
"and I think it's just boiled over!"

I can't claim to have reached such a flash point. But in the weeks
I've had the themes "disability" and "voice" sitting around in my
head, they seem to have converged on their own, without my having
to wrench them together and bind them with hoops of tough rhet-
oric. They *are* related, indeed interdependent, with an intimacy that
has for some reason remained, until now, submerged below the surface of my attention. Forced to juxtapose them, I yank them out of
the depths, a little startled to discover how they were intertwined
down there out of sight. This kind of discovery can unnerve you at
first. You feel like a giant hand that, pulling two swimmers out of
the water, two separate heads bobbing on the iridescent swells, finds
the two bodies below, legs coiled around each other, in an ecstasy
of copulation. You don't quite know where to turn your eyes.

Perhaps the place to start illuminating this erotic connection between who I am and how I speak lies in history. I have known that
I have multiple sclerosis for about seventeen years now, though the
disease probably started long before. The hypothesis is that the disease process, in which the protective covering of the nerves in the
brain and spinal cord is eaten away and replaced by scar tissue,
"hard patches," is caused by an autoimmune reaction to a slow-
acting virus. Research suggests that I was infected by this virus, which
no one has ever seen and which therefore, technically, doesn't even
"exist," between the ages of four and fifteen. In effect, living with
this mysterious mechanism feels like having your present self, and
the past selves it embodies, haunted by a capricious and meanspir-
ited ghost, unseen except for its footprints, which trips you even
when you're watching where you're going, knocks glassware out of
your hand, squeezes the urine out of your bladder before you reach
the bathroom, and weights your whole body with a weariness no

amount of rest can relieve. An alien invader must be at work. But of course it's not. It's your own body. That is, it's you.

This, for me, has been the most difficult aspect of adjusting to a chronic incurable degenerative disease: the fact that it has rammed my "self" straight back into the body I had been trained to believe it could, through high-minded acts and aspirations, rise above. The Western tradition of distinguishing the body from the mind and/or the soul is so ancient as to have become part of our collective unconscious, if one is inclined to believe in such a noumenon, or at least to have become an unquestioned element in the social instruction we impose upon infants from birth, in much the same way we inculcate, without reflection, the gender distinctions "female" and "male." I *have* a body, you are likely to say if you talk about embodiment at all; you don't say, I *am* a body. A body is a separate entity possessable by the "I"; the "I" and the body aren't, as the copula would make them, grammatically indistinguishable.

To widen the rift between the self and the body, we treat our bodies as subordinates, inferior in moral status. Open association with them shames us. In fact, we treat our bodies with very much the same distance and ambivalence women have traditionally received from men in our culture. Sometimes this treatment is benevolent, even respectful, but all too often it is tainted by outright sadism. I think of the bodybuilding regimens that have become popular in the last decade or so, with the complicated vacillations they reflect between self-worship and self-degradation: joggers and aerobic dancers and weightlifters all beating their bodies into shape. "No pain, no gain," the saying goes. "Feel the burn." Bodies get treated like wayward women who have to be shown who's boss, even if it means slapping them around a little. I'm not for a moment opposing rugged exercise here. I'm simply questioning the spirit in which it is often undertaken.

Since, as Hélène Cixous points out in her essay on women and writing, "Sorties,"* thought has always worked "through dual, hierarchical oppositions" (p. 64), the mind/body split cannot possibly be innocent. The utterance of an "I" immediately calls into being its opposite, the "not-I," Western discourse being unequipped to conceive "that which is neither 'I' nor 'not-I,' " "that which is both 'I' and 'not-I,' " or some other permutation which language doesn't

* In *The Newly Born Woman*, translated by Betsy Wing (Minneapolis: University of Minnesota Press, 1986).

permit me to speak. The "not-I" is, by definition, other. And we've never been too fond of the other. We prefer the same. We tend to ascribe to the other those qualities we prefer not to associate with our selves: it is the hidden, the dark, the secret, the shameful. Thus, when the "I" takes possession of the body, it makes the body into an other, direct object of a transitive verb, with all the other's repudiated and potentially dangerous qualities.

At the least, then, the body had best be viewed with suspicion. And a woman's body is particularly suspect, since so much of it is in fact hidden, dark, secret, carried about on the inside where, even with the aid of a speculum, one can never perceive all of it in the plain light of day, a graspable whole. I, for one, have never understood why anyone would want to carry all that delicate stuff around on the outside. It would make you awfully anxious, I should think, put you constantly on the defensive, create a kind of siege mentality that viewed all other beings, even your own kind, as threats to be warded off with spears and guns and atomic missiles. And you'd never get to experience that inward dreaming that comes when your flesh surrounds all your treasures, holding them close, like a sturdy shuttered house. Be my personal skepticism as it may, however, as a cultural woman I bear just as much shame as any woman for my dark, enfolded secrets. Let the word for my external genitals tell the tale: my pudendum, from the Latin infinitive meaning "to be ashamed."

It's bad enough to carry your genitals like a sealed envelope bearing the cipher that, once unlocked, might loose the chaotic flood of female pleasure—*jouissance*, the French call it—upon the world-of-the-same. But I have an additional reason to feel shame for my body, less explicitly connected with its sexuality: it is a crippled body. Thus it is doubly other, not merely by the homo-sexual standards of patriarchal culture but by the standards of physical desirability erected for every body in our world. Men, who are by definition exonerated from shame in sexual terms (this doesn't mean that an individual man might not experience sexual shame, of course; remember that I'm talking in general about discourse, not folks), may—more likely must—experience bodily shame if they are crippled. I won't presume to speak about the details of their experience, however. I don't know enough. I'll just go on telling what it's like to be a crippled woman, trusting that, since we're fellow creatures who've been living together for some thousands of years now, much of my experience will resonate with theirs.

I was never a beautiful woman, and for that reason I've spent most of my life (together with probably at least 95 percent of the female population of the United States) suffering from the shame of falling short of an unattainable standard. The ideal woman of my generation was . . . perky, I think you'd say, rather than gorgeous. Blond hair pulled into a bouncing ponytail. Wide blue eyes, a turned-up nose with maybe a scattering of golden freckles across it, a small mouth with full lips over straight white teeth. Her breasts were large but well harnessed high on her chest; her tiny waist flared to hips just wide enough to give the crinolines under her circle skirt a starting outward push. In terms of personality, she was outgoing, even bubbly, not pensive or mysterious. Her milieu was the front fender of a white Corvette convertible, surrounded by teasing crew-cuts, dressed in black flats, a sissy blouse, and the letter sweater of the Corvette owner. Needless to say, she never missed a prom.

Ten years or so later, when I first noticed the symptoms that would be diagnosed as MS, I was probably looking my best. Not beautiful still, but the ideal had shifted enough so that my flat chest and narrow hips gave me an elegantly attenuated shape, set off by a thick mass of long, straight, shining hair. I had terrific legs, long and shapely, revealed nearly to the pudendum by the fashionable miniskirts and hot pants I adopted with more enthusiasm than delicacy of taste. Not surprisingly, I suppose, during this time I involved myself in several pretty torrid love affairs.

The beginning of MS wasn't too bad. The first symptom, besides the pernicious fatigue that had begun to devour me, was "foot drop," the inability to raise my left foot at the ankle. As a consequence, I'd started to limp, but I could still wear high heels, and a bit of a limp might seem more intriguing than repulsive. After a few months, when the doctor suggested a cane, a crippled friend gave me quite an elegant wood-and-silver one, which I carried with a fair amount of panache. The real blow to my self-image came when I had to get a brace. As braces go, it's not bad: lightweight plastic molded to my foot and leg, fitting down into an ordinary shoe and secured around my calf by a Velcro strap. It reduces my limp and, more important, the danger of tripping and falling. But it meant the end of high heels. And it's ugly. Not as ugly as I think it is, I gather, but still pretty ugly. It signified for me, and perhaps still does, the permanence and irreversibility of my condition. The brace makes my MS concrete and forces me to wear it on the outside. As soon as I strapped the brace on, I climbed into trousers and stayed there (though not in the same trousers, of course). The idea of going around with my bare brace hanging out seemed almost as indecent as exposing my breasts. Not until 1984, soon after I won the Western States Book Award for poetry, did I put on a skirt short enough to reveal my plasticized leg. The connection between winning a writing award and baring my brace is not merely fortuitous; being affirmed as a writer really did embolden me. Since then, I've grown so accustomed to wearing skirts that I don't think about my brace any more than I think about my cane. I've incorporated them, I suppose: made them, in their necessity, insensate but fundamental parts of my body.

Meanwhile, I had to adjust to the most outward and visible sign of all, a three-wheeled electric scooter called an Amigo. This lessens my fatigue and increases my range terrifically, but it also shouts out to the world, "Here is a woman who can't stand on her own two feet." At the same time, paradoxically, it renders me invisible, reducing me to the height of a seven-year-old, with a child's attendant low status. "Would she like smoking or nonsmoking?" the gate agent assigning me a seat asks the friend traveling with me. In crowds I see nothing but buttocks. I can tell you the name of every type of designer jeans ever sold. The wearers, eyes front, trip over me and fall across my handlebars into my lap. "Hey!" I want to shout to the lofty world. "Down here! There's a person down here!" But I'm not, by their standards, quite a person anymore.

My self-esteem diminishes further as age and illness strip from me the features that made me, for a brief while anyway, a good-looking, even sexy, young woman. No more long, bounding strides: I shuffle along with the timid gait I remember observing, with pity and impatience, in the little old ladies at Boston's Symphony Hall on Friday afternoons. No more lithe, girlish figure: my belly sags from the loss of muscle tone, which also creates all kinds of intestinal disruptions, hopelessly humiliating in a society in which excretory functions remain strictly unspeakable. No more sex, either, if society had its way. The sexuality of the disabled so repulses most people that you can hardly get a doctor, let alone a member of the general population, to consider the issues it raises. Cripples simply aren't supposed to Want It, much less Do It. Fortunately, I've got a husband with a strong libido and a weak sense of social propriety, or else I'd find myself perforce practicing a vow of chastity I never cared to take.

Afflicted by the general shame of having a body at all, and the specific shame of having one weakened and misshapen by disease, I ought not to be able to hold my head up in public. And yet I've gotten into the habit of holding my head up in public, sometimes under excruciating circumstances. Recently, for instance, I had to give a reading at the University of Arizona. Having smashed three of my front teeth in a fall onto the concrete floor of my screened porch, I was in the process of getting them crowned, and the temporary crowns flew out during dinner right before the reading. What to do? I wanted, of course, to rush home and hide till the dental office opened the next morning. But I couldn't very well break my word at this last moment. So, looking like Hansel and Gretel's witch, and lisping worse than the Wife of Bath, I got up on stage and read. Somehow, over the years, I've learned how to set shame aside and do what I have to do.

Here, I think, is where my "voice" comes in. Because, in spite of my demurral at the beginning, I do in fact cope with my disability at least some of the time. And I do so, I think, by speaking about it, and about the whole experience of being a body, specifically a female body, out loud, in a clear, level tone that drowns out the frantic whispers of my mother, my grandmothers, all the other trainers of wayward childish tongues: "Sssh! Sssh! Nice girls don't talk like that. Don't mention sweat. Don't mention menstrual blood. Don't ask what your grandfather does on his business trips. Don't laugh so loud. You sound like a loon. Keep your voice down. Don't tell. Don't tell. Don't tell." Speaking out loud is an antidote to shame. I want to distinguish clearly here between "shame," as I'm using the word, and "guilt" and "embarrassment," which, though equally painful, are not similarly poisonous. Guilt arises from performing a forbidden act or failing to perform a required one. In either case, the guilty person can, through reparation, erase the offense and start fresh. Embarrassment, less opprobrious though not necessarily less distressing, is generally caused by acting in a socially stupid or awkward way. When I trip and sprawl in public, when I wet myself, when my front teeth fly out, I feel horribly embarrassed, but, like the pain of childbirth, the sensation blurs and dissolves in time. If it didn't, every child would be an only child, and no one would set foot in public after the onset of puberty, when embarrassment erupts like a geyser and bathes one's whole life in its bitter stream. Shame may attach itself to guilt or embarrassment, complicating their resolution, but it is not the same emotion. I feel guilt or embarrassment for something I've done; shame, for who I am. I may stop doing bad or stupid things, but I can't stop being. How then can I help but be ashamed? Of the three conditions, this is the one that cracks and stifles my voice.

I can subvert its power, I've found, by acknowledging who I am, shame and all, and, in doing so, raising what was hidden, dark, secret about my life into the plain light of shared human experience. What we aren't permitted to utter holds us, each isolated from every other, in a kind of solipsistic thrall. Without any way to check our reality against anyone else's, we assume that our fears and shortcomings are ours alone. One of the strangest consequences of publishing a collection of personal essays called *Plaintext* has been the steady trickle of letters and telephone calls saying essentially, in a tone of unmistakable relief, "Oh, me too! Me too!" It's as though the part I thought was solo has turned out to be a chorus. But none of us was singing loud enough for the others to hear.

Singing loud enough demands a particular kind of voice, I think. And I was wrong to suggest, at the beginning, that I've always had my voice. I have indeed always had *a* voice, but it wasn't *this* voice, the one with which I could call up and transform my hidden self from a naughty girl into a woman talking directly to others like herself. Recently, in the process of writing a new book, a memoir entitled *Remembering the Bone House*, I've had occasion to read some of my early writing, from college, high school, even junior high. It's not an experience I recommend to anyone susceptible to shame. Not that the writing was all that bad. I was surprised at how competent a lot of it was. Here was a writer who already knew precisely how the language worked. But the voice . . . oh, the voice was all wrong: maudlin, rhapsodic, breaking here and there into little shrieks, almost, you might say, hysterical. It was a voice that had shucked off its own body, its own homely life of Cheerios for breakfast and seventy pages of Chaucer to read before the exam on Tuesday and a planter's wart growing painfully on the ball of its foot, and reeled now wraithlike through the air, seeking incarnation only as the heroine who enacts her doomed love for the tall, dark, mysterious stranger. If it didn't get that part, it wouldn't play at all.

Among all these overheated and vaporous imaginings, I must have retained some shred of sense, because I stopped writing prose entirely, except for scholarly papers, for nearly twenty years. I even forgot, not exactly that I had written prose, but at least what kind of prose it was. So when I needed to take up the process again, I could start almost fresh, using the vocal range I'd gotten used to in

years of asking the waiter in the Greek restaurant for an extra an-
chovy on my salad, congratulating the puppy on making a puddle
outside rather than inside the patio door, pondering with my daughter the vagaries of female orgasm, saying goodbye to my husband,
and hello, and goodbye, and hello. This new voice—thoughtful, affectionate, often amused—was essential because what I needed to
write about when I returned to prose was an attempt I'd made not
long before to kill myself, and suicide simply refuses to be spoken
of authentically in high-flown romantic language. It's too ugly. Too
shameful. Too strictly a bodily event. And, yes, too funny as well,
though people are sometimes shocked to find humor shoved up
against suicide. They don't like the incongruity. But let's face it, life
(real life, I mean, not the edited-for-television version) is a cacoph-
onous affair from start to finish. I might have wanted to portray my
suicidal self as a languishing maiden, too exquisitely sensitive to sus-
tain life's wounding pressures on her soul. (I didn't want to, as a
matter of fact, but I might have.) The truth remained, regardless of
my desires, that when my husband lugged me into the emergency
room, my hair matted, my face swollen and gray, my nightgown
streaked with blood and urine, I was no frail and tender spirit. I was
a body, and one in a hell of a mess.

I "should" have kept quiet about that experience. I know the
rules of polite discourse. I should have kept my shame, and the
nearly lethal sense of isolation and alienation it brought, to myself.
And I might have, except for something the psychiatrist in the emergency room had told my husband. "You might as well take her
home," he said. "If she wants to kill herself, she'll do it no matter
how many precautions we take. They always do." *They* always do. I
was one of "them," whoever they were. I was, in this context anyway,
not singular, not aberrant, but typical. I think it was this sense of
commonality with others I didn't even know, a sense of being returned somehow, in spite of my appalling act, to the human family,
that urged me to write that first essay, not merely speaking out but
calling out, perhaps. "Here's the way I am," it said. "How about
you?" And the answer came, as I've said: "Me too! Me too!"

This has been the kind of work I've continued to do: to scrutinize
the details of my own experience and to report what I see, and what
I think about what I see, as lucidly and accurately as possible. But
because feminine experience has been immemorially devalued and
repressed, I continue to find this task terrifying. "Every woman has
known the torture of beginning to speak aloud," Cixous writes,

"heart beating as if to break, occasionally falling into loss of language, ground and language slipping out from under her, because for woman speaking—even just opening her mouth—in public is something rash, a transgression" (p. 92).

The voice I summon up wants to crack, to whisper, to trail back into silence. "I'm sorry to have nothing more than this to say," it wants to apologize. "I shouldn't be taking up your time. I've never fought in a war, or even in a schoolyard free-for-all. I've never tried to see who could piss farthest up the barn wall. I've never even been to a whorehouse. All the important formative experiences have passed me by. I was raped once. I've borne two children. Milk trickling out of my breasts, blood trickling from between my legs. You don't want to hear about it. Sometimes I'm too scared to leave my house. Not scared *of* anything, just scared: mouth dry, bowels writhing. When the fear got really bad, they locked me up for six months, but that was years ago. I'm getting old now. Misshapen, too. I don't blame you if you can't get it up. No one could possibly desire a body like this. It's not your fault. It's mine. Forgive me. I didn't mean to start crying. I'm sorry . . . sorry . . . sorry. . . ."

An easy solace to the anxiety of speaking aloud: this slow subsidence beneath the waves of shame, back into what Cixous calls "this body that has been worse than confiscated, a body replaced with a disturbing stranger, sick or dead, who so often is a bad influence, the cause and place of inhibitions. By censuring the body," she goes on, "breath and speech are censored at the same time" (p. 97). But I am not going back, not going under one more time. To do so would demonstrate a failure of nerve far worse than the depredations of MS have caused. Paradoxically, losing one sort of nerve has given me another. No one is going to take my breath away. No one is going to leave me speechless. To be silent is to comply with the standard of feminine grace. But my crippled body already violates all notions of feminine grace. What more have I got to lose? I've gone beyond shame. I'm shameless, you might say. You know, as in "shameless hussy"? A woman with her bare brace and her tongue hanging out.

I've "found" my voice, then, just where it ought to have been, in the body-warmed breath escaping my lungs and throat. Forced by the exigencies of physical disease to embrace my self in the flesh, I couldn't write bodiless prose. The voice is the creature of the body that produces it. I speak as a crippled woman. At the same time, in the utterance I redeem both "cripple" and "woman" from the shameful silences by which I have often felt surrounded, contained, set apart; I give myself permission to live openly among others, to reach out for them, stroke them with fingers and sighs. No body, no voice; no voice, no body. That's what I know in my bones.

Bells

~≈ ≈~

VED MEHTA

"Wake up, Vedi!" Deoji would say, gently pulling my cheek with his small, cold hand. "It's six o'clock."

I would remember Daddyji's warm and enveloping hand on my forehead in the morning, and I would feel sad. Daddyji used to make many trips into my room to wake me, but each time he tiptoed away. Finally, as he was leaving for the office, he laid his hand on my forehead—so lightly that it seemed to be a hand in a dream—and I woke up.

"Wake up," Deoji would say, his hand pulling my cheek. "Mr. Ras Mohun has rung the wake-up bell."

Mr. Ras Mohun, who was the only person in the school with a watch, was in charge of the bell. Whatever he was doing—looking after Heea upstairs or working in his office downstairs or teaching us or supervising us—he never forgot to ring the bell at the appointed times, and wherever we were in the school we heard him.

"Let me sleep," I would beg Deoji, pulling the bedclothes over my head. "I want to finish my dream."

"The Sighted Master will report you to Mr. Ras Mohun," he would say. "That's the Sighted Master's duty."

I would get down from my bed and quickly wash and dress, just in time to join the hymn line in the boys' dormitory when Mr. Ras Mohun rang the hymn bell. With the Sighted Master prompting us, we would sing in Marathi a few Christian songs, like "When the Saints Go Marching In," that Mr. Ras Mohun had taught us, and we would sing almost in a shout, so that he, in the tower upstairs, and Jesus, Mary, and Joseph, sitting above him, would hear us and give us merit points. Sometimes we would hear the girls shouting from their side, and we would shout louder. I liked to sing the hymns, although Deoji once told me, "I have heard these hymns sung in English a few times, in the church of my missionary mummy and daddy, and they sound very different. There, when you sing 'When the Saints Go Marching In,' you think angels are lifting you up. But here, when we sing them in Marathi, I feel we are a chorus of frogs singing to the bathroom ghost. What a pity that is!"

Sometimes we would hear Mr. Ras Mohun's breakfast bell when we were in the middle of a hymn, and the other boys would rush downstairs to the veranda for their breakfast, while I would run into the sitting-and-dining room for mine. At my separate table, I was usually served porridge, toast, and, occasionally, a soft-boiled egg, which I had learned to eat with a spoon without getting egg all over my bib.

The boys would come back from their breakfast smelling of coconut and groundnuts and spinach—all delicious things that I couldn't have. We would all set about cleaning the boys' dormitory—making our beds and tidying up our boxes, under the supervision of the Sighted Master. At the sound of the class bell, we would go down for our morning class.

The morning class was held in the school's only classroom. I remember that we sat on straight-backed, cane-bottomed, armless chairs—only the teacher's chair had arms—at long tables and studied birds and animals with the pupil-teacher, Miss Mary. I also remember that Miss Mary was partially sighted, was fourteen years old, and had come to the school when she was as small as I was. She had studied up through the fourth standard—as far as the school went. Then she had had nothing to do and nowhere to go, so Mr. Ras Mohun had hired her as a pupil-teacher. At the time he hired her, she was twelve.

I didn't like sitting in a chair. I didn't know what to do with my legs. Every time I moved my legs, they made a noise, and then Miss Mary would tell me to sit quietly, like a good boy. Also, in the class we boys had to sit on one side and the girls on the other. I often wanted to jump across to the girls' side and sit with Paran. But Abdul told me, "Girl-mischief of that kind, if Mr. Ras Mohun comes to know of it, is worth two raps on the knuckles and two swats on the behind with the ruler, and Mr. Ras Mohun's ruler is not your ordinary ruler—thin and flat—but thick and round, like a policeman's swagger stick."

Once, I remember, Miss Mary handed me something fluffy and bulgy and made out of cloth. "What is it, Vedi?" she asked.

"A stuffed bird," I said absently. I didn't feel it carefully, because I was thinking about the touch of Miss Mary's hands—how they were as gentle and slightly moist as Abdul's were rough and dry—and about how sweetly she spoke Marathi.

Everyone laughed.

"Of course, it's a stuffed bird, silly, but what is it called?" Abdul put in.

Miss Mary took it from me and gave it to Reuben, who was sitting next to me. He was eleven and was totally blind. "What is it, Reuben?" she asked.

"A dove, Miss Mary."

I heard Miss Mary's bare feet slap across to Paran's chair. "What is it, Paran?"

"Reuben is wrong," Paran said. "It's not a dove at all. It's a quail."

I heard Miss Mary walk across to Bhaskar's chair. Bhaskar was nine and was half sighted.

"No, Miss Mary, they're all wrong," he said. "It's a pigeon."

She came back to my chair and put the stuffed thing in front of me. "Try again, Vedi," she said. "Can you tell what kind of bird it is?"

"I want to go outside and play," I said, without touching the stuffed thing.

"But you're in a class now," Miss Mary said. "What kind of bird is it, Vedi?"

I picked up the soft, round thing and felt it all over. It had a beak, claws, and a tail.

"It's a myna."

Everybody laughed.

"What's a myna? There is no such thing," Abdul said.

"It's a talking bird."

Everybody laughed again.

"Birds don't talk," Abdul said. "You're the son of an owl."

"Abdul, don't be abusive," Miss Mary said. (In India, the owl is considered to be foolish.)

"If Vedi weren't so small, he would know better," Deoji said.

"Our servant Sher Singh told me about a myna he knew," I said. "She was a bird and she would sit on his shoulder and talk."

"You're a good storyteller," Abdul said.

Miss Mary shushed them. "I think Mr. Ras Mohun taught me that there is a bird in the Punjab that can say a few words, but I'm not sure what it's called. Anyway, you're all wrong. This is a sparrow."

She handed some other stuffed things around, talking all the time. "This is a dove. It's a little bigger than a sparrow. . . . This is a pigeon. It's fatter than the dove. . . . This is a toy buffalo. You feel these horns? . . . This is a toy monkey. He has long arms, which he uses to swing from tree to tree. . . . This is a toy elephant. You can always tell an elephant by its trunk in the front."

"I want to see a real elephant," I said.

"Blind people can never see a real elephant," Miss Mary said. "But if sighted people say to you, 'There goes an elephant,' you should know what they mean."

I wanted to argue the matter with her, but just then we heard the lunch bell.

After lunch, Mr. Ras Mohun would ring the Braille-class bell, for our Braille lesson with the Matron.

I didn't know much about the Matron except that she was the "Sighted Master" of the girls' dormitory—that she slept there and kept order there. I'd never heard the word "matron" before and was struck by its resemblance to "train"; for months I imagined that the Matron had arrived at the school on a train when she was as small as I was, and, like Miss Mary, had stayed on because she had nowhere else to go.

One day, in the Braille class, the Matron set in front of me a wooden slate a little larger than an ordinary sheet of paper, with a couple of nails and a small hinged plate at the top. It had a recessed track of small round holes a couple of inches apart along each side. She leaned over the table from behind me. She had a big stomach, which hung out over her sari, and because she had very short arms it seemed even bigger. Her stomach was damp with sweat, and she smelled of onions and betel nuts.

I tried to slip out from under her, but she caught hold of my hand and began to show me how to align a cardboardlike piece of special Braille paper in the middle of the slate, hook it on the two nails at the top, and lock it in place with the hinged plate. She then handed me something called a guide. It was two metal strips a couple of inches high and a little wider than the slate, connected at one side by a hinge, with two pegs behind the back strip. The Matron took my forefinger and ran it along the front strip of the guide, pointing out two rows of about thirty little openings, each of which just fitted the tip of my forefinger. She then pointed out on the back strip two corresponding rows of little hollowed-out dots in identical groups of six, and told me that each group was called a cell. She showed me how, when the guide was closed and the two strips lay on each other, each opening served as a sort of frame for a cell. She showed me how to slip the back strip under the paper from the left side, fit the pegs into the two top holes of the tracks, and then close the guide, so that the paper was clamped between the two strips.

She then handed me something called a stylus—a small wooden knob with a steel pin on it. She showed me how to hold the stylus in my hand, with the knob in the crook of my right forefinger so that the steel pin was pointing down, and how to punch dots in the paper through the openings in the guide, from the right, using my left forefinger to help direct the pin of the stylus in each cell.

"You're now ready to write the first two lines of Braille on your paper," she said. "But remember that you're punching dots from the back—that Braille is written backward. Different patterns of dots in a cell stand for different English letters. When you have filled two rows of cells with any groups of dots you like, move the guide down to the next holes on the slate, and then you can write two more lines." She had a deep voice and breathed heavily, but she spoke Marathi sweetly, like Miss Mary.

The Matron moved on, and I tried to punch my first line of Braille dots. The head of the stylus was too big for the crook of my finger. So much pressure was required to punch a dot through the thick paper that I had to climb on the chair, hold the stylus with both hands, and press it down with all my weight. When I tried to write in this way, the slate, which was so long that it stuck out over the edge of the table, jabbed me in the stomach. Since my left hand was busy pressing down on the stylus, I couldn't help direct the pin of the stylus, so I couldn't tell what dots I was punching in each cell.

I took the paper out of the guide and out of the hinged plate and turned it over, Braille side up. I touched the Braille dots I had made; each dot was sharp and distinct—not torn and obscure, as when I put a pin through a piece of paper. But I realized I had no idea what the dots meant. Then I heard the Matron exclaim, "There, Vedi! You're reading now!"

I felt excited, and remembered sitting on my rocking horse and rocking away, and playing all the notes on my mouth organ, from one end to the other, and making my first motorcar out of my Meccano set.

"Children who don't know yet how to write Braille," the Matron was saying to the class, "take the paper out of your guide, run your forefinger first down the left side of the first cell of the guide, and then down the right side, and count off with me, from top to bottom, 'Dot one, dot two, dot three—dot four, dot five, dot six.' These six dots, in various combinations, stand for all the English Braille letters. But not all the possible combinations of dots are used up by the twenty-six letters of the English alphabet. So some of these dots and combinations are used for English punctuation marks; dot six before any letter stands for a capital. Other combinations of dots are English contraction signs for everyday words like 'and,' 'for,' 'of.' "

She turned to me. "Can you tell me now, Vedi, what a contraction is?"

"I don't understand anything," I said.

She explained again and repeated her question.

"Contractions are little words like 'and,' 'for,' and 'of,' " I said, repeating what I thought she had said.

"Good boy," she said, patting me on the back. "Now see if you can write some more."

I tried to realign my Braille paper in the slate. The old holes in the paper where it had originally hooked on to the nails under the hinged plate tore, and the paper shifted in the guide. Consequently, the new dots I made went in a crooked line and ran into dots I had made earlier, jumbling everything.

All around me was the clatter of wood, metal, and paper—of Braille dots being punched in the thick paper, of steel pins clicking along the cells of the guides, of guides being shifted down the slate tracks, of hinged plates being opened and snapped shut. Ahead, there was the tick-tick-tick-tick of Deoji (fast, like the pitter-patter of my baby sister Usha's feet); from the left, there was the tick, tick, tick, tick of Bhaskar (lumbering, like the swish-and-jerk of strips of cane being drawn through the chair frames); from the right, there was the tick-tick, tick-tick of Abdul (sudden, like the click-click of Mr. Ras Mohun's shoes).

I remembered the quiet scratchings of my sister Umi's pencil running along in her copybook and the delicate strokes of my sister Pom's fountain pen flowing along her pad. I remembered the soothing, almost imperceptible sound of Sister Umi turning a page of her copybook and the cozy, rippling sound of Sister Pom tearing a page out of her pad.

"Matron!" I cried out. "I want pencil and paper! I want to write like Sister Umi."

"Bhaskar is half sighted, and even he can't write with pencil and paper," the Matron said. "What makes you think that you can?"

"I want pencil and paper!" I shouted, and I flung the guide down on the floor. I would have flung the slate after it except that it was too large and heavy.

"Think of your Braille slate and guide as a new toy," the Matron said, picking up the guide and giving it to me. "You can write a secret message to Abdul."

That idea kept me at my Braille slate for a while, but I soon grew tired of it. I let the stylus drop on the table and sat scratching my legs.

In time—I don't know how many days or weeks or months it was—my stylus finger grew, my hand grew, my strength grew, and I learned to align the paper on the slate properly and write Braille correctly. I remember that in order to memorize which dots stood for which letters I would think of combinations of dots as telephone numbers, and of the letters formed by the combinations as standing for members of my family. When I punched (or dialled) one, three, six, I got "u," for Umi; when I punched one, two, three, four, I got "p," for Pom; when I punched one, three, four, I got "m," for Ma-maji. The Braille letters would race through my fingers into the stylus, along the guide, and down the slate, filling the paper with simple English words, like "cat," "mat," and "sat."

We always knew when the Braille class was over because Mr. Ras Mohun would come into the room ringing the bell. The Matron would leave, and Mr. Ras Mohun himself would start teaching. His subject was Bible stories and general knowledge. It was the only class for which we had a book—a copy for each of us. The book, which was in English, was called "Bible Stories for Boys and Girls." It had a smooth, hard cover, and every time I touched it I thought of a tall marble statue of a mother and child which stood on the mantelpiece in our drawing room at home.

"A good Bible reader is a good Braille reader," Mr. Ras Mohun would say. "And a good Braille reader sits properly. A bad Braille reader reads with the tip of only a forefinger, but a good Braille reader reads with the tips of all eight fingers—with both hands. He doesn't press down hard on the letters. He doesn't move his lips or whisper to himself when he's reading. He keeps his arms straight. He bends his hands slightly, so that his fingers are at an angle to the book. He keeps his book level on the desk."

I paid attention to Mr. Ras Mohun's directions and learned to read "Bible Stories" quickly. Each letter of the book fitted easily under the tip of a finger—the book was embossed without any contraction signs, and there were wide spaces between the lines—and I liked the feel of a line of well-embossed Braille letters. Abdul could read with only his right forefinger, but from the very start I practiced reading like Deoji, with all eight fingers. I used to imagine that each of my fingers was a student—Abdul, Deoji, Bhaskar, Paran—and that they were all competing to see which one of them could read the fastest. The left little finger was the laggard, like Abdul. The right forefinger was the star, like Deoji. To bring the laggard finger up to the level of the star finger, I would practice reading with only the left little finger. But it seemed that, try as I might, there was no way to make the laggard catch up.

"I am determined to become a good Braille reader, even faster than Deoji, so that I can become a doctor, like Daddyji," I said to Abdul one day.

"I would rather be a carpenter than a doctor," Abdul said, referring to a story in the book. In the story, Jesus said that being a carpenter was just as good as being a doctor. Abdul took special delight in the idea because "carpentry and caning are like chair and seat—they go together," he said. "I'd rather cane chairs than read stupid Braille."

Sometimes when I was reading Braille, my hands would get cold, and I would sit on them and wonder if I could ever learn to read Braille with my chin.

Mr. Ras Mohun would conclude the Bible-stories-and-general-knowledge class by ringing the bell from wherever he happened to be standing. Many boys and girls would thereupon go to the veranda for the music class, which was taught by another pupil-teacher, Mr. Joseph, or to the workshop, in the back part of the classroom, to cane chairs under the direction of the Sighted Master.

I wanted to go to the music class, because Deoji went there, and to the caning class, because Abdul went there. I remember that nice sounds of stringed instruments came from the music class, and that once Abdul came upstairs to the boys' dormitory from caning and announced, to great general excitement, that the caning class had received an order to make shirt buttons out of coconut shells.

"I want to make shirt buttons with you," I said.

"Mr. Ras Mohun won't let you," Abdul said.

"Yes, he will."

When I told Mr. Ras Mohun about what I was going to do, he said, "You are not to go to either the workshop or the music class. Your father has forbidden it. Children who cane chairs or play stringed instruments get calluses on their fingers, and then they can't read Braille well. And your father has high hopes for you."

I didn't know exactly what calluses were until Deoji let me feel his fingers after he had started learning to play the *dilrubah* in music class. They had got swollen and hard. "In music class here, we only have cheap instruments with sharp strings, like the *dilrubah*, which is good for street music," Deoji told me. "I am praying to Jesus, Mary, and Joseph that when I grow up I will have a violin, which is played in the drawing rooms of well-to-do homes. It has nice strings and doesn't require too much pressure from the fingers."

As it happened, the shirt-button order was cancelled, because the job proved too difficult for the caning class, but before it was cancelled the workshop acquired a metal bench vise. I remember that I used to slip down to the workshop in the evening and play with it secretly. I would put my fingers between its serrated lips and turn the handle bit by bit to see how much pressure my fingers could stand—all the time hoping that I would get calluses, like Deoji's. I never did, although sometimes I had trouble extricating my fingers, and afterward I would carry the impressions of the serrated lips for a few minutes.

Following Mr. Ras Mohun's class, when everyone else went to the music class or the workshop, I would go down into the cellar and play with Miss Mary. In the cellar, Miss Mary once showed me several heavy wooden bars with wooden balls at the ends. "These are dumbbells," she said. "When you grow big, you will be able to lift them and grow bigger."

She picked me up and showed me metal rings hanging from the ceiling.

I caught hold of the rings and slipped out of her arms and swung like a monkey. "Catch me!" I called out to her, and I swung fast and high until I was giddy. I jumped down and shouted, "Again, Miss Mary!"

Just then, Mr. Ras Mohun rang the tiffin bell, and I ran upstairs to the sitting-and-dining room.

I would swallow my tiffin—a cup of hot milk with soggy pieces of bread in it—as quickly as I could and race down to the back courtyard, where everyone would be waiting for Mr. Ras Mohun to ring the game bell. The back courtyard was so small that if Abdul, Deoji, and I had joined hands, extended our arms, and swung around, we could almost have touched all four walls, but into it a seesaw, a swing, and a combination of climbing bars and a slide had somehow been fitted. During the game period, the Sighted Master and the Matron would see to it that we all got a turn on one or another of these.

After the game period, there would be the relaxing bell, and we boys would all go to the boys' dormitory and sit on our beds and talk. Now and again, Mrs. Ras Mohun would come and get two or three of us and give us a gardening lesson at a patch along one wall of the back courtyard, known as Mrs. Ras Mohun's flower-and-vegetable bed.

I remember that one time we planted a couple of rosebushes, and every morning we went down to feel them. Abdul couldn't understand why the rosebushes had thorns. Bhaskar said that it was because ghosts liked the smell of roses and didn't want us to pick them. Another time, we planted some potatoes, and I couldn't understand why they grew underground. Bhaskar said that it was because ghosts lived underground and liked to eat potatoes.

After the relaxing period, there were two other bells—the dinner bell and the sleep bell.

I remember that once, after the sleep bell, Mr. Ras Mohun caught me out of my bed, and summoned me to his office the next morning.

"Yes? Speak, Vedi, speak," he said. "You have made me very unhappy by being out of your bed after the sleep bell." He tapped what I was sure was his ruler on his desk impatiently, as if his hand were twitching to beat me.

I couldn't find my voice, even though he kept on urging me to speak. I thought what a funny way he had of speaking. He said "yetsh" and "shpeak" and "unhoppy." (He had the same funny way of speaking Marathi; I later learned that the accent was characteristic of many Bengalis.) Yet when he addressed me by name I would start, for it seemed that Mamaji was calling me. Many women's voices were not as high-pitched as his. I remember that he had a thin falsetto voice, which was always pitched on more or less the same note and had a weary quality. Perhaps because he was angry now, his voice was cracking, like Mamaji's. (She had long suffered from asthma, which had clouded her voice, but she had a much greater range of tones than Mr. Ras Mohun did.) I found myself listening to Mr. Ras Mohun's voice and trying to remember Mamaji's voice.

"Shpeak, boy, shpeak."

I jumped. "I was in the boys' common bathroom and couldn't get quickly into my bell—I mean, my bed, Uncle."

Saturdays and Sundays, the boys ordinarily had to stay in the boys' dormitory and the girls in the girls' dormitory. But now and then the Sighted Master and the Matron would organize outings or games for us.

Sometimes we went on outings to Mahim Sea Beach. Those of us who were totally blind walked with the partially sighted, in twos or threes, but boys could walk only with boys, and girls only with girls. Mahim Sea Beach was far away, beyond Dadar Pool and Shivaji Park. Because I was small, I had trouble keeping up with the others and quickly got tired. Sometimes I would sit down on the way and ask to be carried. If I was walking with Bhaskar and Deoji, Bhaskar would get angry and go ahead, but Deoji would stay back with me. Sometimes Deoji and I would reach Mahim Sea Beach only as the others were starting back. Mahim Sea Beach smelled like the boys' common bathroom, the mud underfoot was slippery, and the water was so shallow that I had to sit down even to get my legs wet. Just the same, we always felt refreshed after the outing.

One Saturday, Abdul announced in the boys' dormitory, "The Sighted Master has found a new game for us."

All of us gathered around Abdul to find out what it was.

"It has to do with a long rope," he said.

"They are going to hang Jaisingh, so that the rest of us can sleep," Tarak Nath said.

Everyone laughed at Tarak Nath's remark. None of us liked the deaf, dumb, and blind Jaisingh much, because he cried in the middle of the night for no reason at all; in fact, we scorned him, as we imagined that the sighted scorned all of us.

Bhaskar wanted to know if this was the game he had been dreaming about, in which boys and girls could play together and touch each other.

"No," Abdul said. "There are no such games for the blind. As long as Mr. Ras Mohun has his ruler, such games will not be played here."

We all cursed Abdul for never letting us forget Mr. Ras Mohun's ruler.

That afternoon, the Sighted Master called us all to the postage stamp of a front courtyard for the game. He let us feel a huge rope that was coiled up on the ground. It was rough and abrasive and muddy and so thick that my hands could scarcely go round it. Following the Sighted Master's directions, we uncoiled the rope and laid it out on the ground, organized ourselves into two parties, dug a line across the middle of the muddy courtyard, and took places along the rope, on either side of the line. We held the rope up, nestling it under our arms. The Sighted Master shouted "Go!" and we started pulling. Deoji was very strong and he was on my side of the line, and our team pulled everyone on the other across the line. All of us liked the game very much, because at the end we all fell on each other in a heap in the mud. We begged to play some more, but the Sighted Master said, "This is a tug-of-war. Mr. Ras Mohun says you can hurt yourself, so it must be played only once in a while, under my supervision." It was many weeks before we got a chance to have a tug-of-war again.

The Unification of
Stephen Hawking

MARK O'BRIEN

The opportunities available to the disabled reporter to practice his craft are scant and uninteresting. When *The Fessenden Review* asked this disabled journalist to leave his Berkeley apartment and trek to southern California to interview Elizabeth Bouvia, a disabled woman who demanded medical assistance to help her starve herself to death, I had to say no. I very much wanted to talk with her, but I would have had to rent a van with a wheelchair lift, find accommodations for myself, an attendant or two, and a 900-pound iron lung. I spend most of my time in a 900-pound iron lung because polio has shriveled my lungs. Such a dependence upon the iron lung greatly reduces my mobility, so I told the editor of *The Fessenden Review* that I had to refuse the assignment. Throwing out my Clark Kent fedora, I resumed my career as a small-time poet, freelance book reviewer, and author of an unfinished novel.

Four years ago, I reviewed *Stephen Hawking's Universe* (William Morrow and Company, 1985), a biography of an Englishman who was disabled by amyotrophic lateral sclerosis (ALS) in the 1960s while studying physics and mathematics at Cambridge University. I praised the deft manner in which the author, John Boslough, described Hawking's startling work in theoretical physics, but I expressed disappointment that he failed to say much about Hawking as a person. All Boslough could say on this point was that Hawking was the toughest man he had ever met.

I was fascinated with the idea that one of the world's leading physicists was disabled because the popular image of disabled people has us do nothing besides mope over being disabled. It seemed likely that Stephen Hawking would become, whether he wanted to or not, the most famous disabled person since the death of Franklin Roosevelt. Like Roosevelt, Hawking had become well known more through his work than his disability. Unlike Roosevelt, Hawking never sought to hide the fact of his disability. Where I had the sense that Roosevelt was what a disabled friend of mine had called "a closet crip," I felt no such reticence or shame emanating from Hawking. While not wishing to hide his disability, neither did Hawking seem to regard it as the only important thing in his life. If he was obsessed with anything, it was with the universe—its origin, workings, and destiny. In his own book, *A Brief History of Time* (Bantam Books, 1988), Hawking says he is seeking nothing less than "the unification of physics," the reconciliation of quantum mechanics with relativity and an integration of the four forces (electromagnetism, gravity, and the weak and strong nuclear forces) which would provide an explanation for all phenomena. Given the scope of his ambition and the brilliance of his intellect, it seems likely to me that he will achieve this goal and in the process avoid becoming fixated upon being disabled, a condition a friend of mine calls "being a full-time crip." But Hawking still has to deal with his disability, even if he is just a part-time crip. I wondered how Hawking dealt with becoming severely disabled. How did he get to be so tough? What was it like for him to have a wife and children? What has he done with the feelings of depression which disability usually brings?

So when I learned that Hawking would give a series of lectures on the Berkeley campus of the University of California, I saw my chance. I live a few blocks south of campus, so travel would not present a problem. I phoned the university's public information office and was told that Dr. Hawking (everyone with the university called him Dr. Hawking) would give a press conference the following Tuesday.

I didn't attend Hawking's first lecture (or any of the others) because I felt too tired to get out of the iron lung on those days and because I felt I would have little chance of asking him for an interview in the post-lecture crush that I could envision easily—a swarm of redwood-tall students and T.A.'s elbowing each other, shouting

"Doctor Hawking!" and tripping over my close-to-the-ground wheelchair. No, it would not be pretty. Worse than that, I would not be able to approach Hawking in a calm, dignified manner.

When the morning of the press conference came, I worried that I would not get the interview. Armed only with a cassette tape recorder and a manila envelope stuffed with a formal letter requesting an interview, my disability poems, my science poems, my autobiographical essay, my reviews of *Stephen Hawking's Universe*, and Hawking's new book, I hoped to persuade him to grant me an interview.

I had asked Miguel, my lunch attendant, to come at 10:30 to get me into my wheelchair and push me to the press conference. I worried that he might be late, as he often is, but this time he wasn't. When he lifted me, I screamed much less than usual (getting lifted always scares the sweet bejesus out of me, even if the lifter looks like an Olympic basketball player), because my chief concern was to get to the press conference on time. Miguel took me out into the warm March day while I fretted about my lack of press credentials.

Gentle reader, all of those reporters you see on TV talking about their press credentials are working for some corporation, usually a huge one such as Time, ABC, or *Rolling Stone*. I, being a freelancer, which is to say an unemployed poet and novelist who occasionally deigns to work at journalism when prompted by a desire for thrills or money, had no press credentials at all. When I was a student in the UC Berkeley journalism school, I had been issued a little white card that shrilly insisted I was a bona fide, honest-to-pete reporter for something called the California News Service, a dummy organization invented by the journalism school for the sole purpose of issuing press credentials to its students. But it had been years since I dropped out of J-school and tossed out my CNS cards. I had asked the editor of *The Fessenden Review* to send me press credentials, but they were delayed in the mail. Now I approached the greatest story of my journalistic career with no more press credentials than a hyena. More reason for me to be anxious. What if they demanded proof that I was a reporter? I would sputter "Oh, yeah?" like Tommy Smothers. No, a better idea struck me. I would tell them to phone the editor of *The Fessenden Review*. But what if he wasn't in? What if he was in his office, but the person checking my credentials had never heard of *The Fessenden Review*?

Such trepidations tumbled in my mind like dice as Miguel pushed me into the student union building, where the press conference was to be held in Heller Lounge. Acting as the navigator, for I knew the campus better than Miguel did, I confidently told him that it was on the top floor.

"I remember because it's where I rented my cap and gown for my graduation."

But there was nothing called Heller Lounge up there. When Miguel told a man emerging from a room that we were looking for Dr. Hawking's press conference, the man said he was also going to it and led the way. Downstairs, we entered a long, vaguely defined area which I had always thought of as the student lounge. Miguel pushed me by students lounging, reading, or sprawling across the bright blue sofas in complete exhaustion. Near the end of the lounge, folding chairs had been set up in an open, glass-walled area, presumably as a special accommodation to the able-bodied journalists. On a long table in front of us all were press handouts and a vase of flowers in Cal colors, yellow and blue. No one asked me to produce anything to prove that I was a reporter. I concluded that if you look sufficiently disabled, people will judge you to be harmless.

We were early, so I asked Miguel to grab some handouts and get my cassette recorder out of the red backpack that hangs loosely from the back of my wheelchair like a turkey wattle. Then we waited. The inquisitive reporters looked at each other, at the handouts, at the flowers, and at the view through the tinted glass walls of Lower Sproul Plaza, a barren, concrete space that is afflicted most noons by bands of the heavy metal or acid-punk (or whatever they're called these days) persuasion screeching as though they are being vivisected. But now the bands and their tormentors had the good sense to be absent. In the stark silence, I heard the low buzzing of an electric wheelchair.

"Is that him?" I asked Miguel, who can look around easier than I can.

"No, it's someone else."

Finally, a tall bearded man started talking into the microphone.

". . . Will you please welcome to the university Doctor Stephen W. Hawking."

Applause spattered the room like a sudden rainstorm. Then I saw him to my left, a slight figure moving slowly across the room in a brown, padded wheelchair. Wearing a crumpled houndstooth suit, he looked very English and very academic, happily fulfilling our preconceptions. His face, middle-aged and knobbly, reminded me of a pensive Alfred E. Neuman. Suddenly, his face blessed us with a

smile as dazzling and casual as Jack Kennedy's. A Beatles cut, graying, remained from his student days. After he parked his wheelchair
by the table, the microphone was lowered and placed next to his
voice synthesizer, a plastic and metal device that sits on the wheelchair's lap tray like a large, propped-up book.

"Doctor Hawking," began the first questioner, who proceeded to
ask about a recently discovered supernova.

I wanted to ask my question early to get through my anxiety. I
had decided to ask him what he would say to disabled people who
were stuck in nursing homes or in a room in their parents' house.
I wanted to ask him this because I had spent too many years of my
life stuck in such frustrating, life-stopping places. That I have come
to live in such a jazzy, juicy place as Berkeley astonishes me so much
that I inspect the mailing labels on magazines to make sure that my
name is two lines above BERKELEY, CA.

It took Dr. Hawking a couple of minutes to type his first answer, which came abruptly from the speech synthesizer in a deep
American-sounding voice, impressively human though somewhat
robotic around the edges.

I wanted to get my question in, but Dr. Hawking possesses no
body language to indicate "next?" The other reporters beat me to
it several times. During the long pauses occasioned by Dr. Hawking's
voice synthesizer, photographers scuttled about like hyperactive lob-
sters, standing, kneeling, leaning, trying to get every angle on
Dr. Hawking, whose movements were limited to his cool blue eyes
and that smile. Although his answers were slow in coming, everyone
present had their attention devoted to him. I wondered what the
passersby on the walkway outside the glass wall would make of the
scene—thirty or forty able-bodied people expectantly looking at a
small, thin man in a wheelchair who never moved his lips to speak.

A photographer knelt on the floor, blocking my view of Hawking.
I asked her in a whisper to move, but my whisper was too soft and
I feared that if I asked her in my normal tone of voice, I would
break the eerie silence between questions and answers. I seemed
unable to croak out a medium-sized request, so I asked Miguel to
ask her to move, which she did. Now that I could see Hawking again,
I decided I should ask my question before someone else came along
to block my view. Shimmering with anxiety, I pondered the puniness
of my question. How parochial of me to ask a man who might the
next morning awake with the solution to the universe a question
concerning some Oppressed Minority, even if he were a member of

it. Would Hawking be annoyed that my question would pull him away from the pristine glory of physics and into the sad, ancient swamp of disability? Looking steadily into his halcyon eyes, I pretended to have the courage to ask him my question.

"Doctor Hawking, what can you say to all the disabled people who are stuck in nursing homes or living with their parents or in some other untenable situation and who feel that their life is over, that they have no future?"

As I heard this long question unravel like an ill-mannered ball of yarn, Hawking continued to look at me and typed his answer into the voice synthesizer. I couldn't see his right hand, the one he used to type. I waited. All of us waited. Then the silence was cracked by the voice synthesizer's crisp, booming voice.

It can be very difficult. I know that I was very fortunate. All I can say is that one must do the best one can in the situation in which one finds oneself.

He continued to look at me as his answer was spoken, as though he missed the simultaneity of speech and eye contact. I thanked him, then the other reporters asked questions which veered away from physics, a subject very few of us understood, and toward God, a subject on which we all consider ourselves experts. Hawking told the attentive reporters that he did believe in God, but not in a personal God. At least, that's what I *thought* he said. The final question asked whether Dr. Hawking really wanted the riddle of the universe to be solved. Wouldn't discovering The Answer have the distressing effect of ending a grand quest?

I hope that we will find it, but not quite yet.

We laughed, even though we half-expected such a sly answer.

The press conference over, the able-bodied people got out of their folding chairs to cluster into knots of conversation, which is what able-bodied people do when they are not sure of what they should be doing. Miguel picked my tape recorder off the floor and put it in my backpack. I asked him to give my envelope to someone in Hawking's entourage, but Miguel asked whether I wouldn't rather have him give my envelope directly to Hawking. Suspended in indecision, I thought of how little space there was on the lap tray of Dr. Hawking's wheelchair, the possibility that he might be offended by such naked American chutzpah, and how unlikely it was that I would ever get this close to him again. I thought about this for what seemed to me a day or two. I considered every angle of the problem and after a period the world would count as a second and a half, I felt the cold, sharp gust of "What the hell" blast away my irresolution. I told Miguel to give the envelope to Hawking, who then approached me.

Hello, said Hawking in his calm electronic voice.

"It's such an honor to meet you," I burbled in my tremulous meeting-a-celebrity voice. I explained the contents of the envelope, including the letter asking him for an interview. Rather than wait for him to read my letter, I asked him for an interview right there and then, while the able-bodied reporters towered around us like a circle of curious trees.

Yes. The week of April fourth.

"Good, good. That'll give me time to . . . I have my phone number on the letter, so you . . . you or one of your people can call me to set a time and place."

Yes.

Your people, my people. I was beginning to sound like a CEO.

He left to talk with others amidst the milling, mumbling crowd.

I got it, I got it! I thought. This'll be the biggest story of my journalistic career. Just think. I and *The Fessenden Review* will be quoted by the two dozen companies evoked in the American mind by the trendy and mellifluous word "media."

A balding man leaned down to me, his microphone hungering for my words.

"National Public Radio."

"Are you William Drummond?" I asked, giddy at the thought. Drummond taught at the UC Berkeley journalism school, he had worked for President Ford, as NPR's correspondent in Lebanon he had faced constant danger, and he had met Susan Stamberg, NPR's sultry-voiced, witty anchor. Oh my God, he knows Susan Stamberg!

"No, I'm not Bill Drummond," he said, interrupting my delirium. "Rick McCourt."

Now *that* was a stupid thing for me to say, I thought, chastising myself. Why didn't I just let him introduce himself? But he didn't seem to mind. I told him I had heard his science reports. So what if he hadn't met Susan Stamberg? Maybe he would someday.

Beside him stood a woman who didn't identify herself. She asked me whether seeing Dr. Hawking gave me hope. This struck me as an awfully stupid question. Hope for what? Could Dr. Hawking change my life, make me walk, get me a lover? I tried to think of a polite way to answer her.

"It's not that, so much, as, uh . . . he gives me a sense of 'hurray-for-our-side.' "

What was I saying? God knows. I just didn't want to get sucked into being cast as a Spokesperson for the Disabled in a dreary story headlined "Disabled Inspired by Dr. Hawking." Their interview of me lasted about two minutes. McCourt told me he'd phone me if NPR used his interview with me. Then they left. My celebrity status ended with thirteen minutes left to go.

"I want to go home," I told Miguel, who pushed me through the sunny campus and down Telegraph Avenue back to my apartment.

After a week had passed without any word from Hawking, I grew anxious. He was a busy man in a foreign country and could easily have forgotten about me and my proposed interview. So when I heard that the university's Disabled Students Program was honoring Dr. Hawking with a barbecue, I decided to attend it in the hope of reminding him of the interview.

Miguel took me to the barbecue, which was held in the parking lot behind the old pinkish-red mansion that houses DSP. It was a hot Thursday, the day of Dr. Hawking's third and final lecture on the Berkeley campus. The parking lot was crowded with people in all kinds of wheelchairs, blind people, attendants, deaf people signing at feverish speed, the DSP staff, and reporters from KQED-TV and *National Geographic*. Heat bounced off of the three white buildings that surround the parking lot on three sides. The last thing I wanted was to have a hard, mean, crunchy hamburger pushed into my mouth. This being Berkeley, there was pasta salad, but the good vegetarians of Berkeley had devoured the pasta salad, confident that the pasta salad never said moo, never blinked large brown eyes, and never gave birth to mewling, puking baby pasta salads.

Where was Hawking?

God knew, having a better vantage point than mine, which was in my new and unsteady reclining wheelchair, reclined to almost flat, which put my head about three feet above the hot asphalt.

A man in a tall psychedelic wheelchair bumped into my recliner, causing it to tip backwards maybe an eighth of an inch. Convinced that my skull would be cracked open like an egg and that my brains would fry sunny-side-up on the asphalt, I screamed in falsetto panic. As my wheelchair steadied itself, everyone looked at me.

"Are you all right?" they asked me.

"Yeah."

Now certain in the knowledge that I was having a thoroughly terrible time, I told Miguel I wanted to leave.

"Can you see Hawking? Over there?"

He pointed and I saw him, surrounded by people. He was eating something and looking as though he were enjoying himself in spite of wearing a tweed suit in the ninety-plus heat.

"I'll try to get you over there to see him," Miguel said.

As Miguel knifed my wheelchair through the densely packed crowd, I could see the circle around Hawking break. A DSP official tested the microphone, then said what a privilege it was to have Dr. Hawking present. She then presented the famous disabled physicist tokens of admiration, one of them a T-shirt that proclaimed:

I SURVIVED THE BARBECUE
AT THE UC BERKELEY DISABLED STUDENTS
PROGRAM APRIL 7, 1988

Thinking that I deserved such a T-shirt more than Hawking did, even though he wore that tweed suit, I observed the brief ceremony, which concluded with the announcement that Dr. Hawking would autograph copies of his book at the other end of the parking lot.

A DSP staffer began singing into the microphone as Hawking zoomed by me, two feet to my right. I recognized his wife from her photo in Boslough's book. I had enough cash to buy the book, so Miguel and I waited in the line of people asking Hawking to autograph copies of his book, the sun glaring in my face and raising a bumper crop of skin cancer cells on my potato-pale Irish face. While we waited, Miguel brought one of Hawking's attendants, a tall Englishwoman with curly reddish hair, over to talk with me. When I told her that I wanted to interview Dr. Hawking that Saturday, she said she was terribly sorry, but they were leaving Berkeley the next day.

Was all this for nothing? I asked myself.

"But I can't speak for him," she said. "You should ask him yourself."

At last, Miguel pushed me up to Hawking and, with his assistant's meager encouragement in mind, I asked Dr. Hawking whether he could still give me an interview. Close up, he looked uncomfortable. Was it the heat or was it that I was bugging him? I was rehearsing my yes-I-understand speech when he said *Yes. Half eleven in the lobby of my hotel.*

Once again, I was startled by his willingness to talk with me.

The red-haired attendant pressed Hawking's right thumb into an inkpad, then into the inside cover of his book. I had his autograph.

That Saturday morning, I sat with Miguel in the lobby of the Durant Hotel, a stately green structure which flies an enormous American flag on its roof. Although I had never been in a hotel lobby before, I seemed to recognize the decor and ambience— overstuffed furniture, hushed conversation, men in suits vacuuming the carpet and polishing the brass. I sensed the quiet, genteel bore- dom prized by old money. Perhaps Miguel and I had entered one of the wormholes Hawking writes about, a rent in time-space that leads to unexpected destinations, in this case, the Algonquin Hotel, circa 1924. Was that Robert Benchley reading the *Herald Tribune*? No, it was just a Japanese businessman flipping through the *San Francisco Chronicle*.

Miguel and I looked about, checked my tape recorder, and drummed the fingers of our minds. The two clocks in the lobby went off every fifteen minutes, but had differing ideas of the exact time. Was one right and the other wrong? Were they both wrong?

I was trying to remember whether relativity applied to hotel lob- bies when some men entered the lobby, one of them sitting in a tall and unmistakably psychedelic wheelchair. One of the men was red- haired and seemed to act as attendant to the man in the psychedelic wheelchair. The other two men, one British, the other American, were white-haired. The red-haired man sat atop the back of a pro- foundly upholstered chair, whereupon the group broke up into two groups to provide Miguel and me with polyphonic conversation. The white-haired American talked with the man in the psychedelic wheelchair about the remarkable distribution of ALS, Alzheimer's, and Parkinson's disease on Guam, whose inhabitants come down with either Alzheimer's or Parkinson's on the one hand, or ALS on the other. It seemed that no one on Guam ever got ALS *and* one of the other diseases, and that disorders of the nervous system were so popular on Guam because of all the toxic dreck dumped there by the U.S. military. Through the other channel, I heard the red- haired man talk with the Briton about the bizarre nature of the universe as described by Dr. Hawking at one of his lectures. It struck me that *anyone's* description of the universe must sound bizarre upon a first hearing, but that Hawking's description seemed espe- cially bizarre, what with black holes seeming to radiate gamma rays and the big bang not necessarily signifying any sort of Beginning.

When the two conversations fugued together in my mind, I realized that they were both about aspects of Hawking's life.

Suddenly, I saw Hawking emerge from the elevator with the same attendant who had talked with me at the barbecue. She walked over to tell me she was terribly sorry, but Dr. Hawking would be meeting some people before he could see me. Did I mind? No. It was still only 11:00 or 11:15, depending on which clock you believed. Hawking disappeared down a hallway with his attendant and a group of people who had been sitting in the lobby.

I waited nervously, trying to imagine what I would do if the interview failed to yield me the information I would need to solve the riddle of Stephen Hawking. I knew that I would have only half an hour with him and that it would take him a minute or two to answer each of my questions. When the red-haired woman came to tell me that Dr. Hawking could see me, Miguel pushed me to the meeting as I felt a feeling of this is it, I'm going to hit the beach at Normandy.

Stephen Hawking, sitting beside a long wooden table in a posh conference room, was dressed in a striped T-shirt and brown pants. The walls of the room were paneled in wood and decorated with watercolors of the campus sold by the Berkeley alumni association. As I inhaled the importance of the room and the situation, I noticed that the roseate calm of these paintings clashed with the confusion and clamor I had come to associate with the same scenes in real life. After Miguel set up my tape recorder, I asked him to leave. I was alone with Hawking and his attendant, who helped him drink a glass of tea and occasionally asked me questions as I waited for Hawking's answer to emerge from the voice synthesizer. He seemed preoccupied and would occasionally gag on the tea, which made him seem vulnerable. Telling him that I wanted to ask him personal questions in regard to his disability, I began.

O'BRIEN: It looks like you're becoming a celebrity. Your lectures have drawn overflow audiences. How do you feel about this?

HAWKING: *It may help to sell my book, but I really want to get back to my scientific work.*

O'BRIEN: From what I've read in Boslough's biography of you and other places, meeting Jane Wilde seems to have been an important point in your life. Can you tell me how you were feeling, physically and emotionally, when you met her?

HAWKING: *A bit mixed up.*

O'BRIEN: How did knowing her affect you?

HAWKING: *I wouldn't have been able to do what I have done without her help.*

O'BRIEN: Did you think women wouldn't be attracted to you after you were diagnosed as having ALS?

HAWKING: *I didn't know.*

O'BRIEN: Do you ever feel frustration, rage at being disabled?

HAWKING: *No.*

O'BRIEN: Does your work help you to deal with these feelings?

HAWKING: *Yes. I have been lucky. I don't have anything to be angry about.*

When I asked him how he relates to his children and whether he disciplined them, his attendant asked me whether I knew his children's ages.

"Twenty, seventeen, and seven," I said, relieved that I could recall this information.

"The youngest is nine," she said. "Actually, I don't think he disciplines them enough," she added, smiling at Hawking, who was busy typing his answer. "But that's just my opinion."

HAWKING: *I get along well with them. I'm lucky to have such nice children.*

O'BRIEN: I've read that you've been to Moscow ten times, to the United States twenty-five times to meet with other physicists. Do you find travel to be tiring?

HAWKING: *Yes. I travel a lot. I'm going to Israel and to Russia.*

O'BRIEN: Do you find different attitudes toward disability in different countries?

HAWKING: *People help wherever I go.*

O'BRIEN: Do you find this book-publicizing tour boring?

HAWKING: *I have been meeting colleagues.*

O'BRIEN: Do you read outside of the reading you have to do in physics?

HAWKING: *I don't get much time to read.*

O'BRIEN: Did you derive your idea of an impersonal god from Buddhism, Vedanta, or some other tradition, or have you developed your own religious ideas?

His attendant then told me that I had misunderstood what Dr. Hawking had said at his press conference, which was that he didn't believe in a personal god, not that he believed in an impersonal god.

HAWKING: *It is better not to use the word* god *to describe what I believe, because most people use the word to mean a being with whom one can have a personal relationship.*

O'BRIEN: Do you sense a connection between *how* the universe operates and *why* it exists?

HAWKING: *I don't. If I did, I would have solved the universe.*

Had I succeeded in my quest to solve Stephen W. Hawking, to unify all the forces that made him the man he is? I felt that I had not. His answers were brief and unrevealing. Being disabled myself, I found it difficult to believe that he felt he did not have "anything to be angry about." Had I asked him the wrong questions, questions he considered to be too intrusive? Was it that the slowness of the voice synthesizer tends to make him want to speak laconically? Or, what seems most likely, is he just a shy man wrapped up in his work and his family? Perhaps we demand too much of people when we ask them to turn their lives inside-out to satisfy our raging curiosity about celebrities. The one thing I learned was that Hawking's work succeeds in distracting him from becoming obsessed with his disability, just as Roosevelt's work as governor of New York and president of the United States rescued him from dark years of brooding and frustration. And was I so different with my writing? Didn't my constant work on book reviews, poems, journalism, and my novel take me out of and beyond my wretched body? If the unification of the forces that cause Stephen Hawking is ever achieved, it will teach us the necessity of work not only for those of us who are trapped in unworkable bodies, but for everyone who is trapped in the stark, unyielding prison of time-space.

Renascence

~◉ ◉~

MARGARET ROBISON

On the morning of May 1, 1989, I phoned a friend. I intended to tell her that something was horribly wrong. I intended to ask for help. But when I tried to speak, a garble of some of the most frightening guttural noise that I'd ever heard erupted from me. It was as if some strange animal—wild and terrified—had been set loose in my brain. Speech as I had known it was gone. I was in the process of having the massive stroke that would also paralyze my left arm and leg.

A year and eight months later, I wrote in a letter to Angela Manssolillo, my former speech therapist: *Something happened recently that made me remember my months at Mercy Hospital. I met a woman who also had a stroke. She too is unable to use one arm, and she wears a leg brace like mine. "You speak so bue—tee—ful—lee," this new friend said to me, speaking with slow deliberation, still struggling with every sound seven years after her stroke. "You speak so bue—tee—ful—lee," she said, and I remembered sitting across from you in the small computer room next to the nurses' station. "Will I ever be able to speak without so much effort?" I asked. I had spent half an hour reading to you while you wrote a list of the words I had the most difficulty pronouncing. Please, I thought, please tell me that I will not always have to live with my voice imprisoned like this. Please tell me that I won't always feel exhausted, trapped, fearful. You looked me in the eyes and answered with honesty and warmth—"I don't know."*

After wheeling myself down the hospital corridor for my first appointment with Angela, I stopped abruptly at the doorway to her office. I couldn't make myself cross the threshold into that small, windowless space. *Breathe deeply*, I told myself, trying to do my child-birth breathing exercise, an exercise I'd since used to calm myself before giving poetry readings. *Breathe deeply*. But I couldn't breathe at all. *Maybe*, I thought, *I am suffocating, maybe fear has sucked all the air from my lungs.*

"I can't work in this room," I blurted out.

I don't know what Angela was thinking about the newly para-lyzed, panic-stricken woman facing her from a hospital wheelchair. Did she understand the claustrophobia as a merciful projection of my paralysis onto her office? One could move from an office.

Which is what we did. Angela didn't attempt to reason me out of my fears. She simply smiled warmly and assured me that she would find a space in which I would feel comfortable. The next day we met in the computer room behind the nurses' station. The room wasn't large but it was flooded with light from a large window. Every day for the next two months, for thirty minutes in the morning and thirty minutes in the afternoon I sat next to that window as I worked with Angela, learning to speak again. Initially there were a lot of written tests, though I can remember nothing of them now except that I disliked taking them. I felt like a little child in grade school, nervous about performing well for the teacher. And I told no one that I could no longer recite the alphabet.

Speaking, I rolled my *r*'s, and at each syllable uttered, I spit like an actor in the No Theatre in Japan. Though I had spoken with a thick Southern drawl before my stroke, I now spoke with what sounded like a trace of a German accent. My new speech was squeezed dry of emotion. It sounded flat and mechanical, and was punctuated with struggle-filled hesitations. Often I would kid Angela about going on the road to give poetry readings in this style as if it were something purposefully developed for my performance. In truth I couldn't imagine ever again giving public readings.

To lose my ability to walk was to lose all sense of safety. Who would come when I needed to be propped up in the bed so I wouldn't choke on a sip of water, or when I needed a bedpan or a blanket? To lose my ability to walk was to be thrown back to mem-ories of being an infant left in a closed room for hours, screaming. To lose use of my left arm and hand felt like a cruel amputation. But I have always been in love with the human voice with its tonal variations, hesitations, cadences; with what it holds of the geography of one's beginnings, and of the experiences that lead one to choose the particular words through which one lives. I *needed* my leg. I *needed* my arm. I *needed* my hand. But in a fundamental way I *was* my voice. The loss of that voice felt like a diminishment of soul.

A booklet explaining apraxia lay under a pile of books where I'd hidden it. As long as I didn't read it, as long as I didn't put words to what had happened to my voice, my own acknowledgment of it didn't have to cut so deeply. I could postpone the pain of acceptance. In the meantime, I spent evenings in bed, pronouncing the words with which I'd had the most difficulty that day—*countenance, munificent, ignorance, diminished, eloquent.* I stumbled over sounds, slurred, stuttered, began again.

Six weeks after my stroke, I got the booklet out and read its definition of apraxia—"A movement planning problem involving a disruption in sequencing of voluntary movements. A transmission problem between the brain and the muscle." *Apraxia,* I said aloud, allowing myself to feel the pain evoked at the sound of that word. It was the pain of a grief too large for my body to hold. I felt as if a weight was pressing against my sternum, while in my chest a great and ragged emptiness was struggling against the bone. *Apraxia,* I repeated and felt the pain contract and travel to my throat where it throbbed in a hard knot. My eyes burned. I rolled my wheelchair to the empty dining room and parked at a table near a window. On the fourteenth of June I wrote my first poem after the stroke:

Apraxia

Cars and trucks come and go
along the highway and the trees
are wet. The grass wet too,
and the drenched sky
is a blur of gray. Blackbirds fly,
lyrical and decisive
in their dip and sweep. And so
I search for music to unlock
my damaged speech, some
rhythm I can ride
like birds' wings ride the wind. Or words
like wheels turning in my brain—motion
of language. Creation: In the beginning
was   in the beginning was   In the

                    beginning was
                    the word.
                    The word.

After I'd been in Mercy for nearly two months, my friend Kendall came to visit as she did most afternoons and took me out for a ride around the hospital grounds. As she pushed my wheelchair around the parking lot, she began to sing the song "Side by Side." The mood was light and the words to the song felt poignant, funny, and true. She and I had stood side by side through one of the most difficult periods of our lives and were both more than a little ragged from the effort. Kendall continued to sing. Laughing, I tried to join in. Though what I was doing could hardly be called singing and though my words were much slower in coming out than hers and were not at all clearly spoken, they were the first words since the stroke that I was able to say without wrestling each syllable out of my mouth.

I knew that the music had made this possible. Perhaps I could get my speech back through reading rhythmical poetry. Perhaps I could find some rhythm I can ride *like birds' wings ride the wind.* And as difficult as it was to speak, it made sense to me to practice speaking by reading what I'd loved most.

I have never returned the copy of *The New Pocket Anthology of American Verse* that Kendall brought when I asked her for poetry I could use in speech therapy. A 1955 edition, the book looks much older. The paper is yellowed and brittle, and some animal has chewed through the binding. The second page of Edna St. Vincent Millay's poem "Renascence" has come loose. I couldn't begin to say how many therapy sessions began with, *All I could see from where I stood / Was three long mountains and a wood—*

Because of the music of the poem I was able to read it aloud more easily than most things. I would read as far in its six pages of small print as my energy allowed while Angela sat listening, helping me with pronunciation, making a list of the words with which I had the most difficulty—*infinity, immensity, drenched, joyously, whispering.* Then I would take the list back to my room and practice pronouncing them.

There were other books of poetry from which I read. Just yesterday, when I took my copy of *Norton's Anthology of Poetry* from its shelf, one of Angela's lists fell out. Reading the list—*argument, tedious, chimney, revisions, decisions, scuttling*—I remembered reading

T. S. Eliot's "The Love Song of J. Alfred Prufrock" which, until my stroke, I had not read in many years. I also read Gerard Manley Hopkins's "Pied Beauty." *Glory be to God for dappled things*, I read, struggling, spitting, tripping over words until at the very end I was able get out the final, *Praise him*, with relative clarity.

I read Emerson's "Rhodora," Blake's "The Tyger," Dickinson's *After great pain, a formal feeling comes*—I read Browning's "My Last Duchess," Shakespeare's *When to the sessions of sweet silent thought / I summon up remembrance of things past . . .* I read Roethke's *I wake to sleep, and take my waking slow. / I feel my fate in what I cannot fear. / I learn by going where I have to go.*

I too was learning by going where I had to go. Sometimes, trying to find my way in my damaged brain felt like trying to find my way in a darkened carnival fun house where nothing at all made sense. More than once I recoiled in shame, silence, and confusion after mistaking Angela's left hand for mine as she turned a page of the book in front of me. My own hand lay in my lap, still and forgotten by my brain, my brain which also forgot my son's phone number, many familiar words, what letter came after Q in the alphabet, and much of the left side of my world.

I remember almost nothing about the day I took Kendall's paperback anthology outside with us. After months of work, I was going to try to read Millay's "Renascence" aloud and my mind could hold nothing beyond that intention. Kendall pushed my wheelchair outside and parked it facing a bench on which she seated herself. The book opened naturally to that poem into which I'd poured so much. I gripped the pages between the thumb and fingers of my right hand and—after looking into Kendall's clear blue eyes for an instant—began to read.

All I could see from where I stood / Was three long mountains and a wood, I began. And continued, line after line, page after page while words from Angela's word lists filled my mind—*shrinking sight, immensity, remorse, undefined, swirled, omniscience*.

I know not how such things can be!— / I breathed my soul back into me, I read, seeing the yellow pages of Angela's legal pad, the words in her handwriting, the creative ways she had spelled some of them to communicate pronunciation to my damaged brain. Like Millay's narrator, I too felt that I had tasted my own death, and the coming back. By loss of hope, I too had seen my vision limited. And I had known the heartbreaking beauty of that first spring after my stroke when I wept aloud at the sight of a bough of dogwood blossoms that Kendall broke from the tree and placed on my lap like a prayer. *The world stands out on either side,* I read, *No wider than the heart is wide.* Tears were streaming down Kendall's face. I read the last lines and took a deep breath. The poem was over.

I was still in a wheelchair. My left leg was still paralyzed. I did not have enough balance to stand alone. My left arm hung limp at my side. I was unable to move my hand. But I could read poetry aloud again. Not smoothly, not with the inflection that I wanted, not rapidly enough, and the words weren't always clear. But I had just read all six pages of "Renascence" aloud to Kendall. I felt as if I had been given wings.

Living in an Unstable Body

BARBARA ROSENBLUM

My doctor put it to me very clearly: I had to have chemotherapy, surgery, and radiation, in that order. I had to have chemotherapy for three months before surgery because the tumor in my breast was too large to remove surgically. It had grown too quickly and was now virtually inoperable. Chemotherapy would shrink the tumor, permitting surgery without skin graft. There was another reason for chemotherapy first: the cancer had spread to my lymph nodes, including a supraclavicular node near my collarbone. That was an indicator that metastatic processes were already occurring throughout my body. It was a serious, aggressive cancer and I would require the most aggressive treatment available.

Before the first treatment, my doctor prepared me for the various side effects I might experience: my hair would fall out; I'd have mouth sores; I'd vomit; and I'd lose my period. So after the first treatment, I vomited about thirty times in forty-eight hours, had tired muscles and aching joints, and was exhausted from spasmodic vomiting. And that was just the first week.

The second week, I had low blood counts, extreme fatigue, and breathlessness from the lack of sufficient hemoglobin—and consequently oxygen—in my blood. Almost exactly on the twenty-first day following the first set of three injections, my hair began to fall out. Not just on my head. I lost my pubic hair as well. But I still had my period.

After the second treatment, I had all the side effects again. And I still had my period. I thought for sure I'd beat this: I wouldn't go into menopause.

Following the third treatment, I had all the same side effects but, this time, I had a shorter period. Still I didn't attend to it much because, by this time, my nose and anus were bleeding from chemotherapy and I had grown alarmed. It seemed like I was bleeding from new places and losing the familiar bleeding from familiar places.

Three weeks later, after the fourth treatment, my period stopped. I began to get hot flashes, sometimes as frequently as one an hour. My ears glowed bright red, my face darkened, and sweat collected on the surface of my skin. I felt like a vibrating tuning fork for the next two minutes. Then my internal air conditioning took over, but didn't know when to stop. I got cold; I'd quickly cover myself to avoid the chill of perspiration. I could never find the right amount of clothing because my internal thermostat was completely out of balance. I no longer had any sense of what "room temperature"— that euphemism for a shareable external reality—was. I had no reliable information from my body about the temperature of the outside world. My only information, which I knew was distorted and unreliable, came from deep inside my body.

Then all the hair on my head fell out. Frantically I searched for a good wig before this occurred, but nothing fit my small head. I found a hairdresser who worked for the opera company and he used his connections to get a wig for me. The wig fit but felt foreign and made my scalp hot and itchy. I decided, like many other women who become bald from chemotherapy, not to disguise my loss.

Hats now hang off any available hook in my apartment. I have cotton hats, wool hats, berets, hats with brims, ski caps. Friends have knitted caps for me. And, even now, every time I go into the street, I'm still aware that people look at me. A vital aspect of my social identity has been taken away. In the last six months, I've lost my hair twice. And before that, three times. Practice does not make it easier.

Losing my hair has been much harder than losing my breast. No one can see underneath my clothes. But everyone can see my hair. I never thought my hair was beautiful: it was a simple, brown mop that I combed and washed. It grew out of my scalp. It was a part of me. It was mine.

But as I saw it cover my pillow, as I saw gobs of it come out on the comb, and masses of it clog the shower drain, I sank powerlessly into resignation.

I knew my hair would grow back when I went off the powerful

chemotherapy to another combination of chemicals. It did, but thinly. And then I went off chemotherapy completely and all my hair came back, thick and spiky. But during that time when I didn't take chemotherapy, the cancer spread to my liver and then my lungs. I had to have chemotherapy, the strong stuff, again. Now it is clear that I will never have a full head of hair again. I now lose my hair once a month. I will always look like a Buddhist monk until the day I die.

My pudenda is as smooth as a fig. Even a peach with its infantile fuzziness is too hairy to describe it. Bald, completely smooth except for one Fu Manchu–like hair, straight and long, that resisted decimation. It is a dark, sturdy branch that extends from my skin. It is my mysterious hair, this proud survivor.

Losing my pubic hair, I felt naked and embarrassed, inadvertently returned to pre-pubescence. I was too exposed and didn't want to be touched.

My vagina was changing too. The vaginal tissue was thinning and becoming more sensitive to pressure and friction. It began to hurt when Sandy and I had sex. Then I noticed that my ordinary levels of dampness seemed to be changing: I was becoming less moist. Worst of all I stopped lubricating when I became sexually excited. That single, physiological fact made me realize that the agreements and understandings I had with my body were no longer in effect. If I no longer lubricated when I got sexually aroused, then how could I know I was feeling sexy?

Until I began chemotherapy, my relationship with my body was simple, direct, and uncomplicated. I had a friendly, warm, and pleasurable relationship with my body. Sex was always fun and untroubled. The cycles of my ability to become aroused were exquisitely dependent on my hormones. Ten days before my period, like clockwork, I would begin to feel sexual. This would continue for the next ten days and when my period came the urge would fizzle out. In other words, I had a physiologically based definition of my own sexual excitement: if my body produced some of the sensations that, through experience, had become my standard set of signals for sexual excitement, then I knew what to do with my behavior. But when chemotherapy induced an early and rapidly onsetting menopause and my hormone levels dropped dramatically, I was no longer on a monthly hormone cycle. I could no longer tell when I felt sexy or premenstrual. I got very confused about what I was feeling and when I was feeling it.

These questions of semantic meaning were urgently pre-empted by the necessity of finding practical solutions. Without body clues to signal me as to when and how I was feeling sexy, I consulted my head. Sandy and I re-created situations that had a proven record of creating the right mood in me. We purposefully incorporated the old, reliable environmental cues that had worked so well in the past: excellent food, candlelight, intimate conversation, music. I felt as close as could be, but nothing was happening in my body. We tried romantic meals at cozy restaurants. Nothing. Massage with scented oils. Nothing. Morning hiking in the country followed by steaming coffee and good pancakes. Nothing. Everything in my head told me this should be the right moment to make love but there were no signals coming from my body. Sandy touched me in all the loving, familiar ways. It was soothing and pleasant but not sexy. Nothing. The conclusion: for me sex does not work in the head.

We stopped making love. Instead we found new ways of being intimate. Sandy, who is a very light sleeper and consequently sleeps far away from me so as not to be disturbed by my twists and turns, began to hold me through the night. Our hands found new ways to console each other. I was reminded of how animals touch, lick, and chew each other. They pick at and groom each other, making the other feel secure and loved with their paws. I would touch Sandy's throat in a spot I knew contained all her tears: she would sob. And right in the midst of chemotherapy infusions, when the chemicals were flowing into my veins from huge syringes, Sandy helped me relax by touching my back and neck lightly.

I confess I was still nervous about not making love. Without telling Sandy I still tried to make myself feel sexy. I believed that if I tried hard enough, I could discover a more subtle sexual language in my body. I thought maybe I could pick up these signals when alone. So when Sandy was busy or out of the house, I tried to get in the mood to masturbate. Nothing. But our new intimacy helped ease the passage. I accepted this nonsexual period as part of my life. Ultimately the rock bottom question remains: when facing one's own death, what happens to one's sexuality? I suppose for some women sexual feelings become intensified. They become hungry for life, hungry for life through sex. Erotic energy keeps them alive. I suspect Sandy would have liked it better if I experienced the life force as erotic energy, as libido. But I don't. My life energy comes in another form, in the passion to learn everything, to feel everything, to live every moment with presence and intensity. To study new things. To master new areas of knowledge. To write—alone and with Sandy. Together we have developed a new form that can accommodate our individual and unique voices into a dialogue. We write about things that are important to us. We make love at the typewriter, not in the bedroom.

As I write now, I see that I was learning a new language of the body but it was the language of symptoms, not of sexuality. I became sensitive to when my body was retaining water. I could glance at my various parts, my legs, arms, stomach, and chest and notice a puffiness that had not been there the day before. I learned that when I became puffy, my metabolism was off and that meant my liver wasn't functioning properly. I calculated the ebbs and flows of my energy because my daily activities, as simple as taking a walk, depended on an exact calibration of that energy. I observed how it wavered, how much time I had between the waves, how it disappeared all at once, without forewarning. I discovered how close I could come to throwing up without actually having to do it. I studied the gradations of nausea and their subdivisions, and how to assess when nausea would pass or when I had to take an anti-nausea pill. I learned how to move quickly to the curb while walking the dog, emptying the contents of my stomach there, not on the sidewalk, and how to look reasonably dignified afterward. I learned how to run fast while compressing my anal sphincter muscles so that I wouldn't shit in my pants from the diarrhea that chemo induced. Sometimes I didn't make it.

In the last two and a half years, I peed in my pants three times. Chemotherapy irritates the bladder. That's why doctors tell you to drink half a gallon of liquid whenever you get chemotherapy. The chemicals are so strong that they can even cause cancer of the bladder. On the few occasions I couldn't control my urine, I noticed that I didn't get the usual signal that told me it was time to think about going to the bathroom. It didn't begin as a small pressure or urge, as it normally does, and then build up. No, rather it came on with a burst of urgency, as if I'd been holding it for hours. I had to learn this new language too.

The form of my body changed too. I lost a breast. When I had the mastectomy, I was too worried about my life to worry about my breast. I hoped that the doctors would "get" all the cancer in my breast and that postoperative radiation would control any errant cells that had not been excised by surgery. Losing a breast did alter my body image, as well as my body, but I never felt a diminishment

of my femininity. My breasts were never the center of my woman-
ness.

From the responses of other women in my support group and
also from my cancer counselor, I knew that losing a breast was very
hard for some women. In my cancer support group, most women
were concerned about reconstructive surgery. They swapped names
of good plastic surgeons. They talked about aesthetic criteria for
evaluating a good job, such as the surgeon's ability to make breasts
match in color, tone, weight, density, shape, and identicality of nipple placement with appropriate tones of darkness. To me, they expressed a fetishistic quality in their talk; they were desperate and
afraid.

One woman in the support group told the story of someone
whose husband left her from the time of the mastectomy until she
got her reconstructed breast. She explained matter-of-factly that he
couldn't bear the sight of his wife. Then there's the letter I got from
a distant acquaintance who told me that she, too, had had breast
cancer. She wrote that it wasn't so dangerous now that they could
control it with early detection. She also wrote that, since her surgery
a few years before, she, herself, never got undressed in front of her
husband. When they made love, she always wore her bra with the
prosthesis tucked inside.

I couldn't even imagine how these women might feel about their
partners. I would feel enraged. I cannot count the number of stories
I've heard about couples, both lesbian and straight, breaking up
after a mastectomy. Illness places enormous strains on couples and
many separate afterwards. Each person may feel guilt and abandon-
ment simultaneously.

I'm very lucky. Sandy has been exceptionally steadfast and easy
about the changes in my body. She did not compel me to pay attention to her needs, her anxieties, her worries. She never made me
feel inadequate or freakish. Her face never revealed shock or terror.
She was easy with my scar, touching it delicately. During vomiting
bouts she simply got the bucket, never cringing or complaining. She
was always softly, gently there, through everything.

Signals about hunger also got confused when I began chemotherapy. Up until that time, food was one of the great pleasures of
my life. Over the years I'd become very sophisticated about food
and very knowledgeable about its preparation. Eating was a su-
premely aesthetic experience for me. I always tried to eat and cook

well for myself. Unlike many people who don't cook for themselves when they are alone, I didn't need the company of another person to stimulate me to cook: my own pleasure was sufficient. I would cook sweetbreads in a cream sauce or chicken with lemon and tarragon. Tastes would explode on my tongue, clear and definite tastes.

So when chemotherapy caused painful sores in my mouth and the only thing I could consume was a blenderful of fruit and yogurt, I became despondent. It hurt even to put solid food in my mouth. My appetite and desire for particular flavors and sensations was annihilated. I could no longer tell when I was hungry or when I wanted a specific texture or flavor. All I wanted to do was to get the food down and keep it down and to make sure it didn't hurt as I ate. I treated myself like a hospital patient, making an eating schedule and sticking to it, making sure I had enough protein, liquid, and caloric content.

Now there is never a time in my treatment cycle when my mouth isn't sore or sensitive. I can't have spices—I can't eat hot Chinese food or savor my favorite cuisine, Indian food. My diet resembles that of an ulcer patient: bland and creamy. My relationship to food has been permanently altered and I grieve this loss every day.

In the last two years, my clothes have increased by three sizes. My legs filled with fluid and were puffy and large. My arms and shoulders, usually slender, looked bulky and strong. I remember when Sandy and I saw a beautiful pair of green loafers in a shop window in Amsterdam. They were the first expensive, European shoes I ever owned, but I can no longer wear them. My feet became swollen with fat and fluids. I consulted Shizuko Yamamoto, a well-known macrobiotic practitioner in New York. She slapped my thighs and said in a thick accent, "Water jugs, your legs are like water jugs."

I watched my body stretch to accommodate all the fluid that was collecting in my tissues. I could not believe how rapidly my body shape was changing. I needed new clothes immediately, but going shopping was a horrendous experience. Sandy was kind and patient. She had reached her full height of six feet by the age of thirteen and shopping for clothes that didn't fit was a familiar experience. Turning what was humiliating into an adventure was an old defense for her and now served us both well. I'd be crying from frustration in the fitting room and Sandy would quietly leave and cheerfully return with a few items in the next size.

One day I stopped going to department stores. It was too hard. I decided to go to a shop for larger women. While walking to it, I passed a maternity shop and thought that these clothes might fit me. They did.

The surface of my skin changed too. My veins became more prominent because the fluid in my tissues pressed them against my skin. Even the tiniest capillaries started bursting and my skin became marbled with designs. On my inner thighs, where the pressure was greatest, the capillaries looked like calligraphy. My body oils disappeared and my skin became parched and crusty. Flakes of skin fell from my face. My fingernails first turned black from chemotherapy, then they became ridged with white bands. My fingernails became like alum, soft and whitish, and they ripped rather than broke.

Two and a half years since the first diagnosis and I am still getting chemotherapy six days a month. For two days I'm in the hospital, where I get Adriamycin, and for four days I'm attached to an ambulatory pump filled with Velban, another type of chemotherapy. It hangs from my waist on a velcro belt, buttressed by a safety pin. It looks like a Walkman. Tubes extend from its square form into a one-inch needle that is inserted into my chest. It is attached to a Port-A-Cath, a plastic container that is surgically placed in my chest, the purpose of which is to receive chemotherapy. My veins are too fragile and unstable. They've stabbed me too many times and missed. They have had too many veins burst open with gushing blood. The chemo has burned my veins too many times, making them fibrotic and painfully sensitive.

When I wear the portable pump, I am bombarded by images: of being attached to a bomb, having an artificial limb, having additional plumbing, like there's a giant opening in me, like it's a bionic extension. It's like having shrapnel inside you, like an artificial hip or a metal plate instead of your skull.

My hand rests on the pump: I sense its vibrations and hear it churning along. With the aid of Valium and sleeping pills, I sleep with it tied to my waist. It runs on batteries. It is saving my life. Other people wear pumps too: diabetics get insulin, older people get liquid nutrition, people with AIDS get antibiotics, and people with intractable pain get a continuous infusion of painkilling drugs like morphine. I have cancer and I get chemotherapy. I hate the pump.

Yesterday I called a woman who is on the pump all the time, twenty-four hours a day, 365 days a year, getting chemotherapy for liver cancer. She was helpful and gave me words of encouragement. Maybe I can learn from her.

What is it like to live in a body that keeps on changing? It's frightening, terrifying, and confusing. It generates a feeling of helplessness. It produces a slavish attention to the body. It creates an unnatural hypervigilance toward any and all sensations that occur within the landscape of the body. One becomes a prisoner to any perceptible change in the body, any cough, any difference in sensation. One loses one's sense of stability and predictability, as well as one's sense of control over the body. It forces you to give up the idea that you can will the body to behave in ways you would like. Predictability ends. One grieves over its loss, and that further complicates the process of adjustment to an unstable body. Time becomes shortened and is marked by the space between symptoms.

In our culture it is very common to rely on the body as the ultimate arbiter of truth. We consult our bodies like an oracle. While every emotion may not be consciously available to be experienced, the body knows the truth. We cannot conceal the truth from the body.

We turn to the body to decipher its coded language, to apprehend its grammar and syntax. By noticing the body's responses to situations, we have an idea about how we "really feel about things." For example, if you get knots in your stomach every time a certain person walks into the room, you have an important body clue to investigate. Or if your eyes tear up during a yawn, you might suspect that you may be experiencing some deep and underlying sadness that has not yet come to the surface or, as Wordsworth put it, a thought too deep for tears.

We trust that the body will tell us the truth about emotions that are hidden from consciousness. We trust that the body knows things before the mind does. Our job is to mind the body, to mine the body, to interpret its language.

Interpretations of bodily signals are premised on the uninterrupted stability and continuity of the body. We experience the continuity of the body as taken for granted. Only when there are interruptions does the body become problematic. We usually associate the same continuous sensations with the same stimulations. When the body, like my body, is no longer consistent over time, when it gives different signals every month, when something that meant one thing in April may have a different meaning in May, then it's hard to rely on the stability—and therefore the truth—of the body. And because of that, it's hard to interpret and hard to predict.

I was thrown into a crisis of meaning. I could no longer assess and evaluate what sensations meant. I could no longer measure the intensity of sensations. I was no longer fluent in the language of my body, its signs and symbols, and I felt lost.

Living in the world has become an existential problem for me. How to interpret my very existence is problematic. Am I living because I am alive? Am I dying because I'd be dead in three months without chemotherapy? Am I living and dying? Are all of us living and dying, except that I'm doing it faster?

And all of this confusion is predicated on time because the human mind can experience the simultaneity of the past and the present and can project into the future. The human mind has memory. Time past can color the present and the future. If there were only present time, I could joyfully embrace my body and delight in whatever it brings, whatever form it takes, whatever is given to me. If there were only the past, I would remember swimming naked six months after my surgery in the Pacific waters off the coast of Australia's Great Barrier Reef, when my body, without breast, without much hair, looked whole, healthy, and perfect.

If there were only time past. I remember the time Sandy and I went away with friends of ours who were fighting all weekend. We were at a loss. What could we do to make them stop? Distancing myself from their anger, I put on some old Motown music and started dancing. I had just come out of the hot tub and there I was, naked as a jaybird, having a wonderful time, laughing, singing, and dancing unself-consciously to rock and roll. There I was, with one breast flopping, and one big body dancing. Our friends, stunned at what they called "the life force," stopped fighting and started dancing.

But there is not just the past and not just the present. There is the future. And I can imagine worse scenarios with just as much vividness as I can remember the past. I can envision more chemotherapy, more tubes, more degeneration of body function, more loss of energy and loss of control, more desperation. There may be more physical pain, more ambiguous sensations arising from a body I can no longer interpret, more confusion.

When you have cancer, the body no longer contains the old

truths about the world. Instead you must learn a new language, a new vocabulary, and over time, as symptoms converge and conflate, you learn the deeper structure of its grammar. The patient's task is to learn the new language, hoping that the body will remain stable enough. You can no longer rely on the previous systems of interpreting the body you have used before. When you have cancer, the ground is pulled out from under you. Existence is problematic and anxious. You must look for new, stable ground.

When you have cancer, you have a new body each day, a body that may or may not have a relationship to the body you had the day before. When you have cancer, you are bombarded by sensations from within that are not anchored in meaning. They float in a world without words, without meanings. You don't know from moment to moment whether to call a particular sensation a "symptom" or a "side effect" or a "sign." It produces extreme anxiety to be unable to distinguish those sensations that are caused by the disease and those that are caused by the treatment. Words and their referents are uncoupled, uncongealed, no longer connected. You live in a mental world where all the information you have is locked into the present moment. The past, what the doctors may call "your medical history," is useless and irrelevant for your construction of meanings. Sensations come and go; they disappear for a while and they return; they change. They may add up to something; they may not. They may have meaning; they may not. That pain in my stomach may mean something new or it may not. I must wait until something else happens, until I have an accretion of evidence, until a pattern emerges, if I'm lucky enough to have a pattern. Interpretation of a sensation always depends on having at least two bodily events close enough in time to make meaning of seemingly random events. And most of the time, I live in a world of random body events. I'm hostage to the capriciousness of my body, a body that sabotages my sense of a continuous and taken-for-granted reality.

Sometimes I can hardly use human language to tell how I feel. When I am frightened or feel alone and can't sleep, I need to take sleeping pills because I lie there thinking about dying. I explain to Sandy, "If I were a dog, I'd be shaking and trembling." Animals don't use words; their bodies speak for them. While I'm not mute, I am often frustrated by the way the limits of language circumscribe my ability to communicate events in my body. But I am not an animal. I am a human being, an articulate one at that, who is challenged to find words to apply to sensations I've never had before, challenged to find meaning and stability despite a changing body. I'm caught in a relentless metamorphosis. You cannot imagine how stable and firm and fixed your body looks to me. You cannot imagine that I can actually feel my molecules moving around, wondering what miraculous shape they will prefer next time.

Imperfection Is a Beautiful Thing: On Disability and Meditation

❦

JOAN TOLLIFSON

We should find perfect existence through imperfect existence. We should find perfection in imperfection. For us, complete perfection is not different from imperfection.

—Shunryu Suzuki

I used to dream about being in a world where being disabled was no big deal, where no one considered it a tragedy. No one thought you were inspiring or felt sorry for you. No one stared at you. I imagined what a relief it would be to be seen every day as perfectly ordinary.

I'm missing my right hand and half of my right arm. They were amputated in the uterus, before I was born, by a floating fiber. The question "what happened to your arm?" has followed me through life like some koan-mantra that the universe never stops posing. Total strangers come up to me on the street and inquire. Children gasp in horror and ask. People tell me with tears in their eyes how amazingly well I do things, such as tie my shoes. Or they tell me they don't think of me as disabled (I guess they mean a "real cripple" would be totally incompetent, and I always wonder if they would regard the amputation of their own right arm as no loss at all, no disability). Or people try desperately to pretend that they don't even notice. Nobody says a word. People swallow their curiosity and conceal their discomfort, hoping that the Great Dream of Normalcy is still intact. One of the central memories of my childhood is of children asking me what happened to my arm and the adults instantly silencing them: "ssshhhhhhh!" Taboo.

We are all in such pain, trying to do the right thing, trying not to ask the wrong questions, trying to pretend everything is okay. If we need anything in this world, it's honest seeing and speaking, and the ability to be with the actual truth (including flawed bodies, and flawed responses). That, to me, is love, and the heart of what meditative living is all about: realizing *what actually is* instead of being caught up in and entranced by *what we think would be better.*

Imperfection is the essence of being organic and alive. Organic life is vulnerable; it inevitably ends in disintegration. This is part of its beauty. True meditation delves into this mystery of life and death, discovering (not intellectually, but experientially) how porous and momentary every thing is.

As a child, when I first heard about death and was trying to understand what it was, I used to dream about a person whose arm fell off, then a leg, then the other arm, and so on until nothing was left. Perhaps we fear disability because we fear death. We fear imperfection, loss of control, disintegration.

Growing up, I wanted to dis-identify myself with the image or label of being a cripple. I wanted to be normal. As I grew older, I sought out attractive lovers as a way of establishing my own normalcy. I avoided other disabled people. I refused to see myself as part of that group. I held a great deal of pain and rage inside. I drank excessively, consumed drugs and cigarettes, acted out my anger in violent outbursts, ended up in jails and hospitals. Finally, through some mysterious grace, I woke up and found myself in the company of an excellent therapist.

I remember the first time I actually looked closely at my arm, without looking away. I was twenty-five years old at the time, in therapy, sobering up from my near-suicidal nosedive into substance abuse. It was a terrifying moment. I was drenched in sweat, literally. But amazingly enough, I found that the arm I was seeing was not the loathsome, ridiculous, scary object I had imagined, but something else entirely, a world I had never seen before.

I joined a group of disabled women on the advice of my therapist. I hated the idea, but to my surprise they were marvelous, dynamic women. They shared so many of what I had always thought were my own isolated, personal experiences that I began to realize that my supposedly private hell was a social phenomenon. We had eye-opening, healing conversations. We discovered, for example, that we had all had the experience of being patronized and treated like children even though we were adults. It wasn't simply some horrible flaw in my own character that had provoked such reactions, as I had always believed, but rather, this was part of a collective pattern that was much larger than any one of us. It was a stereotype that existed in the culture at large. Suddenly disability became not just my personal problem, but a social and political issue, as well.

In the late '70s I participated in a month-long occupation of the San Francisco Federal Building demanding the signing into law of the first major civil rights legislation for people with disabilities, the 504 regulations. It was (as far as I know) the longest occupation of a federal building in U.S. history, and we won.

We created a whole society in microcosm inside that building, with work committees, church services, study groups, wheelchair races, long strategy meetings. People laughed, argued, shared their lives; some even fell in love and later married. In this society, you never had to worry about being discriminated against because of your disability. No one was going to tell you that you couldn't do a particular task because you only had one hand or were in a wheelchair. At last, here was a society where being disabled was no big deal. This revealed exactly how disability colored my life (in the way the world saw me, and inside my own head as well).

After a lifetime of isolating myself from other disabled people, it was an awakening to be surrounded by them. For the first time in my life, I felt like a real adult member of the human community. Finally identifying myself as a disabled person was an enormous healing. It was about recognizing, allowing, and acknowledging something I had been trying to deny, and finding that disability does not equal ugliness, incompetence, and misery. If anything, the more disabled you were, the more stature you had in this mini-society. I actually found myself feeling envious of the quadriplegics.

In the years after the 504 sit-in, I took up karate and broke boards with my arm. I studied massage and began doing it for a living, breaking another taboo. You aren't supposed to touch people with a "deformed" body part; it may be disgusting to them. That deep inner feeling of being disgusting still resurfaces every time I touch someone for the first time with my arm. The healing occurs slowly, over a lifetime.

When I began a serious involvement with Zen meditation, the process of awakening took yet another turn. Buddhism is the end of all identification. Meditation is about realizing what is before all identities, what is whole and not limited to or by this body, or any ideas about this body. This is so simple that it gets tricky. It is not about denying the body, or denying particular experiences. Rather, it is about seeing the conceptual grid of thought, image, and belief for what it is: imagination.

Meditation is about being still, listening quietly, openly, experiencing whatever is arising: thoughts, emotions, sounds, smells, sensations. Experiencing it very simply, without adding a storyline, without analysis, without identification (this is "my" anger, "my" problem, "my" peaceful or disturbed mind). If those thought-processes arise, meditation is seeing them for what they are: seeing the story as a story, seeing thought as thought, and not getting caught up in following either one. Of course we do get caught up very easily, but sooner or later we wake up again, we see it. When that happens, can the caught-up-ness simply be seen, without taking off into yet *another* story (what a hopeless case I am, I must try harder, I *will* try harder, Oh No, I failed, I'm on my way to hell)?

Although meditation can happen in any posture, usually in the beginning we sit down and cease all outward activity. Just sit still. If your nose itches, experiment with simply experiencing the sensation fully. Don't scratch it. If your back hurts, just sit with it. (Within reason, that is; don't actually damage your body). But if possible, don't move away from unpleasant sensation, don't chase after pleasant sensation. Just be still and allow whatever comes up to come up and be seen. Listen gently to whatever is there, without judging it as good or bad, not trying to manipulate or control it. You will probably discover that there is a lot of thinking going on. Simply notice that, notice the content of the thoughts, notice that they are thoughts, notice the effects they have on our whole body, our whole mood. Observe all of this.

Notice when there is judgment happening, notice when the mind is trying to get somewhere, notice the internal commands and counter-commands. Listen to the sounds around you, the traffic, the wind, the birds. Experience the breathing, the heartbeat, the temperature. Be exactly right here, right now. This is not something you can capture with thinking. This moment is not some *thing* that can be grasped or possessed. Everything arises and disappears instantaneously, faster than we can think.

The storyline is what gives the illusion of continuity and of a solid, enduring entity called "me" who is "having" all these experiences, the controller, the do-er, the sufferer, the meditator who is making progress or not making progress, succeeding or failing. When we look closely for this "self," we find nothing but shifting thoughts, images, sensations, ideas. What are we really? Without the labels and the stories (I'm a doctor, I'm gay, I'm on welfare, I'm old, I'm young, I'm stupid, I'm brilliant, I've had a hard life, an easy life), without all of that, what remains?

Meditation is returning to pure sensation, pure sound, immediacy of being, undivided by concepts into this or that, self or other, like or dislike, wanting or fearing. It is simply being here, without a story, or a purpose, or an identity. In such aliveness, there is no body. The body is an idea, an afterthought. When I wake up to actual sensate experience, to simply being here this very moment, I can find no place where I end and the outside world begins. There is one whole movement happening. And in this aliveness of being, form becomes transparent, no longer solid. At the same time, everything is more vivid, more obviously miraculous. It is seen.

Human beings seem compelled to make something simple into something complicated. Simple, open listening and immediacy of being gets turned into a "practice" with a method and a dogma. Next thing you know there are costumes and official postures to be in while "doing" it, roles and hierarchies, experts and authorities. When I first got involved in Zen at a major Zen center and went to meditation instruction, there was much concern about what to do with a single hand. Obviously I couldn't form the traditional Zen mudra—the position the hands are supposed to be in while sitting, palms up, left hand atop right hand, thumbs touching, hands forming an oval—so what would I do? This strikes me as ridiculous now, but at the time it seemed like a reasonable and pressing concern. I sat for years with my single hand suspended in midair, forming half of the official mudra, with chronic shoulder pains as a result, until I arrived at Springwater Center, a nontraditional meditation retreat center in rural New York where no one cares about posture and costume anymore, and I discovered the possibility of simply relaxing my arm and hand. How simple!

Back at Zen Center, when I used to imagine myself as a Zen priest, there was always one big catch, namely the realization that it would probably be impossible for me to deal with the traditional robes that priests are supposed to wear. I wouldn't be able to get them on, or function once I was in them. I knew that some adaptation would have been cooked up for me, but the whole point of a uniform is uniformity, and I'd stick out like a sore thumb as usual: different and spotlighted, feeling inferior and slightly humiliated. In retrospect, this might have been just fine—another way of exposing and exploring this whole (mental) phenomenon of "sore thumb" and "sticking out." But I went a different way.

After being at Springwater awhile, I started experimenting with sitting in a chair in the meditation room during retreats. In Zen we were urged to sit on cushions in some kind of lotus posture. Sitting in a chair was tolerated if you had some kind of "problem," but it was made clear that the ideal posture for meditation was on that cushion. It was eye-opening to see the thoughts that came up when I sat down to meditate in a chair for the first time. Back at Zen Center when I'd see people who had to sit in chairs because of back problems, I can remember thinking that if I ever had to do that, I'd give up Zen. It wouldn't be authentic Zen if I was in a chair. (God forbid I should ever have to try to meditate in a wheelchair.)

And now, here I was, meditating in a chair. Sitting in that chair, layers of self-image came to light and dropped away. Images of myself "doing" meditation, doing it correctly, being a perfect meditator, doing something important and spiritual, working to get enlightened, becoming different than what is actually here now, someone who is finally okay. I realized that meditation can happen anywhere, in any position.

Being disabled is a deep wound, a source of pain. But like all wounds, it is also a gift. As Eastern wisdom has always known, it is hard to tell good luck from bad luck. I recall the old story about the farmer who found a beautiful wild horse, and the neighbors said, "What good luck," and the farmer said, "Maybe." Then the farmer's son tried to tame the horse and fell off, breaking his leg. The neighbors all said, "What bad luck," and the farmer said, "Maybe." Then a war started and the army came to conscript all the young men, and they took everyone's sons except the farmer's son with the broken leg. "What good luck," the neighbors said, and the farmer said, "Maybe." And on and on it goes. Life is the way it is, not the way we wish it was, and disability is a constant embodiment of this basic truth.

Having one arm is an endless koan. It is what it is, which is un-knowable, and it attracts a lot of ideas, stories, and images. Caught up in the negative story, I felt ashamed, incomplete, and not okay. I drank to die. Later on, caught up in a more positive story, I felt pride and a sense of identity, and was horrified that medical science would try to eliminate birth defects, as if by doing so they would somehow be eliminating ME. One can look at a quadriplegic or an amputee and feel pity, or in another moment, one can feel attrac-tion and envy, as I had discovered during the 504 sit-in. As the stories begin to reveal themselves as stories—imaginary and ever-shifting—my arm is no longer "my arm" (some solid thing, or some storyline that determines my destiny). In this exact moment, right now, it is nothing at all—empty space, having nothing whatsoever to do with who I really am. That emptiness is creative and free. Anything is possible. The thought-created limitations are dissolved.

In a way, I've gone back to the innocence of a baby. When little babies encounter my arm—the arm that ends just below the el-bow—it is seen as just another interesting shape to explore and put into their mouths. There is nothing scary or creepy or taboo about it. As adults, we can't become babies again. But it is possible to come upon a listening stillness that illuminates all the conditioned con-cepts and judgments that are superimposed by our thinking onto the actual facts, and allows us to once again see the simple shape of what's actually here this moment, before we evaluate it, categorize it, and take a position toward it.

Meditation is that kind of open seeing. Not labeling what appears as either a deficit or an asset, perfect or imperfect, beautiful or ugly, but wondering openly, without conclusions, without trying to get somewhere else. In such open being there is freedom and possibility for the new, even in the midst of what we call imperfection or lim-itation. I don't mean that injustices or painful circumstances disap-pear, but that they no longer bind us in the way that they did. The bondage is in the ideas and the beliefs, the images and stories con-structed by thought. In quiet listening, we discover a presence that is not dependent on conditions being any particular way.

This does not mean that we shouldn't work to change conditions, but rather that we may do that work in a clearer way, and with more ability to be where we are. We can perhaps begin to see and question the strong tendency to polarize and create enemies to blame and hate, the tendency to defend our own opinions as if our life depended on them. We become less identified with our ideas. We develop a greater ability to listen to differing concerns, to notice how we become attached and upset.

The only life that actually exists is right now, this moment. The past and the future only exist if we think about them. Imagination is a great and wonderful power, and it is obviously useful to be able to imagine things that don't exist, to imagine other ways that the world could be. But to the degree that we identify with such pictures and require them to come true, we miss the world that is actually here. We literally don't see it. We live in a mental construction instead, acting out of ideas, convinced that we're right, and easily upset if reality isn't the way we think it should be, which it usually isn't. Meditation begins to loosen all these fixed ideas. When we don't know what anything is, or what to do, or who we are, or who the "others" are, then there is possibility. There is space for something unimaginable to occur, for things to change.

I am grateful for this koan of one arm, even though it is not always pleasant or easy. It teaches me to appreciate the miracle of what is, to feel affection for my actual life. Cardboard ideals of perfection are flat and pale by comparison.

POETRY

Midway: State Fair

JOAN ALESHIRE

People save all year for this—
shooting at those stubborn ducks,
pitching curves at those stone-faced dolls,
eating spun sugar that evaporates
in their mouths. You insist
on playing every game of chance,
like a child determined there's a way
to win. Strings of colored lights
throw shadows that distort
each passing face. I'm afraid
not to stand close to you, though
we've fought all day. A line of men
I ignore lounges outside the girlie show;
laughter erupts from the trailer
that houses the snakeman, no arms
and scales for skin, and gorilla-woman,
all hair except at her breasts.

The funny mirrors make your forehead
a desert, my neck a giraffe's,
before you buy one ticket to the rides,
leave me not knowing the price of admission,
fumbling for the change. "Move it,"
someone mutters. Everyone stares
as my arms slip, unusual
from their concealing sleeves.

The old fear of strangeness breathes
here—how can I say to them
we're different and the same: that riddle,
almost a joke? I'm awkward under their eyes,
until you gesture toward the slowing wheel,
"Will that thing hold us?" Someone laughs,
we all laugh, foolish together, getting aboard

for the seductive lift, abandoning the earth,
screaming as one and hugging each other, as each
little car on top hesitates, like a moment
of awareness, and rattles down.

The X-Rays

They looked like photographs of trees,
except that the terms were reversed—
black for the background, white
for the object itself. And light
shone through the white, making it
insubstantial, subject to change—
but that was my vision, my hope.

There was a smell of hot metal, the charge
of early inventions, and I had to lay
each arm flat on a glossy black plate
that reflected the past and future
with their endless questions. Not to
move, not even to breathe, to act only
as object, so the kindly men, friends
of my father, could hold the film
against the light, admiring the clarity
of their work, admitting the mystery.

No one said *tree* to me, but I saw
the photographs of dancers and the apple trees
they mimicked in "Appalachian Spring,"
curved and twisting; and the cypresses
pressed by wind that Weston took at Point Reyes.

Deformed was the description, and I agreed
since it was simplest to, though that means
unnatural. Trees respond, in the thick joint,
the gnarl, the odd turn, to some force, some
weather. What after all is form
but the giving in, the inch-by-inch bend,
and then the resistance?

The Hemophiliac's Motorcycle

TOM ANDREWS

For the sin against the HOLY GHOST is INGRATITUDE.
— Christopher Smart, *Jubilate Agno*

May the Lord Jesus Christ bless the hemophiliac's motorcycle, the
    smell of knobby tires,

Bel-Ray oil mixed with gasoline, new brake and clutch cables and
    handlebar grips,

the whole bike smothered in WD40 (to prevent rust, and to make
    the bike shine),

may He divine that the complex smell that simplified my life was
    performing the work of the spirit,

a window into the net of gems, linkages below and behind the
    given material world,

my little corner of the world's danger and sweet risk, a
    hemophiliac dicing on motocross tracks

in Pennsylvania and Ohio and West Virginia each Sunday from
    April through November,

the raceway names to my mind then a perfect sensual music,
    Hidden Hills, Rocky Fork, Mt. Morris, Salt Creek,

and the tracks themselves part of that music, the double jumps
    and off-camber turns, whoop-de-doos and fifth-gear downhills,

and me with my jersey proclaiming my awkward faith—"Powered
    By Christ," it said above a silk-screened picture of a rider in a
    radical cross-up,

the bike flying sideways off a jump like a ramp, the rider leaning
    his whole body into a left-hand corner—

may He find His name glorified in such places and smells,

and in the people, Mike Bias, Charles Godby, Tracy Woods, David
and Tommy Hill, Bill Schultz—

their names and faces snowing down to me now as I look upward
to the past—

friends who taught me to look at the world luminously in front of
my eyes,

to find for myself the right rhythm of wildness and precision,
when to hold back and when to let go,

each of them with a style, a thumbprint, a way of tilting the bike
this way or that out of a berm shot, or braking heavily into a
corner,

may He hear a listening to the sure song of His will in those years,

for they flooded me with gratitude that His informing breath was
breathed into me,

gratitude that His silence was the silence of all things, His
presence palpable everywhere in His absence,

gratitude that the sun flashed on the Kanawha River, making it
shimmer and wink,

gratitude that the river twisted like a wrist in its socket of
bottomland, its water part of our speech

as my brother and I drifted in inner tubes fishing the Great White
Carp,

gratitude that plump squirrels tight-walked telephone lines and
trellises of honeysuckle vines

and swallows dove and banked through the limbs of sycamore
trees, word-perfect and sun-stunned

in the middle of the afternoon, my infusion of factor VIII sucked
in and my brother's dialysis sucked in and out—

both of us bewildered by the body's deep swells and currents and
eerie backwaters,

our eyes widening at the white bursts on the mountain ash, at
earthworms inching into oil-rainbowed roads—

gratitude that the oak tops on the high hills beyond the lawns
    fingered the denim sky

as cicadas drilled a shrill voice into the roadside sumac and
    peppergrass,

gratitude that after a rain catbirds crowded the damp air, bees
    spiraling from one exploding blossom to another,

gratitude that at night the star clusters were like nun buoys
    moored to a second sky, where God made room for us all,

may He adore each moment alive in the whirring world,

as now sitting up in this hospital bed brings a bright gladness for
    the human body, membrane of web and dew

I want to hymn and abide by, splendor of tissue, splendor of
    cartilage and bone,

splendor of the taillike spine's desire to stretch as it fills with
    blood

after a mundane backward plunge on an iced sidewalk in Ann
    Arbor,

splendor of fibrinogen and cryoprecipitate, loosening the blood
    pooled in the stiffened joints

so I can sit up oh sit up in radiance, like speech after eight weeks
    of silence,

and listen for Him in the blood-rush and clairvoyance of the
    healing body,

in the sweet impersonal luck that keeps me now

from bleeding into the kidney or liver, or further into the spine,

listen for Him in the sound of my wife and my father weeping
    and rejoicing,

listen as my mother kneels down on the tiled floor like
    Christopher Smart

praying with strangers on a cobbled London street, kneels here in
    broad daylight

singing a "glorious hosanna from the den"

as nurses and orderlies and patients rolling their IV stands behind
   them like luggage

stall and stare into the room and smile finally and shuffle off,
   having heard God's great goodness lifted up

on my mother's tongue, each face transformed for a moment by
   ridicule

or sympathy before disappearing into the shunt-light of the
   hallway,

listen for Him in the snap and jerk of my roommate's curtain as
   he draws it open

to look and look at my singing mother and her silent choir

and to wink at me with an understanding that passeth peace, this
   kind, skeletal man

suffering from end-stage heart disease who loves science fiction
   and okra,

who on my first night here read aloud his grandson's bar mitzvah
   speech to me,

". . . In my haftorah portion, the Lord takes Ezekiel to a valley full
   of bones,

the Lord commands him to prophesy over the bones so they will
   become people . . . ,"

and solemnly recited the entire text of the candlelighting
   ceremony,

"I would like to light the first candle in memory of Grandma
   Ruth, for whom I was named,

I would like Grandma Dot and Grandpa Dan to come up and
   light the second candle,

I would like Aunt Mary Ann and my Albuquerque cousins Alanna
   and Susanna to come up and light the third candle . . . ,"

his voice rising steadily through the vinegary smell and brutal
   hush in the room,

may the Lord hear our listening, His word like matchlight cupped
   to a cigarette

the instant before the intake of breath, like the smoke clouds
  pooled in the lit tobacco

before flooding the lungs and bloodstream, filtering into pith and
  marrow,

may He see Himself again in the hemophiliac's motorcycle

on a certain Sunday in 1975—Hidden Hills Raceway, Gallipolis,
  Ohio,

a first moto holeshot and wire-to-wire win, a miraculously benign
  sideswipe early on in the second moto

bending the handlebars and front brake lever before the
  possessed rocketing up through the pack

to finish third after passing Brian Kloser on his tricked-out
  Suzuki RM125

midair over the grandstand double jump—

may His absence arrive like that again here in this hygienic room,

not with the rush of a peaked power band and big air over the
  jumps

but with the strange intuitive calm of that race, a stillness
  somehow poised

in the body even as it pounded and blasted and held its line
  across the washboard track,

may His silence plague us like that again,

may He bless our listening and our homely tongues.

Little Girl Gone

JOHNSON CHEU

From a Chinese pink prom dress
curly, permed hair, white high heels
she smiles
stares with
shiny, black, pearl, wonder eyes.

Moving overseas
she wears an American maternity dress
Salvation Army fashions
In pained, broken English
she says, "I bleeding, doctor."
Doctor replies, "No, you're not. Don't worry,"
mutters, "Stupid foreigner,"
under breath.

Later, the woman right
baby come early
but too late
damage done.

Years pass
deaf voices
beat
her guilty, etched face.
"Mai-goa-sungh-hoa, tai-shing-koo."
"American life too hard," she says, bitter
stares with
lusterless, black, stone eyes.

Banana Stealing

for Baba

This is not about abuse
    He did not touch me.
This is not about sex
    He did not touch me.
This is not about perversion
    He did not touch me.
This is about love.

My nightly workout with Dad
Ten leg lifts
    One . . . Two
      Sunday, Monday . . . 'Happy Days'
    Three . . . Four
      Tuesday, Wednesday . . . 'Happy Days'
    Five . . . Six
      Thursday, Friday . . . 'Happy Days'
    Seven . . . Eight
      Saturday, what a day,
    Nine . . . Ten
      Oh what a day with you . . . 'Happy Days,' oh 'Happy Days'
Then, my legs frog-style
stretching my abductors
Dad looms over me
    "Oooohhhh, what is this?"
    "Nothing, Baba."
      -wha-da gigi
    "Is it a banana?"
    "No, Baba."
      -wha-da gigi
    "I think I will eat it."
In the air above me, Baba makes hand motions
    mmmm . . . mmmm . . . mmmm
    "Really, Baba."
      -wha-da gigi . . . WHA-da gigi . . . WHA-DA GIGI!

I do not understand, Daddy, this game
We could not play on little league
  could not mow the lawn
  could not join the three-legged race
Is this why you pretended to take my penis away?

In Korea, they play a game
they tweak little boys' penises—call them peppers
    "Look, little red pepper."
    "This one's skinny."
     Tweak . . . Tweak . . . Tweak
"This one's juicy."
 Tweak . . . Tweak . . . Tweak
Do they play this game in China, Daddy?

Chinese say girls are worthless
Girls cannot plow fields
Girls marry
  belong to someone else
Is this the game we played?

We have not played together in years, Daddy
Outside your silence
Outside our shame
I stand
A son
waiting
for my penis
and for happy days.*

* Thanks to Professor Elaine Kim, University of California at Berkeley, for telling me about the Korean penis game.

How to Talk to a New Lover About Cerebral Palsy

ELIZABETH CLARE

Tell her: *Complete strangers*
have patted my head, kissed
my cheek, called me courageous.

Tell this story more than once, ask
her to hold you, rock you
against her body, breast to back,

her arms curving round, only
you flinch unchosen, right arm trembles.
Don't use the word *spastic.*

In Europe after centuries
of death by exposure
and drowning,
they banished us
to the streets.

Let her feel the tension burn down your arms,
tremors jump. Take it slow: when she asks
about the difference between CP and MS,

refrain from handing her an encyclopedia.
If you leave, know that you will ache.
Resist the urge to ignore your body. Tell her:

They taunted me retard, cripple,
defect. *The words sank into my body.*
The rocks and fists left bruises.

Gimps and crips, caps
in hand, we still
wander the streets but now
the options abound: telethons,
nursing homes, and welfare lines.

Try not to be ashamed as you flinch and tremble
under her warm hands. Think of the stories you haven't
told yet. Tension locks behind your shoulder blades.

Ask her what she thinks as your hands shake
along her body, sleep curled against her,
and remember to listen: she might surprise you.

Learning to Speak

Three years old, I didn't talk,
created my own sign language,
didn't walk but stumped
all over the house on my knees
growing thick calluses.
Words slow dance
off my tongue, never leap
full of grace. They hear
blank faces, loud simple replies.
I practiced the sounds *th, sh, sl*
for years, a pianist playing endless
hours of scales. I had to learn
the muscle of my tongue.

G-9

TIM DLUGOS

I'm at a double wake
in Springfield, for a childhood
friend and his father
who died years ago. I join
my aunt in the queue of mourners
and walk into a brown study,
a sepia room with books
and magazines. The father's
in a coffin; he looks exhumed,
the worse for wear. But where
my friend's remains should be
there's just the empty base
of an urn. Where are his ashes?
His mother hands me
a paper cup with pills:
leucovorin, Zovirax,
and AZT. "Henry
wanted you to have these,"
she sneers. "Take all
you want, for all the good
they'll do." "Dlugos.
Meester Dlugos." A lamp
snaps on. Raquel,
not Welch, the chubby
nurse, is standing by my bed.
It's 6 a.m., time to flush
the heplock and hook up
the I.V. Line. False dawn
is changing into day, infusing
the sky above the Hudson
with a flush of light.
My roommate stirs
beyond the pinstriped curtain.

My first time here on G-9,
the AIDS ward, the cheery
D & D Building intentionality
of the decor made me feel
like jumping out a window.
I'd been lying on a gurney
in an E.R. corridor
for nineteen hours, next to
a psychotic druggie
with a voice like Abbie
Hoffman's. He was tied
up, or down, with strips
of cloth (he'd tried to slug
a nurse) and sent up
a grating adenoidal whine
all night. "Nurse . . . nurse . . .
untie me, *please* . . . these
rags have strange powers."
By the time they found
a bed for me, I was in
no mood to appreciate the clever
curtains in my room,
the same fabric exactly
as the drapes and sheets
of a P-town guest house
in which I once—partied? stayed?
All I can remember is
the pattern. Nor did it
help to have the biggest queen
on the nursing staff
clap his hands delightedly
and welcome me to AIDS-land
I wanted to drop
dead immediately. That
was the low point. Today
these people are my friends,
in the process of restoring
me to life a second time.
I can walk and talk
and breathe simultaneously
now. I draw a breath

and sing "Happy Birthday"
to my roommate Joe.
He's 51 today I didn't think
he'd make it. Three weeks
ago they told him that he had
aplastic anemia, and nothing
could be done. Joe had been
a rotten patient, moaning
operatically, throwing chairs
at nurses. When he got
the bad news, there was
a big change. He called
the relatives with whom
he had been disaffected,
was anointed and communicated
for the first time since the age
of eight when he was raped
by a priest, and made a will.
As death drew nearer, Joe
grew nicer, almost serene.
Then the anemia
began to disappear, not
because of medicines, but
on its own. Ready to die,
it looks like Joe has more
of life to go. He'll go
home soon. "When will *you*
get out of here?" he asks me.
I don't know; when the X-ray
shows no more pneumonia.
I've been here three weeks
this time. What have I
accomplished? Read some
Balzac, spent "quality
time" with friends, come back
from death's door, and
prayed, prayed a lot.
Barry Bragg, a former
lover of a former
lover and a new
Episcopalian, has AIDS too,

and gave me a leatherbound
and gold-trimmed copy of the Office,
the one with all the antiphons.
My list of daily intercessions
is as long as a Russian
novel. I pray about AIDS
last. Last week I made a list
of all my friends who've died
or who are living and infected.
Every day since, I've remembered
someone I forgot to list.
This morning it was Chasen
Gaver, the performance poet
from D.C. I don't know
if he's still around. I liked
him and could never stand
his poetry, which made it
difficult to be a friend,
although I wanted to defend
him one excruciating night
at a Folio reading, where
Chasen snapped his fingers
and danced around spouting
frothy nonsense about Andy
Warhol to the rolling eyes
of self-important "language-
centered" poets, whose dismissive
attitude and ugly manners
were worse by far than anything
that Chasen ever wrote.
Charles was his real name;
a classmate at Antioch
dubbed him "Chasen," after
the restaurant, I guess.
Once I start remembering,
so much comes back.
There are forty-nine names
on my list of the dead,
thirty-two names of the sick.
Cookie Mueller changed
lists Saturday. They all

will, I guess, the living,
I mean, unless I go
before them, in which case
I may be on somebody's
list myself. It's hard
to imagine so many people
I love dying, but no harder
than to comprehend so many
already gone. My beloved
Bobby, maniac and boyfriend.
Barry reminded me that he
had sex with Bobby
on the coat pile at his Christmas
party, two years in a row.
That's the way our life
together used to be, a lot
of great adventures. Who'll
remember Bobby's stories
about driving in his debutante
date's father's white Mercedes
from hole to hole of the golf course
at the poshest country club
in Birmingham at 3 a.m.,
or taking off his clothes
in the redneck bar on a dare,
or working on *Stay Hungry*
as the dresser of a then-
unknown named Schwarzenegger.
Who will be around to anthologize
his purple cracker similes:
"Sweatin' like a nigger
on Election Day," "Hotter
than a half-fucked fox
in a forest fire." The ones
that I remember have to do
with heat, Bobby shirtless,
sweating on the dance floor
of the tiny bar in what is now
a shelter for the indigent
with AIDS on the dockstrip,
stripping shirts off Chuck Shaw,

Barry Bragg and me, rolling
up the torn rags, using them
as pom-poms, then bolting
off down West Street, gracefully
(despite the overwhelming
weight of his inebriation)
vaulting over trash cans
as he sang, "I like to be
in America" in a Puerto Rican
accent. When I pass,
who'll remember, who will care
about these joys and wonders?
I'm haunted by that more
than by the faces
of the dead and dying.
A speaker crackles near
my bed and nurses
streak down the corridor.
The black guy on the respirator
next door bought the farm,
Maria tells me later, but
only when I ask. She has tears
in her eyes. She'd known him
since his first day on G-9
a long time ago. Will I also
become a fond, fondly regarded
regular, back for stays
the way retired retiring
widowers return to the hotel
in Nova Scotia or Provence
where they vacationed with
their wives? I expect so, although
that's down the road; today's
enough to fill my plate. A bell
rings, like the gong that marks
the start of a fight. It's 10
and Derek's here to make
the bed, Derek who at 16
saw Bob Marley's funeral
in the football stadium
in Kingston, hot tears

pouring down his face.
He sings as he folds
linens, "You can fool
some of the people some
of the time," dancing
a little softshoe as he works.
There's a reason he came in
just now; *Divorce Court*
drones on Joe's TV, and
Derek is hooked. I can't
believe the script is plausible
to him, Jamaican hipster
that he is, but he stands
transfixed by the parade
of faithless wives and screwed-up
husbands. The judge is testy;
so am I, unwilling
auditor of drivel. Phone
my friends to block it out:
David, Jane and Eileen. I missed
the bash for David's magazine
on Monday and Eileen's reading
last night. Jane says that
Marie-Christine flew off
to Marseilles where her mother
has cancer of the brain,
reminding me that AIDS
is just a tiny fragment
of life's pain. Eileen has
been thinking about Bobby, too,
the dinner that we threw
when he returned to New York
after getting sick. Pencil-thin
disfigured by KS, he held forth
with as much kinetic charm
as ever. What we have
to cherish is not only
what we can recall of how
things were before the plague,
but how we each responded
once it started. People

have been great to me.
An avalanche of love
has come my way
since I got sick, and not
just moral support.
Jaime's on the board
of PEN's new fund
for AIDS; he's helping out.
Don Windham slipped a check
inside a note, and Brad
Gooch got me something
from the Howard Brookner Fund.
Who'd have thought when we
dressed up in ladies'
clothes for a night for a hoot
in Brad ("June Buntt") and
Howard ("Lili La Lean")'s suite
at the Chelsea that things
would have turned out this way:
Howard dead at 35, Chris Cox
("Kay Sera Sera")'s friend Bill
gone too, "Bernadette of Lourdes"
(guess who) with AIDS,
God knows how many positive.
Those 14th Street wigs and enormous
stingers and Martinis don't
provoke nostalgia for a time
when love and death were less
inextricably linked, but
for the stories we would tell
the morning after, best
when they involved our friends,
second-best, our heroes.
J.J. Mitchell was a master
of the genre. When he learned
he had AIDS, I told him
he should write them down.
His mind went first. I'll tell you
one of his best. J.J. was
Jerome Robbins' houseguest
at Bridgehampton. Every morning

they would have a contest
to see who could finish
the *Times* crossword first.
Robbins always won, until
a day when he was clearly
baffled. Grumbling, scratching
over letters, he finally
threw his pen down. "J.J.,
tell me what I'm doing wrong."
One clue was "Great 20th-c.
choreographer." The solution
was "Massine," but Robbins
had placed his own name
in the space. Every word
around it had been changed
to try to make the puzzle
work, except that answer.
At this point there'd be
a horsey laugh from J.J.
"Isn't that *great*?"
he'd say through clenched
teeth ("Locust Valley lockjaw").
It was, and there were lots
more where that one came from,
only you can't get there anymore.
He's dropped into the maw
waiting for the G-9
denizens and for all flesh,
as silent as the hearts
that beat upon the beds
up here: the heart of the drop-
dead beautiful East Village
kid who came in yesterday,
Charles Frost's heart nine inches
from the spleen they're taking
out tomorrow, the heart of
the demented girl whose screams
roll down the hallways
late at night, hearts that long
for lovers, for reprieve,
for old lives, for another chance.

My heart, so calm most days,
sinks like a brick
to think of all that heartache.
I've been staying sane with
program tools, turning everything
over to God "as I understand
him." I don't understand him.
Thank God I read so much
Calvin last spring; the absolute
necessity of blind obedience
to a sometimes comforting,
sometimes repellent, always
incomprehensible Source
of light and life stayed
with me. God can seem
so foreign, a parent
from another country,
like my Dad and his own
father speaking Polish
in the kitchen. I wouldn't
trust a father or a God
too much like me, though.
That is why I pack up all
my cares and woes, and load them
on the conveyor belt, the speed
of which I can't control, like
Chaplin on the assembly line
in *Modern Times* or Lucy on TV.
I don't need to run
machines today. I'm standing
on a moving sidewalk
headed for the dark
or light, whatever's there.
Duncan Hannah visits, and
we talk of out-of-body
experiences. His was
amazing. Bingeing on vodka
in his dorm at Bard, he woke
to see a naked boy
in fetal posture on the floor.
Was it a corpse, a classmate,

a pickup from the blackout
of the previous night? Duncan
didn't know. He struggled
out of bed, walked over
to the youth, and touched
his shoulder. The boy turned;
it was Duncan himself.
My own experience was
milder, didn't make me flee
screaming from the room
as Duncan did. It happened
on a Tibetan meditation
weekend at the Cowley Fathers'
house in Cambridge.
Michael Koonsman led it,
healer whose enormous paws
directed energy. He touched
my spine to straighten up
my posture, and I gasped
at the rush. We were chanting
to Tara, goddess of compassion
and peace, in the basement chapel
late at night. I felt myself
drawn upward, not levitating
physically, but still somehow
above my body. A sense
of bliss surrounded me.
It lasted ten or fifteen
minutes. When I came down,
my forehead hurt. The spot
where the "third eye" appears
in Buddhist art felt
as though someone had pushed
a pencil through it.
The soreness lasted for a week.
Michael wasn't surprised.
He did a lot of work
with people with AIDS
in the epidemic's early days,
but when he started losing
weight and having trouble

with a cough, he was filled
with denial. By the time
he checked into St. Luke's,
he was in dreadful shape.
The respirator down his throat
squelched the contagious
enthusiasm of his voice,
but he could still spell out
what he wanted to say
on a plastic Ouija board
beside his bed. When
the doctor who came in
to tell him the results
of his bronchoscopy said,
"Father, I'm afraid I have
bad news," Michael grabbed
the board and spelled,
"The truth is always
Good News." After he died,
I had a dream in which
I was a student in a class
that he was posthumously
teaching. With mock annoyance
he exclaimed, "Oh, Tim!
I can't believe you really think
that AIDS is a disease!"
There's evidence in that
direction, I'll tell him
if the dream recurs: the shiny
hamburger-in-lucite look
of the big lesion on my face;
the smaller ones I daub
with makeup; the loss
of forty pounds in a year;
the fatigue that comes on
at the least convenient times.
The symptoms float like algae
on the surface of the grace
that buoys me up today.
Arthur comes in with
the Sacrament, and we have

to leave the room (Joe's
Italian family has arrived
for birthday cheer) to find
some quiet. Walk out
to the breezeway, where
it might as well be
August for the stifling
heat. On Amsterdam,
pedestrians and drivers are
oblivious to our small aerie,
as we peer through the grille
like cloistered nuns. Since
leaving G-9 the first time,
I always slow my car down
on this block, and stare up
at this window, to the unit
where my life was saved.
It's strange how quickly
hospitals feel foreign
when you leave, and how normal
their conventions seem as soon
as you check in. From below,
it's like checking out the windows
of the West Street Jail; hard
to imagine what goes on there,
even if you know firsthand.
The sun is going down as I
receive communion. I wish
the rite's familiar magic
didn't dull my gratitude
for this enormous gift.
I wish I had a closer personal
relationship with Christ,
which I know sounds corny
and alarming. Janet Campbell
gave me a remarkable ikon
the last time I was here;
Christ is in a chair, a throne,
and St. John the Divine,
an androgyne who looks a bit
like Janet, rests his head

upon the Savior's shoulder.
James Madden, priest of Cowley,
dead of cancer earlier
this year at 39, gave her
the image, telling her not to
be afraid to imitate St. John.
There may come a time when
I'm unable to respond with words,
or works, or gratitude to AIDS;
a time when my attitude
caves in, when I'm as weak
as the men who lie across
the dayroom couches hour
after hour, watching sitcoms,
drawing blanks. Maybe
my head will be shaved
and scarred from surgery;
maybe I'll be pencil-
thin and paler than
a ghost, pale as the vesper
light outside my window now.
It would be good to know
that I could close my eyes
and lean my head back
on his shoulder then,
as natural and trusting
as I'd be with a cherished
love. At this moment,
Chris walks in, Christopher
Earl Wiss of Kansas City
and New York, my lover,
my last lover, my first
healthy and enduring relationship
in sobriety, the man
with whom I choose
to share what I have
left of life and time.
This is the hardest
and happiest moment
of the day. G-9
is no place to affirm

a relationship. Two hours
in a chair beside my bed
after eight hours of work
night after night for weeks
it's been a long haul,
and Chris gets tired.
Last week he exploded,
"I hate this, I hate you
being sick and having AIDS
and lying in a hospital
where I can only see you
with a visitor's pass. I hate
that this is going to
get worse." I hate it,
too. We kiss, embrace,
and Chris climbs into bed
beside me, to air-mattress
squeaks. Hold on. We hold on
to each other, to a hope
of how we'll be when I get out.
Let him hold on, please
don't let him lose his
willingness to stick with me,
to make love and to make
love work, to extend
the happiness we've shared.
Please don't let AIDS
make me a monster
or a burden is my prayer.
Too soon, Chris has to leave.
I walk him to the elevator
bank, then totter back
so Raquel can open my I.V.
again. It's not even
mid-evening, but I'm nodding
off. My life's so full, even
(especially?) when I'm here
on G-9. When it's time
to move on to the next step,
that will be a great adventure,
too. Helena Hughes, Tibetan

Buddhist, tells me that
there are three stages in death.
The first is white, like passing
through a thick but porous wall.
The second stage is red;
the third is black, and then
you're finished, ready
for the next event. I'm glad
she has a road map, but I don't
feel the need for one myself.
I've trust enough in all
that's happened in my life,
the unexpected love
and gentleness that rushes in
to fill the arid spaces
in my heart, the way the city
glow fills up the sky
above the river, making it
seem less than night. When
Joe O'Hare flew in last week,
he asked what were the best
times of my New York years;
I said "Today," and meant it.
I hope that death will lift me
by the hair like an angel
in a Hebrew myth, snatch me with
the strength of sleep's embrace,
and gently set me down
where I'm supposed to be,
in just the right place.

Four Poems

LARRY EIGNER

November 9 81

big eaves

almost
     walking in the rain
    and it gets harder

June 6 82

quite a ways from the sky

and even the window
  as the dove
rattles the ashcan top
  Is that flight?

July 12 83

flat unroofed body

a white truck longer
  than a house is wide
    delivering goods

     radios

      and radio

     lights

       and the motor going

     1 box spilled

         3 or 4 jars

      and picked up

       in the noonday sun

      learning
       manage this big thing

R v r b r a n c e

in a small room
  tv's
     large   )(for J F and J M

i
 might've

   realized

      prior to
         the reverse

       (how far
         back)

       one world
         in the head

        the window opened

         sometimes cloudless

           or there's one cloud, say,

            in all of the sky

           familiar

       another country

       few or many

        escape to one day

         while in the open air

          and the weather continues bad

      (music

       to hear

for a change

     Haydn)

face to the sun

    spirit

still ok

    still as

were you there when

feet on the ground, head

up at cloud 4 or 5

Gospel so hectic

  of how much use

          it's

  all in Time

  half-lives

    squander

      pass

impossibles

  fade (dwindle

    though one is enough

there's always dawn and sundown

      continuous

   forever?   east and west

        shine

        give

        peace

Excavation

KENNY FRIES

Tonight, when I take off my shoes:
three toes on each twisted foot.

I touch the rough skin. The holes
where the pins were. The scars.

If I touch them long enough will I find
those who never touched me? Or those

who did? *Freak, midget, three-toed
bastard.* Words I've always heard.

Disabled, crippled, deformed. Words
I was given. But tonight I go back

farther, want more, tear deeper into
my skin. Peeling it back I reveal

the bones at birth I wasn't given—
the place where no one speaks a word.

Body Language

What is a scar if not the memory of a once open wound?
You press your finger between my toes, slide

the soap up the side of my leg, until you reach
the scar with the two holes, where the pins were

inserted twenty years ago. Leaning back, I
remember how I pulled the pin from my leg, how

in a waist-high cast, I dragged myself
from my room to show my parents what I had done.

Your hand on my scar brings me back to the tub
and I want to ask you: What do you feel

when you touch me there? I want you to ask me:
What are you feeling now? But we do not speak.

You drop the soap in the water and I continue
washing, alone. Do you know my father would

bathe my feet, as you do, as if it was the most
natural thing. But up to now, I have allowed

only two pair of hands to touch me there,
to be the salve for what still feels like an open wound.

The skin has healed but the scars grow deeper—
When you touch them what do they tell you about my life?

Beauty and Variations

1.

What is it like to be so beautiful? I dip
my hands inside you, come up with—*what?*

Beauty, at birth applied, does not transfer
to my hands. But every night, your hands

touch my scars, raise my twisted limbs to
graze against your lips. Lips that never

form the words—*you are beautiful*—transform
my deformed bones into—*what?*—if not beauty.

Can only one of us be beautiful? Is this your
plan? Are your sculpted thighs more powerful

driving into mine? Your hands find their way
inside me, scrape against my heart. Look

at your hands. Pieces of my skin trail from
your fingers. What do you make of this?

Your hands that know my scars, that lift me to your
lips, now drip my blood. Can blood be beautiful?

2.

I want to break your bones. Make them so
they look like mine. Force you to walk on

twisted legs. Then, will your lips still beg
for mine? Or will that disturb the balance

of our desire? Even as it inspires, your body
terrifies. And once again I find your hands

inside me. Why do you touch my scars? You
can't make them beautiful any more than I can

tear your skin apart. Beneath my scars,
between my twisted bones, hides my heart.

Why don't you let me leave my mark? With no
flaws on your skin—how can I find your heart?

3.

How much beauty can a person bear? Your smooth
skin is no relief from the danger of your eyes.

My hands would leave you scarred. Knead the muscles
of your thighs. I want to tear your skin, reach

inside you—your secrets tightly held. Breathe
deep. Release them. Let them fall into my palms.

My secrets are on my skin. Could this be why
each night I let you deep inside? Is that

where my beauty lies? Your eyes, without secrets,
would be two scars. I want to seal your eyes,

they know my every flaw. Your smooth skin, love's
wounds ignore. My skin won't mend, is calloused, raw.

4.

Who can mend my bones? At night, your hands press
into my skin. My feet against your chest, you mold

my twisted bones. What attracts you to my legs? Not
sex. What brings your fingers to my scars is beyond

desire. Why do you persist? Why do you touch me
as if my skin were yours? Seal your lips. No kiss

can heal these wounds. No words unbend my bones.
Beauty is a two-faced god. As your fingers soothe

my scars, they scrape against my heart. Was this
birth's plan—to tie desire to my pain, to stain

love's touch with blood? If my skin won't heal, how
can I escape? My scars are in the shape of my love.

5.

How else can I quench this thirst? My lips
travel down your spine, drink the smoothness

of your skin. I am searching for the core:
What is beautiful? Who decides? Can the laws

of nature be defied? Your body tells me: come
close. But beauty distances even as it draws

me near. What does my body want from yours?
My twisted legs around your neck. You bend

me back. Even though you can't give the bones
at birth I wasn't given, I let you deep inside.

You give me—*what?* Peeling back my skin, you
expose my missing bones. And my heart, long

before you came, just as broken. I don't know who
to blame. So each night, naked on the bed, my body

doesn't want repair, but longs for innocence. If
innocent, despite the flaws I wear, I am beautiful.

Notes for "Beauty and Variations":
In section 1, the line "What is it like to be so beautiful?" is from "The Mirror" by Louise
Glück in *Descending Figure* (New York: The Ecco Press, 1980). In section 3, "How much
beauty can a person bear?" is from "Baskets" by Louise Glück in *The Triumph of Achilles*
(New York: The Ecco Press, 1985).

The Engines Are Roaring

TERRY GALLOWAY

In this one
there is one last
service the white blanket
of nurses do for the body:
they turn off the intricate machine
and lift it out of my ear.

Before I slept
I read that hearing
is the last of the senses to go.
So in this dream I'm dreaming
they've taken off my hearing aid
and left me here for dead.

I feel them walking, walking, walking
their movement as clear
as the shaking of the floor.

One goes to dampen the washcloth
another to the closet (o what shall I wear)
another to the balcony to tell whoever waits
in the idling car go on
and another . . . this other?
. . . she combs my filthy hair.

The steps, the chatter, the movement of their hands
whirs up like some great engine rising through the air
whirs up making a great din whirs up through the wood,
the metal casters, the cotton of the sheets, the polyester foam
even the thin, wash beaten pillowcase vibrates, hums

as they put my body straight.

They've stripped me bare—
the gown, the glasses, the plastic
band around my wrist, the delicate
machine that fit just so inside my ear—
and left.

But I am here.
The membrane of the silence
that surrounds me twangs,
exults in the boom and the rush.

And around me, even now, around me
the engines are roaring.

       This is the way I dream.
       And how I wake.

People Love Their Freaks

(When I was twelve, I was sent to the Lions Camp for Crippled
Children. I fell in love with a thirteen-year-old girl who was paralyzed
from the neck down. Years later I wanted to get a hold of her to
tell her about a certain triumph in my life. But I couldn't remember
her name.)

Dear Friend, I know just how you feel. Uh, forgive my insensitivity,
but really nobody's the real thing. I mean, just look at me:
no ears, weak eyes, teeth broke, fat butt and these legs!
No, I do not have beautiful legs not even here in New York City.
And of course my speech. A real attention getter. A real foreign
   twang.
Like an eye patch or a limp.

But people love their freaks.
Didn't you know that?
And of course it helps to have a beautiful face.
Which I do.

And how are things in Texas anyway, Beautiful?
I can just imagine.
I mean my folks were worried too
that I might not ever find my rightful place—
you know, no ears, weak eyes, teeth broke, fat butt and these legs!
But it's different somehow out here. Here, people love their
    freaks.
I know you'd find that hard to believe, but just look at me.
Ever since I took up the old trombone my status changed.
And suddenly this—
no ears, weak eyes, teeth broke, fat butt and these legs—
suddenly they are in demand!

And of course it helps to be a wizard on the old trombone.
Which I am.

But I want you to remember this, honey,
when it all starts getting you down,
people love their freaks.

Hey, aren't I speaking from experience here?
People love their freaks.

Well, the band's just starting up so I gotta go.
But I will write you sweetheart, real soon.
And no, I will never forget those beautiful afternoons
when I pushed your wheeled bed
along the banks of the Rio Grande
and moved your head tenderly to the side
so you could see across to the Mexico of your dreams.

Our kisses were the purest love I've ever had.
And I will never forget them or you my darling
even though this busy life pushes me even now
to the four corners.
No, I will never forget them or you. And I will write.
I promise. Real soon.

Cancer Winter

for Rafael Campo and Hayden Carruth

MARILYN HACKER

Syllables shaped around the darkening day's
contours. Next to armchairs, on desks, lamps
were switched on. Tires hissed softly on the damp
tar. In my room, a flute concerto played.
Slate roofs glistened in the rain's thin glaze.
I peered out from a cave like a warm bear.
Hall lights flicked on as someone climbed the stairs
across the street, blinked out: a key, a phrase
turned in a lock, and something flew open.
I watched a young man at his window write
at a plank table, one pooled halogen
light on his book, dim shelves behind him, night
falling fraternal on the flux between
the odd and even numbers of the street.

I woke up, and the surgeon said, "You're cured."
Strapped to the gurney, in the cotton gown
and pants I was wearing when they slid me down
onto the table, made new straps secure
while I stared at the hydra-headed OR
lamp, I took in the tall, confident, brown-
skinned man, and the ache I couldn't quite call pain
from where my right breast wasn't anymore
to my armpit. A not-yet-talking head,
I bit dry lips. What else could he have said?
And then my love was there in a hospital coat;
then my old love, still young and very scared.
Then I, alone, graphed clock-hands' asymptote
to noon, when I would be wheeled back upstairs.

The odd and even numbers of the street
I live on are four thousand miles away
from an Ohio February day
snow-blanketed, roads iced over, with sleet
expected later, where I'm incomplete
as my abbreviated chest. I weigh
less—one breast less—since the Paris gray
December evening, when a neighbor's feet
coming up ancient stairs, the feet I counted
on paper were the company I craved.
My calm right breast seethed with a grasping tumor.
The certainty of my returns amounted
to nothing. After terror, being brave
became another form of gallows humor.

At noon, an orderly wheeled me upstairs
via an elevator hung with Season's
Greetings streamers, bright and false as treason.
The single room the surgeon let us share
the night before the knife was scrubbed and bare
except for blush-pink roses in a vase on
the dresser. Veering through a morphine haze on
the cranked bed, I was avidly aware
of my own breathing, my thirst, that it was over—
the week that ended on this New Year's Eve.
A known hand held, while I sipped, icewater,
afloat between ache, sleep, lover and lover.
The one who stayed would stay; the one would leave.
The hand that held the cup next was my daughter's.

It's become a form of gallows humor
to reread the elegies I wrote
at that pine table, with their undernote
of cancer as death's leitmotiv, enumer-
ating my dead, the unknown dead, the rumor
of random and pandemic deaths. I thought
I was a witness, a survivor, caught

in a maelstrom and brought forth, who knew more
of pain than some, but learned it loving others.
I need to find another metaphor
while I eat up stories of people's mothers
who had mastectomies. "She's eighty-four
this year, and *fine!*" Cell-shocked, I brace to do
what I can, an unimportant exiled Jew.

The hand that held the cup next was my daughter's
—who would be holding shirts for me to wear,
sleeve out, for my bum arm. She'd wash my hair
(not falling yet), strew teenager's disorder
in the kitchen, help me out of the bathwater.
A dozen times, she looked at the long scar
studded with staples, where I'd suckled her,
and didn't turn. She took me/I brought her
to the surgeon's office, where she'd hold
my hand, while his sure hand, with its neat tool, snipped
the steel, as on a revised manuscript
radically rewritten since my star
turn nursing her without a "nursing bra"
from small, firm breasts, a twenty-five-year-old's.

I'm still alive, an unimportant Jew
who lives in exile, voluntarily
or not: Ohio's alien to me.
Death follows me home here, but I pay dues
to stay alive. White cell count under two:
a week's delay in chemotherapy
stretches it out: Ohio till July?
The Nazarenes and Pentecostals who
think drinking wine's a mortal sin would pray
for me to heal, find Jesus, go straight, leave.
But I'm alive, and can believe I'll stay
alive a while. Insomniac with terror,
I tell myself, it isn't the worst horror.
It's not Auschwitz. It's not the Vel d'Hiv.

I had "breasts like a twenty-five-year-old,"
and that was why, although a mammogram
was done the day of my year-end exam
in which the doctor found the lump, it told
her nothing: small, firm, dense breasts have and hold
their dirty secrets till their secrets damn
them. Out of the operating room
the tumor was delivered, sectioned, cold-
packed, pickled, to demonstrate to residents
an infiltrative ductal carcinoma
(with others of its kind). I've one small, dense
firm breast left, and cell-killer pills so no more
killer cells grow, no eggs drop. To survive
my body stops dreaming it's twenty-five.

It's not Auschwitz. It's not the Vel d'Hiv.
It's not gang-rape in Bosnia or
gang-rape and gutting in El Salvador.
My self-betraying body needs to grieve
at how hatreds metastasize. Reprieved
(if I am), what am I living for?
Cancer, gratuitous as a massacre,
answers to nothing, tempts me to retrieve
the white-eyed panic in the mortal night,
my father's silent death at forty-eight,
each numbered, shaved, emaciated Jew
I might have been. They wore the blunt tattoo,
a scar, if they survived, oceans away.
Should I tattoo my scar? What would it say?

No body stops dreaming it's twenty-five,
or twelve, or ten, when what is possible's
a long road poplars curtain against loss, able
to swim the river, hike the culvert, drive
through the open portal, find the gold hive
dripping with liquid sweetness. Risible

fantasy, if, all the while, invisible
entropies block the roads, so you arrive
outside a ruin, where trees bald with blight
wane by a river drained to sluggish mud.
The setting sun looks terribly like blood.
The hovering swarm has nothing to forgive.
Your voice petitions the indifferent night:
"I don't know how to die yet. Let me live."

Should I tattoo my scar? What would it say?
It could say "K.J.'s Truck Stop" in plain English, highlighted with a nipple ring
(the French version: Chez KJ/Les Routiers).
I won't be wearing falsies, and one day
I'll bake my chest again at Juan-les-Pins,
round side and flat, gynandre/androgyne,
close by my love's warm flanks (though she's sun-shy
as I should be: it's a carcinogen
like smoked fish, caffeine, butterfat and wine).
O let me have my life and live it too!
She kissed my breasts, and now one breast she kissed
is dead meat, with its pickled blight on view.
She'll kiss the scar, and then the living breast.

I don't know how to die yet. Let me live!
Did Etty Hillesum think that, or Anne Frank,
or the forty-year-old schoolteacher the bank
robber took hostage when the cop guns swiveled on them both, or the seropositive
nurse's aide, who, one long-gone payday, drank
too much, fucked whom? or the bag lady who stank
more than I wished as I came closer to give
my meager change? I say it, bargaining
with the *contras* in my blood, immune
system bombarded but on guard. Who's gone?
The bookseller who died at thirty-nine,
poet, at fifty-eight, friend, fifty-one,
friend, fifty-five. These numbers do not sing.

She'll kiss the scar, and then the living breast,
and then, again, from ribs to pit, the scar,
but only after I've flown back to her
out of the unforgiving middle west
where my life's strange, and flat disinterest
greets strangers. At Les-Saintes-Maries-de-la-Mer,
lust pulsed between us, pulsed in the plum-grove where
figs dropped to us like manna to the blessed.
O blight that ate my breast like worms in fruit,
be banished by the daily pesticide
that I ingest. Let me live to praise
her breathing body in my arms, our wide-
branched perennial love, from whose taproot
syllables shape around the lengthening days.

Friends, you died young. These numbers do not sing
your requiems, your elegies, our war
cry: at last, not "Why me?" but "No more
one-in-nine, one-in-three, rogue cells killing
women." You're my companions, traveling
from work to home to the home I left for
work, and the plague, and the poison which might cure.
The late sunlight, the morning rain, will bring
me back to where I started, whole, alone,
with fragrant coffee into which I've poured
steamed milk, book open on the scarred pine table.
I almost forget how close to the bone
my chest's right side is. Unremarkable,
I woke up, still alive. Does that mean "cured"?

Back Problems

DAVID MANUEL HERNÁNDEZ

Pain and scar tissue
grid my spine—
the house of broken posture
cracked by misfortune.

In a split second I aged
fifteen years, gained the stoop of
mis abuelos in the fields,
although lettuce never blurred
through my palms
under the shadow of an arched back,
the flavors of pesticides
patiently eating me
from the inside.

Still, I limp now. Because
mal suerte found me hiding
at the rear end of a rotted San Francisco victorian
masquerading with the X generation—
       white college graduates, sour waiters and
       counter hands, unsure of the utility of a literature
       degree and the annual family vacation.

The Mission district stairwell folded,
the porous victim of wood eating
bugs and water rot.
I guess I am "lucky"
not to have been impaled
by the bannister's ancient molding
nor struck on the neck
by a stoned teenager in her twenties
or a potted plant.

"Lucky" to land on my feet—
      like a cat thrown by its tail—
my body compressed into a
balladeer's trusty accordion.

The X-ers were amazed—"Whoa dude"—
at their back porch circus.
So cool, they offered me a joint
and trendy bottled beer for the entertainment
I brought them.
Perhaps a cup of tea for this brown clown
or a cab ride home
would have eased the first day
of a future throbbing with immobility.

"Talking Books"

STEPHEN KUUSISTO

I can still hear that actor's voice
with its bass notes, or the static
and hiss of records played all afternoon.

They'd arrive in black, metallic cartons—
their labels fading: "Matter For the Blind";
or—"Library of Congress."

I'd follow each rhapsodic
twist—Peary tries to find
the path to emptiness

crossing polar ice—
or Huck slips away
from the Widow's fetters,

and the needle would stick—then silence.
I'd flip it over,
feeling for the center

with practiced fingers,
as the Duke and Dauphin hovered
in blackness all the while,

suspended in their violence.
Books might last for days,
but I had them to afford

in half-light, and dark ascensions,
listening without moving.
The machine was government issue,

a veteran of the "New Deal"—
(the blind began to "read" in that Depression.)
It sent off heat like a stove.

I leaned close, clutching a tissue,
and heard the reader's stern appeal—
this book resumes on the next record. . . .

Learning Braille at 39

The dry universe
gives up its fruit,
black seeds
are raining,
Blaise Pascal
dreams of a wrist watch,

and Lord help me,
the metempsychosis
of raised dots
is upon me,
the boy in the monastery
reaches with his fingers

to take the Frenchman's book,
a thing quiescent
as a warm cat,
then feels the old ache
of amazement
under summer stars.

It's a dread thing
to be lonely without reason—
the windows at sunset are open,
and quick, musical laughter
rises from the streets.
I hold grains of the moon in my hands.

Harvest

My Chinese doctor tells me to sit in the park, that green,
the very color, will forestall blindness, and so I sit
under the Hemlocks planted by Baptists.
My temporal task is to hear music,
drink a cup of chrysanthemum tea,
admire the white moon of the morning,
even if my eyes tell me there are two moons.
It's almost a game: this superstition,
my slow idolatry of leaves,
the sparrows hopping as if on fire.
My story is pure vertigo, my eyes
are poppy-petaled, open to the sun.
O cuerpo oscura, I feel my way along the street
and hear voices. Sometimes I ask
what's to regret?
Daylight fails without me.

The Magic Wand
LYNN MANNING

Quick-change artist extraordinaire,
I whip out my folded cane
and change from black man to blind man
with a flick of my wrist.
It is a profound metamorphosis—
From God-gifted wizard of roundball
dominating backboards across America
To God-gifted idiot savant
pounding out chart-busters on a cockeyed whim;
From sociopathic gangbanger with death for eyes
to all-seeing soul with saintly spirit;
From rape driven misogynist
to poor motherless child;
From welfare-rich pimp
to disability-rich gimp;
And from 'white man's burden'
to every man's burden.

It is always a profound metamorphosis.
Whether from cursed by man to cursed by God;
or from scripture-condemned to God-ordained,
my final form is never of my choosing;
I only wield the wand;
You are the magician.

Unsolicited Looking Glass

The Santa Anas had been howling at the tops of their lungs;
Making for one treacherously hot day;
A day when the slightest body contact
produced pools of perspiration

and tight-jawed grimaces on the buses.
A difficult day to keep cool,
Let alone be cool;
An impossible day to be blind and cool.
Nothing like heat agitated automobiles
and sun-limp palm fronds across the face
to magnify the weight of my white cane,
To make me feel repulsively blind
and put upon by life in general.
As I squeezed past the insensate clot of unmoving passengers
to exit the bus,
I wondered if electric cattle prods
made good walking sticks,
Or if laser canes could be cranked up
to *light-sabre* intensity.
As I stepped down to the curb,
a woman's hand lighted on my shoulder.
Her voice was a cool breeze as she said,
"I just want to let you know
that you are looking gooooood today!"

Then she was gone—
Taking with her that terrarium on wheels
and the day's oppressive heat;
Gone, too, were my misanthropic thoughts of mass murder.
My smile was almost decapitating.
There's nothing like unsolicited truth
to clear the path for a brighter day.

The Secret of the Sea Star

EMMA MORGAN

*It would seem that in an animal that deliberately
pulls itself apart we have the very acme of something
or other.* *

—Ed Ricketts,
marine biologist

The mystery of Phataria
is that it breaks itself—
fixes the mainland of its body
to the side of a rock
while one limb bends
at a radical ninety degrees
and starts to walk

The Sea Star's roving arm contorts
twists until it snaps straight off
then ambles to its own death
on the last of its nerve impulses
Science labels this deliberate
although it can't pin down a motive

I understand this mystery
When I was ten a child asked me
why I blinked my eyes too much
I didn't say there was an impulse
and I was tired of resisting
I said, **because I want to**
and we were friends at once

Daily, recalcitrant muscles
threaten the union of my body

* Epigraph from the text of Annie Dillard's *The Writing Life* (New York: HarperCollins, 1990).

writing and pulling
in response to impulses
with no clearer motive
than the arm of a starfish cutting loose

What a relief it must be
to let go a limb

And then I wonder
if she grieves her wayward limbs
the way I grieve the constancy of mine

Attention Deficit Disorder

I

In my world of mental anarchy
the task "to clean the house"
breaks into ten
and ten again
like a seven breaking into two and five
one and six then three and four
each another sum of parts
so that I might wash a dish
dust three shelves
read one page
and return a phonecall
before I finally settle
into sweeping half the stairs
or scouring one sink
with a ferocity of purpose

II

When you speak to me
of Russian borders rearranging—
your hair-do
the glimmer of your nail polish
the dream I had last night
and the pattern on the wallpaper

at your back
vie for my attention
like a class of eager children
sliding off their seats
with the sheer potency of right answers

Your world of global puzzles
loses me in a grand collage of universes
each the size of the pen cap
held between your teeth
But give me just your shoe
or one braided lace
to you a detail—
to me a world of six strands
each a set of threads
the tension of the weave precise
and I can see what isn't visible to you

You couldn't stand to pay attention
in that small world
snaking through the eyelets of your shoe

III

I dismiss the boundaries
of minute, hour, day
until there's only task—
task so focused it becomes world

my mind a sheet of paper
folded in on itself
and again
until it becomes a crane
a Moor on horseback
or a hummingbird
poised on the lip of a blossom
balanced on a stillness
built of motion

Heart Ear

EDWARD NOBLES

To half hear
is to be without direction. Everything moves toward you from the
    right.
Even a lover's kiss, on the earlobe of the
left, is felt, but slightly; the alluring breath
streams around the head and enters at
the other end of night: a spirit's touch
against the window. It flutters there, in the rain,
intent on entry, but it can not knock.

Is it the mystery, or the mistrust,
that the left ear fails to hear?

A child of five, fevered with measles, my heart-ear bled
and bottled-up with wax. The pain was fierce
and good for nothing but my mother's worried eye
which was worth a lot
in a house of seven peers. One night, the ear's shrieking
burnt a hole into the sheet. Or so it seemed, as I held my head
against the pillow and cringed inward; the aching entered
and endured.

Dead now, it treasures more
the subtle world of night. Sometimes,
the good ear's insight is so perfect
I can't bear my present life. It is then
the past crawls
all the way around the rim
of years, to tap lightly, like a spider,
against the senseless drum.

From "Contradictions: Tracking Poems"

ADRIENNE RICH

VII.

Dear Adrienne,
                    I feel signified by pain
from my breastbone through my left shoulder down
through my elbow into my wrist is a thread of pain
I am typing this instead of writing by hand
because my wrist on the right side
blooms and rushes with pain
like a neon bulb
You ask me how I'm going to live
the rest of my life
Well, nothing is predictable with pain
Did the old poets write of this?
—in its odd spaces, free,
many have sung and battled—
But I'm already living the rest of my life
not under conditions of my choosing
wired   into pain
                    rider on the slow train
                              Yours, Adrienne

XI.

I came out of the hospital like a woman
who'd watched a massacre
not knowing how to tell
my adhesions   the lingering infections
from the pain on the streets
In my room on Yom Kippur they took me off morphine
I saw shadows on the wall   the dying and the dead
They said Christian Phalangists did it
then Kol Nidre on the radio   and my own
unhoused spirit   trying to find a home

Was it then or another day
in what order did it happen
I thought　　*They call this elective surgery*
but we all have died of this.

XII.

Violence as purification:　　the one idea.
One massacre great enough to undo another
one last-ditch operation to solve the problem
of the old operation that was bungled
Look:　　I have lain on their tables under their tools
under their drugs　　from the center of my body
a voice bursts　　against these methods
(wherever you made a mistake
batter with radiation　　defoliate　cut away)
and yes, there are merciful debridements
but burns turn into rotting flesh
for reasons of vengeance and neglect.
I have been too close to septic too many times
to play with either violence or non-violence.

XVIII.

The problem, unstated till now, is how
to live in a damaged body
in a world where pain is meant to be gagged
uncured　　un-grieved-over.　　The problem is
to connect, without hysteria, the pain
of any one's body with the pain of the body's world
For it is the body's world
they are trying to destroy forever
The best world is the body's world
filled with creatures　　filled with dread
misshapen so　　yet the best we have
our raft among the abstract worlds
and how I longed to live on this earth
walking her boundaries　　never counting the cost

Open Wound

TOM SAVAGE

To the right eye,
The 20/20 one,
The lid torn,
The white inside
Turned red, raw.
Much itching but
No pain after
Initial epileptic
Impact of head
With pavement.
Once the blood
Stopped flowing, it
Seems I will see with
It again, although
There may be a "defect"
In my sight. But for
Now I must keep it
Closed and rely on the
Other near-or-far-
Sighted one that
Can read but blurs
Beyond ten feet or so.
So this open wound
Should have been sealed
With stitches, but wasn't,
Says Dr. Mitty, the old
Doctor in the surgical
Clinic I went to for
Follow-up because none
Was available to me at
My emergency hospital,
Beth Israel, I being
Medically uninsured and

Not yet back on the
Medicaid dole of
Government necessity.
So now, it's too late,
Two days later, to
Stitch up. What's
A defect to be, to see
In a once-perfect eye?
Will the white in the
Right remain red for
My life long?
Why, then, is there no
Pain, only itching, as
The swelling of lids
And eye shrinks with
Help from passage
Of only Doctor Time?
Does an Emergency Ward
Have a right to be too
Busy on a night to sew
Up the best of my two eyes?
Is this not more than
A severe black eye
Because the first policeman
Who came by didn't want
To call an ambulance
Because he thought I was
An addict o.d.ing?
Fortunately or not, I
Was unconscious then,
My super came along,
Who called the docs.

                              7/31/89

Harmonic Convulsion

This morning at 6:04 AM, New York
City had its strongest earthquake
In thirty years. It measured 4

On the Richter scale and lasted
Less than a minute. At the same time
I had an epileptic seizure in
My sleep, the strongest one in
Several months. How long it
Lasted I can't say. I turned over
And went back to sleep. Three
Hours later, I awoke somewhat more
Permanently with a swollen tongue
And a severe pain in the skull
Fracture scar on the upper right
Side of my head, which persisted
For the rest of the day and into
The evening—a sure sign I'd had
What is called a "grand mal." Thus,
I disagree with the news reports
Which said that no one was hurt
By the earthquake and no damage done.

10/19/85

He Watches the Sky

NANCY SCOTT

My fingers walk across the phases
of the Moon. Waxing, Waning,
Full, New; each month displayed.
One Braille calendar and I
think the Moon is finally
mine. But he speaks of the Old Moon
in the New Moon's arms.
He watches the sky and I
want to know how dark must
it be to see the Moon? What do stars
really look like beyond the points
of light everyone talks
about? Can you see Venus or Mars
or Saturn's rings and does
everything vanish at Sunrise?
I know he knows these things
and may tell me some day
when I am not afraid
to ask or some night
when our differing patience
finds words for this present of seeing.
He watches the sky
and we wait.

Hearing the Sunrise

(This poem is dedicated to the light sensor on my kitchen windowsill.)

The sun rises in B major
to sing one verse of "My Way."
Pitch to remind, tempo to awaken,
twenty-three seconds of song
bordered by silence
serenade through any window I choose
on any morning.
No long gazes.
No missed opportunities.
Twenty-three seconds
is more than enough time
when you hear the light.

FICTION

Wolf
from *Cats Don't Fly*

❧ ❧

MARCIA CLAY

I awoke and sensed the house was empty. I did not feel good, weak, dizzy, and displaced as I rose. My parents were gone; Diane had spent the night out. I pictured my sister stoned and naked under some- one's body, a guy too old for her she'd met at the dance. A residue of makeup on my skin felt sticky and wrong, as the night had been.

But it was another Aimee, a stranger to reluctance, who reached for the crutch at the bedside, secured it, and walked to the bath. She ran water, and as if she'd known it before, breathed in the unfamiliar scent of male sweat on her body. In her pores was the memory of a damp T-shirt pressed against her heart, a first dance with one boy named Ted, his hot breath on her neck, hands tight around her waist, and something firm like wood below.

She didn't want to think of what had happened—how I'd kept the crutch while we danced, afraid I'd fall without it and this boy would have to catch me. *I dropped it. He caught it like a toy and carried me to the closest seat. He took my crutch, swung off on it under the strobes, his grin flashing white at everyone, as if that dance, my first dance, were nothing but a joke on him.* She stopped me short of recalling the shame and tears, and Diane coming for me when the lights went up. Things looked ugly in the light: my spastic bobbing hand, the gaudy bracelets on it, and the old crutch just *there* after all, at my feet. She would not let me dwell on these things.

In the cool shadow of the recessed bath she assessed me. She did not see a sixteen-year-old girl with cerebral palsy, she saw a virgin:

the long flat stomach, dark delta and round mounds above, sub-merged, unchristened. All of these she approved and chastised for their chastity. This Aimee ignored the bobbing arm, a red herring. The yet-removed bracelets she regarded with complicity. Troubled thoughts of Diane sleeping with someone, older, wrong, and strange like the man we'd almost run down on the way to the dance—this other Aimee dismissed. She ignored what was troubling me, the lonely randomness of the thing I'd thought was love. They chose you to dance, or didn't, or saw you sitting under a streetlight in a parked car and came over and said hi. Or they stared deep like they wanted something, the way the no-name man I'd seen hanging around town lately had stared when Diane slammed the brakes to avoid hitting him. He'd just stood there under the trees and looked at us awhile, like we'd fallen into a trap and he'd caught us.

Aimee didn't want to think these thoughts, or other more distant, dreamy things, the fancy party Mama was planning where there'd be live music. How I'd invite Dirk, and he'd come. She wouldn't entertain the daily morning daydream of him either, the true love dream, or stop to wonder with me what *he'd* think of the Ted-sweat on my breast. Sweet Dirk, this strong-bodied boy I studied with, pined over, and was saving myself for, had no scent. Her blood coursed through her faster than usual as she rose restlessly from the tub and reached for the crutch to get out. It was no enemy of hers, that crutch.

This Aimee leaned over the bathroom sink and used Diane's makeup, drew lines on her eyes the way Diane had done. There was intention and defiance in her gestures, an anger that wanted to settle on something—not Ted for his meanness, or Diane for in-sisting on taking me out to a dance I never wanted to go to in the first place. She was mad at me. Why I don't know. For being. For being a cripple.

Does not matter that you're trembling today, she said, a little feverish. Outside is good, go out.

She said these things without speaking, resolute not to pain her-self with my morning speech exercises, aware that no matter how many times I tried to say "Dirk," or "fried eggs," the consonants never stuck to the vowels, or if they did muscular strain in the mouth betrayed my difficulty. Silence was sexier.

Satisfied with the redness of made-up silent lips, she looked in the mirror. At the dresser she dressed. She fastened my peacock choker, dexterous with one hand, and chose a white sweater, a flowing cotton skirt. When we climbed upstairs she was observant but accommodating that there was weakness, inconvenience. We headed for the kitchen and she stopped at the record player, chose Herbie Hancock, and suggested we listen. This is great piano, the best, she said: listen. She showed me the toaster and fridge and said they were there to use. You can make your own toast, Aimee, she said.

The telephone rang. She said not to answer. It's not for you, or it is for you, and it does not matter. I heard ten rings, counted them, and did not answer.

It was only the first transgression.

It might be Diane, in trouble, I argued.

It does not matter.

It might be Mama.

No concern.

It might *be* Diane, it might be Dad, it might be, might be Dirk.

Does not matter, does not matter, does not matter.

The telephone stopped ringing and after a breakfast of fried eggs and toast this other me called a cab.

Of course somewhere in the recesses of my unpadlocked mind, I knew it was a game, an excursion. But the new Aimee said play, and thrust outward. The cab drove past the apartments where I knew Dirk lived, but she did not care. It left us at the bookstore café, and she said, they know us here: order tea and see what happens. Our table was taken and the usual busboy was off that day. No, it does not matter. She ordered tea and found someone to carry it out to the terrace. She put on her sunglasses, slid back in the chair and waited.

I felt hot and weak in the sun. So what, she said: rest.

"Hello, Peacock, can I sit here?" *Let him.* I felt a chill then and trembled.

Peacock has blue eyes? No, green? That's okay, I don't have to see, I can imagine. They're brown, they're purple, man. They're a fucking rainbow. Peacocks have rainbow eyes, don't they, Rainbow? Maybe I'll call you Rainbow, Peacock. No, don't tell me your name. You want to know mine? I'm Wolf, yeah. Like as in big bad. Just kidding. Kidding! I said I'm kidding, don't get shaky on me. You owe me one, almost killed me last night. Nah, I know it wasn't you, it was that Amazon queen you were with. Seen her around before. But you know something—maybe you don't, I bet you don't— you're more my type. Yeah, seen you around. You know I seen you, don't you? I like you, Peacock. Like that thing you wear around your neck. Weren't wearing it last night. I noticed. I like your hair too. Saddle hair. You're a horse girl, Rainbow. You wouldn't have that crutch and that arm how it is you'd be a horse girl, riding thoroughbreds. Yeah, that's your type. Let me buy you something, cake?

I thought. I owed you one—Wolf. How did you get the name? She was careful with the words, got the consonants, and her face didn't flinch.

Ah, you're listening. Very good, very cool. My name, got it in the trees, Peacock—not here, somewhere. You're a cool lady, you know that? I'd like to see you high. Get high? Guess not. Want to? I got some gold, Rainbow, the best. The best for Rainbow. Don't have to go far either, case you don't feel like walking. See that house over there? That one sticking up over the library? Right there. Two hundred paces and you fly. Fly, Peacock, fly.

I looked at the sun-whitened library which seemed painted in place and flat. Above it rising from the wooded hill were shady rectangles, houses climbing like irregular steps, and I did not know to which of them he was pointing. I looked back at the library and wondered if Dirk was there as usual, studying, if he could see us, or would see us should we cross the park together. The white facade of the library seemed pasted in place and unreal. *It does not matter.* I looked at Wolf.

Human. He seemed to have shaven, his hair was the same, long over one eye and the dark glasses. The pants looked new, no holes, plain and black. They hung from his shape, disguised the thinness, as did the dark jacket, the smoky gray shirt. There was a yellow scarf around his neck, silk it seemed, and on his wrist was a thick watchband, gold maybe. But he moved like time was no concern. He smiled a crescent smile, and I knew what *she* was thinking, that I should go with him, find out what being high was like. *Good day for it*, she said. *Flat day today, all flat like paper.*

"I'll finish my tea first. . . . Then we'll go."

Once I agreed, Wolf had less to say. He looked at his watch, it was no longer as if he had all day. "Okay, you finished?" I started to pour what remained in the teapot into my empty cup, pausing to admire my strong wrist, the precision as it tilted the pot. His hand stopped me, knotty fingers pulled mine down and the teapot hit metal with an empty thud. "Tea's cold by now. Cold tea's no good."

"I've never had any, never smoked it. What if we get caught?"

"We won't. It's a house, Peacock, a private residence."

"What if a cop smells something and busts us?"

"That's why we shut the windows."

"What if one just walks in?"

"They don't do that. But that's why we lock the door, Peacock, just in case. Come on. You coming or not?"

Stop shaking, she said, *it will be all right.* I rose.

He did not help in any way, but watched as I rocked the chair backward to make room, and as I rounded the table on my crutch, trying not to tremble. We headed for the park, the short way across. He walked a pace or two ahead. I was conscious of him, imagining what people would think, what Dirk were he watching would conclude at the sight of us. Nothing good, I decided, but Dirk did not seem real to me then, only the moment, the man in dark clothes and the choice to go with him. I kept walking.

The space between us gradually widened. His pace, though slowed I'm sure for my sake, was quicker than mine. He paid no attention to the widening rift, while it grew more disturbing to me with each step. *Why* was I going with him? *She* did not say. *I can't walk like you!* a voice inside screeched. That he *knew* I couldn't keep up, and didn't care, was painful to me. Several paces ahead he lit a cigarette, paused, and looked back. "Take your time," he said. *Turn back*, I thought.

"I think I'll skip it. I'm tired, I—"

He walked over then, sped really. "I'm sorry, Rainbow. Am I going too fast? Hey, I was just spacing out. Look, if you're tired, you are going to feel so much better after a few hits. I guarantee it. You owe it to yourself. Here, we'll walk together, nice and slow, side by side. Come on, that's it. That's it." His hand pressed my back and there was no more thought, only sensation, his touch something like Ted's dancing touch, soothing my angst. I went with him like paper.

We took a side street that wound uphill behind the library. It was peaceful there, lots of tall shady trees, though it was not two hundred paces, but more like a thousand. Just a little way more, he said. He wasn't touching me now but keeping his space as we continued. It was an odd distance, not far enough for the informality of friends, not close enough for the intimacy of partners. But it wasn't the actual distance between us that felt strange, rather my part in it, and willingness. We arrived at the base of a long steep ascending path of steps. They were crudely cut into the hillside and were blocked by rough wood slats. Weeds and wildflowers made a patchwork over them. No railing.

"All the way up there?"

"No, about halfway. It's not that bad, I'll help you." He pointed to a place in deep shadow where there seemed to be a gate. It looked more than halfway to me. Just visible through trees up there was a flickering of movement, someone on the other side of the gate. "Wait a minute, Rainbow, someone's there. May not be cool. This isn't my place, see, I'm just staying here. Wait here, I'll be right back, okay?" He climbed the steps with a kind of indifference. They could have been any steps, anywhere. The person came out and stood waiting as he approached. I couldn't hear but Wolf was gesturing to a house further up, and the person started to climb. It was a woman, I think, wearing something that swayed.

Against the narrow shaded incline he looked lean like a shadow in his dark clothes. He came down slowly, hands in pockets, his long hair falling over one eye. I wondered how he could see, why he kept on his sunglasses. A shaft of sunlight through the trees crossed his shoulders and face, flashing white suddenly, and the yellow scarf around his neck looked startling and bright. I felt something come over me—something important, not good, perhaps irreversible had happened, or was about to.

But his ease, his even pace on the rough steps also evoked in me a kind of trust, the strange willingness to accept whatever might be. "Someone up there, wrong house. It's cool." His arm was around me lifting upward. I felt relinquished of something.

The first few steps I teetered off balance, though he was supporting me on one side, the crutch on the other. The narrow uneven steps made my knees tremble, my body fear, and the way the rubber tip of the crutch caught the slats, didn't plant firmly, slowed us. Every movement felt exaggerated and precarious. "Don't worry," he said, "it's okay." As we climbed he seemed to be lifting more and more of my weight, and I floated, drugged by the movement, a dull fever, and moist shaded air. "Five or six more steps, Rainbow, that's all." His breath and voice blended with the scent of earth and wet growth. There was something familiar and practiced in our rocking ascent, but also timeless, imprecise, and uncultivated. His smooth jacket, the scarf, his sunglasses, my sunglasses, the faint smell of cigarette on his breath, the hard edge of his watchband rubbing my side, the bracelets and the rubber pad under my armpit, were all reminders of an ongoing material present. The heavy trees were not, the pounded earth, the rugged slatted steps, and our swaying were not. They belonged to any time, anywhere. *He was holding me.*

We reached the gate, which he had left open. "No more steps," he said and let go of me. He went ahead and entered the house; the door was unlocked. I expected him to say something, invite me in, but there was nothing. I followed.

The interior was as I had imagined houses in that wooded area: dark beamed ceilings, broad panes of glass and a camouflage of ferns beyond, sparse modern furniture. There were a few throw rugs, a leather couch, a glass table. The house was silent and we were alone there. He sat on the couch, took something from his pocket, and laid it on the coffee table. When he saw that I had entered the room he rose without speaking, walked past me, and closed the front door. I heard it lock. Dizzy from the climb, I pulled over to the couch and collapsed. He came and sat beside me, not saying anything or looking at me. He had removed his glasses; from the side his eyes were small and narrow. With a concentration his short hands plucked weed from a fat new matchbox and sprinkled some into a paper, which he deftly rolled, brought to his lips, licked and sealed.

Two separate people, I thought, and apprehension came out of being there, in a weak state yet doing this—with a strange man. He was a *man.* Sitting close to him I could see that. There were deep creases around his eyes and his face was long healed and pocked. He looked ugly to me, and I thought for a moment that even my sister would not go off with a man this old, this ugly. In some way I felt I wasn't there, sitting next to him; I wasn't a girl who'd do something like this, a desperate like Diane who'd go with almost anyone. But then he touched me, and the sensation of a firm hand rubbing my knee took away the separateness I felt. I was there, and something in me had said it would be all right. *I must make it all right.*

"What do you do?" I asked, seeking form in doubt and silence, but also curious that he, even with such a name, must do something, have done something by his age. When it became too much of an effort to sit forward, watch him, and wait for a response, I dropped back into the couch. He didn't answer but lit the rolled cigarette, inhaled deeply and held it.

"Too tight," his voice squeaked as he finally exhaled a thin stream of strawish-smelling smoke. "Roll great joints, most the time." The words came too late to sound like a response to my question. He tatted at the cigarette. "There, that's better. Your turn, Peacock."

I didn't do it right. He had to instruct me and went for a glass of water when I started to cough convulsively. I didn't want more, but he insisted, said I'd get used to it, that with this stuff, don't worry, a hit or two would get me stoned out of my head. I felt strange and faked the second hit, held it in my mouth. "You didn't take any in, Peacock. Don't waste my weed, okay?" But he was right, one hit was enough.

I watched him smoke and gradually came an uncomfortable feeling that I was in no way connected to my body. I looked at my lap, the patterns on my skirt swirled, and the strong arm seemed far away, the short one close and incongruous. I watched it throb involuntarily in a mild spasm and wondered why it did that, why I couldn't make it stop. "Maa hann's shakin'," I said, control over my speech, too, suddenly lost. Then came hilarity and giggles. "Maa hann's shakin'! Maa hann . . . ii woan, ii woan . . ." He was holding in smoke and looking at me weirdly, I thought, not like I was a person. I wanted him to help me make sense of things. Nothing made sense. An enormous cloud of smoke was released from his nostrils, his thinly parted lips. He didn't look like a person to me either then, but something other.

"Maa leg shakin' too . . . woan staap. . . . Staap! Staap thaa shakin, leg! Shake-shake-shake-shake-shake!" The sounds coming from my mouth weren't like speech or laughter, but a shrill wheeling.

"Shut up."

His words shocked and scared me, and I did become silent then. In sudden self-horror my head throbbed, and I felt ashamed. I wanted to leave, to be home in bed, to curl up like a crawdad and rock myself. But I knew that I could not and was trapped there until something changed. I felt unable to move and drew my legs like folded paper into the corner of the couch, covered them and their shaking with the skirt, and thought of shielding the couch leather from my shoes, so he, so Wolf would not be angry or say anything. I yanked the skirt under the shoes, over them, not wanting him to see my feet, the one elevated sole, the thick ugly rubber. I buried my hand against my chest. That other Aimee, the new one, was nowhere.

He was not watching me, but putting away his things, the matchbox, the papers. Then he took the glass of water and went somewhere and I curled up into what seemed the smallest shape and waited, wedged in the corner of the couch, peering out through tangled hair, humming, fearful, then wanting to laugh again but plugging the urge with my hand. I tried to be very still.

His hand was rubbing my side. "Hey, you alright, Rainbow? Okay, baby? You were making a lot of noise there, you know, like freaked me a little. You okay now?"

He was nice again, nice. He called me baby, *baby*. I listened to the sound of that in my head and told him I was okay.

"Can you walk? Guess not." He sat for a while stroking my side.

"There's something I want to show you here, Rainbow, something I want you to see." He was taking off my shoes, unbuckling the buckles. "Buckles," he said.

"Buckles," I repeated. It was only a word, but I laughed.

"Shhhh." My shoes dropped on the floor. He pulled the bag off my shoulder and dropped it, too. *"Uppppp we go!"* But these were my words. I wanted to make things all right. It would be all right. I was in his arms and there was a swirling sensation as we crossed the floor. Overhead dark beams ran fast like black on white piano keys, and I heard notes in my head, Herbie Hancock all mixed up.

"Where we goin'?" He said nothing. I pointed to the ceiling. "Looks like a piano." I laughed, but softly this time. "Hear it?"

"Shhhh." His face, his arms, were rigid as he carried me. I wanted to soften him, show him I was special, a special sensitive kind of girl who heard music on ceilings. If he saw that, things would be all right.

The high ceiling closed in. We went through a narrow door where it was darker, shady with green light. We were in a small kitchen. There were a few high windows, the sky through them obscured by thick branches. "You're getting heavy, Peacock." He stopped and set me on the rounded end of a wood table and held me there. His breathing sounded like wind. He looked all around us, not at me. On the table were empty plates, crumbs, bread crusts, an open jar of honey. *I should not be on the table*, I thought. *I should be on the chair.*

"Whaa you gonna show me?" I was trying very hard to get the words right, but they felt bulbous. The urge to laugh, though, was gone.

"Nothing, just a window. A beautiful big window, Peacock, down the hall."

"Whaa abou' ii?"

"You can see stuff."

"Whaa?"

"The sky, birds, the town . . . everything. . . . And there's this big tree. It's got roots all over the place. It's hollow, like. Anything you can imagine, Rainbow, you can see right there in that hollow part." His face was close to mine, hollows in his acne-scarred skin sickly and red. He smelled.

"I waan see the tree." He didn't move.

"You don't know things. What people do. Anything you can imagine, Rainbow, they do."

"Show me the tree." His hands were holding on to me, like I might fly away. He didn't move.

"There's no tree. Imagine that now, no tree." Left and right he looked at things on the table, then there were plates sliding, him pushing them away, pressing me down.

"Whaa you doin'?" His hand came over my mouth, pushed, moist and pungent. Small eyes looked down into mine.

"They're green, aren't they, Rainbow? Shhhhh."

His eyes stayed fixed, two dead-looking bugs. I could not look away, feeling they might at any moment multiply, or crawl on me. "It's okay, Peacock. Just be still. Don't *move.*"

His face stared down at my face. The yellow scarf he wore, hanging between us now, tickled my throat. His hair fell over my face, a smell of earth and weedy things, rough skin on my neck pulling at the choker, touching it, tearing it off my neck. The palm on my mouth clammy and warm pushed against cries I couldn't make, and my sweater rose. He suckled my breast.

The tenderness of that new sensation rose against other things: tension in my neck, spasms starting in my hand and leg, and the heavy beams I looked up and saw, lower, darker piano keys, like bars now. His mouth's steady swirling wetness on my nipple swelled through me. A wave. Pleasure, fear, together; I gave into one without freeing myself of the other.

The suckling stopped and I looked down to an intrusion of details: short hurried fingers unlatching his belt, a leather smell, the sound of a zipper, scarred knuckles fumbling, a small slimy-looking thing. I was revulsed by the sight of it, red like the scars on his face and no nicer than a dog's. A smell rose from him, familiar though, coveted, like one left often on my hand at night. With an urgency, and what seemed to be a kind of shame—as if to burrow himself out of view—he pushed up my skirt, yanked down my panties, and forced my legs open. His head was down, his eyes averted.

Now I know, I thought, as he covered my mouth harder, and pushed.

I wanted him off of me. I closed my eyes and saw myself, as if looking down from above, in the ivory between dark keys, a crippled, stunted-armed, stunted-legged virgin, being taken for scraps.

A fight. My arms flailing, crashing things, sharp sounds on the floor, the table, breaking, sticky glass. "Relax!" he said, fighting my hand with his hand. A plate flew.

He stopped. "Goddamn you."

There was silence, then his steps, water running in a sink, him over there washing himself. There was the sound of his zipper again and heavy booted steps coming back. I pushed my skirt down, pulled the stretched sweater. The back of my hand was wet and I saw it was bleeding, gushing from a cut. Shards of glass stuck in the skin. I brought my hand—the good hand—to my mouth and bit one out carefully, spat it, tasting blood and something sweet: honey.

"Fuck!" He walked quickly, collected things: a garbage pail, paper towels, some wetted. I could hear and identify the sounds, but did not look at him. It was a game, guessing each action. I did not want to look at him, but knew exactly what he was doing, swiping the table, picking off pieces of broken glass and dropping them in a trash bin, his movements quick and frantic.

"Move out of the way a little. I've got to clean this shit up. Fucking blood, fuck! I don't need this. I've seen enough *shit*. Move."

"I can't." The consonants were back, I could speak. My thoughts were cogent. Who *was* he; *what* was he? Glass fell upon glass into the trash bin.

"Were you in the war?" The question came from somewhere: *she* asked.

"Don't ask me about that shit." He lifted me like a piece of broken furniture, something inanimate, and set me on a chair. There was a shallow wet throbbing between my legs against the hard seat, like my heart had descended and was beating there. He swiped at the table. "How bad you cut?"

"It's all right." The hand was pressed between my knees, bleeding into the skirt. I watched as he swiped the table, honey there, and discarded the sponge.

"Let me see." His face pale as he unrolled towels in wild rapidity; he wrapped my hand, leaving room for the fingers to move. "Can you walk?" I didn't say but pointed to my panties, a filmy puddle on the floor, like someone had spat them there.

"Put them on." He bent, picked them up, and tossed them on my lap.

"I can't." His fingers ran through his hair, felt pockets and found his cigarettes. Trembling, he lit one and looked at me. Then he knelt, the cigarette shaking between his dry lips, and took my underwear. "Lift your foot." I didn't.

"I said, lift your foot!" I thought of what feet meant in a war—survival, what with one's wits could keep a person alive in a jungle. I thought of how his feet had shifted instinctually, just enough the night before, to avoid my sister's reckless turn. He must have been a good soldier, capable of precision. I clung to this thought as the smoke from his cigarette rose between us, dispelling something, the tension we both felt.

"Okay, lift your butt."

"Don't look."

"I'm not." He didn't look. It was a small thing, but I think I forgave him something then. Not doing it—right—for my first time.

He gathered my things, buckled my shoes. Leaving the house he did not lock the door. I wondered if he really knew the people who lived there. He looked up, down the steep steps, as if anticipating an enemy. Trembling the whole way, tilting, he brought me back down to the road. "You going to be all right, Peacock?" Released from his support, I stood against the crutch a moment before folding into the last step, exhausted.

Wolf looked down at me, away: left, right, into the woods, out toward the road. "You're going to be all right." He adjusted the yellow scarf on his neck, then pulled something from his pocket, my choker, and ran his fingers over it. "Souvenir," he said and slid it back in.

His pace walking away was easy and even. There was no trace of a past in it, no future.

My thoughts traced the way home but held back from considering consequences, and how I'd explain the way I looked.

The park was empty when I crossed. Out of a state of disorientation emerged a medicating sensation of euphoria. Every slow-moving moment, every element caressed. The crutch was smooth and weightless under my arm, the smell of its rubber tip rising from damp grass familiar and pleasing. The all-blue sky, usually distant and laminated, was near, palpable. On the quiet streets white cars passed with slow formality, like brides. The café, cast in shade now, looked benign and rested as if after a long sweat.

I thought of Dirk, his strong, unspoiled body and gentle ways. I wondered if he'd called, if the ten rings this morning had been his. I told myself they were, and that today would have been different had I answered. The shade surrounding me, the sky close overhead, promised nothing and hung immutable. *This day cannot be changed.* And knowing this was so, I asked myself if *now* I could have a boy like Dirk.

I'd invite him to the big party Mama was planning.

Across from the café a cab waited, bright and yellow in the sun. I clenched the crutch under my arm and swung forward in pursuit. My heart pounded and the ease I had experienced moments earlier was lost to a terrible urge to escape. But the other Aimee looked coolly at the driver, who sat lax, smoking and in no hurry.

Slow down, she said. *Take your time.*

Dancing After Hours

FOR M.L.

⌘

ANDRE DUBUS

Emily Moore was a forty-year-old bartender in a town in Massachusetts. On a July evening, after making three margaritas and giving
them to Kay to take to a table, and drawing four mugs of beer for
two young couples at the bar, wearing bathing suits and sweatshirts
and smelling of sunscreen, she went outside to see the sun before
it set. She blinked and stood on the landing of the wooden ramp
that angled down the front wall of the bar. She smelled hot asphalt;
when the wind blew from the east, she could smell the ocean here,
and at her apartment, and sometimes she smelled it in the rain, but
now the air was still. In front of the bar was a road, and across it
were white houses and beyond them was a hill with green trees. A
few cars passed. She looked to her right, at a grassy hill where the
road curved; above the hill, the sun was low and the sky was red.

Emily wore a dark blue shirt with short sleeves and a pale yellow
skirt; she had brown hair, and for over thirty years she had wanted
a pretty face. For too long, as a girl and adolescent, then a young
woman, she had believed her face was homely. Now she knew it was
simply not pretty. Its parts were: her eyes, her nose, her mouth, her
cheeks and jaw, and chin and brow; but, combined, they lacked the
mysterious proportion of a pretty face during Emily's womanhood
in America. Often, looking at photographs of models and actresses,
she thought how disfiguring an eighth of an inch could be, if a
beautiful woman's nose were moved laterally that distance, or an eye
moved vertically. Her body had vigor, and beneath its skin were firm
muscles, and for decades her female friends had told Emily they

envied it. They admired her hair, too: it was thick and soft and fell in waves to her shoulders.

Believing she was homely as a girl and a young woman had deeply wounded her. She knew this affected her when she was with people, and she knew she could do nothing but feel it. She could not change. She also liked her face, even loved it; she had to: it held her eyes and nose and mouth and ears; they let her see and hear and smell and taste the world; and behind her face was her brain. Alone in her apartment, looking in the mirror above her dressing table, she saw her entire life, perhaps her entire self, in her face, and she could see it as it was when she was a child, a girl, a young woman. She knew now that most people's faces were plain, that most women of forty, even if they had been lovely once, were plain. But she felt that her face was an injustice she had suffered, and no matter how hard she tried, she could not achieve some new clarity, could not see herself as an ordinary and attractive woman walking the earth within meeting radius of hundreds of men whose eyes she could draw, whose hearts she could inspire.

On the landing outside the bar, she was gazing at the trees and blue sky and setting sun, and smelling the exhaust of passing cars. A red van heading east, with a black man driving and a white man beside him, turned left from the road and came into the parking lot. Then she saw that the white man sat in a wheelchair. Emily had worked here for over seven years, had never had a customer in a wheelchair, and had never wondered why the front entrance had a ramp instead of steps. The driver parked in a row of cars facing the bar, with an open space of twenty feet or so between the van and the ramp; he reached across the man in the wheelchair and closed the window and locked the door, then got out and walked around to the passenger side. The man in the wheelchair looked to his right at Emily and smiled; then, still looking at her, he moved smoothly backward till he was at the door behind the front seat, and turned his chair to face the window. Emily returned the smile. The black man turned a key at the side of the van, there was the low sound of a motor, and the door swung open. On a lift, the man in the wheelchair came out and, smiling at her again, descended to the ground. The wheelchair had a motor, and the man moved forward onto the asphalt, and the black man turned the key, and the lift rose and went into the van and the door closed.

Emily hoped the man's injury was not to his brain as well; she had a long shift ahead of her, until one o'clock closing, and she did not want the embarrassment of trying to speak to someone and listen to someone whose body was anchored in a chair and whose mind was afloat. She did not want to feel this way, but she knew she had no talent for it, and she would end by talking to him as though he were an infant, or a dog. He moved across the parking lot, toward the ramp and Emily. She turned to her right, so she faced him, and the sun.

The black man walked behind him but did not touch the chair. He wore jeans and a red T-shirt, he was tall and could still be in his twenties, and he exercised: she guessed with medium weights and running. The man in the moving chair wore a pale blue shirt with the cuffs rolled up twice at his wrists, tan slacks, and polished brown loafers. Emily glanced at his hands, their palms up and fingers curled and motionless on the armrests of his chair; he could work the chair's controls on the right armrest, but she knew he had not polished the loafers; knew he had not put them on his feet either, and had not put on his socks, or his pants and shirt. His clothes fit him loosely and his body looked small; *arrested*, she thought, and this made his head seem large, though it was not. She wanted to treat him well. She guessed he was in his mid-thirties, but all she saw clearly in his face was his condition: he was not new to it. His hair was brown, thinning on top, and at the sides it was combed back and trimmed. Someone took very good care of this man, and she looked beyond him at the black man's eyes. Then she pulled open the door, heard the couples in bathing suits and the couples at tables and the men at the dartboard; smells of cigarette smoke and beer and liquor came from the air-conditioned dark; she liked those smells. The man in the chair was climbing the ramp, and he said: "Thank you."

His voice was normal, and so was the cheerful light in his eyes, and she was relieved. She said: "I make the drinks, too."

"This gets better."

He smiled, and the black man said: "Our kind of place, Drew. The bartender waits outside, looking for us."

Drew was up the ramp, his feet close to Emily's legs; she stepped inside, her outstretched left arm holding the door open; the black man reached over Drew and held the door and said: "I've got it."

She lowered her arm and turned to the dark and looked at Rita, who was watching from a swivel chair at the bar. Rita Bick was thirty-seven years old, and had red hair in a ponytail, and wore a purple shirt and a black skirt; she had tended bar since late morning, grilled and fried lunches, served the happy hour customers, and now was drinking a straight-up Manhattan she had made when Emily came to work. Her boyfriend had moved out a month ago, and she was smoking again. When Emily had left the bar to see the evening sun, she had touched Rita's shoulder in passing, then stopped when Rita said quietly: "What's so great about living a long time? Remote controls?" Emily had said: "What?" and Rita had said: "To change channels. While you lie in bed alone." Emily did not have a television in her bedroom, so she would not lie in bed with a remote control, watching movies and parts of movies till near dawn, when she could finally sleep. Now Rita stood and put her cigarette between her lips and pushed a table and four chairs out of Drew's path, then another table and its chairs, and at the next table she pulled away two chairs, and Drew rolled past Emily, the black man following, the door swinging shut on the sunlight. Emily watched Drew moving to the place Rita had made. Rita took the cigarette from her lips and looked at Drew.

"Will this be all right?"

"Absolutely. I like the way you make a road."

He turned his chair to the table and stopped, his back to the room, his face to the bar. Rita looked at Emily and said: "She'll do the rest. I'm off."

"Then join us. You left two chairs."

Emily was looking at the well-shaped back of the black man when he said: "Perfect math."

"Sure," Rita said, and went to the bar for her purse and drink. Emily stepped toward the table to take their orders, but Kay was coming from the men at the dartboard with a tray of glasses and beer bottles, and she veered to the table. Emily went behind the bar, a rectangle with a wall at one end and a swinging door to the kitchen. When Jeff had taught her the work, he had said: When you're behind the bar, you're the ship's captain; never leave the bar, and never let a customer behind it; keep their respect. She did. She was friendly with her customers; she wanted them to feel they were welcome here, and were missed if they did not come in often. She remembered the names of the regulars, their jobs and something about their families, and what they liked to drink. She talked with them when they wanted her to, and this was the hardest work of all; and standing for hours was hard, and she wore runner's shoes, and still her soles ached. She did not allow discourtesy or drunkenness.

The long sides of the bar were parallel to the building's front and rear, and the couples in bathing suits faced the entrance and, still talking, glanced to their right at Drew. Emily saw Drew notice them; he winked at her, and she smiled. He held a cigarette between his curled fingers. Kay was talking to him and the black man, holding her tray with one arm. Emily put a Bill Evans cassette in the player near the cash register, then stepped to the front of the bar and watched Kay in profile: the left side of her face, her short black hair, and her small body in a blue denim skirt and a black silk shirt. She was thirty and acted in the local theater and performed on nights when Emily was working, and she was always cheerful at the bar. Emily never saw her outside the bar, or Rita, either; she could imagine Rita at home because Rita told her about it; she could only imagine about Kay that she must sometimes be angry, or sad, or languid. Kay turned from the table and came six paces to the bar and put her tray on it; her eyelids were shaded, her lipstick pale. Emily's concentration when she was working was very good: the beach couples were talking and she could hear each word and Evans playing the piano and, at the same time, looking at Kay, she heard only her, as someone focusing on one singer in a chorus hears only her, and the other singers as well.

"Two margaritas, straight up, one in a regular glass because he has trouble with stems. A Manhattan for Rita. She says it's her last."

Dark-skinned, black-haired Kay Younger had gray-blue eyes, and she flirted subtly and seriously with Rita, evening after evening when Rita sat at the bar for two drinks after work. Rita smiled at Kay's flirting, and Emily did not believe she saw what Emily did: that Kay was falling in love. Emily hoped Kay would stop the fall, or direct its arc toward a woman who did not work at the bar. Emily wished she were not so cautious, or disillusioned; she longed for love but was able to keep her longing muted till late at night when she lay reading in bed, and it was trumpets, drums, French horns; and when she woke at noon, its sound in her soul was a distant fast train. Love did not bring happiness, it did not last, and it ended in pain. She did not want to believe this, and she was not certain that she did; perhaps she feared it was true in her own life, and her fear had become a feeling that tasted like disbelief. She did not want to see Rita and Kay in pain, and she did not want to walk into their pain when five nights a week she came to work. Love also pulled you downhill; then you had to climb again to the top, where you felt solidly alone with your integrity and were able to enjoy work again, and food and exercise and friends. Kay lit a cigarette and rested it on an ashtray, and Emily picked it up and drew on it and put it back; she blew smoke into the ice chest and reached for the tequila in the speed rack.

The beach couples and dart throwers were gone, someone sat on every chair at the bar, and at twelve of the fifteen tables, and Jeff was in his place. He was the manager, and he sat on the last chair at the back of the bar, before its gate. A Chet Baker cassette was playing, and Emily was working fast and smoothly, making drinks, washing glasses, talking to customers who spoke to her, punching tabs on the cash register, putting money in it, giving change, and stuffing bills and dropping coins into the brandy snifter that held her tips. Rita took her empty glass to Emily; it had been her second Manhattan and she had sipped it, had sat with Drew and the black man while they drank three margaritas. There were no windows in the bar, and Emily imagined the quiet dusk outside and Rita in her purple shirt walking into it. She said: "Jeff could cook you a steak."

"That's sweet. I have fish at home. And a potato. And salad."

"It's good that you're cooking."

"Do you? At night."

"It took me years."

"Amazing."

"What?"

"How much will it takes. I watch TV while I eat. But I cook. If I stay and drink with these guys, it could be something I'd start doing. Night shifts are better."

"I can't sleep anyway."

"I didn't know that. You mean all the time?"

"Every night, since college."

"Can you take a pill?"

"I read. Around four I sleep."

"I'd go crazy. See you tomorrow."

"Take care."

Rita turned and waved at Drew and the black man and walked to the door, looking at no one, and went outside. Emily imagined her walking into her apartment, listening to her telephone messages, standing at the machine, her heart beating with hope and dread; then putting a potato in the oven, taking off her shoes, turning on the television, to bring light and sound, faces and bodies into the room.

Emily had discipline: every night she read two or three poems twice, then a novel or stories till she slept. Eight hours later she woke and ate grapefruit or a melon, and cereal with a banana or berries and skimmed milk, and wheat toast with nothing on it. An hour after eating, she left her apartment and walked five miles in fifty-three minutes; the first half mile was in her neighborhood, and the next two were on a road through woods and past a farm with a meadow where cows stood. In late afternoon she cooked fish or chicken, and rice, a yellow vegetable and a green one. On the days when she did not have to work, she washed her clothes and cleaned her apartment, bought food, and went to a video store to rent a movie, or in a theater that night watched one with women friends. All of this sustained her body and soul, but they also isolated her: she became what she could see and hear, smell and taste and touch; like and dislike; think about and talk about; and they became the world. Then, in her long nights, when it seemed everyone on earth was asleep while she lay reading in bed, sorrow was tangible in the dark hall to her bedroom door, and in the dark rooms she could not see from her bed. It was there, in the lamplight, that she knew she would never bear and love children; that tomorrow would require of her the same strength and rituals of today; that if she did not nourish herself with food, gain a balancing peace of soul with a long walk, and immerse herself in work, she could not keep sorrow at bay, and it would consume her. In the lamplight she read, and she was opened to the world by imagined women and men and children, on pages she held in her hands, and the sorrow in the darkness remained, but she was consoled, as she became one with the earth and its creatures: its dead, its living, its living after her own death; one with the sky and water, and with a single leaf falling from a tree.

A man at the bar pushed his empty glass and beer bottle toward Emily, and she opened a bottle and brought it with a glass. Kay was at her station with a tray of glasses, and said: "Rita left."

"Being brave."

Emily took a glass from the tray and emptied it in one of two cylinders in front of her; a strainer at its top caught the ice and fruit; in the second cylinder she dipped the glass in water, then placed it in the rack of the small dishwasher. She looked at each glass she rinsed and at all three sides of the bar as she listened to Kay's order. Then she made piña coladas in the blender, whose noise rose above the music and the voices at the bar, and she made gin and tonics, smelling the wedges of lime she squeezed; and made two red sea breezes. Kay left with the drinks and Emily stood facing the tables, where the room was darker, and listened to Baker's trumpet. She tapped her fingers in rhythm on the bar. Behind her was Jeff, and she felt him watching her.

Jefferson Gately was a tall and broad man who had lost every hair on top of his head; he had brown hair on the sides and back, and let it grow over his collar. He had a thick brown mustache with gray in it. Last fall, when the second of his two daughters started college, his wife told him she wanted a divorce. He was shocked. He was an intelligent and watchful man, and at work he was gentle, and Emily could not imagine him living twenty-three years with a woman and not knowing precisely when she no longer wanted him in her life. He told all of this to Emily on autumn nights, with a drink after the bar closed, and she believed he did not know his wife's heart, but she did not understand why. He lived alone in a small apartment, and his brown eyes were often pensive. At night he sat on his chair and watched the crowd and drank club soda with bitters; when people wanted food, he cooked hamburgers or steaks on the grill, potatoes and clams or fish in the fryers, and made sandwiches and salads. The bar's owner was old and lived in Florida and had no children, and Jeff would inherit the bar. Twice a year he flew to Florida to eat dinner with the old man, who gave Jeff all his trust and small yearly pay raises.

In spring Jeff had begun talking differently to Emily, when she was not making drinks, when she went to him at the back of the bar. He still talked only about his daughters and the bar, or wanting to buy a boat to ride in on the river, to fish from on the sea; but he sounded as if he were confiding in her; and his eyes were giving her something: they seemed poised to reveal a depth she could enter if she chose. One night in June he asked Emily if she would like to get together sometime, maybe for lunch. The muscles in her back and chest and legs and arms tightened, and she said: "Why not," and saw in his face that her eyes and voice had told him no and that she had hurt him.

She had hurt herself, too, and she could not say this to Jeff: she wanted to have lunch with him. She liked him, and lunch was in daylight and not dangerous; you met at the restaurant and talked and ate, then went home, or shopping for groceries or beach sandals. She wanted to have drinks and dinner with him, too, but dinner was timeless; there could be coffee and brandy, and it was night and you parted to sleep; a Friday dinner could end Saturday morning, in a shower that soothed your skin but not your heart, which had opened you to pain. Now there was AIDS, and she did not want to risk death for something that was already a risk, something her soul was too tired to grapple with again. She did not keep condoms in her apartment because two winters ago, after one night with a thin, pink-faced, sweet-eyed man who never called her again, she decided that next time she made love she would know about it long before it happened, and she did not need to be prepared for sudden passion. She put her box of condoms in a grocery bag and then in a garbage bag, and on a cold night after work she put the bag on the sidewalk in front of her apartment. In a drawer, underneath her stacked underwear, she had a vibrator. On days when most of her underwear was in the laundry basket, the vibrator moved when she opened and closed the drawer, and the sound of fluted plastic rolling on wood made her feel caught by someone who watched, someone who was above this. She loved what the vibrator did, and was able to forget it was there until she wanted it, but once in a while she felt shame, thinking of dying, and her sister or brother or parents finding the vibrator. Sometimes after using it, she wept.

It was ten-fifteen by the bar clock that Jeff kept twenty minutes fast. Tonight he wore a dark brown shirt with short sleeves, and white slacks; his arms and face and the top of his head were brown, with a red hue from the sun, and he looked clean and confident. It was a weekday, and in the afternoon he had fished from a party boat. He had told Emily in winter that his rent for a bedroom, a living room, a kitchen, and bathroom was six hundred dollars a month; his car was old; and until his wife paid him half the value of the house she had told him to leave, he could not buy a boat. He paid fifteen dollars to go on the party boat and fish for half a day, and when he did this, he was visibly happier. Now Emily looked at him, saw his glass with only ice in it, and brought him a club soda with a few drops of bitters; the drink was the color of Kay's lipstick. He said: "I'm going to put wider doors on the bathroom." Their faces were close over the bar, so the woman sitting to the right of Jeff could not hear unless she eavesdropped. "That guy can't get in."

"I think he has a catheter. His friend took something to the bathroom."

"I know. But the next one in a chair may want to use a toilet. He likes Kay. He can feel everything, but only in his brain and heart."

She had seen Drew talking to Kay and smiling at her, and now she realized that she had seen him as a man living outside of passion. She looked at Jeff's eyes, feeling that her soul had atrophied; that it had happened without her notice. Jeff said: "What?"

"I should have known."

"No. I had a friend like him. He always looked happy and I knew he was never happy. A mine got him, in Vietnam."

"Were you there?"

"Not with him. I knew him before and after."

"But you were there."

"Yes."

She saw herself facedown in a foxhole while the earth exploded as close to her as the walls of the bar. She said: "I couldn't do that."

"Neither could I."

"Now, you mean."

"Now, or then."

"But you did."

"I was lucky. We used to take my friend fishing. His chair weighed two hundred and fifty pounds. We carried him up the steps and lifted him over the side. We'd bait for him, and he'd fold his arms around the rod. When he got a bite, we'd reel it in. Mike looked happy on a boat. But he got very tired."

"Where is he now?"

"He died."

"Is he the reason we have a ramp?"

"Yes. But he died before I worked here. One winter pneumonia killed him. I just never got to the bathroom doors."

"You got a lot of sun today."

"Bluefish, too."

"Really?"

"You like them?"

"On the grill. With mayonnaise and lemon."

"In foil. I have a grill on my deck. It's not really a deck. It's a landing outside the kitchen, on the second floor. The size of a closet."

"There's Kay. I hope you had sunscreen."

He smiled and shook his head, and she went to Kay, thinking they were like that: they drank too much; they got themselves injured; they let the sun burn their skin; they went to war. The cautious ones bored her. Kay put down her tray of glasses and slid two filled ashtrays to Emily, who emptied them in the garbage can. Kay wiped them with a paper napkin and said: "Alvin and Drew want steak and fries. No salads. Margaritas now, and Tecates with the meal."

"Alvin."

"Personal care attendant. His job."

"They look like friends."

"They are."

Emily looked at Jeff, but he had heard and was standing; he stepped inside the bar and went through the swinging door to the kitchen. Emily rubbed lime on the rims of glasses and pushed them into the container of thick salt, scooped ice into the blender and poured tequila, and imagined Alvin cutting Drew's steak, sticking the fork into a piece, maybe feeding it to him; and that is when she knew that Alvin wiped Drew's shit. Probably as Drew lay on his bed, Alvin lifted him and slid a bedpan under him; then he would have to roll him on one side to wipe him clean, and take the bedpan to the toilet. Her body did not shudder, but she felt as if it shuddered; she knew her face was composed, but it seemed to grimace. She heard Roland Kirk playing tenor saxophone on her cassette, and words at the bar, and voices from the tables; she breathed the smells of tequila and cigarette smoke, gave Kay the drinks, then looked at Alvin. Kay went to the table and bent forward to place the drinks. Drew spoke to her. Alvin bathed him somehow, too, kept his flesh clean for his morale and health. She looked at Alvin for too long; he turned and looked at her. She looked away, at the front door.

It was not the shit. Shit was nothing. It was the spiritual pain that twisted her soul: Drew's helplessness, and Alvin reaching into it with his hands. She had stopped teaching because of pain: she had gone with passion to high school students, year after year, and always there was one student, or even five, who wanted to feel a poem or story or novel, and see more clearly because of it. But Emily's passion dissolved in the other students. They were young and robust, and although she knew their apathy was above all a sign of their being confined by classrooms and adolescence, it still felt like apathy. It made Emily feel isolated and futile, and she thought that if she were a gym teacher or a teacher of dance, she could connect with her students. The women and men who coached athletic teams or taught physical education or dance seemed always to be in harmony with themselves and their students. In her last three years she realized she was becoming scornful and bitter, and she worked to control the tone of her voice, and what she said to students, and what she wrote on their papers. She taught without confidence or hope, and felt like a woman standing at a roadside, reading poems aloud into the wind as cars filled with teenagers went speeding by. She was tending bar in summer and finally she asked Jeff if she could work all year. She liked the work, she stopped taking sleeping pills because when she slept no longer mattered, and, with her tips, she earned more money. She did not want to teach again, or work with teenagers, or have to talk to anyone about the books she read. But she knew that pain had defeated her, while other teachers had endured it, or had not felt it as sharply.

Because of pain, she had turned away from Jeff, a man whom she looked forward to seeing at work. She was not afraid of pain; she was tired of it; and sometimes she thought being tired of it was worse than fear, that losing fear meant she had lost hope as well. If this were true, she would not be able to love with her whole heart, for she would not have a whole heart; and only a man who had also lost hope, and who would settle for the crumbs of the feast, would return her love with the crumbs of his soul. For a long time she had not trusted what she felt for a man, and for an even longer time, beginning in high school, she had deeply mistrusted what men felt for her, or believed they felt, or told her they felt. She chronically believed that, for a man, love was a complicated pursuit of an orgasm, and its evanescence was directly proportionate to the number of orgasms a particular man achieved, before his brain cleared and his heart cooled. She suspected this was also true of herself, though far less often than it was for a man.

When a man's love for Emily ended, she began to believe that he had never loved her; that she was a homely fool, a hole where the man had emptied himself. She would believe this until time healed the pain. Then she would know that in some way the man had loved her. She never believed her face was what first attracted these men; probably her body had, or something she said; but finally they did like her face; they looked at it, touched it with their hands, kissed it. She only knew now, as a forty-year-old woman who had never lived with a man, that she did not know the truth: if sexual organs were entities that drew people along with them, forcing them to collide and struggle, she wanted to be able to celebrate them; if the heart with intrepid fervor could love again and again, using the sexual organs in its dance, she wanted to be able to exalt its resilience. But nothing was clear, and she felt that if she had been born pretty, something would be clear, whether or not it were true.

She wanted equilibrium: she wanted to carry what she had to carry, and to walk with order and strength. She had never been helpless, and she thought of Drew: his throbless penis with a catheter in it, his shit. If he could not feel a woman, did he even know if he was shitting? She believed she could not bear such helplessness, and would prefer death. She thought: *I can walk. Feed myself. Shower. Shit in a toilet. Make love.* She was neither grateful nor relieved; she was afraid. She had never imagined herself being crippled, and now, standing behind the bar, she felt her spine as part of her that could be broken, the spinal cord severed; saw herself in a wheelchair with a motor, her body attenuating, her face seeming larger; saw a hired woman doing everything for her and to her.

Kay's lighter and cigarettes were on the bar; Emily lit one, drew on it twice, and placed it on the ashtray. Kay was coming out of the dark of the tables, into the dim light at the bar. She picked up the cigarette and said: "Oh, look. It came lit."

She ordered, and Emily worked with ice and limes and vodka and gin and grapefruit juice and salt, with club soda and quinine water, and scotch and bottles of beer and clean glasses, listening to Roland Kirk and remembering him twenty years ago in the small club on the highway, where she sat with two girlfriends. The place was dark, the tables so close to each other that the waitresses sidled, and everyone sat facing the bandstand and the blind black man wearing sunglasses. He had a rhythm section and a percussionist, and sometimes he played two saxophones at once. He grinned; he talked to the crowd, his head moving as if he were looking at them. He said: "It's nice, coming to work blind. Not seeing who's fat or skinny. Ugly. Or pretty. Know what I mean?"

Emily knew then, sitting between her friends, and knew now, working in this bar that was nearly as dark as the one where he had played; he was dead, but here he was, his music coming from the two speakers high on the walls, coming softly. Maybe she was the only person in the bar who heard him at this moment, as she poured gin; of course everyone could hear him, as people heard rain outside their walls. In the bar she never heard rain or cars, or saw snow or dark skies or sunlight. Maybe Jeff was listening to Kirk while he cooked. And only to be kind, to immerse herself in a few seconds of pure tenderness, she took two pilsner glasses from the shelf and opened the ice chest and pushed the glasses deep into the ice, for Alvin and Drew.

Kirk had walked the earth with people who only saw. So did Emily. But she saw who was fat or ugly, and if they were men, she saw them as if through an upstairs window. Twenty years ago, Kirk's percussionist stood beside him, playing a tambourine, and Kirk was improvising, playing fast, and Emily was drumming with her hands on the table. Kirk reached to the percussionist and touched his arm and stepped toward the edge of the bandstand. The percussionist stepped off it and held up his hand; Kirk took it and stepped down and followed the percussionist, followed the sound of the tambourine, playing the saxophone, his body swaying. People stood and pushed their tables and chairs aside, and, clapping and exclaiming, followed Kirk. Everyone was standing, and often Kirk reached out and held someone's waist, and hugged. In the dark they came toward Emily, who was standing with her friends. The percussionist's hand was fast on his tambourine; he was smiling; he was close; then he passed her, and Kirk was there. His left arm encircled her, his hand pressing her waist; she smelled his sweat as he embraced her so hard that she lost balance and stood on her toes; she could feel the sound of the saxophone in her body. He released her. People were shouting and clapping, and she stepped into the line, held the waist of a man in front of her; her two friends were behind her, one holding her waist. She was making sounds but not words, singing with Kirk's saxophone. They weaved around tables and chairs, then back to the bandstand, to the drummer and the bass and piano players, and the percussionist stepped up on it and turned to Kirk, and Kirk took his hand and stepped up and faced the clapping, shouting crowd. Then Kirk, bending back, blew one long high note, then lowered his head and played softly, slowly, some old and sweet melody. Emily's hands, raised and parted to clap, lowered to her sides. She walked backward to her table, watching Kirk. She and her friends quietly pulled their table and chairs into place and sat. Emily quietly sat, and waitresses moved in the dark, bent close to the mouths of people softly ordering drinks. The music was soothing, was loving, and Emily watched Kirk and felt that everything good was possible.

It would be something like that, she thought now, *something ineffable that comes from outside and fills us; something that changes the way we see what we see; something that allows us to see what we don't.*

She served four people at the bar, and Jeff came through the swinging door with two plates and forks and knives, and went through the gate and around the bar to Alvin and Drew. He stood talking to them; Alvin took the plate Jeff had put in front of Drew, and began cutting the steak. Jeff walked back to the bar, and Emily opened two bottles of Tecate and pulled the glasses out of the ice chest. Jeff said: "Nice, Emily."

Something lovely spread in her heart, blood warmed her cheeks, and tears were in her eyes; then they flowed down her face, stopped near her nose, and with the fingers of one hand she wiped them, and blinked and wiped her eyes, and they were clear. She glanced around the bar; no one had seen. Jeff said: "Are you all right?"

"I just had a beautiful memory of Roland Kirk."

"Lucky man." He held the bottle necks with one hand, and she put the glasses in his other hand; he held only their bottoms, to save the frost.

"I didn't know him. I saw him play once. That's him now."

"That's him? I was listening in the kitchen. The oil bubbled in time."

"My blood did, that night."

"So you cry at what's beautiful?"

"Sometimes. How about you?"

"It stays inside. I end up crying at silly movies."

He took the beer to Alvin and Drew, and stood talking; then he sat with them. A woman behind Emily at the bar called her name, and the front door opened and Rita in a peach shirt and jeans came in, and looked at Drew and Alvin and Jeff. Then she looked at Emily and smiled and came toward the bar. Emily smiled, then turned to the woman who had called; she sat with two other women. Emily said: "All around?"

"All around," the woman said.

Emily made daiquiris in the blender and brought them with both hands gripping the three stems, then went to Rita, who was standing between two men sitting at the bar. Rita said: "Home sucked." She gave Emily a five-dollar bill. "Dry vermouth on the rocks, with a twist."

Emily looked at Jeff and Alvin and Drew; they were watching and smiling. She poured Rita's drink and gave it to her and put her change on the bar, and said: "It's a glorious race."

"People?" Rita said, and pushed a dollar toward Emily. "Tell me about it."

"So much suffering, and we keep getting out of bed in the morning."

She saw the man beside Rita smiling. Emily said to him: "Don't we."

"For some reason."

"We get hungry," Rita said. "We have to pee."

She picked up the vermouth and went to Jeff and Alvin and Drew; Jeff stood and got a chair from another table. Alvin stuck Drew's fork into a piece of meat and placed the fork between Drew's fingers, and Drew raised it to his mouth. He could grip the French fries with his fingers, lift them from the plate. Kay went to their table and, holding her tray of glasses against her hip, leaned close to Rita and spoke, and Rita laughed. Kay walked smiling to the bar.

When Alvin and Drew finished eating, Drew held a cigarette and Rita gave him a light. Emily had seen him using his lighter while Rita was at home. He could not quite put out his cigarettes; he jabbed them at the ashtray and dropped them and they smoldered. Sometimes Alvin put them out, and sometimes he did not, and Emily thought about fire, where Drew lived, then wondered if he were ever alone. Jeff stood with their empty plates and went to the kitchen, and she thought of Drew, after this happened to him, learning each movement he could perform alone, and each one he could not; learning what someone else had to help him do, and what someone else had to do for him. He would have learned what different people did not like to do. Alvin did not smoke, or he had not tonight. Maybe he disliked touching cigarettes and disliked smelling them burning to the filter in an ashtray, so sometimes he put them out and sometimes smelled them. But he could empty bags of piss, and wipe shit. Probably he inserted the catheter.

Two summers ago a young woman came to work as a bartender, to learn the job while doing it. Jeff worked with her, and on her first three days the noon crowd wanted fried clams, and she told Jeff she could not stand clams but she would do it. She picked them up raw and put them in batter and fried them, and they nauseated her. She did not vomit, but she looked all through lunch as if she would. On the fourth day, Jeff cooked, but when she smelled the frying clams while she was making drinks, she could see them raw and feel them in her hands and smell them, and she was sick as she worked and talked with customers. She had learned the essential drinks in four days and most of the rare ones, and Jeff called a friend who managed a bar whose only food was peanuts, to make the customers thirsty, and got her a job.

So, was anyone boundless? Most of the time, you could avoid what disgusted you. But if you always needed someone to help you simply live, and that person was disgusted by your cigarettes, or your body, or what came out of it, you would sense that disgust, be infected by it, and become disgusted by yourself. Emily did not mind the smell of her own shit, the sight of it on toilet paper and in the water. There was only a stench if someone else smelled it, only disgust if someone else saw it. Drew's body had knocked down the walls and door of his bathroom; living without this privacy, he also had to rely on someone who did not need him to be private. It was an intimacy babies had, and people like Drew, and the ill and dying. And who could go calmly and tenderly and stoutly into his life? For years she had heard married women speak with repugnance of their husbands: their breath, their farts, their fat stomachs and asses, their lust, their golf, their humor, their passions, their loves. Maybe Jeff's wife was one of these; maybe she had been with him too long; maybe he took home too many fish.

Kirk had said: "Know what I mean?" To love without the limits of seeing; so to love without the limits of the flesh. As Kirk danced through the crowd, he had hugged women and men, not knowing till his hand and arm touched their flesh. When he hugged Emily, she had not felt like a woman in the embrace of a man; she melded; she was music.

Alvin stood and came to the bar and leaned toward her and said: "Are we close to a motel?"

"Sure. Where did you come from?"

"Boston."

"Short trip."

"First leg of one. He likes to get out and look around." He smiled. "We stopped for a beer."

"I'm glad you did. You can use the bar phone."

She picked up the telephone and the book beside the cash register and put them on the bar. She opened the Yellow Pages. Alvin said: "We need the newest one."

"Are the old ones bad?"

"Eye of a needle."

"Are you with him all the time?"

"Five days a week. Another guy takes five nights. Another the weekend, day and night. I travel with him."

"Have you always done this work?"

"No. I fell into it."

"How?"

"I wanted to do grand things. I read his ad, and called him."

"What grand things?"

"For the world. It was an abstraction."

Now the bar was closed and they had drawn two tables together; Emily was drinking vodka and tonic, Louis Armstrong was playing, and she listened to his trumpet, and to Drew; he was looking at her, his face passionate, joyful.

"You could do it," he said. "It's up in Maine. They teach you for—what?" He looked at Alvin. "An hour?"

"At most."

Kay said to Alvin: "Did you do it?"

"No. I don't believe in jumping out of airplanes. I don't feel good about staying inside of one, either."

"Neither do I," Emily said.

"You could do it," Drew said, watching Emily. He was drinking beer, but slowly, and he did not seem drunk. Alvin had been drinking club soda since they ate dinner. "You could come with me. They talk to you; then they take you up." Emily saw Drew being carried by Alvin and other men into a small airplane, lowered into a seat, and strapped to it. "They told me there was a ground wind. They said if I was a normal, the wind wouldn't be a problem. But—"

Jeff said: "They said 'a normal'?"

"No. What the guy said was: 'With your condition you've got a ninety percent chance of getting hurt." Drew smiled. "I told him I've lived with nine-to-one odds for a long time. So we went up in their little plane." Emily could not imagine being paralyzed, but she felt enclosed in a small plane; from inside the plane she saw it take off. "The guy was strong, very confident. Up in the air he lifted me out of the seat and strapped me to him. My back to his chest. We went to the door of the plane, and I looked at the blue sky."

"Weren't you terrified?" Emily lit one of Drew's cigarettes and placed it between his fingers. When she had cleaned the bar and joined them at the table, she had told him and Alvin her name. Drew Purdy. Alvin Parker. She shook their hands, Alvin rising from his chair; when Drew moved his hand upward, she had inserted hers between his fingers and his palm. His hand was soft.

"It felt like fear," Drew said. "But it was adrenaline. I didn't have any bad pictures in my head: like the chute not opening. Leaving a mess on the ground for Alvin to pray over. Then he jumped; we jumped. And I had this rush, like nothing I had ever felt. Better than anything I ever felt. And I used to do a lot, before I got hurt. But this was another world, another body. We were free-falling. Dropping down from the sky like a hawk, and everything was beautiful, green and blue. Then he opened the chute. And you know what? It was absolutely quiet up there. I was looking down at the people on the ground. They were small, and I could hear their voices. I thought I heard Alvin. Probably I imagined that. I couldn't hear words, but I could hear men and women and children. All those voices up in the sky."

Emily could see it, hear it, and her arms and breast wanted to hug him because he had done this; her hand touched his, rested on his fingers; then she took his cigarette and drew on it and put it between his fingers and blew smoke over his head.

Kay said: "I think I'd like the parachute. But I couldn't jump out of the plane."

Drew smiled. "Neither could I."

"I don't like underwater," Rita said. "And I don't like in the air."

"Tell them what happened," Alvin said.

"He didn't think I should do it."

"I thought you should do it on a different day, after what he told you. I thought you could wait."

"You knew I couldn't wait."

"Yes." Alvin looked at Emily. "It's true. He couldn't."

"I broke both my legs."

"*No,*" Emily said.

Jeff said: "Did you feel them?"

Rita was shaking her head; Kay was watching Drew.

"No," Drew said. "They made a video of it. You can hear my legs break. The wind dragged us, and I couldn't do anything with my legs."

"He was laughing the whole time," Alvin said. "While the chute was pulling them on the ground. He's on top of the guy, and he's laughing and shouting: 'This is great, this is great.' And on the video you can hear his bones snapping."

"When did you know?" Jeff said.

"On the third day. When my feet were swollen, and Alvin couldn't get my shoes on."

"You never felt pain?" Rita said.

"Not like you do. It was like a pinball machine, this little ball moving around. So in the hospital they sent me a shrink. To see if I had a death wish. If a normal sky dives and breaks some bones, they don't ask him if he wanted to die. They ask quads. I told him if I wanted to die, I wouldn't have paid a guy with a parachute. I told him it was better than sex. I told him he should try it."

"What did he say?" Jeff said.

"He said he didn't think I had a death wish."

Rita said: "How did you get hurt?"

"Diving into a wave."

"Oh my God," Emily said. "I love diving into waves."

"Don't stop." He smiled. "You could slip in the shower. I know a guy like me, who fell off his bed. He wasn't drunk; he was asleep. He doesn't know how he fell. He woke up on the floor, a quad."

She was sipping her third drink and smoking one of Rita's cigarettes, and looking over Jeff's head at the wall and ceiling, listening to Paul Desmond playing saxophone with Brubeck. Rita's face was turned to Kay, and Emily could only hear their voices; Jeff and Alvin and Drew were planning to fish. She looked at them and said: "Paul Desmond—the guy playing sax—once lost a woman he loved to an older and wealthy man. One night he was sitting in a restaurant, and they came in, the young woman and the man. Desmond watched them going to their table and said: 'So this is how the world ends, not with a whim but a banker.' "

Rita and Kay were looking at her.

"I like that," Drew said.

"He was playing with a T. S. Eliot line. The poet. Who said 'April is the cruelest month.' That's why they called him T. S."

They were smiling at her. Jeff's eyes were bright.

"I used to talk this way. Five days a week."

"What were you?" Drew said.

"A teacher."

She was looking at Drew and seeing him younger, with strong arms and legs, in a bathing suit, running barefoot across hot sand to the water, his feet for the last time holding his weight on the earth, his legs moving as if they always would, his arms swinging at his sides; then he was in the surf, running still, but very slowly in the water; the cold water thrilled him, cleared his mind; he moved toward the high waves; he was grinning. Waves broke in front of him and rushed against his waist, his thighs, his penis. A rising wave crested and he dived into it as it broke, and it slapped his legs and back and turned him, turned him just so, and pushed him against the bottom.

Alvin asked Rita to dance, and Kay asked Jeff. They pushed tables and chairs and made a space on the floor, and held each other, moving to Desmond's slow song. Emily said: "When this happened to you, who pulled you out of the water?"

"Two buddies. They rode in on the wave that got me. They looked around and saw me. I was like a big rag doll in the water. I'd go under, I'd come up. Mostly under."

"Did you know how bad it was?"

"I was drowning. That's what I was afraid of till they came and got me. Then I was scared because I couldn't move. They put me on the beach, and then I felt the pain; and I couldn't move my legs and arms. I was twenty-one years old, and I knew."

Last night Emily had not worked and yesterday afternoon she had gone to the beach with a book of stories by Edna O'Brien. She rubbed sunscreen on her body and lay on a towel and read five stories. When she finished a story, she ran in the surf, and dived into a wave, opened her eyes to the salt water, stood and shook her hair and faced the beach, looking over her shoulder at the next wave coming in, then dived with it as it broke, and it pushed and pulled her to the beach, until her outstretched hands and then her face and breasts were on sand, and the surf washed over her.

John Coltrane was playing a ballad, and Jeff looked at her and said: "Would you like to dance?"

She nodded and stood, walked around tables, and in the open

space turned to face him. Rita and Alvin came and started to dance. Emily took Jeff's hand and held him behind his waist, and they danced to the saxophone, her breasts touching his chest; he smelled of scotch and smoke; his mustache was soft on her brow. She looked to her left at Drew: he had turned the chair around, and was watching. Now Kay rose from her chair and stood in front of him; she bent forward, held his hands, and began to dance. She swayed to the saxophone's melody, and her feet moved in rhythm, forward, back, to her sides. Emily could not see Drew's face. She said: "I don't know if Kay should be doing that."

"He jumped from an airplane."

"But he could feel it. The thrill anyway. The air on his face."

"He can feel Kay, too. She's there. She's dancing with him." He led Emily in graceful turns toward the front wall, so she could see Drew's face. "Look. He's happy."

Drew was smiling; his head was dancing: down, up to his right, down, up to his left. Emily looked at Jeff's eyes and said: "You told me your friend always looked happy and you knew he was never happy."

"It's complicated. I knew he couldn't *enjoy* being a quad. I knew he missed his body: fishing, hunting, swimming, dancing, girls, just *walk*ing. He probably even missed being a soldier, when he was scared and tired, and wet and hot and thirsty and bug-bit; but he was whole and strong. So I say he was never happy; he only looked happy. But he had friends, and he had fun. It took a lot of will for him to have fun. He had to do it in spite of everything. Not because of everything."

He turned her and dipped—she was leaning backward and only his arms kept her balanced; he pulled her up and held her close.

"On a fishing boat I lose myself. I don't worry about things. I just look at the ocean and feel the sun. It's the ocean. The ocean takes me there. Mike had to do it himself. He couldn't just step onto a boat and let the ocean take him. First he had to be carried on. Anybody who's helpless is afraid; you could see it in his eyes, while he joked with us. I'm sure he was sad, too, while we carried him. He was a soldier, Emily. That's not something he could forget. Then out on the ocean, he couldn't really hold the rod and fish. And his body was always pulling on him. He had spasms on the boat, and fatigue."

Coltrane softly blew a low note and held it, the drummer tapping cymbals, and the cassette ended. Emily withdrew her hand from Jeff's back, but he still held hers, and her right hand. He said: "He told me once: 'I wake up tired.' His body was his enemy, and when he fought it, he lost. What he had to do was ignore it. That was the will. That was how he was happy."

"Ignore it?"

"Move beyond it."

He released her back and lowered her hand, and shifted his grip on it and held it as they walked toward the table; then Jeff stopped her. He said: "He had something else. He was grateful."

"For what?"

"That he wasn't blown to pieces. And that he still had his brain."

They walked and at the table he let go of her hand and she stood in front of Drew, and said: "You looked good."

Kay sat beside Rita; Jeff and Alvin stood talking.

"My wife and I danced like that."

"Your wife? You said—" Then she stopped; a woman had loved him, had married him after the wave crippled him. She glanced past him; no one had heard.

"Right," he said. "I met her when I was like this."

"Shit."

He nodded. She said: "Would you like a beer?"

"Yes."

She walked past the table, then stopped and looked back. Drew was turning his chair around, looking at her now, and he said: "Do you have Old Blue Eyes?"

"Not him," Rita said.

"He's good to dance to," Kay said.

"I've got him," Emily said. "Anybody want drinks?"

She went behind the bar and made herself a vodka and tonic. Kay and Rita came to the bar, stood with their shoulders and arms touching, and Emily gave them a Tecate and a club soda, and they took them to Drew and Alvin. They came back and Emily put in the Sinatra cassette and poured vermouth for Rita and made a salty dog with tequila for Kay. While she was pouring the grapefruit juice, Kay said to Rita: "Can you jitterbug?"

"Girl, if you lead, I can follow."

Kay put her right hand on Rita's waist, held Rita's right hand with her left, then lifted their hands and turned Rita in a circle, letting Rita's hand turn in hers; then, facing each other, they danced. Kay sang with Sinatra:

> *Till the tune ends*
> *We're dancing in the dark*
> *And it soon ends*

Emily sang:

> *We're waltzing in the wonder*
> *Of why we're here*
> *Time hurries by, we're here*
> *And gone—*

Emily watched her pretty friends dancing, and looked beyond them at Jeff and Alvin, tapping the table with their fingers, watching, grinning; Drew was singing. She smiled and sang and played drums on the bar till the song ended. Then she poured Jeff a scotch on ice and went to the table with it, and he stood and pulled out the chair beside him, and she sat in it.

She looked at Drew. She could not see pallor in the bar light, but she knew from his eyes that he was very tired. Or maybe it was not his eyes; maybe she saw his fatigue because she could see Jeff's friend, tired on the fishing boat, talking and laughing with Jeff, a fishing rod held in his arms. Rita and Kay sat across from her, beside Alvin. Emily leaned in front of Jeff and said to Drew: "How are you?"

"Fine."

Her right knee was touching Jeff's thigh, her right arm resting on his, and her elbow touched his chest. For a moment she did not notice this; then she did; she was touching him as easily as she had while dancing, and holding his hand coming back to the table. She said to Drew: "You can sleep late tomorrow."

"I will. Then we'll go to Maine."

"You're *jump*ing again?"

"Not this time. We're going to look at the coast. Then we'll come back here and fish with Jeff."

She looked at Jeff, so close that her hair had touched his face as she turned. She drew back, looking at his eyes, seeing him again carrying a two-hundred-and-fifty-pound wheelchair with a man in it up the steps to the wharf, and up the steps to the boat: Jeff and

Alvin and someone else, as many men as the width of the steps would allow; then on the boat at sea, Jeff standing beside Drew, helping him fish. She said: "Really? When?"

"Monday," Jeff said.

She sat erectly again and drank and glanced at Kay and Rita in profile, talking softly, smiling, their hands on the table, holding cigarettes and drinks.

Sinatra was singing "Angel Eyes," and Kay and Rita were dancing slowly, and Jeff and Alvin were in the kitchen making ham and cheese sandwiches. Kay was leading, holding Rita's hand between their shoulders, her right hand low on Rita's back; they turned and Emily looked at Rita's face: her eyes were closed. Her hand was lightly moving up and down Kay's back, and Emily knew what Rita was feeling: a softening thrill in her heart, a softening peace in her muscles; and Kay, too. She looked at Drew.

"You danced with your wife, you—" She stopped.

"Are you asking how we made love?"

"No. Yes."

"I can have an erection. I don't feel it. But you know what people can do in bed, if they want to."

Looking at his eyes, she saw herself with the vibrator.

"I was really asking you what happened. I just didn't have the guts."

"I met her at a party. We got married; we had a house. For three years. One guy in a *hun*dred with my kind of injury can get his wife pregnant. Then, wow, she was. Then on New Year's Eve my wife and my ex-best friend came to the bedroom, and stood there looking down at me. I'd thought they spent a lot of time in the living room, watching videos. But I never suspected till they came to the bed that night. Then I knew; just a few seconds before she told me the baby was his, I knew. You know what would have been different? If I could have packed my things and walked out of the house. It would have hurt; it would have broken my heart; but it would have been different. On the day of my divorce it was summer, and it was raining. I couldn't get into the courthouse; I couldn't go up the steps. A guy was working a jackhammer on the sidewalk, about thirty yards away. The judge came down the steps in his robe, and we're all on the sidewalk, my wife, the lawyers. My lawyer's holding an umbrella over me. The jackhammer's going and I can't hear and I'm saying:

'What? What did he say?' Then I was divorced. I looked up at my wife, and asked her if she'd like Chinese lunch and a movie."

"Why?"

"I couldn't let go."

She reached and held his hand.

"Oh, Drew."

She did not know what time it was, and she did not look at the clock over the bar. There was no music. She sat beside Jeff. Drew had his sandwich in both hands; he bit it, then lowered it to the plate. Alvin was chewing; he looked at Drew; then as simply as if Drew's face were his own, he reached with a paper napkin and wiped mustard from Drew's chin. Drew glanced at him, and nodded. *That's how he says thank you,* Emily thought. One of a hundred ways he would have learned. She picked up her sandwich, looked across the table at Kay and Rita chewing small bites, looked to her right at Jeff's cheek bulging as he chewed. She ate, and drank. Kay said: "Let's go to my house, and dance all night."

"What about your neighbors?" Rita said.

"I don't have neighbors. I have a house."

"A whole house?"

"Roof. Walls. Lawn and trees."

"I haven't lived in a house since I grew up," Rita said.

"I've got to sleep," Drew said.

Alvin nodded.

"Me, too," Jeff said.

Rita said: "Not me. I'm off tomorrow."

"I won't play Sinatra," Kay said.

"He *is* good to dance to. You can play whatever you want."

Jeff and Alvin stood and cleared the table and took the plates and glasses to the kitchen. Drew moved his chair back from the table and went toward the door, and Emily stood and walked past him and opened the door. She stepped onto the landing, and smelled the ocean in the cool air; she looked up at stars. Then she watched Drew rolling out and turning down the ramp. Kay and Rita came, and Jeff and Alvin. Emily turned out the lights and locked the door and went with Jeff down the ramp. At the van, Emily turned to face the breeze, and looked up at the stars. She heard the sound of the lift and turned to see it coming out of the van. Kay leaned down and kissed Drew's cheek, and Rita did; they kissed Alvin's cheek, and Jeff shook his hand, then held Drew's hand and said: "Monday."

"We'll be here."

Emily took Alvin's hand and kissed his cheek. Jeff pointed east and told him how to drive to the motel. Emily held Drew's hands and leaned down and pressed her cheek against his; his face needed shaving. She straightened and watched Drew move backward onto the lift, then up into the van, where he turned and went to the passenger window. Alvin, calling good night, got into the van and started it and leaned over Drew and opened his window. Drew said: "Good night, sweet people."

Standing together, they all said good night and waved, held their hands up till Alvin turned the van and drove onto the road. Then Kay looked at Emily and Jeff.

"Come for just one drink."

Emily said: "I think it's even my bedtime. But ask me another night."

"And me," Jeff said.

"I will."

"I'll follow you," Rita said.

"It's not far."

They went to their cars, and Rita drove behind Kay, out of the parking lot, then west. Emily watched the red lights moving away, and felt tender, hopeful; she felt their hearts beating as they drove.

"Quite a night," she said.

"It's beautiful."

She looked at him; he was looking at the stars. She looked west again; the red lights rose over a hill and were gone. She looked at the sky.

"It is," she said. "That's not what I meant."

"I know. Do you think if Drew was up there hanging from a parachute, he could hear us?"

"I don't know."

He looked at his watch.

"You're right," he said. "It's four o'clock."

He walked beside her to her car; she unlocked it and opened the door, then turned to face him.

"I'm off Monday," she said. "I want to go fishing."

"Good."

She got into the car and closed the door and opened the window and looked up at Jeff.

"The bluefish are in," he said. "We'll catch some Monday."

"You already have some. Let's eat them for lunch."

"Today?"

"After we sleep. I don't know where you live."

"I'll call and tell you. At one?"

"One is fine," she said, and reached through the window and squeezed his hand. Then she drove east, smelling the ocean on the wind moving her hair.

From *"Her Sense of Timing"*

꧁ ꧂

STANLEY ELKIN

"All I can say," Schiff told Claire, "is you've got a hell of a sense of timing, a *hell* of a sense of timing. You've got a sense of timing on you like last year's calendar."

"Timing, Jack? Timing? Timing has nothing to do with it. Time maybe, that it's run out. This has been coming for years."

"You might have told a fella."

"Oh, please," Claire said.

"Oh yes, you might have prepared a chap."

"I just did."

"Given *fair* warning I mean. Not waited till the last minute."

"Two weeks' notice?"

"Ain't that the law?"

"For the help."

"You *were* the help, Claire."

"Not anymore."

"I can't afford to be single."

"Tough," she said.

"Tough," Schiff said. "Tough, yeah, that should do me."

"All you ever think you have to do is throw yourself on the mercy of the court."

"Well, ain't mercy of the court the law too?"

"For juveniles and first offenders. You're close to sixty."

"So are you."

"I don't talk about 'fair.' "

"Very refined, very grown-up. Come on, Claire, put down the suitcases."

"No. The others are all packed. I'll send UPS for them when I'm settled."

"I won't let the bastards in. The door to this house is barred to the sons of bitches."

"Oh, Jack," Claire said, "the things you say. Stand up to delivery people? You? Painters and repairmen? But you're such a coward. The man who comes to read the meter terrifies you. Tradesmen do, the kid who brings the pizza."

"Why are they blue collar? This is America, Claire."

"Is that my cab?" She looked down out their bedroom window and waved.

"This is really going to happen?"

"It's happened," she said, leaned over the bed to kiss her husband on the cheek, and just upped and walked out the door on their thirty-six-year marriage.

"Wait, hey wait," Schiff called after her, taking up his walker and moving toward the window. By the time he got around the bed Claire was already handing the driver two big valises. Schiff, bracing his hands on the sill, stood before the window in his shorty pajamas. "Excuse me," he called to the man. "Sir? Excuse me?" The fellow shaded his eyes and looked up. "Where are you taking her?"

The driver, a young man in his twenties, looked at Claire, who shook her head. "Sorry," he said, "destinations between a fare and her cabbie are privileged information."

Schiff held up his walker. "But I'm a cripple, I'm handicapped," he said. "I'm close to sixty."

"Sorry," the man said, shut the trunk in which he'd put Claire's suitcases, and got into his cab.

"That," Schiff called after the taxi, "was no fare, that was my wife."

And thought, Her sense of timing, her wonderful, world-class, championship sense of timing. Leaving me like that. Just like that. Just get up and go. Just got up and gone. Don't tell *me* she forgot tomorrow's the party.

Schiff's annual party for his graduate students, though by no means a tradition—Schiff, who was a professor of Political Geography, had started it up only two or three years ago when, during a fit like some cocktail made of equal parts of sentimentality and pique, he realized that though it was barely a few years until retirement he had had only a stunningly scant handful of students who ever wrote him once they were done with their studies, let alone any who might regard him as a friend—had become, at least in Schiff's diminishing circles, one of the hottest tickets in town. Admittedly, it was not like Creer's annual anti–Thanksgiving Day bash, or one of Beverly Yaeger's famous feminist dos in honor of the defeat anywhere of a piece of anti-abortion legislation, but unlike the old manitou he could not claim Indian blood or, unlike Ms. Yaeger, even the menstrual stuff. Unlike any of his fabulous colleagues he was axless, out of it, their long loop of rage, degrees below the kindling point of their engagement. Outside all the beltways of attention and the committed heart. In point of fact so *un*committed that one of the next things he would do, once he struggled back to bed, would be to call his guests and explain that his wife had left him suddenly, the party was off.

They'd understand. He did none of the work for it himself, never had—my handicap, my handicap and footicap, he liked to say—and would simply set forth for them the now impossible logistics, freely giving Claire the credit for the splendid spread they put out——— not one but *three* roasts, rare through dark medium, turkey, sliced cheeses like slivery glints of precious metals, pâtés riddled with gemmy olives and crumbs of spice, breads and pastries, cakes and ale. Put out and gave away, in doggy bags and Care packages, Schiff—who addressed them in class as "Mister," as "Miss"—avuncularizing at them and propped up in the doorway forcing the uneaten food on his departing, liquored-up guests like some hearty, generous Fezziwig. Schiff's all-worked-and-played-out Bob Cratchits, his pretty young Xmas Carols. It was a strain. It was more. Not just another side but a complete counterfeit of his character and, while he generally enjoyed the masquerade, he couldn't help but wonder what his students made of his impersonation. Many sent thank-you notes, of course—a form Schiff regarded as condescending—but few ever actually mentioned the parties to him because the only other times they saw each other were in class, where it was business as usual, where the smoking lamp was never lit, and it was Mister and Miss all over again.

What he feared for was his dignity, protecting that like some old-timey maiden her virginity. The annual party, to Schiff's way of thinking, was pure ceremony, obligatory as hair let down for Mardi Gras, candy and trinkets tossed from the float, insignificant gelt on the anything-goes occasions. But only, they would surely see, *voluntarily* obligatory, obligatory for as long as his mood was up for it. This was what the great advantage of his age came down to. Added to the other great advantage of his disenabling condition, Schiff practically had it made. A cheerful, outgoing older man might have genuinely enjoyed it. Bargains struck with the Indians for Manhattan, a kind of openhanded heartiness done strictly on spec. Even— he's thinking about his rough bluff brusqueness with them—the flirting—the men as well as the women—— Schiff's sandpapery humours. (Well, it was in the nature of the profession to flirt, all profs engaged in some almost military hearts-and-minds thing.) Schiff *would* have enjoyed it. He *had* enjoyed it. In the days before he'd been struck down, when even at twenty-five, when even at forty and for a few years afterward, all this curmudgeon business had been merely a dodge, style posturing as temperament and all, he suspected (almost remembered) the customary mishmash of mush skin-deep beneath it. Because, again, the only thing that stood between him and his complete capitulation—he could not revert to what he had not really come from in the first place—to type, was that brittle dignity he had practically lain down his life for. Pretty ironic, he'd say, even in as ironic a world as this one, to have had stripped from him (and by mere pathology) the physical bulwark of his great protective formality and fastidiousness. (Completely toilet trained, according to family legend, at nine months.)

And now he has a choice to make: whether to wiggle-waggle on the walker (with no one in the house to help him should he fall) the thirty or so steps to the bathroom, or to scoot crabwise up along the side of his bed toward the nightstand, where he keeps his urinal, Credé his bladder by pressing up on it with his good hand, priming piss like water from a pump till it flowed, not in anything like a stream but in nickel-and-dime dribs and petty drabs from his stunted, retracted penis (now more like a stuck elevator button than a shaft). They tell him he must use his legs or lose them, but it's his nickel, his dime—— his, he means, energy, and he sidesaddles the bed, bouncing his fists and ass on the mattress in some awkward, primitive locomotion somewhere between riding a horse and potato-racing. Vaguely he feels like a fellow in a folk song, a sort of John Henry, or as if he is somehow driving actual stitches into the bedding and thinks, and not for the first time, that he ought to be an event in the Olympics.

His head within striking distance of the head of the bed, Jack Schiff laid into gravity and fell back on the pillow, then, with his palms under his left thigh, he pulled his almost useless leg up after him. The right one still had some strength and he kicked it aboard, leaned over to open the door to the nightstand, and took out the green plastic basin and thin urinal, angled, tipped at its neck (always reminding Schiff somehow of a sort of shellfish, indeed actually smelling like one, of the shore, its filthy musks and salts and iodines, its mixed and complex seas gone off like sour soup). It's into this, once he's snapped back its plastic lid, Schiff must thread his penis, hold it in place, pushing up on the bottom of his abdomen, jabbing and jabbing with his thumb until he feels the burn. (Taking pleasure not just in the release of his water but in the muted, rain-on-the-roof sound it makes once it begins to come.) Only recently has he noticed the bruise on the skin of his lower stomach where he's been punching himself silly. He examines it now, reading the yellowish black and blue like a fortune-teller. What, thought Schiff, a piece of work is man, and blotted at his pee with a Kleenex. Then he measured his output in cubic centimeters on the bas relief plastic numerals outside the urinal. His secret wish was to piss a liter, but the most he's ever done was six hundred cubic centimeters. This time it's under two hundred. Not even average, but he's relieved because the fact is Schiff can't stand even seventy-five cc of discomfort, not even fifty. For a man as generally incapacitated and uncomfortable as Schiff is he's a sort of snob, but pissing is something he can do something about. Schiff is very conscientious about pissing.

And only now does his new situation have his full attention.

For the truth is Schiff has always been very organized. Even before he was a cripple he was organized. (Schiff believes in a sort of cripple's code——— that one must never do anything twice. It's a conservation-of-energy thing, an anti-entropy thing, scientific, almost Newtonian, and now, in an age of raised environmental consciousness, recycling, of substitution and cut corners, the golden age, he supposes, of the stitch in time, of taken pains and being careful in the streets, he finds—for a cripple—he's not only, given his gait, in step with his times but practically a metaphor for them. It's a conservation-of-energy thing and a nine-months-of-toilet-training thing.)

Of course—he's thinking of his new situation, he's thinking of the carefully trained guns of his full attention, he's thinking of the inescapable fallout of the world, he's thinking of synergy, of the unavoidable garbage created not only out of every problem but out of each new solution—the pisser—he knew this going in, he couldn't help himself, by nature he was a list maker—will have to be emptied, especially this particular pisser with its almost caramel-colored urine. (Schiff prefers a clearish urine, something in a dry white wine, and what, he wonders, is the liquid equivalent of anal retentive?) This had been—even with the handle of the urinal attached to the walker's wide aluminum crossrail his wild limp would not have permitted him to take five steps without setting up the dancing waters, a rough churn of spilled piss—Claire's job, and though he doesn't really blame Claire for leaving him—had their roles been reversed, take *away* his nine-month toilet training and his incremental, almost exponential squeamishness, he'd have bugged out on her long ago—he understands that, should this thing stick, in the future he will have to think twice, three times, more, before using the urinal. (Or maybe, thinks the list maker, he can arrange for a *case* of urinals, keep them in the nightstand, turn it into a kind of wine cellar. Nah, he's kidding. Well he is and he isn't. It's something to think about, another thing he'll have to run past the cripple's code, the garbage potential latent in all solutions.)

But he set all that aside for the moment and took up the phone to see if he could get some idea where he stood.

The dispatcher at the cab company—Schiff had made a mental note of the number on Claire's taxi—said he'd like to help but the computer was down. (Schiff, who didn't believe him, wondered what the fallout would come to from such solutions.) He checked with the airlines, but since he couldn't give them Claire's destination, let alone times or flight numbers, they couldn't help him. (Couldn't or wouldn't. He insisted that even without the specifics they ought to be able to punch up her name on their computers. Claire Schiff, he said to one agent, how many Claire Schiffs could there be riding on their airplanes? She was his wife, for God's sake, and he didn't know of another Claire Schiff in all of America. Suppose this had been a *real* emergency. A *real* emergency? "Sure. If the plane went down, God forbid. If there'd been a hijacking." "If the plane went down, if there's been a hijacking?" the agent said slyly. "God forbid," said Schiff. "She's your wife," another agent said, "and you don't even have a destination for her?" "Well, my girl." "Oh, now she's your 'girl.'" "My daughter," he said, "we think she's run off." "Your daughter, is she?" the agent said. "Listen, you," Schiff, getting defensive, said aggressively, "I happen to be a Frequent Flyer on this airline. I have your platinum card, more than a hundred thousand uncashed miles and enough bonus points to practically charter my own goddamn plane. Either look up Claire Schiff for me or let me speak to your supervisor." The son of a bitch hung up on him. They'd whipped him. "I have to find her," he told the very last agent he spoke to, "I'm disabled and we're giving a party.") He probably spent thirty or forty dollars on long-distance fishing expeditions. Their friends, proclaiming no knowledge of her plans, went on fishing expeditions of their own. "No," he'd say, putting them off, "no trouble. As for myself, my condition's pretty much unchanged, but I think Claire may be getting a little spooked. Well," he said, still fairly truthfully, "we're both getting on. Hell," he said, "I'm close to sixty. So's Claire, for that matter. Maybe she thinks she won't be able to lift me much longer." But finally as cavalier with the truth as he'd been with the airline son of a bitch who'd hung up on him. "She's been depressed," he said. "I've got her meeting with a psychiatrist three, sometimes four times a week. We're starting to think about institutions. We're starting to think, now they've got a lot of the kinks worked out, about electroshock therapy. Life's a bitch, ain't it? Yeah, well, if you should happen to hear anything, anything at all, you have my number, give me a ring. Dr. Greif and I want to get this thing settled as soon as we can. Tell Marge hi for me."

No longer bothering to pick up the litter he left after these flights of fancy, no longer even thinking about it. Just working his new situation. And was still working his new situation when the idea came to him to call Harry Ald in Portland. Once he thought of it he didn't screw around.

"Harry, it's Jack. Is Claire with you?"

"With me? Why would she be with me?"

He recognized the tone in Harry's voice. It could have been the tone in his own voice when he was handing out his God forbids to the airline agents and transforming his wife's identity into his girlfriend's and then declining that one into some daughter's.

"Why? Well, for starters, I think she may still have a thing for you, you big lug."

"That was years ago, Jack. Christ, man, I'm sixty years old. We ain't high school kids any longer."

"Is she with you, Harry?"

"Jack, I swear on my life she isn't."

"Yeah, all right, it's a four-hour plane ride to Portland. Is she on her way?"

"Honor bright, Jack, I'm telling you that as of this minute I have absolutely no idea where she is."

So, Schiff thought, she's run off to play out her life with her old sweetheart.

"Okay, Harry. Hang tough. Stonewall me. Just you remember. I'm a helpless old cripple with a degenerative neurological disease who has to be strapped into the chair when he goes down the stairs on his Stair-Glide."

"Oh, Jack," Harry said.

"Oh, Harry," said Jack, and hung up.

It wasn't that satisfactory but at least now he knew where he stood. (Well, he thought, *stood.*) What he'd told his wife had been true. He *couldn't* afford to be single. Not at the rate his exacerbations had been coming. Only a little over a year ago he'd still been able to manage on a cane, he'd still been able to drive. He'd owned a walker—a gift from the Society—but hadn't even taken it out of its box. Now they had to tote him around in a wheelchair he hadn't enough strength in his left arm to propel by himself. Now he had to go up and down stairs in contraptions on tracks——— Schiff's little choo-choo. Now he couldn't stand in the shower, there were grab bars on the sides of his handicap toilet, a bath bench in his tub, he had to sit to pee, and couldn't always pull the beltless, elastic-waistband pants he wore all the way up his hips and over his ass. (Now, for the same reason, he didn't even wear underwear.) There were ramps at both the front and rear of the house. And every other month now there was some elaborate new piece of home health equipment in the house. Indeed, where once it had been a sort of soft entertainment for him to go into the malls and department stores, now it had become a treat to drop into one of the health supply shops and scope the prosthetics. On his wish list was the sort of motorized wheelchair you'd see paraplegics tear around in, a van with a hydraulic lift in which to put it, and one of those big easy chairs that raised you to a standing position. Also, although in his case it was still a little premature to think about just yet, he had his eye on this swell new electronic hospital bed. He found himself following ads for used hospital beds in the Society's newsletter. ("Don't kid yourself," he told colleagues, "it takes dough to be crippled and still have a lifestyle.")

You could be crippled or you could be single. Schiff, though he made a pretty good living at the university—Check, he reminded himself, the savings and money-market accounts, see if she cleaned you out before she split—didn't know anyone who could afford to be both. Oh, maybe if you went into a *home* maybe, but unless you had only three or four years to live that was prohibitive, too. (Wasn't everything up front? Didn't you have to sign your life savings over to those guys? He should have known this stuff, but give him a break, until this morning he hadn't even known his wife would be running out on him.) And, though he'd never actually been in one, he didn't think he'd like the way it would smell in the corridors.

So he was checking his options. Still working his new situation, he meant, still, he meant, thinking about the blows he would be taking in his comfort, he found his mind drifting back to that wish list. He found himself idly thinking about the skeepskin whoosies crips draped over the furniture and across their wheelchairs and sheets to help prevent lesions and bedsores. It was astonishing what one of those babies could go for in a wicked world. (It varied actually. They came in different grades, like wool rugs, fur coats, or diamonds. Lambskin was the most expensive, then ewes, then adult males, but it wasn't that simple. There were categories within even these categories, and certain kinds of sheep—castrated fully-grown males were an example—could sometimes be more expensive than even the finest virgin lambskin. Once you really got into it, it was a waste, a waste and a shame, thought Schiff, to be crippled-up in such an interesting place as the world.) Oh well, he thought, if he really needed them he could afford all the sheepskins he wanted. Sheepskin deprival wasn't his problem. His wish list wasn't. He *had* been drifting, he *had* been thinking idly. With Claire gone his problem was the real and present danger he was in, his problem was singleness and emergency.

He picked up his cordless phone and called Information. (Another thing he didn't understand about his wife. Since his disease had been first diagnosed, even, that is, when he was relatively asymptomatic, he'd asked the telephone company, and with a supporting letter from his neurologist received, for its free Unlimited Information Privilege. For years now he hadn't cracked a phone book. Claire had telephone numbers written down in a small, worn black spiral notebook she kept in a drawer in the kitchen. When she wanted the number of a plumber, say, or the man who serviced their air conditioners, she'd go all the way downstairs for it rather than call Information. Recently, it was the cause of some of their biggest fights. "Ask Information," Schiff offered expansively, almost like a host pressing food or drink on a guest. "The number's in my book," she'd say. "Why not ask Information? It's free." "I've got the number downstairs. Information has better things to do." "It's their *job*, for Christ's sake. What do you think the hell else they have to do?" "That's all right, I don't mind." "*I* mind," Schiff would say, and he'd be shouting now. "*Why?*" he'd yell after her. "*This is some passive-aggressive thing, isn't it? Sure,*" he'd shout, "*this is some lousy passive-aggressive thing on your part. Just your way of showing me who the cripple is in this outfit!*" Sometimes, out of spite and with Claire as witness, checking what was playing at all the movie houses, when the feature was scheduled to begin, he'd rack up a dozen or so calls to Information at a time. Or patiently explain to her, "You know, Claire, the Information operators don't actually look anything up. It isn't as if they were ruining their eyes over the tiny print in the telephone directory. It's all computers nowadays. They just punch in an approximate spelling and the number comes up on the screen." "It's wasteful," Claire might say. "It's free." "It's a drain on the electricity, it's wasteful." "You clip goddamn coupons for shampoos and breakfast cereals and shit we wouldn't even eat unless you got fifteen or twenty cents off the price of the goddamn box! *That's* wasteful! Do you know what they charge for a call to Information? *Forty-five cents, that's what! Forty-five cents!* They're ripping you off. I'll tell you the truth, Claire, I feel sorry for people who aren't handicapped today, I really do. I probably save us a dollar eighty cents a day. You know what that comes to over the course of a year? Practically six hundred fifty dollars a year! Go buy yourself a designer dress, Claire, go get yourself a nice warm coat." "*Big man!*" "*Big fucking passive aggressive!*")

"S.O.S. Corporation," a woman said when the number rang through. "How may we help you?"

"I've seen your ads on TV and I'd like to speak to one of your sales representatives," Schiff said.

"Bill isn't busy just now. I'll put you through to Bill."

"I'm disabled," Schiff told Bill. "My wife of thirty-six years skipped out on me today to be with an old boyfriend in the Pacific Northwest and left me high and dry and all alone in the house, pretty much a prisoner in it, in fact. Claire left me the car, and I have my handicap plates—my 'vanity plates,' I call them, with their stick-figure, big-wheeler wheelchairs like a kid's toy—but I haven't driven in over a year and don't even know whether I still can."

The salesman started to explain his company's services but Schiff interrupted him. "Yes," he said, "I've seen your ads on TV," and continued, teaching Bill his life and current situation. Then the good political geographer went on to explain what he called "choke points" in his home, fault lines along which he could be expected most likely to fall, how close these were to the various telephones in the house. When he was done, the fellow, if he'd been paying attention at all, could have passed, and might even have aced, any pop quiz on the material that Schiff cared to give him.

"Yes sir," Bill said, "that's pretty clear. I think we'll be able to serve you just fine."

"I think so," Schiff said, "I've seen your ads on TV, I've heard them on the radio."

"Pretty effective spots," Bill said.

"Long-time listener, first-time caller," said Schiff.

"Hey," said the salesman, "you can rest easy. We could get the equipment over to you and set you up today."

"Well, I do have *some* questions."

"Oh," Bill said, disappointed, realizing things had gone too smoothly, sensing the catch, "sure. What's that?"

Schiff wanted to know if he could wear the thing in the shower, whether there was any chance he would be electrocuted. The shower was one of the major choke points; if he was going to be electrocuted the deal was off.

"No chance at all," Bill, who'd actually often been asked this same question, said brightly. "The emergency call button works on the same principle as the waterproof watch. Besides, everything in it, the case, the working parts, are all made of high-grade, bonded, heavy-duty plastic. The only metal part is the copper wire that carries the signal, and that's locked in bonded, heavy-duty, high-grade plastic insulation."

Schiff said that that was good, that people his age had been known to recover from broken hips, but that he couldn't think of anyone who'd ever come back from an electrocution. Bill chuckled and, feeling his oats, wanted to know if Professor Schiff had any other questions. Well, yes, as a matter of fact, he had. If he wasn't near a regular phone would it work on a cordless? The salesman was ready for him. He slammed this one right out of the park. "Yes, absolutely. So long as it's in the On mode. Then of course, since the battery tends to drain down in that position, it's your responsibility to see to it that you keep your phone charged."

"I could do that, I'm not completely helpless, you know," said Schiff, who, from the salesman's quick answer to what Schiff thought a cleanly unique question, suddenly had a sad sense of himself as a thoroughly categorized man.

"Of course not," Bill said. "Anything else?"

There was the question of price. Bill preferred to wait until he had a chance to meet Schiff in person before going into this stuff—there were various options——— if a doctor accompanied the paramedic on a call, whether Schiff would be using some of the other services the company offered, various options—but the professor was adamant. He reminded Bill of all he had yet to do if he was going to call off that party for his graduate students. He wouldn't budge on this one. The salesman would either have to tell him what it cost right then and there or lose the sale. Bill gave him the basic monthly rates, installation fees, what it would cost Schiff if they had to put in additional phones. He broke down the costs to him of the various options and offered a price on specific package deals. It was like buying a good used car.

It was expensive. Schiff said as much.

"Is it?" Bill said. "Do you have a burglar-alarm system in your house there, Professor?"

"No."

"Sure," Bill said, "and if that's what you have to pay to see to it your hi-fi ain't stolen or they don't clear out your spoons, isn't your very life worth a few dollars more to you than just making sure they don't get your tablecloth?"

"I said I *don't* have a burglar-alarm system," Schiff said.

"Whether you do or you don't," the salesman said. "It's the same principle."

On condition that all of it could be put in that day he ended up picking one of the S.O.S. Corporation's most all-inclusive plans. He got a bit of a break on the package.

"You won't be sorry," Bill told him sincerely. "They dealt you a rotten hand. In my business I see it all the time, and I agree, it's a little expensive, but you'll see, it's worth it. Even if you never have to use us, and I hope you don't, it's worth it. The sense of security alone. It's worth it all right. Oh, while I still have you on the phone, is there something else you want to ask, can you think of anything you'd like to know?"

Schiff figured the man was talking about credit arrangements, but he didn't care about credit arrangements. It was expensive, more expensive than Schiff would ever have thought, but not *that* expensive. If the bitch hadn't cleaned out his accounts—something he'd have to check—he could afford it. But there *was* something else. Schiff brought it up reluctantly.

"Would I have to shout?" he asked. "On the TV, that lady who falls down shouts."

"Well, you take a nasty spill like that you could just as well be screaming as actually shouting."

"I think she's shouting," Schiff said. "She's pretty far from the phone, all the way across the room. It sounds to me like she's shouting."

"Well," Bill said gently, "shouting, screaming. That's just an example of truth in advertising." And Schiff knew what Bill was going to tell him next. He braced himself for it. And then the salesman said just exactly what Schiff thought he was going to say. "Maybe," he said, "her phones aren't sensitive enough, maybe they're not wired for their fullest range. That's one of the reasons I want to be on the site, why I don't like to quote a customer a price over the telephone."

He has me, thought the political geographer, they dealt me a rotten hand—he's in the business, he knows—and he has me.

If it wasn't one thing it was another. Or no, Schiff, remembering his theory of consequences, fallout, the proliferation of litter, corrected. First it was one thing, *then* it was another. Once you put the ball into play there was nothing for it but to chase it. He had to find out about his funds, whether there were enough left to take care of it if S.O.S. insisted on payment for their service up front. (Claire paid the bills, he hadn't written a check in years. Except for a couple of loose dollars—it was awkward for him to get to his billfold, finger credit cards from a wallet or handle money—for a coffee and sweet roll when he went to school, he didn't even carry cash anymore. Even in restaurants Claire paid the check, figured the tip, signed the credit-card slip. His disease had turned him into some sort of helpless, old-timey widow, some nice, pre-lib, immigrant lady.) He knew the names of the three banks with which they dealt, but wasn't entirely certain which one they used for checking, which handled their trust fund, which was the one they kept their money-market account. (There was even a small teacher's credit-union account they'd had to open when the interest rates were so high on certificates of deposit a few years back and they took a loan out on an automobile Claire didn't think they should pay for outright.)

Information gave him the bank's number, but the bank—they might have been suspicious of his vagueness when he couldn't tell them what kind of account he was asking about—wouldn't tell him a thing without an account number.

"Jesus," he said, "I'm disabled, I'd have to go downstairs for that. My wife usually takes care of the money. Normally I wouldn't even be bothering you with something like this, but she walked out on me today. Just left me flat."

"I don't like it," the bank said, "when people take the name of the Lord in vain."

He knew where to find the stuff, in the top drawer of a high, narrow cabinet in the front hall—for reasons neither could remember they called it "the tchtchk"—the closest thing they had in the house to an antique, and except for the fact that two of its elaborate brass handles were missing it might have been valuable. The only thing was, getting there would not be half the fun. Even with the Stair-Glide Claire had to help him. Always she had to swivel and lock the seat, folded upright like a seat in a movie theater, into position for him at the top of the stairs. On days he was weak she had to lift Schiff's feet onto the little ledge—less long than his shoes—and pull down its movable arms held high in the air like a victim's in a stickup. Even on days he was strong she had to fold and carry his aluminum walker down the stairs for him. The logistics seemed overwhelming. He'd really have to think about this one.

He was in bed. He was lying down. Lying down, sitting, he was any man's equal. He didn't know his own strength. Literally. He had no sense of weakness, his disease. He could be in remission. Unless he tried to turn on his side, or raise himself into a sitting position, he felt fit as a fiddle. At rest, even his fingers seemed normal. He could have counted out money or arranged playing cards. Really, the logistics seemed overwhelming. He was as reluctant to move as a man in a mine field. Inertia had become almost a part of his disease, almost a part of his character. His character, Schiff thought, had become almost a part of his disease. A man's gotta do what a man's gotta do, he thought, and heaved himself upright. So far, so good. Not bad, he thought, and pushed himself up off the bed and, preparing to move, leaned into his walker. Not bad, he thought again, pleased with the relative crispness of his steps, but soon his energy began to flag. By the time he'd taken the thirteen or so steps to the Stair-Glide (the twenty-six or so steps, actually, since his movement on the walker could be broken down—to keep his mind occupied, he really *did* break it down—this way: push, step, pull; push, step, pull, each forward step with his right leg accompanied by dragging the left one up alongside it, *almost* alongside it. He felt like someone with a gaping hole in his hull). Push, step, rest, pull, he was going now; then push, rest, step, rest, *pull. Rest!* He lived in slow motion, like someone bathed in strobe light or time-lapse photography. He could have been the subject of time-motion studies.

In repose, folded out of the way against the wall, the Stair-Glide looked like a torso on a target on a rifle range. Gasping, Schiff fumbled with the lever that swiveled it into position and, almost losing his balance as he took a hand off the walker, had practically to swipe at its shallow little theater seat to get it down. With difficulty he managed to lower the chair's arms and wrap them about himself—there was a sort of elbow on each arm that loosely encircled his body and was supposed to keep him from falling too far forward—and lower the tiny footrest. (They design this shit for kids, Schiff thought. They think of us as a bunch of Tiny Tims.) He didn't know what to do, whether to pull his feet up on the footrest and then try to collapse the walker, or to collapse the walker and then worry about getting his feet up. (They're right, he thought. We *are* kids. We need nursemaids. Or wives. Boy, he thought angrily, her sense of timing. Her world-class, son-of-a-bitch sense of timing. Briefly, it occurred to him that he might be better off homeless, find himself a nutso, broken-down bag lady with whom he could bond and who would take care of him, or, if it was still too soon for him to make a commitment, get involved, or even too early for him to start dating again, some streetsmart, knowledgeable old wino with a feel for the soup kitchens, the ground-floor, handicap-friendly shelters. He had money. Surely she'd left *something* for him, though even if she hadn't there was the house. He could sell it, split the proceeds with her, and have enough left over to pay the wino or bag lady for their trouble. What could it cost him———— ten bucks a day, fifteen? Hell, if he didn't save almost that much on the calls he made to Information, he saved almost *almost* that much. I was already crippled, Schiff thought, now I'm crazy, too.) It was a dilemma, a whaddayacallit, Hobson's choice. This ain't going to happen, he told himself. If I bring my feet up and fold the walker, my feet will slide off the footrest and I'll never get them back on it again. If I fold the walker and hold it I won't have the use of my hands to lift up my feet. Then, out of the blue, it came to him. He raised his feet onto the footrest and moved the chair into its glide mode. He leaned over and picked up the still uncollapsed walker. He didn't even *try* to fold it. With his arms on the armrests and the heel of his hand pressed against the button that made the Stair-Glide go, he raised the lightweight aluminum walker around his body and up about level with the top of his head and, to all intents and purposes, proceeded to *wear* it downstairs!

By the time he'd made it the eight steps to the landing—his hand kept slipping off the button and stopping the chair—a second walker—one he could keep permanently set up at the bottom of the stairs—had gone on his wish list. When the Stair-Glide slowly started its turn into the second flight—he'd timed it once, it took exactly one minute to do the trip—the telephone began to ring. He knew it would stop ringing before he could get to it. I'm in farce, he thought. I take to farce the way ducks take to water. But, even in farce, Schiff was a hopeful man—a man, that is, obsessed with solutions, even though he tried always to live by the cripple's code with all its concomitant notions about the exponentiality of litter and his grand ideas about every solved problem creating a new one. Now, for example, he had still more items for his wish list. He could leave cordless phones all over the house, in every out-of-the-way place he was likely to be when a phone started to ring, by the shelf where the toilet paper was kept, along the tops of tables, between the cushions of the sofa, in the gap between his pants pocket and the side of a chair, beside potted plants on windowsills——— in each inconvenient closet, pantry, alcove, and cuddy, adjunct to all the complicated, nesty network of random space.

The minute was up. He was at the bottom of the stairs. He disrobed himself of the walker and set it down, aware at once (by the relief he felt, that suffused him like a kind of pleasure) of how rough it could be, how heavy it became if one wasn't up to the burdens of aluminum. The burdens of aluminum. And, still seated in the Stair-Glide, already accustomed to his relief, no longer surprised by the return of his off-again, on-again energies, restored—so long as he remained seated—to health, which after the ordeal of the stairs he intended to savor a while longer, not even tempted by the telephone which he suddenly realized had never stopped ringing. It's Claire, he thought. Only Claire knew he was alone in the house, how long it took him to get to a phone. Then he thought, No, that's not true, plenty of people know, Claire's driver, even the dispatcher at the taxicab company, the agents at the airlines, the woman at the bank, friends to whom he'd spilled the beans, Harry in Portland, Bill at S.O.S. Even, when it came right down, Information. God, he hoped it wasn't Information. Then he realized he was wrong about that one too. He hoped it *was* Information. They could be checking up on him to see if he was still crippled. He wanted Information on his side and decided not to pick up. The phone stopped ringing. Though, actually, Schiff thought once it had stopped, it *could* have been anyone. Thieves checking to see if the house was empty so they could come out and strip it, take what they wanted. If it was thieves, Schiff thought, it was probably a good thing he hadn't yet had time to do anything about his wish list——— that second walker, the dozen or so extra cordless telephones he'd thought he might buy. And suddenly scratched the cordless telephones and had another, less expensive, even better item for the wish list——— an answering machine. They didn't have an answering machine— Schiff felt clumsy speaking to them and didn't like to impose on others what he hated to do himself—but he had to admit, in his new circumstances, under his novel, new dispensation, an answering machine could be just the ticket. It might just fill the bill. The problem with an answering machine as Schiff saw it was the message one left on it to tell callers you couldn't come to the phone. If the device caught important calls you didn't want to miss, it was also an open invitation to the very vandals and thieves he was concerned to scare off. "I can't come to the phone just now, but if you'll just . . ." was too ambiguous. It wouldn't keep the tiger from your gates. A good thief would see right through the jesuiticals of a message like that and interpret it any way he wanted. Schiff wouldn't take it off the wish list but he'd first have to compose an airtight message for the machine before he ever actually purchased one. An idle mind is *too* the devil's workshop, Schiff thought, and rose from the chair, plowed—he often thought of his walker as a plow, of his floors and carpets as fields in which he cut stiff furrows—his way to the tchtchk and, quite to his astonishment, found almost at once statements from the banks with their account numbers on them. These he put into his mouth, but he couldn't go up just yet, couldn't yet face the struggle with the walker on the Stair-Glide; he had to rest, build strength, and decided to go into the living room for a while and sit down.

Coitus Interruptus

~℧℃ ℃℧~

MIKE ERVIN

Sometimes I wonder if I did the right thing. But everything happened so fast.

I made that phone call to the Thurgood Marshall legal clinic because I was furious. About an hour later I was calmed down and ready to forget about it. I never expected anything to come of it.

But I was so mad I'm lucky I didn't have a stroke. It's not like Linda and I were fornicating on top of the desk of the nurses' station like a couple of dogs in heat. We were down in the basement in the boiler room, down there in private and minding our own business. They never lock the boiler room door for some reason so that's where you went at Hillcrest when you wanted to sneak off somewhere with your girlfriend. Joe Houston was the one who went down there mostly, or so he said. I wouldn't doubt it. That was the kind of thing he would do. Joe Houston was bound to be a lifer at the Hillcrest Convalescent Center youth ward (under age fifty-five). No reason for it, really. All Joe Houston was was a one-leg amputee. He could stand and hop and his arms were strong as a lumberjack's. Joe Houston was about forty-two and he had a face like Abe Lincoln's, drawn and creased and weather-beaten. Or maybe it was his beard that gave him that Lincoln look, a beard with no mustache like the Amish. He always wore a battered black cowboy hat and an enormous Harley-Davidson belt buckle. He had an Oklahoma drawl. He had stacks of biker magazines with women with big breasts sitting on motorcycles naked. Joe Houston had been living on the Hillcrest "youth wing" for ten years and he was bound to be a lifer because around there he could be the grand wizard. Alpha wolf. He could be everybody's hero. He always had a big wad in his money clip, even though he was on social security like the rest of us. I think maybe it was a bunch of ones wrapped in a twenty. Around there Joe Houston could be a trendsetter. I think that's why so many guys on the ward smoked Marlboros like him.

I'd never been to the boiler room. I never was very good with women to begin with and it seemed like a hopeless cause getting one to go down there anyway. The only kind of women I could imagine who would come into a place like Hillcrest and go down to the boiler room were ones like those biker mamas that came in to see Joe Houston. There was that one named Shoshanna, the bottle blond with a little rose tattoo just above her heaping cleavage. And I would have felt like I should have warned any woman who did agree to go down there that if word got out that she didn't mind putting out for guys in wheelchairs she'd be marked and all the guys on the youth ward would be swarming over her like they were drug-sniffing dogs and she had a pound of heroin in her pants.

So to get Linda to go down to the boiler room was a major breakthrough for me. It was the first time I'd been with a female since my diving accident. Linda was one of the volunteers from the Catholic high school. I don't know how old she was. I didn't even ask. She looked like a senior. First time I met her was one of those days when no one came around to get me out of bed until noon. She brought in my breakfast tray. "Do you want me to feed you?" she said. I didn't need to be fed any more than the man in the moon. But it was a chance for me to have a young woman all to myself by my bed for a half hour so I said what the hell. And she was such a flirtatious feeder, the way she'd wipe my lips and chin and brush the hair out of my eyes. So on the mornings when she was on the volunteer schedule I'd pray no one would come around to get me up until noon or if they would I'd fake a bladder infection or something so I could stay in bed. I'd have to stay in bed all day but it was worth it. And she'd always bring me my breakfast tray. I think she looked forward to it as much as I did because she was always there with my tray right on time. She'd say, "Sick again? Poor baby!" with a giggle. That's what I think she liked about it. The forbiddeness. For her I think it was like cutting out on home economics class for a rendezvous with a married man. And pretty soon she started pulling the curtain around the bed so we could be alone. And when she'd wipe my lips and chin she'd lean way over and I could see her breasts stuffed in her black bra inside her pink, seersucker uniform. And pretty soon she was sitting on my bed and feeding me. And when she'd lean over to wipe my lips and chin her chest would press up against mine.

So finally I told her about the boiler room. We snuck down there on a Sunday when everybody was busy watching football. Linda ripped open the snaps of her uniform in one motion and wiggled her panties off. Then she lay back on the engineer's big metal desk and I pulled my chair up close and buried my face in her warm, wet vagina. And she stiffened a little and gasped when I first did and soon her thighs were on my shoulders and squeezing harder and harder and she was bearing down and squirming and panting. And then there was a knock on the door and I knew it had to be a nurse because it was a sharp and perturbed knock with the edge of a quarter. And it was Mrs. Crockett's voice on the other side saying, "You better come out of there, Rudy! That girl ain't barely eighteen years old!" And I can't believe I just yelled out "Fuck off!" but like I said I was so mad I was about to pop a gasket. Mrs. Crockett said, "I'm gonna get security!" and I said, "They can fuck off too!" That wasn't like me at all. So she went to get security but by that time Linda was mortified and she wrestled on her uniform and ran out. And by the time I got back upstairs she was gone. And I never saw her again.

Mrs. Crockett said she was going to write me up which meant I'd have to explain myself to the nursing supervisor in the morning and there might be a shrink there too. So I went straight to the pay telephone and called that Thurgood Marshall legal clinic. I'd heard about these lawyers on the news that represented prisoners and people in police brutality cases and things like that. But because it was a Sunday the answering machine said the office was closed and to either call back Monday or leave a message or if it was an emergency to call the beeper number. So I called the beeper number because I was so mad I was crazy and a few minutes later the pay phone rang and when I answered a calm, young woman's voice said, "Did someone page the Thurgood Marshall legal clinic?" And I said, "Yes. I live in the Hillcrest Convalescent Center and I want to sue!" And the woman said, "OK. Why don't you tell me your name. Mine's Jane." So I told her my name and I told her I was twenty-eight years old and I went to college but I might as well be ten around here for all it was worth because I didn't even have the right to be with my girlfriend in private. I told her what happened with Linda. I told her about the boiler room and how they burst in on us and embarrassed the hell out of us and I wanted to sue them for it. I remember I said, "Even fucking prisoners have rights to conjugal visits for God's sake!" I told her about my accident and how this was the first woman to flirt with me since and they ruined it and that's what made me most mad!

I must have gone on for a half hour about what a fucking Gestapo hellhole this place was and she didn't interrupt me once. I told her I didn't even belong in this place but my family just basically dumped me here after I broke my neck. "I get social security," I said, "and it all goes to the damn nursing home except for fifty bucks a month which I get to keep to buy toothpaste and cigarettes and shit like that! What the hell can anybody do with fifty bucks a month! For as much as they're charging the government for me to live here, I could be living at the goddam Ritz! You know what time they put me in bed last night! Seven! That's when they came to get me so that's when I had to go! I'm a man! Men don't go to bed at seven! But the orderlies and nurse's aides wanted to have plenty of time before quitting time to go sit on their fat asses! They sit on their fat asses more than the queen of England!" I must have been livid because I didn't even care who might walk by the pay phone and hear what I was saying. She even asked a few questions like she was taking it all down. The background noise where she was sounded like a restaurant so I'd probably pulled her away from her brunch but she still never blew me off so I took it as a good sign that maybe they were interested. But after I hung up I felt like a fool because I thought that probably the only reason Jane stayed on the phone for so long was because they probably have a staff meeting first thing every Monday morning at the Thurgood Marshall legal clinic. And they probably start off each week with a good laugh by having whoever was on emergency call that weekend tell about all the maniac crackpots who called on the beeper, swearing up and down it was life or death. I was probably this week's grand prize winner! Fuck it all, I said to myself. I wasn't going to be in this place forever like most of these pathetic mopes! My settlement from my accident lawsuit would be in in about six months or so and I'd be out the door so fast I'd whip up a cyclone! So in the meantime I would just shut up and try not to say anything more to anybody than I had to! When I got my settlement, I was going to buy myself a condo and a van with a wheelchair lift on it to get around in and I was going to hire a Polish lady to come in and cook and clean. I'd take trips to California. To the beach. To the Caribbean.

And about a month later I got a call on the pay phone. And the woman on the line said, "This is Jane Sapperman" and that didn't mean a thing to me until she mentioned the Thurgood Marshall legal clinic. "We've been wanting to do something in the arena of the rights of the disabled and we think yours might make an excellent test case. Might I make an appointment to come in and discuss it with you?"

I remember the first thing I felt was a quick nervous nausea. So even though I said "Sure," I must not have sounded like I really meant it because she said, "Don't worry. I won't dress like a lawyer. I can be your cousin." Because having a lawyer come in here from a place with a name like the Thurgood Marshall legal clinic would cause an earthquake like the time they say state inspectors showed up here. A cerebral palsy woman named Darla who lived on the female side called them and after they left she got sent to the crazy house for it, Joe Houston said, in that low tone he uses when he's giving you sage advice not to rock the boat.

Jane and I made an appointment for that Saturday, which was only three days later, but about ten times during those three days I started to go to the pay phone to tell her to just forget the whole thing because it was just too damn perverted. I pictured myself on the witness stand telling everybody all about the boiler room. And then the judge pounds his gavel and sends me to the nut house. And all I had to do was survive six more months until my settlement came in so why do anything so stupid? And then sometimes I felt as righteous as Thurgood Marshall himself. Someday there'd be a legal clinic named after me! It took all I could do to not say anything to anybody about how I was going to sue their asses. Especially when they'd come to put people to bed at 7:30 or when I'd lift the plate lid on the dinner tray and it would be tuna with elbow macaroni. More goddam elbow macaroni! I'd wanted to tell them all they'd better have their fun now because they were going to be real sorry real soon but I kept my mouth shut like Jane Sapperman said I had to do no matter what. But when I went along with things it didn't eat me up as much because I knew I'd get even soon for me and for everybody else who had ever been in this goddam place. Sometimes I felt ecstatic like the mad bomber who knows there's a bomb in the basement about to go off. And let them try to put me in the nut house, I'd say to myself, defiantly. They'd have to get past Jane Sapperman first. Was that her name? And anyway all I had to do was survive six more months.

Jane Sapperman showed up wearing a University of Michigan sweatshirt and blue jeans and a Yankees hat. She had a yellow backpack. She looked more like a college student than a lawyer. She might've been younger than me. "Hello, Rudy," she said. "Long time no see." I didn't play along very well.

"Really," I said.

"I came to town for my grandma's birthday," she said.

"That's good," I said. And then I thought I'd better take her outside onto the patio before I said something else stupid and blew the whole thing.

The first thing I said to myself about Jane Sapperman was I bet any money she used to be a nun. It stuck in my mind how much she reminded me of Sister Peggy. Sister Peggy was the first nun I met who wore civilian clothes. She even wore makeup and she played guitar and sang folk songs like "Blowin' in the Wind." I was a freshman in high school and she was the music teacher and I had it real bad for Sister Peggy. There was just something really sexy about a nun that didn't look or act anything like a nun.

And Jane Sapperman didn't look or act anything like a lawyer. She had a short, simple, modest hairdo like Sister Peggy and her same earnest expression. She had that same discreet sophistication where you could picture her just as easily at an opera or in the bleachers at a baseball game. That's why she was good at coming in here and not looking like a lawyer. But I had it so stuck in my mind that she must have been a drop-out nun who quit the convent so she could really work for the poor that I really didn't listen to what she was saying until she said, "We need you to be a Jackie Robinson. In order for a case like this to succeed we need somebody who's going to stick it out. Somebody who's got guts." I told her that was me, I sure got guts, and at the moment I really meant it. With her around I felt ready to take them all on. She really charged me up.

"Great," she said. "Then we need to do an intake." She pulled a small tape recorder out of her backpack. "I'll tape all your information and fill it in later so they don't see us messing with a bunch of papers." She pushed the record button, set it on the table between us and placed the baseball hat over it. She had this all figured out. And after I answered all her questions she slipped me a blank form on the side to sign. I signed real quick before I could change my mind. "Don't worry," she said. "We'll get you those conjugal rights." And when she left she gave me a big hug. I assumed it was because she wanted it to look like she was my cousin. But it was a hard hug, harder than when she came in, like she meant it this time, like maybe she was trying to say that when this is all over she might be interested in me.

Jane filed a suit on my behalf with the state human rights commission. In it she said that Hillcrest's "blatant harassment" of me on the day I went to the boiler room constituted a "grievous violation" of my human rights. It was beautiful! I knew the day Hillcrest got served notice because the only time the owner showed up was when there was trouble or if inspectors were coming. His name was Ralph and he wasn't much older than me either. That day he came huffing in wearing his jogging suit and talking on his flip phone. "You deal with it!" he barked to whoever he was talking to. "I got enough shit on my mind!" Ralph makes me laugh when I think back on him because he was the slick-looking wheeler-dealer politician type right out of central casting, big pinky ring and wrap-around shades and all. But back then I was scared like hell of him but I didn't crack when I got called into the head nurse's office. I just sat there stone-faced like Jane Sapperman said I had to do if something like this ever happened. "Remember," she said. "Name, rank and serial number." So when Ralph shook the papers and said "What the fuck is this!" I was so scared they were going to drag me off to the loony bin that my skin was trembling but I sat there and just said, "This is an ex parte communication and you'll have to speak to me through my attorney." That was the line Jane Sapperman gave me to use. I'd practiced it over and over in my head. "You wanna just fuck anywhere you feel like?" Ralph said. "Is that what you want?" I used the line over and over. I felt like a prisoner of war. I thought next they would start torturing me. But then Ralph tried acting like Mr. Reasonable. "Look," he said, real calm. "If it was all guys like you, I wouldn't have a problem. But what about the retarded ones! One of them gets pregnant and I get sued!" I just kept using my line over and over until he told me to get the hell out. And they didn't mess with me again, probably because Jane Sapperman called them up the next day and said if they did it again they'd be real sorry.

Then came the weirdest day of my life. Weird as the day of my diving accident. It was about six months later. I didn't end up in the nut house. I ended up in a downtown law office, in this room that looked like a corporate boardroom. Big windows with a panoramic view of the city. A table about fifty yards long. It was a catered affair. Men dressed like Pullman porters brought in trays of cheese and fruit and vegetables and a whole salmon with the head on it on a silver platter. I ate like a pig. I drank a lot of wine.

It was the law firm of Biddle, Brooks and some other guys, attorneys for Horizons Incorporated, owners and operators of Hillcrest and about three dozen other "quality long-term care centers." Their lead lawyer was Herbert Amos. He was ebony black and his beard and hair were dusted with white. There was a formality of contemptuousness in everything about him, his words and tone of voice and gestures. He always addressed me as "sir" or "Mr. Wilson" and always made it sound like a sarcastic putdown. I had some nuns for teachers who were good at that. Amos had a whole bunch of other lawyers swarming in and out too like a video running in fast motion backward, but Amos was the one who did all of the talking.

Jane Sapperman was at my side of the table. And in the middle was Martin Bernstein. Martin Bernstein was the chief mediator for the human rights commission. He was just like my uncle Buddy. He didn't look anything like my uncle Buddy. Uncle Buddy was a burly bald truck driver and Martin Bernstein was gangly and intellectual looking. He had wild hair like Einstein's. He was in his fifties. His suits were kind of shabby. But he was just like my uncle Buddy in the way he always looked like he was in a state of intense worry. He always looked like he just found out he has six months to live. But Jane Sapperman thought he was the greatest. "He's quite brilliant. He could craft a settlement out of anything. He should be a diplomat. And he really cares too."

The human rights commission sent Martin Bernstein because the first thing they do is always try to mediate a settlement. He got us together once before at the Thurgood Marshall legal clinic. That wasn't anything like Biddle, Brooks Etc. Clinic was a good word for it because that's what it looked like. It looked and felt like a dingy unemployment office. The conference room was also the lunchroom. There was a microwave and a coffeemaker and a little fridge like I had in my college dorm room.

That time was a disaster. Herbert Amos was such an arrogant ass. He said, "It is our position that this is not a civil rights issue but an issue of privacy. We must weigh your alleged right to sexual intimacy with the right of the patient in the next bed to not be subjected to the sights and/or sounds of such activity. That can be very traumatizing." But what really set me off was when he said, "There are also liability issues. For many of the residents of Hillcrest who are exceedingly frail, willy-nilly coitus can be a very risky proposition." And I was so mad I said, "How can a guy who went to Harvard be such a stupid ass!" And that's about as far as the meeting went. Martin Bernstein said that was a cheap shot but I said I didn't care and Herbert Amos said I was being "overly emotional" and left. After everyone was gone I apologized to Jane Sapperman for letting her down. I wished I had a chance to do it all over again not because I didn't think Amos deserved it but because by now I was crazy in love with Jane Sapperman and the whole episode reinforced how unworthy I was of her. I knew who her dream man was. Thurgood Marshall. I bet if she could make a list of all the men in history she'd most like to seduce, he'd be on top. And it just went to show how far away I was from him. He would never call a lawyer arguing before the Supreme Court stupid ass, no matter how much he deserved it. He'd be more sophisticated than that. I was afraid Jane Sapperman might be ready to bite my head off and tell me to forget the whole thing. But all she said when I apologized was "Well, it certainly wasn't very productive. But he'll get over it." Can you see why I was so in love with her? She made me feel fearless!

A couple weeks later Jane Sapperman came over to see me at Hillcrest with big news. "I told you Martin would come up with something!" she said as she slid me a stack of papers. On top was a memo from Bernstein to Amos and Jane and it read:

> *I've reflected a great deal upon our impasse. I've heard the plaintiff's concerns about establishing his right to conjugal relations between consenting adults. On the other hand, I've heard the defendant's misgivings over the administrative chaos that can result from, as Mr. Amos put it, willy-nilly coitus. So I've drafted something for your consideration that I believe provides us a basis for compromise. It affirms the plaintiff's right to conjugal visits within a regulatory framework that I believe is administratively feasible.*

Across the top of the next page it said PROPOSED CONSENT DECREE. In Martin Bernstein's proposal it said "defendant Hillcrest shall establish a separate and private conjugal room in which residents who are consenting adults may enjoy private sexual relations. This room shall be clearly marked on the door and its purpose and availability shall be explained to all residents as part of their patient orientation." And later on it said, "Defendant may retain certain administrative prerogatives, including but not limited to the establishment of hours of operation and scheduling functions."

"Scheduling functions?" I said.

"It means there may have to be a sign-up sheet," Jane Sapperman said, dismissing it as a petty detail with a wave of her hand. "But Amos has already agreed to the concept of a conjugal room, which means there's been significant movement on their part." It sounded like a bunch of bullshit to me. I had this vision of that room down by the elevator that was marked JANITOR'S CLOSET instead marked CONJUGAL ROOM. Beneath that sign was an airplane-bathroom sliding OCCUPIED sign. And right outside was a nurse, sitting in one of those college student chairs with the long wooden slab protruding from one arm, like a stern hall monitor. She had a stopwatch and when it went off she knocked like the FBI. But Jane was so excited I didn't have the heart to disappoint her.

And so we all got together in the posh law office when Amos had a counterproposal for us to consider. And the reason I say it was the weirdest day of my life is because when I broke my neck I imagined I would end up in all kinds of places. I imagined I could be in for all kinds of things. At first I was convinced I would spend the rest of my life flat on my back on some army cot like in a DMZ wounded ward among a bunch of moaning mummies and vegetables. But I began to feel hope again when I realized I could sue the city and the county and the lifeguard for millions and travel around the world like some playboy. I could end up on top of Mount Everest. There were always stories in the papers about blind guys and paralyzed guys who did stuff like that. But I never could have in any way imagined that I would end up eating caviar hors d'oeuvres in a swanky law office engaged in intense negotiations about my sex life.

It was like some really ridiculous nightmare. I'd probably swear it was if I didn't still keep the consent decree that came out of that day in a folder in my file cabinet. I show it sometimes to certain of my friends. I suppose it represents some kind of a breakthrough that I can do that. For a long time I was ashamed of it. It made me feel like I was a part of a Ripley's freak show. But now I can appreciate it for the science fiction that it is. Arnold, my old mechanic, the only thing he ever does is complain about what a hard time he has getting laid. So finally I said to him, "You think you got it rough! I once had to get a court order!" He didn't believe me so I bet him twenty-five bucks and I brought it in and showed it to him and he thought it was the funniest thing he ever saw. And even though I don't go to him anymore he still calls me every now and then and says, "Hey, I bet a buddy of mine about your court order thing. Can you send me a copy?" So last time I faxed it to him so he could have a copy to keep.

I've got the funniest parts highlighted in yellow, like the part about the liability waivers. And the bestiality clause. I remember how Amos and I almost came to blows about it. I'd had a lot of wine so I wanted to punch him out the minute he strode into the conference room with his entourage, like the great matador. And one of his serfs carried a pile of stapled pages and he set it on the table and dealt them to us from the top of the deck. And on the first page it was stamped CONFIDENTIAL in red. Amos struck a very judgmental pose, tilted slightly back in his big stuffed swivel chair and clutching its arms firmly. And then he said, "As I've indicated previously, my client, in the interest of avoiding protracted litigation, finds Mr. Bernstein's concept of a conjugal room potentially palatable in theory. We've taken Mr. Bernstein's proposal and flushed out the parameters a bit so as to reflect what we feel to be a good-faith settlement."

If I would have had any brains back then I would have kept a copy of the proposal so I could remember the exact wording because it was so vintage. The first thing that struck me was how his proposal referred to "conjugal privileges" wherever Bernstein had referred to "conjugal rights." And the way Amos had it set up the conjugal room would operate on a point system. So like if we ate all our vegetables or something we would get five points or if we didn't make our beds we would lose five points and once you got a hundred points or so you could turn them in for an hour in the conjugal room, provided whoever was going in there with you also had a hundred points, unless it was someone from the outside. And the encounter would have to have been "heterosexual in nature and devoid of deviant manifestations including but not limited to sado-masochism and bestiality." I remember those words exactly because I laughed out loud when I read them and Amos cocked an angry eyebrow at me like the presiding librarian and Bernstein's eyes widened with dread.

And the way Amos had it set up, even if you had a hundred points, you and whoever you wanted to go into the conjugal room with would have to fill out a form at the nurses' station stating that you were indeed consenting adults plus sign a waiver absolving Hill-crest of all responsibility for "death or injury that may occur during the encounter." And then, after all that, the loving couple would then schedule a time but it would have to be a time at least two days ahead because Amos had in there a forty-eight-hour "cooling off period." That part made me laugh out loud too.

Well, I don't know what it was but after I finished reading it something had me all stoked up again. Maybe it was the wine because the Pullman porter kept refilling my glass before it was even empty and I was feeling immortal. Or maybe it was sitting so close to Jane Sapperman and the faint peach smell of her body lotion and her sleek neck. Or maybe it was just because Amos was such an incredible ass.

It was probably some of all that, but I wasn't afraid of anything right then, and before Bernstein could even ask if we had any comments I said, "So does this mean I can't take a sheep in there if I want to?"

Amos kept his cool and placed his glasses on the tip of his nose. "You're referring to the bestiality clause, I presume?"

"I'm referring to life in general. Don't I have the right to fuck a sheep?"

Bernstein said, "That's not the issue here. The issue is—"

"I mean, you've got that right, don't you, Amos? So why don't I? This is America, right? People fought and died for it!"

Amos removed his glasses, put on a smile of great disdain, and said to Jane Sapperman, "Would you control your client, please."

Jane Sapperman reached over and squeezed my biceps, but I said, "Can't we at least make it a privilege? If I clean up my room and do all my chores, then can I fuck a sheep? Pretty please!"

"That's it!" Amos said, and he bolted to his feet. All his henchmen popped up too, like jack-in-the-boxes.

Jane Sapperman put her hand over my mouth. Bernstein sprung up too, horrified. "Wait! Herbert! Let's take a brief recess! Let me talk to you in your office!" And he ran out after Amos.

When it was just Jane Sapperman and I alone in the room, I said, "Doesn't that asshole know a metaphor when he hears one? Some Harvard boy!"

"That was really stupid what you did," she said.

"I don't care! I wasn't wrong!"

"I didn't say you were wrong," she said, sternly enunciating. "I said you were stupid."

That one really cut deep. I was so goddam jealous of Thurgood

Marshall right at that moment. I hated him! "Well, I'm sorry I'm not Mr. Universe!"

"Look, Martin is working very hard here—"

"What was your nun name?" I said.

Long, bewildered pause. "What?"

"Sister Mary What?" In my drunken state I struck myself as exceedingly clever.

"I think we need to get you sobered up," she said, sliding my wineglass away.

And soon Bernstein came bustling back in, a vague and nervous hope in his erratic stride. "I was able to calm him down," Bernstein said, "but the bestiality appears to be a deal breaker. And frankly, I don't see the problem."

Jane Sapperman said, "If we—"

"It's the goddam principle!" I said.

"Be pragmatic," Bernstein said. "I respect your convictions, but do you really want to go to court over it? What judge would side with you on that?"

"Thurgood Marshall would!" I said. I nodded to Jane. "Right?" But by now I'd had so much wine that the next time I evoked the name of Thurgood Marshall it came out Thurgood Martian. So Jane Sapperman took over and told Bernstein to go back and tell them they'd have a deal if they took out all the point system crap and all the stuff about deviant manifestations and the liability forms and the cooling-off period. So Bernstein dashed off notes on his yellow pad and scurried off.

I was alone in the room with Jane Sapperman again. She was rejuvenated. "Keep you fingers crossed," she said, and then she popped grapes into her mouth, so sexy and confident.

But I was feeling a panic, like time was running out. What if we had a deal? Would we just sign it and toast and that would be it and I'd never see Jane Sapperman again, like Linda?

"Can I ask you something?" I said.

"Of course. I'm your attorney."

"I don't mean like that." Hot wax burned inside my stomach. "I mean . . . if we get this conjugal room . . . I wouldn't mind if you and me could go inside."

Jane Sapperman took a quick deep breath and held it nervously for a second. "Um . . ."

"Why not!"

She cleared her throat and tidied up her papers. For the first time she was losing her cool.

"I'm nuts for you!" I said.

"Oh, and I admire you too!" She was so nervous her voice squeaked when she said it!

"Admire!" I said. She couldn't have picked a crueler word.

"Oh, yes!" she said, all heartfelt and sincere, trying to wiggle off the hook. "More than you realize!"

Then that damn Bernstein came drooping back in. His hanging face made him look like an emergency room doctor coming to tell the family the valiant surgery had failed. But Jane looked just the opposite. She looked like she was going to run up and throw her arms around him, like he'd just rescued her.

Bernstein said, "There's some flexibility on the rights versus privileges concept and the waiting period. But I'm afraid they're adamant on the deviant manifestations and the liability waivers."

"OK," said Jane Sapperman, jumping right in. "We'll give you bestiality and sadomasochism. Drop the heterosexual part and you've got a deal." She asked me if that was all right. I just about told them to forget the whole thing because I could suddenly see what the problem was here. I bet the only reason I couldn't get anywhere with her was because she was hot and heavy with Bernstein! How dense could I have been! He could be her dream man too! He's quite brilliant, you know! And he really cares! I was about to show them how damn brilliant he was by storming out of there but I just waved my hand in a "whatever" motion. I didn't give a damn anymore.

And when Bernstein left Jane jumped up and went over to the hors d'oeuvres table. Her back was turned to me. "Sounds like we're getting close, huh," she said, her voice still squeaking.

"I'm getting a big settlement, you know!" I said.

"Yes!" Jane squeaked, clearing her throat incessantly. "You told me."

"So I'm not just some deadweight cripple!"

"Indeed not!" Jane said. By now she'd piled a mountain of cheese cubes on her plate.

"Whenever I see you," I said, "it takes me three days to recover. It's like a hangover!"

"Well, I've really enjoyed working with you too!" she said. And then she set her plate down and said, "I need to check in with the office! Be back shortly!" And she shot out of there like her pants were on fire.

And there I sat alone. I just wanted to go home and go to bed and not talk to anybody any more than I had to until my settlement came in. And I was concentrating on not throwing up.

Jane didn't come back in until about two seconds before Bernstein did. I knew we had a deal by the way Bernstein came strutting back in like a drum major. Amos and his ducklings followed behind. Amos didn't share Bernstein's ebullience. His brow was still cast down in an angry pout.

I suppose I shouldn't keep dwelling on whether or not I sold out by going along with it all. I'm long gone from there now. It took about two years for my settlement to come through and it wasn't nearly as much as I'd hoped but it was enough to get the hell out of there and that was the important thing. And I'm pretty much over Jane Sapperman now, but it took me forever. That day in the conference room was the last I saw of her. A lawyer named Jeff took over the case after that.

When word of the conjugal room got back to the youth wing I was a big hero like Douglas MacArthur. Or at least I was on the male wing. Or at least I was to Joe Houston. You'd swear it was the armistice or something, the way he kept whooping and hollering and slapping me on the back about it. What more could he ever want? Three squares a day and a warm place to screw. He spent a lot of time and money decorating it like it was his bachelor pad. When it first opened all they did was clear out the old medical records alcove and shove in a hospital bed. But over time Joe Houston put in one of those bead curtains and red and yellow lightbulbs and an old eight-track player and an incense burner. He's probably grand wizard around there still because the thing he lives for is to pick one of the guys, especially if it's a new guy or a Down's syndrome guy or someone he thinks is a virgin, and hire a woman from the escort service for him for the conjugal room. So if you're on his good side, he might pick you. It makes him feel like a humanitarian. The way he sits back satisfied and smokes after he pulls one of those off, his hands cupped behind his head and his elbows spread like wings, you'd swear he was the one who just came out of the conjugal room. Joe Houston always took special pride in the way he corrupted Dale, the spina bifida albino kid who was a Jehovah's witness when he came in. He had him smoking Marlboros and reading biker magazines and everything. He follows Joe Houston around like he's his bodyguard.

Joe Houston got it in his head, and he wouldn't get it out, that on the day the conjugal room officially opened for business I should be the one to christen it. I'll admit that I thought about that a lot. But I couldn't bring myself to do it because Joe Houston and the guys were bound to make a big parade out of it and what woman would subject herself to that? Or that's what I told myself. Maybe I was worried I'd be too distracted to do anything. It would be like trying to do it in Grand Central.

So on the day of the grand opening of the conjugal room, I faked a bladder infection and stayed in bed all day with the curtain pulled around my bed because by that time I was sick to death of the whole damn thing and I knew that was the only way I could get out of it. It officially opened at six o'clock and I could hear the crowd Joe Houston gathered outside counting down the last ten seconds like it was New Year's Eve. Then suspenseful silence fell as Joe Houston raffled off Shoshanna. The picture I had in my mind was of Joe sitting in front of the conjugal room like a big city mayor with a big scissors ready to cut the ribbon, Shoshanna sitting on his lap. And on her lap is Joe's turned-up cowboy hat. Joe had been selling raffle tickets all week for a quarter apiece.

The sapphire sun was setting into the blue Caribbean. "Mmmm," Jane Sapperman sighed, stretched across my beach blanket, her head resting on my leg. She wore her University of Michigan sweatshirt and blue jeans. "You win, angel. This tops Paris."

"Who's the lucky boy, darlin'?" I heard Joe Houston say.

I stroked Jane Sapperman's neck and hair. "Just wait'll you see Aruba." I offered up a toast with my champagne glass. "Here's to my settlement."

And then I heard Shoshanna say, "And the winner is—"

Jane Sapperman loomed above me on our canopied bed, perched on the flesh mound of my chest. She wore a Yankees cap, a lacy black bra, and panties, garters holding up red fishnets. She offered up a toast with her champagne glass. "To a true pioneer!" She downed her champagne, throwing back her head so smooth and sophisticated.

"Dale!" Shoshanna said.

Dale whooped. There was a lot of commotion. "Fix! Goddam fix!" someone yelled.

"Make way for Dale," Joe Houston boomed.

Jane Sapperman and I were naked on a roller coaster.

Helen and Frida

ANNE FINGER

I'm lying on the couch downstairs in the TV room in the house where I grew up, a farmhouse with sloping floors in upstate New York. I'm nine years old. I've had surgery, and I'm home, my leg in a plaster cast. Everyone else is off at work or school. My mother re-covered this couch by hemming a piece of fabric that she bought from a bin at the Woolworth's in Utica ("Bargains! Bargains! Bargains! Remnants Priced As Marked") and laying it over the torn upholstery. Autumn leaves—carrot, jaundice, brick—drift sluggishly across a liver-brown background. I'm watching the *Million Dollar Movie* on our black-and-white television: today it's *Singin' in the Rain*. These movies always make me think of the world that my mother lived in before I was born, a world where women wore hats and gloves and had cinched-waist suits with padded shoulders as if they were in the army. My mother told me that in *The Little Colonel*, Shirley Temple had pointed her finger and said, "As red as those roses over there," and then the roses had turned red and everything in the movie was in color after that. I thought that was how it had been when I was born, everything in the world becoming both more vivid and more ordinary, and the black-and-white world, the world of magic and shadows, disappearing forever in my wake.

Now it's the scene where the men in blue-jean coveralls are wheeling props and sweeping the stage, carpenters shouldering boards, moving behind Gene Kelly as Don Lockwood and Donald O'Connor as Cosmo. Cosmo is about to pull his hat down over his forehead and sing, "Make 'em laugh . . ." and hoof across the stage, pulling open doors that open onto brick walls, careening up what appears to be a lengthy marble-floored corridor but is, in fact, a painted backdrop.

Suddenly, all the color drains from the room: not just from the mottled sofa I'm lying on, but also from the orange wallpaper that looked so good on the shelf at Streeter's (and was only $1.29 a roll), the chipped, blue willow plate: everything's black and silver now. I'm on a movie set, sitting in the director's chair. I'm grown-up suddenly, eighteen or thirty-five.

Places, please!

Quiet on the set!

Speed, the soundman calls, and I point my index finger at the camera, the clapper claps the board, and I see that the movie we are making is called "Helen and Frida." I slice my finger quickly through the air, and the camera rolls slowly forward toward Helen Keller and Frida Kahlo, standing on a veranda, with balustrades that appear to be made of carved stone, but are, in fact, made of plaster.

The part of Helen Keller isn't played by Patty Duke this time; there's no *Miracle Worker* wild child to spunky rebel in under one hundred minutes, no grainy film stock, none of that Alabama sun that bleaches out every soft shadow, leaving only harshness, glare. This time Helen is played by Jean Harlow.

Don't laugh: set pictures of the two of them side by side and you'll see that it's all there, the fair hair lying in looping curls against both faces, the same broad-cheeked bone structure. Imagine that Helen's eyebrows are plucked into a thin arch and penciled, lashes mascaraed top and bottom, lips cloisonnéd vermilion. Put Helen in pale peach *mousseline de soie,* hand her a white gardenia, bleach her hair from its original honey blond to platinum, like Harlow's was, recline her on a *Bombshell* chaise with a white swan gliding in front, a palm fan being waved overhead, while an ardent lover presses sweet nothings into her hand.

I play the part of Frida Kahlo.

It isn't so hard to imagine that the two of them might meet. They moved, after all, in not so different circles, fashionable and radical: Helen Keller meeting Charlie Chaplin and Mary Pickford, joining the Wobblies, writing in the *New York Times,* "I love the red flag . . . and if I could I should gladly march it past the offices of the *Times* and let all the reporters and photographers make the most of the spectacle. . . ."; Frida, friend of Henry Ford and Sergy Eisenstein, painting a hammer and sickle on her body cast, leaving her bed in

1954, a few weeks before her death, to march in her wheelchair with a babushka tied under her chin, protesting the overthrow of the Arbenz regime in Guatemala.

Of course, the years are all wrong. But that's the thing about the *Million Dollar Movie*. During Frank Sinatra Week, on Monday Frank would be young and handsome in *It Happened in Brooklyn*; on Tuesday he'd have gray temples and crow's feet, be older than my father; on Wednesday, be even younger than he had been on Monday. You could pour the different decades in a bowl together and give them a single quick fold with the smooth edge of a spatula, the way my mother did when she made black-and-white marble cake from two Betty Crocker mixes. It would be 1912, and Big Bill Haywood would be waving the check Helen had sent over his head at a rally for the Little Falls strikers, and you, Frida, would be in the crowd, not as a five-year-old child, before the polio, before the bus accident, but as a grown woman, cheering along with the strikers. Half an inch away, it would be August 31, 1932, and both of you would be standing on the roof of the Detroit Institute of the Arts, along with Diego, Frida looking up through smoked glass at the eclipse of the sun. Helen's face turned upwards to feel the chill of night descending, to hear the birds greeting the midday dusk.

Let's get one thing straight right away. This isn't going to be one of those movies where they put their words into our mouths. This isn't *Magnificent Obsession*: blind Jane Wyman isn't going to blink back a tear when the doctors tell her they can't cure her after all saying, "and I thought I was going to be able to get rid of these," gesturing with her ridiculous rhinestone-studded, cat's-eye dark glasses (and we think, "*Really*, Jane,"); she's not going to tell Rock Hudson she can't marry him: "I won't have you pitied because of me. I love you too much," and "I could only be a burden," and then disappear until the last scene when, lingering on the border between death and cure (the only two acceptable states), Rock saves her life and her sight and they live happily ever after. It's not going to be *A Patch of Blue*: when the sterling young Negro hands us the dark glasses and, in answer to our question "But what are they for?" says, "Never mind, put them on," we're not going to grab them, hide our stone Medusa gaze, grateful for the magic that's made us a pretty girl. This isn't *Johnny Belinda*; we're not sweetly mute, surrounded by an aura of silence. No, in this movie the blind women have milky eyes that make the sighted uncomfortable. The deaf women drag metal against metal, oblivious to the jarring sound, make odd cries of delight at the sight of the ocean, squawk when we are angry.

So now the two female icons of disability have met: Helen, who is nothing but, who swells to fill up the category, sweet Helen with her drooping dresses covering drooping bosom, who is Blind and Deaf, her vocation; and Frida, who lifts her skirt to reveal the gaping, cunt-like wound on her leg, who rips her body open to reveal her back, a broken column, her back corset with its white canvas straps framing her beautiful breasts, her body stuck with nails: but she can't be Disabled, she's Sexual.

Here stands Frida, who this afternoon, in the midst of a row with Diego, cropped off her jet black hair ("Now see what you've made me do!"), and has schlepped herself to the ball in one of his suits. Nothing Dietrichish and coy about this drag: Diego won't get to parade his beautiful wife. Now she's snatched up Helen and walked with her out here onto the veranda.

In the other room, drunken Diego lurches, his body rolling forward before his feet manage to shuffle themselves ahead on the marble floor, giving himself more than ever the appearance of being one of those children's toys, bottom-weighted with sand, that when punched, roll back and then forward, an eternal red grin painted on their rubber faces. His huge belly shakes with laughter, his laughter a gale that blows above the smoke curling up toward the distant, gilded ceiling, gusting above the knots of men in tuxedos and women with marcelled hair, the black of their satin dresses setting off the glitter of their diamonds.

But the noises of the party, Diego's drunken roar, will be added later by the Foley artists.

Helen's thirty-six. She's just come back from Montgomery. Her mother had dragged her down there after she and Peter Fagan took out a marriage license, and the Boston papers got hold of the story. For so many years, men had been telling her that she was beautiful, that they worshiped her, that when Peter declared himself in the parlor at Wrentham, she had at first thought this was just more palaver about his pure love for her soul. But no, this was the real thing: carnal and thrilling and forbidden. How could you, her mother said. How people will laugh at you! The shame, the shame. Her mother whisked her off to Montgomery, Peter trailing after the two of them. There her brother-in-law chased Peter off the porch with a good old southern shotgun. Helen's written her poem:

What earthly consolation is there for one like me
Whom fate has denied a husband and the joy of
    motherhood? . . .
I shall have confidence as always,
That my unfilled longings will be gloriously satisfied
In a world where eyes never grow dim, nor ears dull.

Poor Helen, waiting, waiting to get fucked in heaven.

But not Frida. She's so narcissistic. What a relief to Helen! None
of those interrogations passing for conversation she usually has to
endure. (After the standard pile of praise is heaped upon her—I've
read your book five, ten, twenty times, I've admired you ever since—
come the questions: Do you mind if I ask you: Is everything black?
Is Mrs. Macy always with you?) No, Frida launches right into the tale
of Diego's betrayal. ". . . Of course, I have my fun, too, but one
doesn't want to have one's nose rubbed in the shit . . . ," she signs
into Helen's hand.

Helen is delighted and shocked. In her circles, Free Love is believed in, spoken of solemnly, dutifully. Her ardent young circle of
socialists want to do away with the sordid marketplace of prostitu-
tion, bourgeois marriage, where women barter their hymens and
throw in their souls to sweeten the deal; Helen has read Emma, she
has read Isadora; she believes in a holy, golden monogamy, an un-
fettered, eternal meeting of two souls-in-flesh. And here Frida speaks
of the act so casually that Helen, like a timid schoolgirl, stutters:

"You really? I mean, the both of you, you . . . ?"

Frida throws her magnificent head back and laughs.

"Yes, really," Frida strokes gently into her hand. "He fucks other
women and I fuck other men—and other women."

"F-U-C-K?" Helen asks. "What is this word?"

Frida explains it to her. "Now I've shocked you," Frida says.

"Yes, you have. . . . I suppose it's your Latin nature. . . ."

I'm not in the director's chair anymore. I'm sitting in the audience of the Castro Theatre in San Francisco watching this unfold.
I'm twenty-seven. When I was a kid, I thought being grown-up would
be like living in the movies, that I'd be Rosalind Russell in Sister
Kenny, riding a horse through the Australian outback or that I'd
dance every night in a sleek satin gown under paper palms at the
Coconut Grove. Now I go out to the movies, two, three, four times
a week.

The film cuts from the two figures on the balcony to the night sky. It's Technicolor: the pale gold stars against midnight blue. We're close to the equator now: there's the Southern Cross, and the Clouds of Magellan, and you feel the press of the stars, the mocking closeness of the heavens as you can feel it only in the tropics. The veranda on which we are now standing is part of a colonial Spanish palace, built in a clearing in a jungle that daily spreads its roots and tendrils closer, closer. A macaw perches atop a broken Mayan statue and calls, "I am queen / I am queen / I am queen." A few yards into the jungle, a spider monkey shits on the face of a dead god.

Wait a minute. What's going on? Is that someone out in the lobby talking? But it's so loud—

Dolores del Rio strides into the film, shouting, "Latin nature! Who wrote this shit?" She's wearing black silk pants and a white linen blouse; she plants her fists on her hips and demands: "Huh? Who wrote this shit?"

I look to my left, my right, shrug, stand up in the audience and say, "I guess I did."

"Latin nature! And a white woman? Playing Frida? *I* should be playing Frida."

"You?"

"Listen, honey." She's striding down the aisle toward me now. "I know I filmed that Hollywood crap. Six movies in one year: crook reformation romance, romantic Klondike melodrama, California romance, costume bedroom farce, passion in a jungle camp among chicle workers, romantic drama of the Russian revolution. I know David Selznick said: 'I don't care what story you use so long as we call it *Bird of Paradise* and del Rio jumps into a flaming volcano at the finish.' They couldn't tell a Hawaiian from a Mexican from a lesbian. But I loved Frida and she loved me. She painted 'What the Water Gave Me' for me. At the end of her life, we were fighting, and she threatened to send me her amputated leg on a silver tray. If that's not love, I don't know what is—"

I'm still twenty-seven, but now it's the year 2015. The Castro's still there, the organ still rises up out of the floor with the organist playing "San Francisco, open your Golden Gate. . . ." In the lobby now, alongside the photos of the original opening of the Castro in 1927, are photos in black and white of lounging hustlers and leather queens, circa 1979, a photographic reproduction of the door of the women's room a few years later ("If they can send men to the moon, why don't they?" Underneath, in Braille, Spanish, and English: "In the 1960s, the development of the felt-tip pen, combined with a growing philosophy of personal expression caused an explosion of graffiti. . . . Sadly unappreciated in its day, this portion of a bathroom stall, believed by many experts to have originated in the women's room right here at the Castro Theatre, sold recently at Sotheby's for $5 million. . . .").

Of course, the Castro's now totally accessible, not just integrated wheelchair seating, but every film captioned, a voice loop that interprets the action for blind people, over which now come the words: "As Dolores del Rio argues with the actress playing Frida, Helen Keller waits patiently—"

A woman in the audience stands up and shouts, "Patiently! What the fuck are you talking about, patiently? You can't tell the difference between patience and powerlessness. She's being *ignored*." The stage is stormed by angry women, one of whom leaps into the screen and begins signing to Helen, "Dolores del Rio's just come out and—"

"Enough already!" someone in the audience shouts. "Can't we please just get on with the story!"

Now that Frida is played by Dolores, she's long-haired again, wearing one of her white Tehuana skirts with a deep red shawl. She takes Helen's hand in hers, that hand that has been cradled by so many great men and great women.

"Latin nature?" Frida says, and laughs, "I think perhaps it is rather your cold Yankee nature that causes your reaction. . . ." And before Helen can object to being called a Yankee, Frida says, "But enough about Diego . . ."

It's the hand that fascinates Frida, in its infinite, unpassive receptivity: she prattles on. When she makes the letters *z* and *j* in sign, she gets to stroke the shape of the letter into Helen's palm. She so likes the sensation that she keeps trying to work words with those letters in them into the conversation. The camera moves in close to Helen's hand as Frida says, "Here on the edge of the Yucatan jungle, one sometimes sees jaguars, although never jackals. I understand jackals are sometimes seen in Zanzibar. I have never been there, nor have I been to Zagreb nor Japan nor the Zermatt, nor Java. I have seen the Oaxacan mountain Zempoaltepec. Once in a zoo in Zurich I saw a zebu and a zebra. Afterwards, we sat in a small café and ate cherries jubilee and zabaglione, washed down with glasses of zinfandel. Or perhaps my memory is confused: perhaps that day we ate jam on zwieback crusts and drank a juniper tea, while an old Jew played a zither. . . ."

"Oh," says Helen.

Frida falls silent. Frida, you painted those endless self-portraits, but you always looked at yourself level, straight on, in full light. This is different: this time your face is tilted, played over by shadows. In all those self-portraits, you are simultaneously artist and subject, lover and beloved, the bride of yourself. Now, here, in the movies, it's different: the camera stands in for the eye of the lover. But you're caught in the unforgiving blank stare of a blind woman.

And now, we cut from that face to the face of Helen. Here I don't put in any soothing music, nothing low and sweet with violins, to make the audience more comfortable as the camera moves in for its close-up. You understand why early audiences were frightened by these looming heads. In all the movies with blind women in them—or, let's be real, sighted women playing the role of blind women—Jane Wyman and Merle Oberon in the different versions of *Magnificent Obsession*, Audrey Hepburn in *Wait Until Dark*, Uma Thurman in *Jennifer 8*, we've never seen a blind woman shot this way before: never seen the camera come in and linger lovingly on their faces the way it does here. We gaze at their faces only when bracketed by others, or in moments of terror when beautiful young blind women are being stalked. We've never seen before this frightening blank inward turning of passion, a face that has never seen itself in the mirror, that does not arrange itself for consumption.

Lack = inferiority? Try it right now. Finish reading this paragraph and then close your eyes, push the flaps of your ears shut, and sit. Not just for a minute: give it five or ten. Not in that meditative state, designed to take you out of your mind, your body. Just the opposite. Feel the press of hand crossed over hand: without any distraction, you feel your body with the same distinctness as a lover's touch makes you feel yourself. You fold into yourself, you know the rhythm of your breathing, the beating of your heart, the odd independent twitch of a muscle: now in a shoulder, now in a thigh. Your cunt, in all its patient hunger.

We cut back to Frida in close-up. But now Helen's fingers enter the frame, travel across that face, stroking the downy mustache above Frida's upper lip, the fleshy nose, the thick-lobed ears.

Now, it's Frida's turn to be shocked: shocked at the hunger of these hands, at the almost feral sniff, at the freedom with which Helen blurs the line between knowing and needing.

"May I kiss you?" Helen asks.

"Yes," Frida says.

Helen's hands cup themselves around Frida's face.

I'm not at the Castro anymore. I'm back home on the fold-out sofa in the slapped-together TV room, watching grainy images flickering on the tiny screen set in the wooden console. I'm nine years old again, used to Hays-office kisses, two mouths with teeth clenched, lips held rigid, pressing stonily against each other. I'm not ready for the way that Helen's tongue probes into Frida's mouth, the tongue that seems to be not so much interested in giving pleasure as in finding an answer in the emptiness of her mouth.

I shout, "Cut," but the two of them keep right on. Now we see Helen's face, her wide-open eyes that stare at nothing revealing a passion blank and insatiable, a void into which you could plunge and never, never, never touch bottom. Now she begins to make noises, animal mewlings, and cries.

I will the screen to turn to snow, the sound to static. I do not want to watch this, hear this. My leg is in a thick plaster cast, inside of which scars are growing like mushrooms, thick and white in the dark damp. I think that I must be a lesbian, a word I have read once in a book, because I know I am not like the women on television, with their high heels and shapely calves and their firm asses swaying inside of satin dresses waiting, waiting for a man, nor am I like the women I know, the mothers with milky breasts, and what else can there be?

I look at the screen and they are merging into each other, Frida and Helen, the dark-haired and the light, the one who will be disabled and nothing more, the other who will be everything but. I can't yet imagine a world where these two might meet: the face that does not live under the reign of its own reflection with the face that has spent its life looking in the mirror; the woman who turns her rapt face up toward others and the woman who exhibits her scars as talismans, the one who is only, only and the one who is everything but. I will the screen to turn to snow.

Ten Reasons Why Michael and Geoff Never Got It On

〜❦ ❦〜

RAYMOND LUCZAK

1. Their Physiques Differed from Each Other's.

Geoff was six-one with broad shoulders and a thick back; he didn't like to think too much about his growing pot belly. He recently had to go out and buy a whole week's worth of 38-inch underwear, and the other morning after a shower it struck him that through his blondness he was balding in very much the same pattern as his father's.

Michael was five-eleven with narrow shoulders. No matter what he ate, he just couldn't add another pound, and it had taken him a long time to feel comfortable enough to play volleyball at a nudist beach the previous summer. Some men had found the different colors of hair on his body fascinating: the blondness of his short bangs, the redness of his beard, the blackness of his chest hair, and the brownness of the hair on his arms and legs. Michael's red beard complements the shape of his slightly weary face very well. He dresses as if everything is an afterthought; no one at work minds, because he works in Creative at an advertising agency in the East Forties.

Michael is something of an oddity where he works, though. He wears a hearing aid in one ear and his speech is clumsy, sometimes incomprehensibly nasal. He figures that as long as hearing people already realize that he's slightly different because of this, he will refuse to hide his hearing aid in a mass of his strawberry blond hair. He keeps his hair cut around his ears.

They both desired a physically bigger, older man. Michael was 23; Geoff, 32. But when they first saw each other, each had thought the other was older. Later, when they were introduced, Michael was relieved to find that Geoff didn't mind the fact that Michael was nine years younger; after all, Michael was used to being taken for 30 because of his full beard.

When Michael first saw Geoff in the copy room on his floor, he had thought, He must be at least three years older than me. Geoff was clean-shaven, had slightly curly blond hair, and an eaglelike nose.

And when they first saw each other, their eyes locked.

2. Their Ambitions Were Too Different.

Michael was a graphic arts student at Gallaudet University in Washington, D.C.; he was able to sell a few of his collages, and they were included in a group show here in New York. But he'd come to the point where he wanted very much to be in the same position as Lorraine Louie, who had her name printed on the back covers of Vintage Contemporary Books and Random House's *Quarterly*. He felt some of her stuff was beginning to look contrived, but her graphic style was instantly identifiable, which counted for something. That was the kind of reputation he longed for. Otherwise he was content where he was, working as a storyboard artist. He agreed with the aphorism his younger sister had once repeated to him when he became frustrated because he couldn't understand the deejay's voice on "America's Top 40": "Keep your hopes high, but keep your feet on the ground." He knew he wanted to continue making those collages: People kept saying that they'd make him famous. He wasn't sure he wanted fame. It was far more important to find a man who didn't treat his deafness as something cute but as just another part of him. And for the time being he was very content to live where he was, on the northwestern fringe of Park Slope in Brooklyn; the apartment was generously large for the rent.

Geoff had for years been a pipe dreamer, but lately he'd decided to make money. That was his biggest reason for putting in so many hours in the first six months at the agency before bypassing three positions to become budgeting supervisor for six of the company's biggest accounts. He was fairly pleased with himself, considering he'd never actually completed his finance degree at Washington University in St. Louis. Maybe in two years' time he'd have enough for the first down payment on a nice co-op somewhere on the Upper West Side. He would've preferred to live on the Upper East Side, but he knew that neighborhood was completely unaffordable. If only he could meet a handsome rich man. . . .

3. Neither Could Avoid Michael's Hearing Loss.

Geoff does not remember seeing Michael's hearing aid at all until they happened to ride down the elevator together at the end of the day. Geoff had run to make the elevator as its doors were closing, and he stepped in right next to Michael. "Oh hello," he said. They'd never spoken.

It was then he saw the hearing aid up close, a flesh-colored comma perched on Michael's ear. The earmold caught a little of the fluorescent lighting from the elevator's ceiling, and Geoff wondered how much Michael could hear. He knew something about deaf people; his sister Ruth had told him some about her deaf students in White Plains, north of New York City. He didn't know any sign language, and he wasn't even sure if Michael knew it. Well, he'd find out soon enough.

Michael nodded and smiled slightly.

Geoff noticed how easily Michael blushed. Michael's freckles seemed awash in that peculiar pinkness; seeing this turned him on. While they didn't speak any, Geoff was suddenly very aroused by noticing the way Michael was trying not to look more closely at him. He thought, *I have to know this guy.*

When they got off the elevator, Michael nodded again while they moved through the revolving door out of the lobby. Michael wanted to follow Geoff, but he didn't know what to do, so he walked uptown, with furtive glances back at Geoff, who was walking the other way to his subway station.

A few days later, when they met again, homeward bound, alone on the elevator together, Michael surprised him by extending his hand. "I'm Michael Osbourne, and you are . . . ?"

After such a bold introduction, Geoff was relieved that he couldn't blush. "Geoff Linnesky."

"I'm really busy tonight but let me give you my number. I'm not so deaf that I can't use the telephone."

"Sure. Sure." Geoff watched Michael scribble his number. He was struck by the volume of Michael's voice, and the slightly pinched enunciation.

"Here. Now it's all up to you." Michael smiled.

Geoff took the number and thought, *He wants me to take care of everything. But if Michael made the first move, he was supposed to call, wasn't he?*

The third time they boarded the elevator together a few days later, Michael leaned over and said, "I didn't catch your name the last time. How do you spell it?" He had his pad out already.

Geoff wrote it down and smiled. "Are you busy tonight?"

They ended up walking through Central Park. It was May, and the evening was warm. They walked through Midtown, and in their conversations about their lives, Geoff noticed how difficult it was for Michael to lipread him. He had never heard "What? Pardon? I'm sorry, I didn't catch that," so many times in the space of a few hours. A comment from Ruth came back to him with some force: "You have very expressive eyes, it's too bad you have to mumble so much." Of course he'd always been interested in sign language ever since he learned how to fingerspell as part of his Boy Scout training—why couldn't he remember the letters now that he needed to? He felt somewhat frightened because he could understand Michael's speech well enough to know what he was talking about, and that created a feeling of inadequacy: *I can understand him but he can't understand me.*

So Geoff asked Michael to show him various signs, and among these was "fuck." When Geoff repeated back to Michael, he felt giddy when he saw how Michael blushed.

As they reached Columbus Avenue, Michael said he had two tickets for that evening's spring production given by the National Theater for the Deaf. Geoff agreed to go, once Michael told him it would be voice-interpreted. Michael also said he knew quite a few of the people who would be there, and he assured Geoff that he could show Geoff a few conversational signs—besides "fuck" and "asshole." Michael told him that if he showed that he was willing to try to use sign language, he'd do just fine. Geoff nodded, not wanting to wonder too closely: What if he didn't know how to read a sign? Or what if he fumbled with his hands the way he mumbled? Or . . . ?

Before the play began, Michael tugged Geoff over to a small group of friends. He introduced Geoff to them, and they nodded and smiled, but then they all had curious, waiting looks on their faces, as if they had expected something more from Geoff.

Geoff felt suddenly intimidated. What was the sign for "Sorry"? He didn't know, or he had forgotten, or both, and he wished he were somewhere else. He wanted just to stand around and talk and laugh the way he usually did in the lobby before a show began. He felt even more lost when he watched deaf people hug their friends and sign so quickly, and even though he tried to watch them closely, he just couldn't understand them. What were the signs Michael had taught him? He felt like he was treading around the lobby with useless hands. He just nodded, "How do you do?"

During the play, though, Geoff felt deeply aroused by the way Michael pressed his fingers warmly under Geoff's elbow; he was afraid to look at Michael when he did that. Finally, he did look, and he saw that Michael's unblinking eyes were shining brightly from the lights from the stage. He had never felt such warmth shiver up his spine, and he grinned. He wished he could learn the sign for that shimmer in Michael's eyes; there had to be a way. He'd seen enough of Michael's signs to believe that hands could most certainly convey such specifics.

Geoff found the play itself touching—not so much the play, which was a rendering of a Restoration farce, but how clear and comprehensible the deaf performers were on stage. He heard the voices, but his eyes were riveted on the deaf actors. There was a logic, a beauty to what they were doing. He found himself wondering why he had been so intimidated by the notion of interacting with deaf people. They laughed at themselves, but he still felt a little embarrassed when he laughed too. He could tell that his laugh was among the few that sounded "normal" among the dozens that were raw and strange and howling—but primal in the pleasure they took from the visual jokes. They weren't afraid of their bodies, either. Maybe that was what seemed to make Michael so different, Geoff thought.

At the reception afterwards, Michael took Geoff around again and introduced him to his friends. Geoff just nodded, mumbling, "How do you do?" He had forgotten how to sign, "Nice to meet you."

When they left the theater, Michael said, "You could've at least *tried* to sign something. I showed you how to greet. . . . Deaf people do really appreciate it if you just *try*."

"I'm sorry."

Michael said nothing for a while as they walked toward the Times Square subway stop. "I wanted them to like you as much as I do. I just feel like shit for going to all that trouble for nothing."

Geoff looked down. "I'm sorry."

"Please."

"What?"

"Don't look away from me when you talk to me. Otherwise, how can I read your lips?"

"I'm sorry, okay?" In that moment Geoff forgot how warm he'd felt while he watched Michael's eyes shining so brightly during the play, drinking in the performers; he forgot about asking Michael to come to his apartment that night. He said instead, as they parted to their own trains home, "I'll see you tomorrow."

While Michael took the long ride to Brooklyn, he continued to feel like shit. He knew it would've been better to attend the play alone and not have to worry about enunciating clearly for Geoff. He could have just let his hands do everything. *Fuck.* He should've waited till he knew Geoff better.

He took out his hearing aid and fingered it a little inside his denim jacket pocket, hoping that he would run into Geoff tomorrow.

They would have to talk about this.

4. They Were Both Loners.

Geoff had never gotten along with his parents. He never went back to synagogue after his bar mitzvah. In the seventies, he grew his hair into a weird afro, sought sex in bathhouses, and fell in love with pot. He left St. Louis for New York only two months before he would have received a B.S. in Finance. At the time, he thought, *Why not? Fuck everybody.* He could graduate somewhere else.

Through the years, he found he enjoyed being alone, yet he was beginning to get tired of drifting around. In New York, he gradually became the consummate sexual drifter: He knew which porn movie theaters had the best dark places, which doors in which peep booths could lock or not, which hours attracted greater numbers in which places. He never actually thought much about these things; they had simply become part of his routine. He was too much the hunter to worry about the annoying flashlight checks of the attendants. He had thought, when he first started frequenting the same kinds of places in St. Louis, that he might eventually find love. He could at least expect to chat a while with regulars, but even that made him feel uncomfortable. He didn't see himself as a regular patron of these places; yet he was. Although he couldn't admit it, he was absolutely terrified of the fact that he'd evolved into leading a double life: by day, an openly gay man with a good-paying job, and by night, a guy who was willing to grope just about anybody in the dark. Still, the allure of these encounters, the efficient pleasure they provided, and the ongoing possibility of connecting—he'd exchanged phone numbers with over fourteen eligible guys—made returning to these sexual emporiums seem sensible enough.

Michael had grown up reading. Books were a land where he never had to lipread; he could eavesdrop on everything. He grew up in a family of seven children, yet he felt alone; he was used to people turning their faces toward him, whenever they spoke to him, but from an early age he began to feel set apart. If everyone turned their faces toward each other whenever they talked, then he wouldn't feel so different.

As for sex, he couldn't talk about it. It wasn't in his nature to brag, or to wish that a man he'd met would call again; he had been let down far too many times. He eventually decided that some men wanted to sleep with him only because they found the idea of tricking with a deaf man exciting in some way, but none of them seemed to care for anything more. Michael quickly got enough of drifting around.

Michael wasn't like some of his deaf friends who were eager and willing to accept whatever hearing people said at—so to speak—face value, and this actually became a kind of burden for Michael himself. Why weren't there more intelligent deaf men out there? And why couldn't an intelligent hearing man be willing to learn sign language? He often shuddered at the prospect of misunderstandings during an argument, and because of this, he decided that his next lover would have to learn it. If not, then he'd have to leave. He was used to being alone anyway.

5. Each Was Concerned How the Other Would Appear to His Friends.

By the time Geoff had lived in New York for nearly a decade, he had accumulated a small group of friends either from having slept with them, or from finding they had similar interests. Most of them were concerned with making money and living well, while Geoff had lived in his cramped apartment on Ludlow Street for over eight years.

He thought often about the feeling he had whenever he entered their apartments: how beautiful, how white, and how spacious their places were. He remembered waking up the morning after meeting one of them, and thinking, *If I could be his boyfriend, then everything would be just perfect.* He concentrated on making a go of it, but he found each man unwilling to be more serious. But how could any-one with money take him seriously once he told them that he lived on the Lower East Side?

Whenever he received invitations to weddings and housewarming parties, he felt envious, but he was careful not to talk about it. "Lucky you." People always laughed. "You're still single, you're still eligible, you can sleep with anyone you want."

Not only that, he felt he wanted somehow to become closer again to his sister Ruth. When he'd moved to New York, she let him stay with her, and she'd showed him around the city. Walking the streets of Manhattan, they'd become very close, talking always about what they hoped their future boyfriends would be like. The similarities of their hopes were often a revelation.

But when Ruth met John, everything changed. She married him, and now he'd become some kind of an executive for a large food company in White Plains. She got a teaching job at the local resi-dential school for the deaf, and the school in White Plains was so much nicer than the one in New York. John told both of them that he knew all about Geoff's "lifestyle," and he kept himself at a dis-tance, much to Ruth's chagrin. Geoff didn't much care; as far as he was concerned, John was a complete asshole.

Meanwhile, Ruth began trying to convince Geoff to stop working at his low-paying accounting firm job downtown and to start looking for a higher-paying job. "You have to dress well to attract the kind of man you want, so how else will you be able to do it? Steal?"

In truth, it was rather obvious from his clothes that Michael didn't appear to care about making a whole lot of money.

Michael wanted just enough to live on comfortably; when he met Geoff, he began to fret: Should he dress up like him, or should he dress the way he always had?

After much thought, Geoff decided not to tell Ruth about Michael, even though she might be tickled by the idea of him falling for a deaf man. She was fluent in sign language: he had thought about asking her for some pointers on how to communicate better with Michael, but decided against it. It would be a waste of time: Michael could never fit in with Geoff's friends anyway, or even with Ruth and John. No, it was better that Ruth didn't know about Michael.

And Michael was sure his deaf friends would surely turn stony toward him whenever Geoff was around: Geoff was so hard to lipread, and he was so unsure of Geoff's ability to sign with them. Maybe they still resented the fact that he could communicate with almost any hearing person he liked. They couldn't do that so easily. Still, they were his friends because they shared the language. Unlike anyone else, they understood how separated from the rest of the world life could feel because one couldn't hear the radio, or because one had to wait to watch a TV news report that was close-captioned. Michael knew from experiences growing up that something that's funny—in a group conversation—is killed when it's repeated so soon after its first occurrence. The joke is no longer spontaneous; it sounds contrived. So Michael had always felt ambivalent about having a joke repeated. Having to endure such secondhand humor all the time without asking was bad enough.

Michael wished more than anything else that Geoff would take a sign language class at the Chelsea School of American Sign Language, where he taught two nights a week; he had even teased Geoff about being his teacher there. If Geoff didn't try to learn sign language, then all his friends would whisper among themselves, Why did Michael pick *him*, when it seemed so obvious that Geoff just wanted to use him, the way a lot of hearing guys always did?

But why couldn't they be patient with Geoff?

6. Michael Drew a Caricature of Geoff.

Michael rarely did caricatures of anyone he knew, but one afternoon when he stepped out of the 3rd Street exit of the West 4th Street subway station he saw the portrait artists and cartoonists lining up on Sixth Avenue. This gave him an idea.

At home, after trying many approaches, he finally settled on patterning Geoff after James Bond in his trademark tuxedo, substituting Geoff's head for Sean Connery's. As he sketched carefully in charcoal and added dramatic touches with India ink, he found himself unable to stop smiling.

One morning as they happened to step aboard the same elevator, Michael said, "Can I show you something in my office?"

"Sure, sure." Geoff was curious to see how Michael might decorate his office. It was like anyone else's, festooned with posters of Prince and wiggly Keith Haring drawings; Geoff noticed a light-flasher switchbox near his telephone.

Michael took out the drawing. "It's for you."

Geoff coughed. *The craft was amazing, but really, this was too much.* "Well, I don't know what to say," he said. "I—I like it, though."

As Michael gauged Geoff's reaction, he immediately wondered why he'd even bothered. He nodded instead, and said, "I'm glad you like it."

Later that day, when Geoff took the Second Avenue bus downtown to the Lower East Side, he thought, *Michael is a romantic.* He remembered the men he had dated and how they had set up their apartments in candlelight with a rose in a slender vase on the table between them—and how extremely uncomfortable he'd felt. He didn't like the idea of going through all that trouble to make everything so romantic. Geoff thought, *Last thing I need is another romantic in my life.*

7. Their Definitions of the Ideal Lover Were Different.

Geoff was most attracted to men who were tall, rather clean-shaven but with a healthy spurt of dark hair out of the collar just below the neck, and slightly older. The ideal lover would be muscular, monied, and masculine in his interests; he would be interested in the woods and not care so much for shopping at Bloomie's. He would be well read in many areas, and would be able to conduct intelligent conversations about anything. He would also have a sarcastic sense of humor. He wouldn't feel the need to tickle Geoff, because that always made him feel more tense afterward. He would want to live in a very nice co-op on the Upper East Side, and have a great group of friends who were always a blast whenever they got together. They would smoke joints now and then, and giggle away their highs together. His ideal lover would be well versed in classical music, Mozart and Verdi most of all. He would be a great fan of experimental films, and he would beg to see another Almadovar movie if one was being shown in New York. They would play Trivial Pursuit occasionally and make the most passionate love. His ideal lover would have a big dick, and a very hairy and very round ass, and nipples that got hard whenever Geoff's fingers touched them through his Ralph Lauren shirt. His ideal lover would have style and an elegantly casual way of looking at things. He would never grow into a tacky old queen with friends who never quite made it to the altar; he'd stay very virile while they grew old together.

And Michael was most attracted to a man who was tall, had a nice beard, and was slightly older. His ideal lover would be hearing and have a natural ability to learn sign language easily and quickly; he would be very affectionate with Michael in public and in private; he would enjoy their strolls through art museums together. He would enjoy cooking gourmet meals, he would prefer to rent close-captioned videotapes than attend nonsubtitled movies at the theater, he would buy a TDD—a Telecommunication Device for the Deaf which would transmit through the phone whatever the person on the other end typed on the screen—so he could talk with Michael anytime without having to rely on the TDD/voice relay service; no matter that he would also have a crystal-clear voice easily understood over the phone. He would never mumble. He'd be very expressive in his humor. He'd tickle Michael under his feet because that was one of Michael's favorite turn-ons. And his ideal lover would love books. He would enjoy going to sign-interpreted theater performances and deaf theater productions. And everyone who met him would accept him as one of them. Not only that, he would be propositioned often, and he would shrug them off in ASL with, "Me-sorry but me-taken. Ask Michael first." And of course, no one would dare ask Michael for permission. They'd live together in the Village, and their neighbors would be couples who wanted to be couples and who wanted to learn sign language too, and they would play pinochle and have elaborate dinner parties at each other's place. . . .

8. Both Had Lived with a Lover a Few Years Before.

Michael had lived with a deaf lover for over two years, long before he'd moved to New York; in fact, his sudden move to New York was his attempt to lessen his ex-lover Tom's fierce sense of unrequit-edness.

Geoff had lived for four years with Nick, who was six years older, and it had taken him two years since the breakup to concede that it had been a very bad relationship, that Geoff had been cheated on so often, and that he'd hoped for too much too soon. But he sometimes thought about Nick, only because he hadn't yet found anyone who really wanted to live as a couple, to build a home.

So, while Michael and Geoff were both willing to try again—this time with someone new and different—each arrived in the other's life with a separate set of expectations, and each felt like—though they weren't—damaged goods.

9. Michael Was Too Direct for Geoff's Comfort.

During one of their lunch breaks at a public fountain on East 50th Street, which turned out to be their last together, Michael asked, "Did you have a chance to look at the schedule of sign language classes? You know, the one the Chelsea School sent you?"

"I just don't have the time."

"Well, if you need to borrow some money to go, I'd be happy to help you out. I'm just tired of guessing what's on your lips." His eyes didn't seem to Geoff to shine as brightly as they had before. "I can arrange a discount for you, if that's a problem."

"I'm sorry." Geoff wondered again why Michael had to make him feel so inadequate. What about Geoff's *own* needs, goddammit? Couldn't he just talk about anything and not worry about being misunderstood or having to repeat some things twice? Why couldn't they just be telepathic, the way all true lovers were supposed to be? "You know how busy I am," Geoff said at last.

Michael said, "Well, I believe that if something is important enough, I make the time for it. I'm busy too, but if you're willing to make the time for us, I'm willing too."

Geoff said nothing for a moment. Finally he said, "You're too romantic."

"What was that?"

"I said, *You're too romantic.*"

"I don't understand what you mean by that."

"It's like—you want flowers, poems, and all that, and I'm just not that type of guy—"

"You have an ideal lover in mind, right?"

"Well, who doesn't?"

"Lots of people don't. But people who *do*, I call them romantics. And they seldom admit it." Michael stood up, his sandwich half-eaten. "You're a romantic, Geoff. Fuck you if you think I'm too romantic for you. Ideals change. We could have been wonderful."

And Michael left the sound of the fountain thundering in Geoff's ears.

10. Geoff Did Not Know How to Approach Michael.

After that, Geoff stayed more and more in his office, knowing how Michael liked being outside for lunch. He kept an occasional eye on the pedestrian traffic below his office window; it was the only time he could observe Michael without him knowing it. He went instead to the company cafeteria for lunch, chatting almost listlessly with his co-workers and trying not to remember.

One morning Geoff was standing at a urinal in the men's room when Michael came in. Michael looked away as he stepped into a stall. Geoff shook off his dick and zipped up. But he took his time, washing his hands with soap and glancing back under the stall door where the jeans were crumpled atop Michael's black Reeboks. He wondered what kind of underwear Michael wore, and then it occurred to him that Michael must be waiting for him to leave.

Then there were those elevators in the morning. Michael stood at a distance while they waited in the lobby, smiling hellos to everyone except Geoff. Meanwhile, Geoff would pull his *Times* over his face until they arrived at their floors. Such scenes repeated themselves in Geoff's mind all day: Why couldn't Michael live and let live?

He wants to be able to say, "I'm sorry," but he doesn't know the signs.

Geoff starts to see other men, but it's not the same. The *men* are the same as before, but something about Michael will not let go. He looks at the small handbook of signs and realizes the only sign he remembers is for "fuck."

He stares after Michael now and then as he walks down the corridors of their office building, and feels his heart opening a little again. *No.* He must go on looking. And no, he is *not* a romantic, goddammit.

In time, Geoff does leave for a better job, this time on Madison Avenue. He has mostly forgotten about Michael, until one day he notices a messenger in Spandex shorts pulling out a package of storyboards for the receptionist. He recognizes that it is unmistakably Michael's artwork; he closes his office door quickly.

Michael also notices Geoff's absence and goes on to date other men occasionally. But it's not the same. When Michael falls asleep beside them, he imagines himself curling a little closer to Geoff's chest, trying to hear the sound of his own heart beating.

How Much It Hurts

DAVID MIX

After every game the slow-pitch team went to The Travelers, and I usually tagged along. We scraped tables together and raised dust off the wood floor that mixed with dust the players slapped off their uniforms. Our voices boomed up to the tin ceiling and disturbed regulars at the bar who hunched low on their stools and surrounded their drinks as if they could hide from the noise we made. Once we had the tables together, we passed pitchers of beer and re-played the game.

That was how it started one Tuesday. After softball we talked about where all the salmon had gone and the size of the deer herd, but for some reason the regular subjects wore out early. Everyone paused, sipped their beer, then all at once came at me in a rush. They wanted to know what it was *really* like over there, whether I was scared and did I kill anyone, questions they had asked before. This time I was surprised. I thought the subject was dead, but I leaned forward anyway and cleared my throat, ready to trot out one of the old regulars when Red, our lanky third baseman, beat me to it.

"What was that story about the sergeant who stole a jeep and drove to a town and went to a whorehouse?" They all laughed and went on to tell the story about the sergeant being in bed with a whore when the VC attacked the hotel and how he fired his rifle back through the door while he was still on top of her.

"Shotgun," I said.

"You're trying to tell me some drunk is on top of a woman handling a gun with a bunch a crazies trying to break in and kill him?" That was Orloe, the veteran pitcher. He never looked at me but went on as much as calling me a liar. "And he doesn't miss a beat let alone keeps it up through all that?" Orloe shook his head.

Red came right back. "Sure he can. Look, he's on his elbows, and he's got the rifle sighted under the gal's chin, like this." Red showed us with his elbows on the table and his eye squinted down the sight.

"That ain't the hard part," Orloe said.

"You old vets forget how it used to be."

"I'd like to see *you* do it."

"Okay. Go see if Helen's in a friendly mood. I'll show you."

Red nodded toward the woman who ran The Travelers sitting at the bar with a cigarette dangling between her fingers. She glanced our way and we all laughed.

"Can you picture it?" Bill the right fielder said. "Spent casings flying past her face, bullets blasting back through the door, and all the time he's in the saddle banging away."

What could I add to a story they already knew by heart? The trouble was they knew all my stories, and there is nothing worse than a worn-out war story all dog-eared and bent out of shape from too many tellings.

The guys laughed themselves out, but there was always one who wouldn't quit. "Man," he said looking at me, "you must have been pissed when you got back and saw all that crap on TV, the demonstrations and all that."

And then Red again. "How'd you feel about those peace marches and all that, after what you'd been through?"

I shrugged. "I didn't care about any protests. I was flat on my back and so happy to be alive I didn't care what those freaks did."

But I thought of a story they had not heard, one that happened in Philadelphia six months after I got back. I told them how four of us from the Navy Hospital went out to celebrate one Saturday night. I think Ed was scheduled for surgery in a few days to clean out an infection in his stump. Ed's team got caught in the open and when one of his men went down, Ed crawled back out to rescue him and they emptied a .30 cal. machine gun on him, forty or fifty rounds at point-blank range and they only hit him once, but that one round all but blew his leg off. Ed was stuck out in the mud all day and half that night and by then he had picked up a catalogue of untreatable infections.

But maybe Ed's surgery isn't why we were celebrating that Saturday. One of us was always getting ready for an operation or getting over one, and most of the time we weren't really sick. They just stuck us in the hospital until we healed enough so they could kick us out of the Marine Corps for good. I'm not complaining. Our life was easy. We came and went as we pleased, but we were bored. I had already been at Philadelphia six months, and I was the junior man. John, with his right leg gone above the knee, had been there almost ten months, Ed the same, and Marty, his leg gone at the hip and a head wound that left him half crazy and totally blind, had been in Philadelphia and other military hospitals for almost two years.

When we went out it was a real zoo, a whole carload of cripples with twice as many crutches as legs. One of us was always assigned to lead Marty along the icy sidewalks, but he usually got left behind anyway and then we would wait and cheer while he ran into buildings and street signs, or people. They used to do some desperate dances to get out of his way, like it was against the rules to take his arm and help him. Sometimes it got embarrassing when Marty cussed. He couldn't see who was around to object so he didn't care, but most of all we loved the shocked look of civilians when all we did was laugh. I can still see Marty on his crutches tangled up with a parking meter, the rest of us clapping and cheering.

That night we went to Mickey Finn's, and naturally we drank too much. That was the idea. It was a sing-along place with a five-piece honky-tonk band, and once you got into the spirit of things you could pour a gallon of beer down your throat before you knew what happened. It was late by the time they played the Marine Corps Hymn and we stood and sang as loud as we could. John beat time with his stump on top of the table, slamming it so hard the peanut shells and beer mugs bounced and as I recall he had terrible phantom pains for months after that night.

Anyway, we left Mickey Finn's on a roll. Nearby patrons gave us plenty of room as we assembled our crutches and put on our coats. John, whose good leg was none too steady with most of the calf and thigh muscle blown away, was trying to get his crutches set when he lost his balance. He grabbed for the nearest support which happened to be some poor guy's head. The guy was probably in his early forties, a generation older than any of us, wearing a suit and tie, and bald, and he was talking to a sharp blond when John grabbed hold and wrapped both arms around the guy's ears and across his face. I don't know what the guy thought, but John had a grip like a lynch mob's noose, and the guy's little neck muscles twitched and strained under John's weight.

We helped John to get straightened out and pointed Marty toward the door, with me bringing up the rear on my old wooden crutches. I swung ahead but was laughing so hard I missed my armpits. Suddenly I had no support and fell flat on my face, not even getting my arms out to break the fall. I was too relaxed to get hurt, but I was still laughing when I hit the floor and got a mouthful of peanut shells. There was plenty of help to get me back on my feet, spitting my lips clear, with Marty asking, "What happened? What was that?"

We were still laughing when we headed down Broad Street on our way back to the hospital in South Philly, Ed driving his big Pontiac with me in front and John and Marty in back. We tried to explain to Marty what had happened, but we kept interrupting each other and cracking up. Ed was trying to describe the look on the bald guy's face, when all at once John yelled, "Turn here!"

Naturally, Ed turned and then he asked, "Why?"

"Another block," John said. "Over there, on the left."

It was a block of old stores, narrow little groceries, a cleaners, a florist, a dusty old shoe repair shop. Tucked between them a store where in the middle of the plate glass window someone had painted a giant peace sign.

John told us it was where they counseled draft dodgers, showed them how to get deferred or helped them get to Canada if they wanted to run. Pricks, we said. Assholes. Someone said, Let's get that place. I don't remember who said it first, probably because we all thought the same thing at once, except maybe not Marty who never quite knew what was going on.

The narrow street was lined on both sides with parked cars, but there was no traffic. We cruised down another block, the brick building fronts, the dark glass and small piles of sooty snow on the sidewalks, all of it fixed like a still photo by the streetlights overhead. We were quiet. We didn't know what to do, but we all felt the same.

I think Ed spoke first. "Let's break in. You know, do like they do, spill blood on draft records and piss on their files."

I said shit would be better.

"Burn the fucking place down," Marty said. "But wait till morning when it's full of long-hairs." If he could have found the place and if he had a match, I think he would have done it.

As we turned another corner and approached the store again from the other direction, John yelled for Ed to stop, which he did, double-parked in the narrow street, and John jumped out of the back door and fished his crutches out with him.

"Wait," we said. "What are you going to do?"

Marty wanted to know what was going on.

"Come on back," we called. "You can't do anything. You'll just make it worse."

John looked over his shoulder. "Don't get excited. All I want to do is look the place over. I want to see what they're like." He shaded both eyes and leaned against the glass.

We asked him what he saw.

"Nothing. It's just a crummy office."

Ed behind the wheel was pretty nervous and leaned across toward my window and called for John to get back in. I got out to drag John back, but before I got my crutches set he turned away from the window and started toward us. I told him to hurry up and ducked to get back in the car, but John stopped in the middle of the sidewalk and turned to look back at the store. We yelled at him to stop screwing around.

Instead of coming back what John did was raise his head and scream at the top of his lungs, "Chickenshit motherfuckers!" His cry echoed up and down the cold brick storefronts.

Ed was swearing to get him back in the car or he would leave him, and since I was closest I might have stopped him. But all we could do was watch, all except Marty who wanted to know what was going on, when John took his arm back and threw the crutch like a spear straight for the center of the window, and with his follow-through sprawled flat on his face in the middle of the sidewalk.

"Jesus," both Ed and I said.

Breaking glass clanged up and down the street like a big bell.

"What's that?" Marty said.

"Glass," I said.

John had been a pitcher in college and some pro teams were interested before a grenade screwed up both his legs, so his arm was plenty strong enough to throw a metal crutch.

I helped John back to the car and we got out of there as fast as we could and I looked back as we turned the corner and saw the street as quiet as ever. We went another block before anybody said anything, before John said, "My crutch."

"Too bad," we said.

"We can't just leave it. It's evidence."

We argued a little, said no way we could go back now and he said it had hospital markings on it and even those Navy doctors would notice a patient who was one crutch short and we said he would have to steal another one and he said they could trace it to us. Not us, we said, but Ed had circled back toward the store as we always figured he would even while he said it was stupid, dangerous, unnecessary, but that was probably why he did it.

I was scared and felt my stomach tighten and begin to burn in a way I hadn't expected to feel again in this life. We came to a stop at a corner and all took a couple of deep breaths and then turned and coasted down the deserted street. We watched for lights that had come on or a face peering out of an upstairs window, but everything was dark and quiet.

John borrowed my crutches and I hopped along behind with his one remaining crutch for balance. The other one was on the floor inside the office in the midst of broken glass just beyond the frame of light. It was well beyond our reach. I was ready to call it a loss and get back to the car, but John began to poke at the pointy shards with one of my crutches. The noise was deafening, like a midnight alarm that defied the still empty street.

"Come on, help," John hissed.

It went faster with both of us working, and in a few seconds I was boosting him over the low ledge and John swung into the shadows and picked up his crutch and then disappeared farther into the darkness.

"What the hell are you doing?" I said.

"I got to piss."

"Are you nuts?"

"What the hell, I'm here."

I could have gone back to the car to wait, but I stood by the window and watched the street. I whispered for him to hurry, and when I looked back to tell Ed what was taking so long, I saw a cop car stop at the red light two blocks up on Broad Street. I was ready to hop back to the car, but the light changed and the cops made a right turn off Broad and came straight for us.

I had no choice, and anyway it wasn't right to leave John alone in the office, so I balanced with care and stepped over the ledge and onto the slippery pieces of glass. Once inside I could see John finishing up after pissing all over one of the desks and into the drawers.

He zipped up and looked at me. "Hey, you gotta go too?"

"Asshole. The cops are here."

"Aw, shit. Really?"

He didn't seem to realize what could happen if we got caught. The cops could charge us, or they could turn us over to the commanding officer of the hospital, some hard-ass doctor who would send us up before a court-martial because the military was very sensitive about the constitutional rights of civilians, especially anti-war shitheads. We could even get a bad-conduct discharge.

We hid behind a desk as the police stopped beside Ed's car, and later Ed told us he didn't see the cops until they were next to him because Marty was throwing one of his fits. Marty took medication for seizures and wasn't supposed to drink, but that never stopped him.

Ed told the cops he was on his way back to the hospital when he spotted the broken window. The cops ordered Ed and Marty out of the car, but when they saw the missing legs and the crutches and the Frankenstein scar across Marty's face their tone changed.

One cop said, "Vietnam?" and then asked how long they had been there and where they had operated and how they got wounded, and he made a speech about scumbag protesters and shipping whole trainloads off to Canada where they belonged. The other cop inspected the window with his flashlight and sprayed the beam around the interior.

John and I tried to be perfectly still with the beam searching over our heads and on the wall behind us, but John slipped, knocked me sideways and started to giggle. He would have been great on an ambush.

"Sorry," he whispered.

"You dumb shit," I more or less hissed back.

I figured we'd had it, but the flashlight went out and when I peeked over the desk both cops were standing by Ed's car, very friendly, asking what it was like in a real combat zone and telling him how bad it was in South Philly, family squabbles, drunks and dopers. They shook their heads. South Philly, they said, the asshole of the world.

I got tired of kneeling on one knee and sat with my back against the desk. John kept a rigid lookout, his head just high enough to see over the top of the desk, his eyes split so wide they were round. I was calmer by then, not really mad anymore, but John was more keyed up than ever. I could hear him swallow, loud clunks in his throat like he was trying to swallow something solid, and then he would lick his lips, first the top and then the bottom.

"You know, this is like an ambush we were on once," I whispered. I wanted to relax things a little. "It was up near Hue in all this elephant grass. Huge stuff, three feet over your head. You couldn't see five feet, but it made all kinds of noise if you moved. We got everyone spread out and settled in, then the captain calls. 'We got a report of a gook regiment moving toward your position,' he says. Great, I tell him, me with twenty-five men, fifteen rifles and couple of machine guns. We're supposed to hold off three, four hundred regulars." I closed my eyes and smiled and thought how silly it was to get caught in a draft-dodgers office.

I said, "What's going on out there?"

"Nothing."

Beads of sweat had formed on his upper lip and his jaw was quivering. He looked down at me from above the desk with huge eyes and asked, "What happened?"

"Huh? Oh, one of my men signaled he had movement in front of him. Then another man from the other side of the perimeter says the same thing, gooks all around us. God, I was scared."

John sat on the floor next to me. "What did you do?"

"What the hell you think! Nothin. My biggest worry was one of the men would get nervous and open up. That would have done it. But those guys were smart. They gooks knew we were there too, but they didn't want contact either, and— What's wrong?"

John was taking long deep breaths that shook his whole body as if he was getting sick and about to start calling Ralph with the cops not thirty feet away. Great, I thought, and waited for the retching to start and begged him to hold it down when all at once I realized he wasn't sick. He was crying.

"What the hell?" I said.

"I'm sorry."

"Forget it," I said but I hate sloppy drunks.

"No, it's not what you think, getting caught here like a fool. It's everything. I never told you but I hardly saw any action. I was in-country for less than a week. Five days, to be exact. One patrol. All that training, all that crap and getting all psyched up for combat, then you don't even use all the cigarettes you brought from home."

"I thought you were in-country three, four months."

John hiccuped. "I lied."

I peeked over the top of the desk and saw the cops still talking to Ed and Marty. They must have been the friendliest cops in the city. I was tired of being trapped and especially I was tired of John's tear-laced confessions, how he was put in a recon company, and how one night he tagged along with a patrol, and how they walked into an ambush.

"Rounds were popping everywhere," he said. "All I could see was tracers and flashes. There I was, crouched behind this little bush, like they do in the movies. I said to myself, 'You dumb ass, this bush ain't no protection,' so I made a dive for a trench and just then a grenade went off by my feet. And that was it, my whole military career."

"No shit?" I had to cover up a smile.

"I'm sorry."

"For what? I wish to hell you would stop being sorry."

"For this. Everything I do turns out like this. I'm sorry I got you and the other guys in it too. I'm sorry about everything."

I lost my temper. I rolled to my good knee and grabbed the front of his shirt and pulled him so close our noses bumped. "Stop apologizing. I don't want to hear no more apologies. Ever." My voice filled the office and a little late we both crouched low behind the desk, but I didn't care if the cops heard me. I was so mad I could have strangled him.

Look where we were, stuck in the dark like a couple of rat-cowards or like kids on a Halloween prank and apologizing for what? What did we have to be sorry for? Like this kid in my platoon who picked up a dud one day on patrol. It was normal curiosity, a little lapse, but one little touch and it blew. By the time I kneeled beside him he was barely conscious, bleeding from everywhere. I tried to tell him to relax, a medevac chopper was on the way, but he wouldn't let me talk. "Lieutenant," he said, "I'm sorry." He had a hole in his chest the size of my fist with blood bubbling and turning to foam when he talked, but he wouldn't shut up. He had to tell me how sorry he was he screwed up, sorry he slowed the patrol, sorry he got killed. I couldn't take it, not then and not a second time from John in that goddamn peace office.

That's what I told the guys at The Travelers. That was how I felt when I got back from that war, aside from the personal loss, all the close calls and the pain and the fear, and all we do is apologize like there was no honor in what we did, no value, no purpose.

I stopped talking and looked at the slow-pitch team, their powder blue uniforms, their hats back on their heads, their eyes down or focused away from me. They didn't like this story. It didn't have a punch line or a clean end.

I could have told them how the cops were decent and let Ed go, how John and I snuck out a back door and found our way to Broad Street, where Ed drove by a little later and took us back to the hospital. But that didn't matter. I didn't tell the story for entertainment.

I jumped up and the chair tipped back on two legs and then returned to hit me behind the knee. The circle of faces watched me with some interest like maybe this was part of the story, but they wouldn't get it if I jumped across the table and grabbed Red by the throat. So I turned and hobbled past the bar and out through the front door.

Outside I faced a street lined with cars, dull chrome and dull paint. I leaned against the clapboard wall and looked up for a view of the night. I wanted stars, an infinity of space, but all I got was the fluttering neon sign leaning out on rusted chains from the front of the building, the faded Travelers half burned out.

I closed my eyes. I finally understood those Marines who go crazy, the ones who climb towers and shoot people at random, or who lock themselves in a house and hold off a battalion of cops before they kill themselves. What I should have done that night in Philly was stand up, march outside and tell those cops I did it. I broke the goddamn window and I was proud of it.

Or better yet, come out with a gun blazing. Fire from the hip and blast everyone in sight, cops who wanted to know what real combat was like, people asleep with their pleasant dreams, who wouldn't wake up for battles fought right in the streets below where they lived, and even my friends at The Travelers who only wanted a good time, a little fun before they went home to their wives and kids. Blast them all and watch them bleed like that kid in my platoon, whose name I can't remember, and tell them, Now do you see? Now do you understand?

The Interview

～⊙ ⊙～

JEAN STEWART

Claire hurried into the bathroom when the doorbell rang, to tidy her disheveled hair. Let Leo answer it; somehow their lovemaking had not disheveled him. (She listened to the mechanical racket of his automatic door opener.) Anyhow it was his interview, not hers, though she might pop her head in, out of curiosity.

Yesterday for the fifth time she'd sat in—at Leo's invitation—on an interview with a candidate who was, like the four preceding him, desperate for work. For Claire, who had nothing at stake, the interviews were compelling drama; she liked seeing Leo in action, observing what he looked for in an applicant, what kinds of questions he asked. She tried to imagine that melancholy young man—his wife and two small children still back in Guatemala, awaiting the day when he would be able to send for them—assisting bon vivant New York-born-and-raised Jewish funnyman/celebrity art museum curator Leo, whose arms and legs had been amputated at the age of five as a result of what the textbooks called "congenital malformations." Tried to visualize the fellow spooning Leo's oatmeal into his mouth, fitting the prosthetic legs on his thigh stumps, helping him negotiate New York City's stairs and curbs and potholes, hauling him up from the pavement when he fell.

Twenty minutes later the interview was over, though Claire suspected, vaguely sideswiped by guilt, that her nosy presence and eagerly interjected questions had prolonged a process that Leo sensibly regarded as drudgery, one he wanted to dispatch quickly. It was not, after all, her business who he hired to replace, temporarily, his daytime aide, who was about to leave for six months' back-packing in Europe.

The bathroom mirror was a good place to take inventory. Al-though she'd only been back from her last South American trip for three days, already Claire's face was smoothing itself out. Having moved in with Leo four months ago, she had begun to notice that certain muscles in her cheeks and brow tended to knot like clenched fists whenever she went away on research trips, giving her a grim *I'll-get-through* look of embattlement. By now those fists had released their grip, the whole face softening, easing, like a curtain parted in a dark room, letting in light.

Was it just the lovemaking? Claire could remember little of the past three days other than tangled bodies and sweat and whispered endearments, starting almost the instant her plane arrived at Ken-nedy Airport. Dreamily she replayed the scene: Leo's face in the crowded terminal as she walked through the gate, the hunger that blazed behind his darkly sexual eyes when he caught sight of her. Claire thought they were the most *male* eyes she'd ever seen: they stripped, they penetrated. Other women seemed to agree; he was a remarkable sexual magnet. He'd led the way, swinging along on his prosthetic legs (Claire knew he'd be wearing his legs today, though sometimes he preferred sitting legless in a wheelchair or—alone with her at home—walking on his stumps) toward a bathroom marked with a blue access emblem. Apparently he'd scoped it out earlier while waiting for her flight, which was delayed; now he hus-tled her inside the small empty one-person room, locked the door behind her, and looked at her. In the next moment he was pressing her against the wall—she almost lost her footing and fell, as often happened when Leo's passion superseded Claire's unsteady cerebral palsy gait—his lips on her throat, tongue sliding between her teeth, groin hard against her belly.

If it wasn't just the lovemaking, what else was it? He uncreased her brow. He always did, sooner or later, every time she arrived home from a field trip. Claire put the question to herself: How do men acquire such power? They get to play God, molding the fea-tures of another human face as if it were clay.

Well, he'd done a decent job with hers, Claire thought, brushing her hair. No more than that: decent. Briefly—she hated narcis-sists—Claire studied the rumpled, bereft-looking (but not creased) woman in the mirror, who wore no makeup, wondering what Leo saw when he looked back at her, what it was that lit such fire in him. Cerebral palsy had gently tugged her mouth upward on one side, giving her an ironic glint. In fact, CP had slightly tilted everything about her—her speech (which issued from the upturned side of her mouth, so that when she spoke she looked—the boys in high school used to point out—like Popeye), her shambling walk, her intelligence, which, a college English professor had once commented in a note scribbled on her thesis paper, reminded him of Emily Dickinson's imperative: *Tell it slant.*

All in all, her presence seemed to Claire unfinished, a body with no focus; graying unruly curls formed a messy nimbus that surrounded her features and added to the overall lack of definition. You expected such a blur in a thirteen-year-old, groping her way through the minefields of adolescence; in a near-fifty ethnomusicologist it seemed incongruous, an embarrassment. It was as though one of Leo's artists had drawn her in pastels and then had run a finger through the chalk. Only her large brown eyes contradicted the overall vagueness; CP had given them a fixity more penetrating than that of nondisabled folk. People tended to look away from her unsettling gaze.

Claire used to think that physical beauty was not an attribute of people with CP. CP held its shapeless cargo captive; the arrangement of one's body made style, angularity, bold dramatic line impossible, out of the question. She no longer subscribed to such views; they now seemed a form of self-hatred, "an internalization" (she'd announced to Leo) "of the nondisabled world's phobic social constructs about disability." (Leo had gazed at her, bemused, vaguely surprised that she regarded this as a fresh insight.) Her observations in so-called third world countries where her work had taken her, countries where wheelchairs seemed nonexistent and disabled people invisible, had furnished Claire the soil in which to plant her own shyly evolving disability identity.

Yes! CP pride, CP grace! The fact that she had not yet (today) reconfigured proud graceful Claire did not mean—she told herself—that pride and grace were unavailable, only that at this moment she felt tired, empty, delineated not so much by who she was as by what she was missing.

Gazing out the bathroom window at Leo's tiny backyard, Claire reflected that even now, four months after moving in, the precipitousness of her decision to leave her own sunny, high-ceilinged apartment and live with a man she'd met sixty days before still astonished her. It was unlike the Claire she thought she knew, the one who'd evolved an elaborate modus operandi to defer all life transitions, denying their urgency and discounting their legitimacy on the grounds that the contemplated new life (new apartment, new job, new man) would prove to be the same as whatever preceded it. Here *is where one must take one's stand,* she habitually chided herself, *not forever foraging in the realm of impossibility.* Accordingly, the act of leaving something in order to move on to something else had long been dismissed as "an escape fantasy." The diabetic, she reasoned, dreams of a chocolate bar, right?

As for Claire, for thirty years she'd dreamt of *being* the chocolate bar, of stirring some man to ravenous, devouring need. None of the men in Claire's life—there'd been several, including a husband—had seemed, in choosing Claire, to be reaching for their chocolate-bar dreams. Or rather, that was the problem: they'd *reached.* One *lunges* for chocolate. They'd settled, that was all; they'd liked her quirky nature, admired her probing intellect. A few had pitied her, including her husband, whose pity had lost its zeal when someone else had come along—someone sans CP—and kindled in him a flame Claire had not known was there.

Leo lunged, bless his soul. Every night, every morning. There seemed no end to his hunger. Nonplussed, Claire mused that perhaps he was so preoccupied with the in-and-out of it—with the necessity of proving he could?—that he simply hadn't noticed her CP. Would he wake one hard-edged winter morning, glance at the figure beside him—left side of her mouth drooping, a spidery thread of sleep-spittle wandering from open lips to pillow—and leap from the bed, appalled? Claire acknowledged, rinsing her face clean of Leo's salty musk, peering into the mirror, that she could hardly be considered a conquest.

Leo, on the other hand, seemed to those around him, quadruple amputee notwithstanding, to be the man who was missing nothing. Claire pondered Leo's sexiness, which seemed to reside not only in his dark eyes but in his wildly energetic New York style. Leo's humor, for instance, had a way of shielding people from, and at the same time refracting, his intellect. The engine that powered it was storytelling, which relied on perfect recall, exquisite timing and ingratiating charm; his trove of elaborate jokes and assorted trivia of all genres produced a stuporous effect, as if his audiences had just been helplessly snared in a web of inarticulate amnesia, as if their own tongues and brains had thickened into woolly lumps of meat in the presence of dazzling verbal gymnastics.

Claire stared out at a reedy gingko tree in the backyard, its delicate fan-shaped leaves now yellow, loosening. *Leo's audiences.* An odd concept, that: friends, lovers, colleagues, acquaintances transmogrified into audience. Claire as audience. Claire above all. It was one of the many ironies of their coupling that the more time they spent together, the deeper their intimacy, the more steadfastly Claire was relegated to the role of undifferentiated, anonymous audience by Leo's endless, endlessly repeated stories. Usually there was some kind of signal—a minute twitch at the corners of his mouth, a glitter in the eye—just before he amped into performance gear. It reminded Claire of reports she'd read by migraine survivors describing the "aura" that would presage an attack. Once a story was under way he seemed out of control, unable to stop himself.

Yesterday, for instance, he'd recounted a comic tale about the time he was invited to loan several paintings from the museum collection to an exhibit being mounted in Madrid. There was a lot of back and forth on the phone between Leo and the Spanish-speaking curator regarding shipping and insurance matters; they also differed as to which paintings would best represent the artist's *oeuvre.* Often the curator would call when Leo was out, and his live-in aide, Mike, an all-American college student, would answer. "I don't speak Spanish," Mike would blurt, hanging up the phone.

Patiently Leo tried to coach his ill-mannered aide, who seemed still to be recovering from the humiliation of one thoroughly flunked high school Spanish class. His head was filled with scraps of vaguely recalled words and phrases which he'd frantically string together, with sometimes disastrous results.

Leo finally resorted to a handwritten script taped to the answering machine. In the event of a call from Señor Romero, the script directed Mike to say, in Spanish: "THIS IS SEÑOR WALINSKY'S AIDE, I DON'T SPEAK SPANISH, CAN YOU CALL BACK, PLEASE?"

Weeks passed; Leo, busy with a major Picasso exhibition, forgot about the gallery in Madrid. One morning Mike breezily asked, while spooning Leo's oatmeal, "So, did you and Señor Romero finally work things out?"

Leo paused. "Señor Romero! I forgot all about him. When was the last time he called?"

"I haven't taken a call from him in over two weeks, not since I learned that Spanish message you wrote out. I recited it to him by memory," Mike added proudly.

When Leo called Madrid and identified himself, he couldn't help noting the chill in Señor Romero's voice. "Since I haven't heard from you in some time, I—" Leo began.

Señor Romero interrupted crisply. "I don't know why you would expect to! Your aide told me 'Please don't call back if all you speak is Spanish!' "

Leo, who spoke five languages with exquisite precision, told the tale with great charm and zest; Claire defused her boredom at hearing it for the third time by admiring the perfectly inflected punch line, delivered in Spanish.

Plucking Leo's dark curly chest hairs from the bathtub, Claire granted the obvious: his storytelling gift was nonpareil. So was his skill at moving through the world; he knew, and tended to get, what he wanted. And assumed he would get it, assumed those in positions of power would rearrange the world in such a way as to secure for him what he required. Apparently one of the perks that went with high-level art world hobnobbing, this sense of entitlement seemed to Claire an entirely male domain. She had never, in all her own maundering years, experienced anything remotely resembling Leo's certainty that the final checkmate would be his, *because he deserved it.*

Oh, he had his middle-of-the-night moments; but these seizures of doubt seemed to Claire the exceptions that proved the rule, for even his worst attacks seemed to turn *outward*: "I'm being considered to curate the 'Matisse to Diebenkorn' show at the Modern but I know I won't get it, Harvey will get it because he worked for them, they feel they have to give it to him out of loyalty. But everyone knows my curating is superior to Harvey's."

In the end, of course, he got the curatorship; every silver spoon that one ordinarily associates with rich white nondisabled men seemed somehow to find its way to Leo's mouth. (Claire smiled, her palm full of Leo's wiry curls, thinking of his mouth. In her private heart she very much liked the eccentric, appealingly compact body birth "defects" had molded for Leo. She couldn't help wondering what would be "the content of his character" if disability hadn't tossed its banana peel across his path. More cocky? Or less? And would he choose to be with her?)

(And who would *she* be without CP? The question of whether, absent CP, she would choose to be with Leo seemed fatuous; Leo's past was littered with nondisabled women who had not—according to Leo—found him wanting; why should Claire be different? There had, of course, been dozens who'd discreetly run the other way, aghast at his interest in them, but Claire knew she'd never have been one of *those*, CP or no.)

What killed Claire was his apparent *expectation* that: (a) the spoons would be his, and (b) they'd all be silver. This despite the overwhelming evidence that people with bent or nonfunctioning or missing limbs/eyes/brains/what-have-you were, as far as Claire could tell, not only *not* offered spoons of silver; they (*we*, she flared inwardly, *Leo too*, for she knew what he went through, living his life) weren't offered spoons at all. *Let them eat cake—from the plate.*

Well, you'd never guess that Marie Antoinette was alive and well in New York City by listening to Leo's stories, which were not about the daily assault of banal, petty discrimination dealt one of the city's more prominent disabled citizens. They were about each catalog essay or fancy coffee table art book introduction he'd been asked to write, each quote attributed to him in the art pages of the *New York Times*; they described in detail, with nary a modest bat of eyelash, what some art world high muckety-muck said to a packed ballroom by way of introducing Leo's keynote speech at a banquet. Each inflection, every pause—not to mention the adulatory words themselves—became a structural part of Leo's storytelling craft.

Irritably leafing through an art magazine she remembered noticing on the toilet tank the day she'd moved in, Claire concluded that apparently it was okay to brag if you did it with panache. And if, she thought—recalling Virginia Woolf's *I, I, I* marching across every page of men's writing, the letter casting tall shadows in which women darkly scrabbled for identity—you were a man. It puzzled Claire that Leo had emerged from a childhood of astonishing misery and oppression—the oppression that only severely disabled children can know—into adulthood marked by such unwavering . . . faith. Hastily she shuffled the cards, having almost called it arrogance. . . . But no, that was surely her own envy talking.

Certainly one couldn't envy Leo's childhood. He remembered with piercing clarity the moment his parents first abandoned him, parking him in a hospital bed, waving goodbye, turning, leaving the room. They were leaving forever, he knew. After that they came to visit often, and each time they visited they left, and each leaving, like the one before it, was forever. Skinny little Leo, up to his eyeballs in amputations, would gag on grief and fear and rage.

Anyway there was nothing arrogant about Leo's unalloyed passion for art. Though he schmoozed with New York's *haute monde*, Leo was marked by an unusual absence of greed. He often purchased a work for his personal collection specifically to support some gifted, underrecognized artist; most of his pieces were eventually donated to his own museum or to libraries.

Doing her best to impersonate proud grace, Claire stepped from the bathroom to meet whatever poor slob was being interviewed. (Leo had again invited her to sit in; she hoped she'd missed the dull business part—job description, hours, pay.) Not that Leo grilled his applicants; he gently coaxed them into whatever degree of ease was possible, given the situation. He was, all in all, gracious and kind; but you could reasonably assume that these were desperately unemployed people, otherwise they wouldn't be sitting here, hoping to get a job cooking and cleaning for another human being, bathing and dressing him—Leo had tried prosthetic arms and hated them—working variable hours at low pay and occasionally sleeping over in the spare room whenever his night aide had to cancel.

As Claire approached the living room, she recalled the handful of less conventional respondents who'd phoned after seeing Leo's ad. In an attempt to screen out inappropriate candidates, Leo had engaged them in conversation. Claire remembered three who'd made it past the first cut, all of whom were due to be interviewed: there was the amateur opera singer who'd developed polyps; the Filipino with advanced degrees in history and law who was tired of working for the IRS; the anthropologist on leave who "needed a change of pace" and was "looking for meaningful work." In the split second before making her entrance Claire winced, imagining herself as someone else's "meaningful work." She wondered if Leo reacted similarly to the locution.

Perched on an arm of the stuffed chair by the window, Leo was looking across the living room at Job Candidate Number Six. Claire's eyes followed his line of vision to locate, seated on the sofa, a slender woman in her thirties, her dark hair sleekly gathered at the back of her neck. Though Claire had missed some ten minutes of interview, it seemed clear that Leo's alchemy had not yet succeeded with this applicant, who sat with her legs crossed, hands folded in her lap, still wearing her coat which was long and full, dove-colored, with elaborate shoulder pads. Her expression was one of decorous neutrality.

Having sat in on five of these rituals, Claire had by now observed a certain basic pattern: the interviewees' initial discomfort (with Leo's disability? with his convivial cheer? with Claire's presence?) tended to be ill concealed and blessedly short-lived; Leo's warmth was a foolproof social softener. Though as for that (Claire glanced sidelong at the candidate again), this particular interview—if interview it was—seemed from the start likely to surprise. Perhaps this woman was not applying for a job at all; had Claire gotten Leo's schedule mixed up? Was she a gallery owner? A museum administrator? An artist?

"Claire, meet Natasha!" Leo chimed, and Claire imagined the expansive gesture he'd make, if he had arms. His tone of voice seemed to offer martinis all round, on the house.

Natasha turned her long-stemmed neck in acknowledgment, took in Claire and turned back, continuing to Leo, ". . . but of course it's hard to get funding for that sort of work." She smiled primly.

Leo clucked commiseration, interrupting his own train of thought to offer, as Claire tacked her way toward a chair: "Can we take your coat?"

Confused—who *was* this woman?—obediently taking her cue, Claire changed course, heading for the sofa. "Here, let me get that," she murmured, but Natasha had already slipped the coat off her shoulders and draped it elegantly beside her. Claire couldn't help staring; before recrossing the room toward her chair she turned and saw Leo, his lips parted, examining in silence the stranger who, no longer hidden by her greatcoat, sat revealed, snappily dressed in navy blue, her tailored skirt ridden up above the midpoint of sheer-navy-blue-stockinged long thighs, which were now no longer crossed. For a split second Claire shivered, imagining he was looking at *her*, for his expression was the privatest one in his repertoire. An endless pause filled the room before Leo boomed, "Tell her about the work in Peru!"

Ah, the anthropologist. Claire was attempting to unravel the mystery of her own response to Leo's pronoun, *her*—why did it trip her so, hearing herself thus referred to by Leo?—when Natasha said, smoothly patient despite having to repeat herself, "I do culture conservation." She continued to face Leo; her head did not turn.

"Culture conservation," Claire echoed stupidly.

"I try to document those aspects of a culture that I think are in danger of disappearing, dying out."

Claire felt herself rallying. *Thank God! Good work! Honorable, necessary work. None of the rest of it matters,* she addressed herself—*that glossy dark hair and* your *graying shapeless jumble, those long blue athletic thighs that don't seem to want to stay together and* your *drunken gait, her trim blue linen and* your *nightgown-sized pink T-shirt with the bleach stain on one shoulder, her young sculpted cheekbones and* your *wintry unfocused face—none of these things matter. What matters is, she's doing good work!*

Awash with equal portions of relief and shame, Claire found eager conversation now crowding her tongue. She too had recorded vanishing cultures. . . . She'd mention, when the time was right, the Hopi and Navajo reservation schools where she'd filmed song, dance, and native languages that were already well on their way to extinction. . . . She'd talk about the Indians' struggle to keep those schools open against all odds, and especially she'd tell about the tapes she'd made in South America of fiestas from the Altiplano region—Bolivia, Ecuador, Peru. . . .

Sudden images of Peru bombarded Claire, acutely physical, vividly detailed, prickling her chest: haunting stray melodies on *siku* and *quena*, delicate figurations—like finest lace—of the South American harp, urgent rhythmic brilliance of *charango*, now crafted of wood to spare the armadillo its shell . . . Heavy wet-wool smell of striped brown serapes, couples dancing *marineras* . . . And the haunting *huaynos* . . .

"Leo mentioned your work in Peru—?"

"None of Peru's museums have catalogued their artifacts. I'm documenting and recording them all, which has to be done before they can be catalogued." Natasha was doing this by means of video, a novel approach which she said was quicker and cheaper than more conventional methods. Addressing Leo, she went on to describe the more high-tech aspects of the work in some detail, periodically splashing her no-longer-prim smile across the floor space between stuffed chair and sofa.

"Do you do any culture conservation in the U.S.?" Leo asked, splashing back.

"This is such a *young* country, by European standards I mean. . . . You see my background is Spanish/Russian. . . ." She added this as a generous aside to latecomer Claire, since Leo—beaming and nodding—obviously already knew. "The U.S. is barely two hundred years old! I don't see any cultural artifacts that are in danger of disappearing in a country that young." She paused, glancing long enough in Claire's direction to read, or think she read, what was written there.

"And as for the Native Americans," she continued, "I know them *very well* . . . I *lived with* them. . . . And they made it very clear they don't want any outsiders touching their things." Another brief silence. "Anyway," eyes flickering back in Claire's direction, "I really don't believe they're endangered."

Claire was absorbing the full impact of this statement, wondering if perhaps Leo had already told her something about Claire's work? Was she baiting Claire? Words lined themselves up at the threshold of her teeth, about to tumble out, words which would undoubtedly embarrass Leo, sabotage his interview. Before they could, Leo leapt to the rescue. "Do you enjoy the work in Peru?" (*Whose rescue?* Claire wondered.)

"It's very hard." Natasha shook her head. "I have to live in Lima for months at a time. . . ." She laughed, lifting her hands from her lap in a little it-can't-be-helped gesture, shrugging. "It's very dirty. Let's face it, Lima's not the South of France. It seems"—she paused, gazing directly at her questioner—"I have a taste for the exotic." Her eyes having by now abandoned all pretense of traveling in the direction of the bleach-stained pink T-shirt, Natasha anchored her body firmly on course, blue thighs aimed directly at the stuffed chair by the window. "And I get tired," she added, "of speaking their language all the time."

"Didn't you say you're partly Spanish?" Claire had been on the verge of excusing herself and leaving the room, but a morbid curiosity now held her.

"Yes, Spanish from Spain." Natasha's answer tilted across the room, as if not Claire but Leo had asked the question, as if they were having a private conversation. "Mine is Castilian, The Mother Tongue, *la lengua madre*. It appalls me to hear what passes for Spanish in these Latin American countries. It's embarrassing."

Claire looked across the room at her lover, whose work he himself had once characterized, in an interview, as "a process of honoring and dignifying the vessels—art, language—into which humans pour their deepest, fullest selves." She was watching for his *Let's-leave-this-party, shall-we?* signal. Leo's eyes, in certain situations, could be counted on to lock onto hers across rooms full of people, silently commenting on whatever had just been said or whoever had said it, conveying appreciation, kindly good humor, boredom, a slightly crazed impatience, contempt. . . . The current that rippled from his eyes to hers or hers to his always completed its circuit, its message shared, reciprocal, buzzing back and forth, high voltage. What tended to happen after the initial communication had traveled its arc always came as a surprise to Claire: message number one melted, unbidden, into message number two, as explicit as the first and as mutual: pure lust: *I want you I want you I want you.* The air between them would crackle; later, arriving home, Leo would tear off her blouse with his teeth—Claire racing to unbutton ahead of him— before they'd even reached the bedroom.

She searched now for Leo's eyes but they were elsewhere, pre-occupied; for the very first time since she'd met him six months ago, they didn't return her signal. He seemed oblivious not only to Claire but to his own mouth which—though no one in the room was listening—was speaking words, a river of words, their tone dryly comical: "You know, speaking of the brutalizing of *la lengua madre,* a few years back I was asked by a Spanish curator to loan some paintings to an exhibit being mounted in Madrid. . . ." The imaginary cocktail in his hand had long been drained and refilled and drained again. Leo was tunneling along a muscular blue corridor, warm, sweet-smelling, toward the prize at its end. And nothing mattered, nothing on God's green earth, except that he get there.

The afternoon light seemed to change, deepening, clearing. Graceful, proud Claire (elusive grace, elusive pride) lurched into the bedroom, pulled her well-worn suitcase from the closet, and began to pack.

THEATER

Selected Scenes from: P.H.*reaks: The Hidden History of People with Disabilities

Adapted by Doris Baizley and Victoria Ann-Lewis

from writing by:

ISAAC AGNEW

MARY MARTZ

BEN MATTLIN

PEGGY OLIVERI

STEVE PAILET

VINCE PINTO

JOHN PIXLEY

PAUL RYAN

LESLYE SNEIDER

BILL TRZECIAK

TAMARA TURNER

YOUNG WOMAN IN WHEELCHAIR—Sister Elizabeth—The Half-Lady—Telethon Girl—Beth—Jailed Activist.

YOUNG MAN IN WHEELCHAIR (Speech impaired)—Wild Man—Zoltan the Wild Man—Jailed Activist—Joey.

WOMAN OF SMALL STATURE—Princess Angie.

MAN IN WHEELCHAIR—Andreos the Legless Wonder—Telethon Star—Jailed Activist.

OLDER MAN—Father John—The Talker—Telethon Development Person—Doctor—Matisse—FDR's Old Bodyguard—Unemployment Clerk.

YOUNGER MAN—Joshua—Louis-Michel—Old Bodyguard—Joey's Attendant.

WOMAN—Woman Doctor—FDR's New Bodyguard—New Guy—Attendant.

Company plays various other voices, HEW and WPA demonstrators and hecklers.

NOTE:

The first four roles must be played by actors with disabilities.

In the initial presentations of *P.H.*reaks*, WOMAN IN WHEELCHAIR was a quadriplegic, MAN IN WHEELCHAIR a paraplegic and YOUNG MAN IN WHEELCHAIR had cerebral palsy with speech impairment. While innovative casting is encouraged, the script will resist too much variation from these descriptions. In addition, YOUNG MAN IN WHEELCHAIR used a variety of mobility aids: a sports wheelchair, crutches, and a cart on wheels for Andreos.

1. MAGIC.

The Saint. Slide: A stained glass window. In a side chapel of a medieval cathedral. SISTER ELIZABETH *(WOMAN IN WHEELCHAIR) sits behind a bank of candles. She wears flowing white robes. A brass bowl of coins is on the floor.*

ELIZABETH: Come, come here. Touch me. Look in my eyes. I can see you. I know you. Your sufferings, your hopes, your fears. I know your longings.

Sound: Shouting mob, barking dogs, cathedral doors slamming shut.

WILD MAN *(YOUNG MAN IN WHEELCHAIR) enters, roaring. He wears beggar's rags and a wild wig. His speech is difficult to decipher.*

ELIZABETH: Yes?

WILD MAN *circles her, screaming.*

ELIZABETH: What is it? What dogs of hell are trapped in your body? Come . . . light a candle. Drop a coin in the bowl. I can help you.

WILD MAN *blows out the candles.*

ELIZABETH: Stop. No. These are God's candles. These are the hopes and fears of human souls.

WILD MAN *blows out more candles. Overturns the bowl of money.*

ELIZABETH: You want the money? Go ahead. I don't need the money. You want to touch me, don't you? (WILD MAN *looks at her, calm now.*) Come here. Light a candle—one candle and the Light will come to you . . . and you will know comfort and peace . . . Just light the candle.

WILD MAN *tries to light a candle.*

ELIZABETH: Light it. Go ahead. That's it. Can you light the candle? Good. Light it. Light the candle . . .

He struggles with the candle.

ELIZABETH: LIGHT THE FUCKING CANDLE!

WILD MAN *backs away from her. She rings bell.* FATHER JOHN *enters.*

FATHER JOHN: Back to the streets, you monster. Filthy thing. You dirty this place.

As WILD MAN *goes out,* FATHER JOHN *points after him.*

FATHER JOHN: These are the same devils that roar in the deaf man's ears so he cannot hear the words of Light. These are the same darknesses that curl inside the hunchback's burden. Have you not smelled the sulphur as these monsters pass?

Slides: Old woodcuts of ancient gods, acts of bestiality; satyrs, fauns, and devils.

FATHER JOHN: The devil still comes to tempt. Some weak souls fall. Pretending to sleep, they invite Lucifer himself into their beds and find him beautiful. But when the woman sees the repulsive issue of that union, when the monster claws out between her legs, she is grateful for the kindness that ties her filthy body to the stake and burns it clean.

Slides: Giants, dwarves, gnomes, mermaids, and hunchbacks, including Danny De Vito as the Penguin in Batman.

Slide: Penguin being thrown to his death.

FATHER JOHN: Beware careless souls: mark the devil's easy entry into the world. This is why our earthly kings protect monsters at their feet.

*Slide: Court dwarfs, 17th century changes to modern freak shows.
Sound: 17th-century court music changes to sideshow music.*

On stage: LITTLE PRINCESS ANGIE, *THE FREAK SHOW PER-
FORMER, enters.* FATHER JOHN *removes his habit to become the
freak show talker, wearing a sweat-stained, wrinkled jacket and old
straw hat.*

TALKER: Oh yeah. Let's give a big hand to Little Princess Angie.
Highest paid little lady on the midway. Just a sample of what we
got here . . . Come and see 'em folks, come on and see. Strangest
human beings in the world today. We got 'em all here. And
they're all alive. Keep your eyes up here—and we'll bring 'em out
to give you a sample. No laughter or rude remarks. Try not to be
shocked at what—here they come—here they come now—

ELIZABETH, ANDREOS, *and* WILD MAN *enter, wearing faded,
turn of the century circus garb. They line up next to* ANGIE *as*
TALKER *continues:*

TALKER: Here's Elizabeth—America's Only Living Half-Lady. Can't
use her arms can't use her legs. Why? Only God knows, folks. She
was born that way . . . Next you have Andreos the Legless Acrobat.
How does he do it? Come and see. Come and see—and Special
tonight—we've got Zoltan the Wild Man, Half-Man Half-Beast.

WILD MAN *starts grumbling.*

TALKER: Hear those sounds? That's animal language. That's right.
Don't be scared. That's animal talk—straight outta the jungle—

WILD MAN: I said—When's lunch???

TALKER: BACK, WILD MAN! BACK! You'll get your live chickens
later. (*To audience.*) Two dollars extra to see him at feeding time.
No pregnant women or children under twelve allowed. Come and
see 'em. We got 'em all here . . .

WILD MAN *starts to chase him.*

ANDREOS: Hey!

TALKER: Ladies and Gentlemen—Before your very eyes—Mighty
Andreos! The World's 8th Wonder and Greatest Legless Acrobat—Captured by pirates in the Gulf of Persia, thrown into
the shark-infested Caribbean and raised by reptiles in the

Everglades—you've read his inspiring True Life Story, now see the Human Wonder Himself . . .

ANDREOS *performs an acrobatic trick.*

ANDREOS: Hey!

TALKER: Just a sample of what we've got here. Ask questions. Go ahead. Look as long as you want. Ask about anything. Let your mind wander. Don't feel guilty. You paid for the privilege. Wanna peek backstage for a closer look . . . ?

Lights change to:

Backstage. ANGIE *in bathrobe, taking off makeup.* JOSHUA *enters, holding a bottle of bourbon.*

JOSHUA: Angie . . . Angie . . . ?

ANGIE: Who's there?

JOSHUA: It's me, Joshua. Haven't you seen me around? I've been here every night this week. (*Holds up the bottle.*) I thought you might like to have a drink with me.

ANGIE: Looks like you've had a few without me.

JOSHUA: Yeah, I guess I have. I've been waiting awhile. It's good stuff, my grandpa made it. Here, try some. (*Trips and falls, holding the bottle upright.*) Didn't spill a drop. Maybe you could use me in the show.

ANGIE: We're all pros here. You're out of your league.

JOSHUA: I'm a professional too.

ANGIE: Yeah, what do you do?

JOSHUA: I'm a doctor.

ANGIE: I haven't met many doctors who operate out of a bottle. Where's your little black bag?

JOSHUA: I left it in my office. This wasn't an official visit.

ANGIE: So you've been coming around every day since we opened. Why?

JOSHUA: Curious, just like everyone else I guess.

ANGIE: Curious people come once and then talk about us for a month at dinner. You've got other reasons. Talk.

JOSHUA: Sure, I've got more than a passing interest. I'm interested for medical reasons—what can be done to help prevent or cure these sorts of things.

ANGIE: You gonna put me on a rack and stretch me?

JOSHUA: Sure, after I soak you in alcohol to loosen you up.

ANGIE: (*Taking the bottle.*) So that's what this is for?

JOSHUA: Just to loosen your tongue for now.

ANGIE: What do you want to know?

JOSHUA: Why you put yourself on display, allow yourself to be exploited like this?

ANGIE: I don't believe it, another bleeding heart idiot. I was just starting to like you, too. Maybe you should go.

JOSHUA: I'm sorry if I offended you. Maybe I'm just a stupid hick from a small town, but I really don't understand.

ANGIE: Listen, smart boy, it's easy—we're always on display. You think that if I walked down the street of your stinking little nowhere town people wouldn't stare at me? Damn right they would, and tell their neighbors and friends and talk about me over dinners and picnics and PTA meetings. Well, if they want to do that, they're going have to pay me for that privilege. You want to stare at me, fine, it's twenty-five cents, cash on the barrel. You want a picture, that's another quarter. My life story? Pay me. You think I'm being exploited? You pay to go to a baseball game, don't you? What's the difference if you watch some big oaf hitting a ball with a stick or me pretending to be a princess?

JOSHUA: You mean you're not?

Pause. They both burst out laughing. He leans over and kisses her.

ANGIE: You always get fresh with your medical specimens?

JOSHUA: You're not just any specimen.

He leans over to kiss her again. She ducks away.

ANGIE: You know, you're a pretty interesting specimen, too. Mind if I examine you?

JOSHUA: Go right ahead.

ANGIE: Stand up. Close your eyes.

He complies and she kicks him in the shins.

JOSHUA: Ow!

ANGIE: Just checking your reflexes. Now close your eyes again. Don't worry, I'm not going to kick you. (*Takes a pin out of her hair and starts poking him in the legs and buttocks.*) Can you feel this? How about this? Stand still, this is important. Does this feel sharp?

JOSHUA: Yes, yes, ow, that's enough!

ANGIE: Not so much fun being on the receiving end is it?

JOSHUA: No, I guess not.

ANGIE: Come over here, I'm not finished yet.

JOSHUA: I think I am.

ANGIE: Oh, don't be such a baby. I won't hurt you anymore, I promise. Come over and sit down. Please. (*Rubbing his shoulders and neck.*) Just relax, there, isn't that better?

JOSHUA: Yes, much better.

ANGIE: You're a fascinating case, I want to examine you further . . . Don't worry, no more tricks. Here, have some medicine.

She tips the bottle to his mouth. She slowly unbuttons his shirt. He tries to reach for her but she pushes his hands down.

ANGIE: Uh-uh. I'm the doctor. I'll do the examining. I think you need more anesthesia.

She tips the bottle to his mouth. She puts her arms around him from behind and starts rubbing his chest.

ANGIE: Oh yes . . . This is more serious than I thought . . .

She has him mesmerized. She reaches down and slips his wallet out of his pocket.

ANGIE: Yes, I'm afraid it's hopeless.

She gives him a long kiss, then runs off. He lies there for a second, then sits up, sees she's gone, and exits.

Slide: Telethon—rehearsal.

YOUNG WOMAN IN WHEELCHAIR *enters with* TELETHON DEVELOPMENT PERSON *(the TALKER, still in a sweaty jacket, now he's wearing a headset).*

DEVELOPMENT/TALKER: He's gonna love this. A few little touches and you're done.

He puts a bow in the woman's hair. The TELETHON STAR *(MAN IN WHEELCHAIR) enters.*

DEVELOPMENT/TALKER: OK. It'll begin something like this—music starts, then lights come up on the girl—

STAR: On *me* and the girl.

DEVELOPMENT/TALKER: Exactly. Then you say—

YOUNG WOMAN *starts to speak.*

DEVELOPMENT/TALKER: Not you. He says . . . "Look at this, folks. *Can* you look at this. . . . ?"

He points to YOUNG WOMAN IN WHEELCHAIR.

DEVELOPMENT/TALKER: "Imagine what their daughter's disease has done to a wonderful, happy family. Please. Don't let this happen to any more children—"

STAR: Where's the family?

DEVELOPMENT/TALKER: What?

STAR: HER FAMILY! Mother. Father. You know. A nice-looking normal mom and dad standing there crying, "How could this happen to people like us???" She can't just sit there looking like she got here on her own.

YOUNG WOMAN *starts to speak again but—*

DEVELOPMENT/TALKER: She did. She flew out here yesterday—

STAR: She doesn't even look like a kid.

DEVELOPMENT/TALKER: Well . . . she's not actually—

STAR: I WANT A FAMILY. GET A FAMILY HERE NOW!!!

DEVELOPMENT/TALKER: They're in Cincinnati. That could get expensive. We've got a budget.

STAR: A family or you're fired.

> STAR *and* DEVELOPMENT *exit.* WOMAN DOCTOR *enters and puts a hospital gown on the* YOUNG WOMAN IN WHEELCHAIR.

WOMAN DOCTOR: You'll be in Examination Room 115.

> WILD MAN *comes through with newspaper.*

WILD MAN: ANGIE! Angie? Did you read this?

> ANGIE *enters.*

ANGIE: Did I read what?

> *Slide: Sad news for circus freaks—no more human wonders for the big show this year.*

WOMAN DOCTOR: (*To WOMAN IN WHEELCHAIR.*) The nurse will help you take off all your clothes, and leave the gown open in front.

ANGIE: Oh my god—Andreos!

2. MEDICINE.

Hospital sounds. Slide: Hospital examination lights. YOUNG WOMAN IN WHEELCHAIR *moves to center spotlight.*

Split scene: Freaks remain onstage reading from an old newspaper.

WOMAN DOCTOR: Lie on the table, please.

ANDREOS: "The Hall of Human Curiosities has been canceled from the Ringling Brothers circuit indefinitely."

WOMAN DOCTOR: I'm just going to measure you now.

ANDREOS: "The cruel exhibition of these poor unfortunates is distasteful to an increasingly refined and educated public."

WOMAN DOCTOR: OK. Good. Now turn over.

ANDREOS: "Most of these individuals, whose sole means of livelihood is the exhibition of their physical infirmities to a gaping crowd, are pathological rarities: The Giant presents a severe case of acromegaly. The Half-Lady—Quadriplegia. The Princess Angie—acromisomilia. The Wild Man—cerebral palsy."

WILD MAN: Fuck 'em.

WOMAN DOCTOR: Try not to move please! Let's get rid of this gown.

ANDREOS: Bastards!

WOMAN DOCTOR: OK. That's better. Hmmm.

ANDREOS: They didn't even mention me.

WOMAN DOCTOR: Good. Now. I'm just going to ask in a few of my colleagues to observe here.

MAN DOCTOR *enters (TALKER in sweaty jacket, with stethoscope and an examining light on his forehead).*

WOMAN DOCTOR: OK, this is what I told you about. Interesting isn't it? It's three quarters of an inch.

DOCTOR/TALKER: I'd say half an inch.

WOMAN DOCTOR: Measure, you'll see.

DOCTOR/TALKER: You're right. Just like that case in Detroit.

WOMAN DOCTOR: Yes, but here it's more severe.

DOCTOR/TALKER: But the muscle tone is better.

WOMAN DOCTOR: OK, turn over. Now, you see?

DOCTOR/TALKER: Yes, it's clearer from the front. What is this, a tenodesis?

WOMAN DOCTOR: Yes, two years ago.

DOCTOR/TALKER: Not bad. Graft?

WOMAN DOCTOR: No, repair.

DOCTOR/TALKER: And now.

WOMAN DOCTOR: I think a laminectomy.

DOCTOR/TALKER: Fenestration?

WOMAN DOCTOR: No, decompression. OK, turn again, please. Good.

DOCTOR/TALKER: Interesting.

WOMAN DOCTOR: You can see it better here.

DOCTOR/TALKER: Like the case in Detroit.

WOMAN DOCTOR: More severe.

DOCTOR/TALKER: But the muscle tone is better.

BOTH DOCTORS: Good.

DOCTOR/TALKER: Thank you.

WOMAN DOCTOR: That will be all.

DOCTORS *exit.*

ANDREOS: "Curiosities they may be. What they are more certainly is sick."

DOCTOR'S VOICE (*Offstage.*) You may get dressed now.

BETH *exits as we see:*

Slide: 1911—City of Chicago Ordinance prohibits any person who is diseased, maimed, mutilated or deformed in any way so as to be an unsightly or disgusting object from exposing himself to public view.

ANDREOS *exits.*

Slide: 1919—Wisconsin school board expels an eleven-year-old boy with cerebral palsy because his teachers and other students find him depressing and nauseating. The Wisconsin Supreme Court upholds the expulsion.

WILD MAN *exits.*

Slide: 1927—The U.S. Supreme Court upholds state sterilization laws "to prevent those who are manifestly unfit from continuing their kind."

ANGIE *exits. Lights change to:*

Slides of Franklin D. Roosevelt: At the wheel of his car, at the tiller of his sailboat, standing at a podium. Sound: One of FDR's fireside chats on the radio.

FDR'S VOICE: I speak therefore tonight to and of the American people as a whole. My most immediate concern is in carrying out the purposes of the Great Work Program just enacted by Congress. Its first objective is to put men and women, now on the relief rolls, to work . . .

The White House. A life-sized dummy sits in the wheelchair. NEW GUY (WOMAN) does jumping jacks as OLD GUY (YOUNG MAN) takes notes on a clipboard.

NEW: Seventy-three—four—five—

OLD: Your dad got hurt in a crash or something right?

NEW: (*As he jumps.*) Yessir. He got crippled in a combine accident. Seventy-eight—nine—eighty. (*Stops jumping.*) There.

OLD: Give me ten more.

NEW GUY *starts more jumping jacks.*

OLD: Used a wheelchair?

NEW: Huh?

OLD: Your father.

NEW: Yeah.

OLD: You helped him get up and around and all?

NEW: Yes sir. (*Finishes jumping jacks.*) OK, what now?

OLD: (*Checking clipboard.*) Says here you're left-handed.

NEW: That's right. What gives? Why all this?

OLD: Security. You're replacing the President's right-hand man. We lost our right-hand man in the incident. We need a strong left-hander.

NEW: Right. So when do we go to the firing range?

OLD: After the wheelchair.

NEW: The wheelchair???

OLD: OK, you got clearance. Guess it's OK to tell you. (*Pause, confidential.*) There's a lot more about being FDR's bodyguard than providing security . . .

NEW: OK . . .

OLD: You know the President got polio.

NEW: Right. So?

OLD: I mean—he *really got polio.*

NEW: So what? He never lets it get him down.

OLD: Well, it got him down more than anyone knows. Crippled him up considerably.

NEW: You're sayin' the President's *a cripple?*

OLD: I'm not sayin' he *is* a cripple, it just affected his body.

NEW: Whatta you mean? Either he is or ain't a cripple—

OLD: OK, it's this way. What do you think when you see someone with polio?

NEW: I dunno.

OLD: Well, you never admired 'em, did you?

NEW: No—I feel sorry for them.

OLD: Now how about the President? Feel sorry for him, do you?

NEW: No sir.

OLD: Right. Probably admire him too. Probably wouldn't mind being more like him either.

NEW: I never thought of him as a cripple.

OLD: Now you got it! We go to a lot of trouble to see that no one does. Now we do the stand and walk.

He goes to the dummy in the wheelchair.

OLD: You take the right side I take the left. Get him up and out of the chair. (*As NEW GUY lifts dummy.*) NOT LIKE THAT! You look like you're lifting.

NEW: You said get him up—

OLD: But you can't look like it. You're just a guy talking to him, see? You bend down. Look like you're whispering something in his ear. You take his right elbow. Weight on your left arm. Slowly rise. He'll be with you. (*As they stand the dummy upright.*) Don't lift— just support. He's got great upper body strength. That's it. Stay in close for the walk. (*As they walk the dummy.*) Keep the conversation going. Blah blah blah—up to the podium. Blah blah blah —away from the podium.

NEW: I don't believe it. I'da sworn I seen him walk in the newsreels.

OLD: All part of our job. Around here we perform magic. He's only as helpless as people think he is.

NEW: Press much of a problem?

OLD: Nah. Occasional new guy. Rule is: no pictures of him in the chair or below the waist. And never of him being helped. By anyone. Be nice but firm.

NEW: And if they persist?

OLD: (*Dropping the dummy back in the chair.*) I make sure they don't.

NEW: So—are you gonna tell me? About the "incident." Was it really an assassination attempt?

OLD: So they're buying it, huh? That's good.

NEW: What really happened? How come I'm replacing the other guy?

OLD: It was a fund-raising dinner at the Mayflower. Joe and I were walking him out the side door when we run into the DuPonts. The President tells us to leave him on his crutches while he talks. Then outta nowhere comes this bellhop walking six or seven dogs on their nightly constitutional. There we are—dogs milling everywhere. I'm thinking any minute one of these mutts is gonna cut a crutch out from under him. They finally move on. He's finished talking and we head for the car. Then I spot it . . . a steaming pile of dog shit near FDR's left crutch tip. He don't see it, plants his crutch and turns. He slips—but before he can fall, Joe lunges under him yelling: "HEY—OUT THERE! HE'S GOT A GUN!" As everybody looks out, Joe falls onto the dog pile, passes me the crutch, and I prop the Prez back up. Joe threw his back out. Not to mention the mess with the suit. He won't be back on the job for a while.

NEW: What a yarn. Wait'll Sally hears about this—

OLD: Hey. That's classified. (*Pause, listens to radio.*) OK. He's almost finished. We'll walk him out after the radio crew leaves. Oh yeah. Keep this with you at all times. (*Hands NEW GUY a small can and brush.*) Black paint for his braces and crutches. Can't have them drawing attention in the photographs. Come on. It's time for you to meet the President of the United States.

They exit.

FDR's VOICE: We have, in the darkest moments of our national trial, retained our faith in our own ability to master our own destiny. Fear is vanishing. Confidence is growing.

Slide: Unemployment office. TALKER *enters as* CLERK *in glasses and wig. Freaks enter as applicants.*

CLERK/TALKER: May I help you?

ELIZABETH: Yes, we're here to get jobs.

CLERK/TALKER: Name please.

ELIZABETH: I'm the Half-Lady.

CLERK/TALKER: Name?

ELIZABETH: I'm Elizabeth America's Only Living Half-Lady and this is Princess Angelica—

CLERK/TALKER: I said *name*!!!

ANGIE: Sure, how many you want? Countess Angela, Queen Angelina, Empress Angelissima—

ANDREOS: Andreos the Legless Wonder.

ELIZABETH: And this is Zoltan the Wild Man—

WILD MAN: Joey—

CLERK/TALKER: I beg your pardon?

WILD MAN: My name is Joey.

CLERK/TALKER: Would somebody tell him, I ASKED FOR YOUR *NAMES.*

ELIZABETH: He heard you.

WILD MAN: My name is Joey.

CLERK/TALKER: Back in line please. Let's try that again. Your names as they appear on your birth certificates.

ELIZABETH: My mother burned mine.

ANDREOS: I was raised by reptiles in the Everglades.

ANGIE: You can read about me all the way back to my great great great—ask Will—he's got it all written down.

WILD MAN: My name is—

ANDREOS: Forget it, Joey. You're better off as the wild man.

CLERK/TALKER: We will have to have some official identification before we can process you.

WILD MAN *lunges at the* CLERK/TALKER.

CLERK/TALKER: Now—job desired . . .

ANGIE: What's wrong with my old job???

ELIZABETH: I'll take whatever pays the rent.

ANDREOS: What have you got for a Wonder?

CLERK/TALKER: Before we go any further with this, you're all going to have to have a complete physical examination. Medical history and description . . .

ELIZABETH: Spinal cord injury, C5–6. Quadriplegia.

ANGIE: Acromisomilia dysplasia.

ANDREOS: Spinal cord injury. T12–21. Partial paraplegia. Hey!

WILD MAN: What about jobs???

CLERK/TALKER: Oh, that's a shame.

ELIZABETH: He said what about jobs?

CLERK/TALKER: Restricted activities?

ANDREOS: I use this board—I've also got crutches—

CLERK/TALKER: So that would mean limited ambulation?

ANDREOS: I'll get to work on time, if that's your question.

CLERK/TALKER: Do you require any assistance in your daily living?

ELIZABETH: Hold on a minute. This isn't anybody's business. We're here to find jobs.

ANGIE: Yeah. When do we hear about our jobs?

CLERK/TALKER: Classification: P.H. Physically Handicapped. Substandard Unemployable. Your relief checks will be mailed to your home or institutional addresses.

Blackout.

3. MOVEMENT.

Slides: 1936 Headlines and photos of the League of the Physically Handicapped picketing in Washington, D.C. Company enters in 1930s street clothes.

TALKER: Now ladies and gentlemen, I will show you something so astounding you'll wonder how it ever came to pass—in 1936, in Washington, D.C., these odd remnants of human miscellanea lumbered out onto public streets and uttered their strange, chilling cry—

VOICES: WE WANT JOBS—NOT TIN CUPS! WE WANT JOBS— NOT TIN CUPS!

TALKER (*on tape*): Ladies and gentlemen, look if you dare at the ragtag battalion of despair—the League of the Physically Handicapped.

DEMONSTRATORS: We want jobs! Not tin cups!

DEMONSTRATOR: The WPA promised jobs for everybody! Why not us?

DEMONSTRATOR: P.H. doesn't stand for Put at Bottom of Stack.

DEMONSTRATOR: We won't leave Washington till we talk to Harry Hopkins.

DEMONSTRATOR: We demand satisfaction from the WPA.

DEMONSTRATOR: We'll stay in the street, we'll sleep in his office if we have to!

DEMONSTRATOR: We don't need relief, we're trained to work. WE WANT JOBS!

HECKLER: Communist Cripples!

HECKLER: Freaks!

HECKLER: You oughtta be ashamed—

HECKLER: Using your crutches to get sympathy.

HECKLER: Shame!

DEMONSTRATOR: We don't want sympathy—we want jobs!

DEMONSTRATOR: A group of us went to the Commissioner in charge of the Civil Service examinations. He told us one of his reasons for keeping us out of civil service was that he disliked the sight of an employee who limped through the halls.

HECKLERS: Freaks!

HECKLER: They oughtta string up the whole bunch on telegraph poles.

HECKLERS: Shame!

DEMONSTRATOR: You think they put P.H. on Mr. Roosevelt's job file? You think they made him take a physical exam?

HECKLERS: TWISTED BODIES—TWISTED MINDS!

Pause. DEMONSTRATORS *freeze, facing the audience.*

DEMONSTRATOR: Go ahead and stare. We're staring back.

Lights fade on them.

TALKER *brings on an antique wheelchair.*

TALKER: Fame, fortune, beauty, talent—the grace of God—the hand of fate or a good doctor? What fine line separates us from them, my friends? Witness the heartbreaking story of Henri M . . .

Slide: MATISSE *in wheelchair (1940s).*

TALKER: A brilliant artist—at the height of his career—on intimate terms with the Muse herself—struck down to the basest level of human capacity—from the Olympian heights of productive imagination—to this—

TALKER *collapses into the chair to become* MATISSE *as he is joined by his assistant,* LOUIS-MICHEL.

LOUIS-MICHEL: M. Matisse, is this the right color? (*MATISSE nods*) I'm finished with the blues. Do you want me to start on the reds?

MATISSE/TALKER: I have a piece for the cut-out. Place it like this, below the oval. This is her torso.

Split scene: An ATTENDANT *joins the* YOUNG WOMAN IN WHEELCHAIR.

YOUNG WOMAN IN WHEELCHAIR: Well, are you ready to start?

ATTENDANT: Yes. OK, I turn on the water while it is warming up, rinse out your cup, put toothpaste on the toothbrush, and then fill your cup up with warm water.

YOUNG WOMAN: Great. OK give me the roll of toilet paper. No, don't unroll it. I'll do it myself.

ATTENDANT: I'm sorry. I can pull some off for you. I think I can handle that.

YOUNG WOMAN: I know. But if I do it, then I can fold it the way it's easiest for me.

ATTENDANT: Now what?

YOUNG WOMAN: Vitamins—and then go fix the bed.

LOUIS-MICHEL: I am so amazed by the difference in style between your paintings and these cut-outs. Is there a reason for your change?

MATISSE/TALKER: The scissors, please, Louis-Michel.

ATTENDANT: Are you sure you don't want me to brush your teeth for you?

YOUNG WOMAN: No thanks.

LOUIS-MICHEL: Let me help. If you draw your shapes on the paper, I'll cut them out for you. Then you won't need to hold the heavy scissors.

MATISSE/TALKER: Louis-Michel, give me back the scissors.

LOUIS-MICHEL: I was only trying to help. I want to save your energy.

MATISSE/TALKER: Yes, that is most understandable. Take the shape and place it on the cut-out.

ATTENDANT: I happened to see you brushing your teeth and it looked so difficult and uncomfortable. That's what I'm here for—to help you with anything you can't do.

YOUNG WOMAN: Oh. Well. Thank you. But I can brush my teeth. I just don't do it the same way you do.

ATTENDANT: OK. There are your vitamins. Now your pajama top?

YOUNG WOMAN: Yes. Pull my shirt up in the back and then over my elbow.

MATISSE/TALKER: Move it a little to the right . . . No. That's a little too far . . . Back to the left a little . . .

YOUNG WOMAN: No—wait—just over my elbow. I'll get the rest.

LOUIS-MICHEL: That's just where I had it.

MATISSE/TALKER: More to the right . . . Tip the bottom to the right a little bit.

LOUIS-MICHEL: It doesn't look any different from the way I first had it.

MATISSE/TALKER: It is different. Where you have it now is fine. Please come and get these pieces.

ATTENDANT: I didn't mean to offend you.

YOUNG WOMAN: That's OK. Now let me pull my shirt over my head myself. I will completely take it off and then put it on the bed.

LOUIS-MICHEL: Here, let me clean up the scraps around your chair. This mess must bother you.

MATISSE/TALKER: No, don't touch them. I will tell you when I want my papers cleaned up.

LOUIS-MICHEL: Ahh. Forgive me . . .

ATTENDANT: My grandpa—

YOUNG WOMAN: Now open up my pajama top—

ATTENDANT: He feels sorry for you people.

YOUNG WOMAN: I will slide my arms in—

ATTENDANT: He says he can't understand how you do it—

YOUNG WOMAN: And pull it over my head myself—

ATTENDANT: Having people dress you, feed you—

YOUNG WOMAN: Pull it down in the back—

ATTENDANT: Helping you go to the bathroom . . .

YOUNG WOMAN: You can put the shirt in the dirty clothes.

ATTENDANT: What a struggle to live.

MATISSE/TALKER: When I cut into a color, it has a certain effect on me. A certain blue enters my soul; a certain red affects my blood pressure and another color wakes me up. I do not cut the oranges and reds the same way I cut the greens and blues. Here, this is ready. Place it above the torso so it looks as if soon it will touch but for now it floats.

YOUNG WOMAN: My wrist bands go in the middle drawer on the right.

LOUIS-MICHEL: How's that?

MATISSE/TALKER: No. That's not it. That's a collision. Much higher and on a slight diagonal. No, higher. (*Beat.*) Not on the ceiling!

ATTENDANT: He says if it was him—

YOUNG WOMAN: I need some lotion.

ATTENDANT: He couldn't do it.

YOUNG WOMAN: Squirt one drop on my palm. I'll rub it in myself.

ATTENDANT: He says he'd want to kill himself.

YOUNG WOMAN: OK, we're ready to transfer. Slide one arm underneath my knees to your elbow, push against the cushion with your other hand. Now pull me out a little—

LOUIS-MICHEL: Is this how you want it? . . . Am I doing it right? . . . Is this EXACTLY how you want it?

ATTENDANT: How is this?

MATISSE/TALKER: That is fine.

YOUNG WOMAN: Good.

LOUIS-MICHEL: Are you sure?

MATISSE/TALKER: Fine.

YOUNG WOMAN: Sit me up.

MATISSE/TALKER: Only a few more pieces are needed.

YOUNG WOMAN: Grip one arm around my lower back and cup your other hand underneath my butt. Use your knees and stand up. (*A beat.*) Whoa—whoa! Wait—wait—we need to stand and wait so the spasms don't throw us off—and so I can have weight bearing on my legs.

ATTENDANT: The physical therapist I worked for said it's bad to do that because your legs are so brittle and I shouldn't take the chance of breaking them.

YOUNG WOMAN: It's called osteoporosis. It will get worse if I can't get weight bearing and then you *will* break my leg. Ask *my* therapist.

LOUIS-MICHEL: M. Matisse . . . this work is so tranquil . . . Why don't we try more tension?

ATTENDANT: You're telling me to throw my knowledge out the door?

MATISSE/TALKER: There are sufficient bothersome things in the world. I do not wish to add to them. I want my art to be like a good armchair.

LOUIS-MICHEL: An armchair?

YOUNG WOMAN: Now we need to swing my legs onto the bed. Support under my knees and ankles please.

MATISSE/TALKER: A place to rest from physical fatigue.

LOUIS-MICHEL: But Monsieur Matisse, truly great work must be dangerous, disturbing.

ATTENDANT: You are so stubborn. Why can't you take any suggestions?

MATISSE/TALKER: Louis-Michel, I need your help because I can no longer stand, but my art must still be my creation.

YOUNG WOMAN: I'm not stubborn. I've been in a chair twelve years. I've learned what works best for me.

LOUIS-MICHEL: Why have you never done a piece about your illness, your pain? We could create one. That would be a great work.

MATISSE/TALKER: To express my pain for others to see? . . . No . . . That is not my art. My art is light. It is open, free, bright. Pain is heavy, like a blanket of dark lead. It has taken away my freedom, robbed me of vitality. But I will not let it rob me of my creativity.

YOUNG WOMAN: And as far as your grandpa is concerned, I think I have a pretty incredible life.

MATISSE/TALKER: I have created a little garden on the wall around my bed, where I can walk. In this garden I have put familiar things: leaves, fruit, a bird, a nude figure. Surrounded by my cut-outs I am never alone.

YOUNG WOMAN: I like my adventures. I have plenty to live for. It's too bad your grandpa would want to kill himself. I feel sorry for him.

MATISSE/TALKER: Take this. Above the blue and a little to the left. And swivel it to the right. Back a fraction. Fine. Good.

ATTENDANT: OK, I think that's it for tonight.

LOUIS-MICHEL: Is this piece finished . . . Is it finally finished?

YOUNG WOMAN: Thanks. See you tomorrow.

MATISSE/TALKER: Ah, Louis-Michel, you are so young. One has only one life, and one is never finished.

Slide of MATISSE *cut-out. Then black.*

Slides: 1970s demonstrations. Sit-in at the Health, Education, and Welfare Federal Building in San Francisco. COMPANY *enters as 1970s* DEMONSTRATORS.

DEMONSTRATOR: These are the facts. In 1972 Congress passed the Rehabilitation Act which was our first civil rights act. By 1977 the regulations were drawn up, but HEW chairman Califano still hadn't signed them. April 4 was our deadline. When nothing happened, we moved into ten federal buildings across the U.S. In most places the sit-ins lasted only a few hours, but in San Francisco we stayed for—28 days!

DEMONSTRATOR: Nobody expected it to last that long. I mean some of us had sleeping bags—but even that wasn't official because we couldn't let anyone know we were planning to stay. But 28 days!

DEMONSTRATOR: I'd wake up on the floor—me who *had* to use a hospital bed at home—I'd wake up on this skimpy mattress on the floor with my two cups of coffee in front of my nose. And then my attendant would move on to help four other people. Everyone was acting as an attendant—sign language interpreters—deaf people—blind people.

DEMONSTRATOR: I'd never felt so safe and powerful in my life. It was so—well—PEOPLE FELL IN LOVE. I'm not kidding. I could name quite a few couples who met there.

DEMONSTRATOR: Some of them are still together.

DEMONSTRATOR: I hated being dirty. There was no shower. Toward the end Mayor Moscone sent in a portable shower gizmo—the joy of it!

DEMONSTRATOR: The bathrooms weren't accessible. It took great ingenuity to go to the john. There were long lines for the one stall we had removed the door from.

DEMONSTRATOR: And no privacy. People would be lying a foot away from you, naked, getting a sponge bath, but nobody cared.

DEMONSTRATOR: Lining up with our dimes to use the one accessible phone—nobody cared.

DEMONSTRATOR: There were 200 of us and we were there for ourselves and about 35 million other disabled people—

DEMONSTRATOR: —and that's not an exaggeration.

DEMONSTRATOR: For many of us it was, and is, the most important thing we'd ever done with our lives. I mean so much so, that our final political crisis after we won was that a whole group refused to leave the building. They didn't want to go back to the real world even if there were regs now.

DEMONSTRATOR: We fiddled with the media, told them we had to clean up the building like the good citizens we were—

DEMONSTRATOR: And gently we coaxed our comrades through the doors with us . . . and out to the waiting crowd.

Slide: DEMONSTRATORS *leaving building.*

Lights change to:

Jail. JOEY *(YOUNG MAN IN WHEELCHAIR) and* MAN IN WHEELCHAIR *behind bars, wearing a placard: Free our people! Down with nursing homes!*

MAN IN WHEELCHAIR: Since 1983 Joey and I—between the two of us—have been arrested 43 times doing civil disobedience for disability rights. Joey lived in a nursing home for the first 25 years of his life. He had to sue the state to get out. The only difference between a jail and a nursing home is the color of the uniform. They use a night-stick in jail, medication in a nursing home.

He exits. BETH *(WOMAN IN WHEELCHAIR) enters, moves to* JOEY.

Slide: A motel. A rumpled motel bed. An ATTENDANT *helps* JOEY *into bed, next to* BETH. *(Scene can be played in chairs.)*

ATTENDANT: OK, let's go . . . easy . . . relax . . . easy does it . . . Oh sure, like now is the time to relax.

JOEY *begins to laugh.*

ATTENDANT: God, you would have to laugh now. Get those spasms going, that's the last thing we need now . . . we have to work on our foreplay—

BETH: You shut up about foreplay!

JOEY: Foreplay? You ain't seen nothing yet!

ATTENDANT: Yeah-buddy! You tell her she ain't seen nothing yet. That's my bud! Go for it!

BETH: You guys shut up—both of you!

ATTENDANT: OK, if you two are all set . . . Shelley or I'll be right outside so just call if—you know, you need something.

BETH: Sure. Thanks.

JOEY: Yeah. Hey, thanks a lot, Mike.

ATTENDANT: Sure thing. I'll leave you two . . . have at it!

JOEY: fuck off, Mike!

ATTENDANT: What?

BETH: He said fuck off, Mike. He'll see you later.

ATTENDANT: (*as he exits*) OK, OK, I'm outta here. See ya!

BETH: Not bad. Not bad. I knew we could pull it off. Now if one of us could get a double bed at home we wouldn't be stuck with this thirty-five dollar a night scene—

JOEY: I know. I know. But this is just the beginning.

BETH: Yeah, it is the beginning . . . We'll have plenty of time to work out stuff later. You can come closer, you know. I won't bite. Maybe nibble a bit. Love bites.

He moves closer.

BETH: Oh, Joey, easy!

JOEY: What? You all right?

BETH: I'm all right. Just take it easy. Like we talked about.

JOEY: Sure?

BETH: Sure. Easy. Nice and slow. Nice. More like it. Mmmmm . . . I feel you.

JOEY: Yeah . . . you . . . you're warm.

BETH: You're warm too. (*Suddenly.*) Joey! Joey! Your foot—you're kicking me!

JOEY: Shit. Sorry.

BETH: No, come back. No, you're doing fine. We can work it out. And besides, this is your first time.

JOEY: Yeah, but shit . . .

BETH: You're doing fine. Just nice and easy . . . It's tickling me, you know. I feel you.

JOEY: Yeah . . .

BETH: Mmmmm . . . amazing . . . just a little . . .

JOEY: Right . . .

BETH: LET GO! Joey! Damn it! Let go!

JOEY: Beth? . . . Beth? . . . You OK?

BETH: I'm . . . I'll be fine . . .

JOEY: I'm sorry . . . I didn't mean—

BETH: I know. I know you didn't mean to, Joey. We just have to learn . . . explore . . . how to be . . . enjoy each other . . .

JOEY: Sure, but . . . it's hard. I want to . . .

BETH: What?

JOEY: I . . . want . . . I want to . . .

BETH: Do you want to be with me . . . ?

JOEY: Yeah. I want to be with you.

BETH: Then why don't you scoot that bod of yours on over here. You know . . . the way you scoot—it's so sexy . . . it's a real turn-on . . . (*As Joey moves closer.*) That's it. This is where it's at. There you are. You're tickling me again.

JOEY: Yeah . . .

Lights change.

Jail. WOMAN IN WHEELCHAIR *behind bars.*

COMPANY *gathers around her.*

WOMAN IN WHEELCHAIR: November 20, 1992. We're barricading McDonald's—and this disabled guy yells at me from down the street, "BEHAVE YOURSELF. You make a bad name for us."

This one woman in a chair told me she wished I was dead because I was fighting Special Transit to get all the city busses accessible. She likes Special Transit the way it is because she doesn't know the names of the streets—and she doesn't want to learn them.

We've made a lot of progress in Denver. See in Denver I'm part of the picture for the bus driver—a *regular* pain in the ass, not a *special* pain in the ass . . . Just another pain in the ass.

Lights to black.

The End.

Blue Baby
A Play in One Act

KATINKA NEUHOF

Who will unsnarl my body
Into gestures of love?
—by Vassar Miller

Note on the crutches and on the wheelchair:

Because of Jo's disability, she must use her Canadian Crutches when she isn't sitting in the wheelchair. She has no balance and cannot walk without her crutches. Although she doesn't need to use a wheelchair to be independent, Jo uses it to have her hands free, to move more easily around the apartment, to relax.

The wheelchair should be a standard, functioning wheelchair, the kind often seen in hospitals. It must have removable armrests and foot pedals. It must be blue. The wheelchair is old and worn. Perhaps the seat is ripped and has been taped together. One turning rim is missing, spokes are loose. Once the wheelchair and crutches have been introduced, they are to remain on stage and must be visible to the audience at all times.

If a nondisabled actress is cast as Jo, I strongly suggest that she seek out people with cerebral palsy in order to better understand the nature of the disability. I am especially concerned that she look and move and speak in the ways that people with CP do. While there are many different types of cerebral palsy, those of us who use Canadian Crutches share many similarities within our vocabulary of movement.

CHARACTERS

JO: Early twenties, small, strong. A catherine wheel of emotion and energy.

LEON: Early twenties, strong. Southerner. Graceful, flickering gestures.

SETTING

An apartment in New York City. The cramped space can hardly contain the possessions of two people. On the floor are stacks of identical dictionaries. On a small desk there is a rotary phone, pencils, pens and several long lists printed on computer paper. Lined on shelves, and on the floor, all over the apartment is equipment familiar to magicians. This may include: rings, several packs of cards, both opened and unopened, scarves, rope, balls of all shapes and sizes, etc. There is a tall hat, and clustered here and there, colorful juggling pins of various sizes. Behind the couch a large window opens to a fire escape. The bars on the windows have been partially removed to allow access to the fire escape. The action that takes place out there must be seen by the audience. The room should give the sense of two people trying to make the best of run-down conditions. The walls need painting. Whatever hangs on the walls is there to hide cracks. All of the objects in the apartment are arranged to create space for the wheelchair.

TIME

The present. Summer. Early evening.

SCENE ONE

LEON *and* BLUE BABY *out on the fire escape. The armrests are attached to the wheelchair. The wheelchair is filled with magician's props. LEON is practicing his juggling. As he juggles, he recites several verses from the bible. When he drops a pin, he repeats the same passages and continues to juggle. LEON juggles and recites for a while before JO enters. When he hears JO, LEON stops reciting aloud. He does not stop juggling.*

JO *is heard unlocking the door. She slams the door behind her, throws her keys and her bag to the floor. She wants to sit, but moves restlessly. She notices something different about the room.*

JO: *(Shouting.)* LEON! LEON! GET IN HERE! LEON! GIVE HER BACK! NO USE TAKING WHAT'S TOO BIG TO HIDE! LEON! TAKING WHAT DOESN'T BELONG TO YOU! *(Pause.)* Leon? (LEON *appears at the window.*) Where's Baby?

LEON: Right out here.

JO: What is she doing outside? She shouldn't be outside. What if it rains? She'll rust. She cries when she gets wet. She'll cry, the super will hear and we'll be out on the street.

LEON: Baby don't so much as whisper.

JO: Yes, but what if it rains?

LEON: Ash dry for three weeks. *(He disappears.)*

JO: IT ISN'T RIGHT, LEON. TAKING WHAT ISN'T YOURS TO KEEP. I'M MAROONED. YOU HEAR ME? MAROONED. DON'T LEAVE ME IN HERE! I NEED THE BABY. MY KNEES WILL DROP OFF. MY KNEES WILL DROP OFF AND ROLL ACROSS THE FLOOR AND MY LEGS ARE SURE TO FOLLOW. I'LL COME APART IN PIECES. ALL THE KINGS HORSES, LEON. *(JO moves impatiently around the apartment and suddenly slips, loses her balance and falls. She stays on her back.)* JESUS TO HELL GOD-DAMN CHRIST! *(Silence.)* AND WHAT ABOUT THE AIR IN THIS PLACE. THERE IS NO AIR IN THIS HOT BOX. IT MUST BE A HUNDRED AND SEVENTY-FIVE DEGREES IN HERE. *(LEON reappears at the window. He drops the equipment into the apartment. He lifts the wheelchair, BLUE BABY, inside.)*

LEON: Jo?

JO: Here.

LEON: Y'alright?

JO: I'm fine.

LEON: Nothing broken?

JO: Go to hell.

LEON: I was only inquiring as to the general state of your health. . . .

JO: Help me up.

LEON: Uh huh.

JO: Leon?

LEON: The Lord's name. . . .

JO: Oh no. . . .

LEON: The Lord's name in vain. . . .

JO: I'm sorry. Okay? I'm sorry.

LEON: Don't say it to me.

JO: Aw no. . . .

LEON: I'll juggle over here for a while.

Jo: I want to get up.

Leon: Course you do. *(He juggles.)*

Jo: Lord Jesus, please forgive me for taking your name in vain. Amen.

Leon: That was good. That was real good.

Jo: Goddamn Christ. Help me up.

Leon: Praise the Lord.

Jo and Leon: One . . . two . . . three . . . *(On "three" LEON pulls JO to her feet. They have done this many times before. It must appear synchronized and nearly effortless. LEON gradually lets go as JO regains her balance. She shakes him off.)*

Leon: You gonna tell me?

Jo: No.

Leon: That bad huh.

Jo: Scratch. To the left. Down.

Leon: Here?

Jo: Ah. Ah.

Leon: There you go.

Jo: He put his hands on me.

Leon: Who?

Jo: My prospective employer.

Leon: His hands?

Jo: He reached for my knee.

Leon: He touched your knee.

Jo: His palm rested.

Leon: Where?

Jo: There.

Leon: What did you do?

Jo: I lifted his stubby, sweaty, inconsequential little fingers—

LEON: You touched him?

Jo: I left.

LEON: Good.

Jo: I hate interviews.

LEON: I'll punch him. I'll go now.

Jo: No, no. It gets better.

LEON: It does?

Jo: He offered me money.

LEON: He didn't.

Jo: Forty dollars. Cash. Can you believe it? Here, he said, take a cab. Get home safe. My pinstriped interviewer. I almost kicked him.

LEON: Did you take a cab?

Jo: I took the bus. (JO *shows him the money.*)

LEON: You sure you're all right?

Jo: Here. (JO *points to her elbow.* LEON *kisses her elbow.* JO *points to different parts of her body and* LEON *kisses where she points.*) Taking what doesn't belong to you.

LEON: I only borrowed her.

Jo: Thief.

LEON: Kept her near me out on the fire escape.

Jo: She's got her arms on.

LEON: I know.

Jo: Take them off.

LEON: I know. (*He pulls off the armrests and invites her to sit.* JO *sits.*)

LEON: Don't you see it?

Jo: What?

LEON: The Baby. Look at her.

JO: What? *(During this next segment of dialogue,* LEON *helps to undress* JO. *They work together to take off her interview clothes and put on summer clothes. There should be no break in their exchange.)*

LEON: She's clean. I took some soap and water to her. A bucket filled to the lip and one of those rough scratch pads with soap in the middle of it. You've never given her a second look. She's got layers on her, no hope in hell would burn off. Old food stuck between the vinyl seams. Crusts of dust baked on the spokes of the wheels. It soured my stomach to scrape that crud off but she's clean now. Not a stain on her. Folks seeing Baby for the first time might remark to themselves on her cleanliness. See the sparkle on those rims? Ain't she clean and pretty?

JO: Listen to you talking like some damn hausfrau about the virtues of a well-kept home. Baby looks the same to me. She looks the same. A standard lousy piece of equipment. An Everett Jennings, worth in her former glory approximately three hundred dollars.

LEON: Your feet are cold. How can that be? No less than ninety-eight degrees outside and your feet wouldn't feel the difference. What must I do to keep the blood pumping in these spiny legs of yours? *(He rubs her legs and feet vigorously. When* JO *touches him he stops and rests his head in her lap.)*

JO: Do I look like a homeless person?

LEON: Not in that interview suit.

JO: This morning I was walking toward the bus stop, burning holes in my shoes because I didn't want to be late for yet another interview, and I stopped to take the correct change out of my bag. The bag, needless to say, which perfectly matches my orthopedically correct shoes and my freshly pressed suit. I reach for the money, and a man, a stranger wearing a suit of his own, shoves a bundle of bills under my nose and says, "Here. Take it." At first, I didn't know what he was talking about. I stared at his face. "Hey," he said, "You were standing there. I thought you were one of those people . . ."

LEON: What people?

JO: "What people?" I ask not daring to anticipate the answer. Three possibilities spring to my mind: a tart, a cripple, a recent graduate from the neighborhood asylum. All three of course sporting perfect identical interview suits.

LEON: No. . . .

JO: "No! No! One of those people." One of those people holding out an empty coffee cup ready to sing for their supper. . . .

LEON: *(He climbs onto her lap. He sits facing her, his legs straddling the sides of the wheelchair. As they talk, they touch, kiss and gradually grow more passionate.)* You don't look like a homeless person. . . .

JO: Not in this interview suit.

LEON: Folks been throwing money at you all day. Maybe you should go to the races and place a few bets.

JO: I took the bus. I went to an interview. I talked to a man who wanted to know whether I fell off a horse as a child.

LEON: I remember the first time I saw you fall.

JO: Leon. . . .

LEON: Two summers ago.

JO: Not again, Leon.

LEON: The first time you talked to me. As God is my witness, I will never forget it. I was juggling in the middle of the steps in front of the Metropolitan Museum, the folks were friendly but not enthusiastic, they were coming and going, minding their own, and who do I see but this crazy little girl making her way up that long flight of steps. You had two crutches, one big heavy bag around your neck and a look on your face like this was easy and you do it all the time.

JO: I do.

LEON: Well, I didn't know that. Nobody else did neither. You were carrying one crutch and holding on to the bannister, taking one step at a time. First the right foot then the left, and these people kept coming up to you and saying—

JO: —Can I help you in any way? May I help you? Do you need any help? Can I carry your bag—

LEON: —Can I take off your shoes? I can call a guard. Let me get you a policeman—

JO: —What's your name? Does it hurt? Mommy, why does she walk that way? You must have the strongest arms. Can you have children?

LEON: Can you have sex?

JO AND LEON: Yes!

JO: I bet you've got polio. My cousin twice removed on my mother's side he had polio. Iron lung you know. I broke my leg once. Can I carry your crutch?—

LEON: —Cerebral what?—

JO: —Let me spell it for you: C-E-R-E-B-R-A-L. Cerebral. P-A-L-S-Y. Palsy.—

LEON: —There's an accessible entrance right next door. I can carry you up the stairs. Sack of potatoes. Over my shoulder. And to each person you said, "No thank you. It's all right. This won't take long. Thank you." Smiling a big Sunday picnic sort of smile. Meanwhile it was taking a heck of a long time only because people were tripping all over themselves in front of you. And I juggled pretending it was just another ordinary day in New York City.

JO: It was.

LEON: Not to me it wasn't. I had never seen anybody as determined to get up a flight of stairs. And never before had I witnessed the people of New York City acting that kind or that stupid all at the same time. It was a revelation. And finally two steps from the top, you were just about there, the doors were wide open, crowds going in, coming out. You were two steps from the top. This man, this brainless idiot, comes running out of the museum. Without even stopping to ask he grabs the crutch you were carrying and dashes with it down the stairs.

JO: He was just trying to be helpful.

LEON: Except that you can't get anyplace with one crutch and the jerk pulled you along with him. I had never seen anything like it. You were doing full somersaults backwards down the steps of Metropolitan Museum. It must've been the momentum, God knows, but you didn't stop on the landings, you kept rolling, the bag, the crutch turning, turning with you. It stopped when you and the sidewalk met. Such screams, such gasping, such ensuing pandemonium, I had never before experienced. And you, legs in the air, crutch twisted, you in the middle of a growing crowd, lying on the sidewalk, had a smile on your face.

Jo: It was fantastic!

Leon: It was horrible. I dropped my pins, I dropped everything and pushed my way through. I thought you were dead but you smiled.

Jo: It was the closest I will ever come to flying. . . .

Leon: And from the sidewalk, smiling, you told the folks that you were all right. You were all right and you were going to stay right where you were until you caught your breath. And everybody went on their way. Nobody noticed anymore. You could've been stark raving naked and singing like a whippoorwill. . . .

Jo: But you stayed. You held my hand.

Leon: Not your hand. Your ankle. It was bigger than a phone book. I rubbed your ankle and got you to your feet.

Jo: You did it well.

Leon: It seemed easy after what I had just seen. One, two, three. You insisted on walking on back up the stairs. This time, I carried your bag, I carried your crutch—

Jo: I wanted you to carry me!

Leon: When you got to the top of the steps, you didn't go inside—

Jo: I didn't. I sat on the steps to watch you do your tricks.

Leon: Lord, I was nervous.

Jo: You dropped your pins. Over and over again. They rolled down the steps and you chased them. Juggle, drop, roll, juggle, drop, roll. Like you were reenacting a secret ritual in front of me. *(Pause.)* Leon? When I left that office, after the interview, I walked back to the bus stop. The only thing I thought about was, "It's all right. It's okay. Leon is home. Leon will save me."

Leon: *(Gets off her lap.)* You going to work tonight?

Jo: What? Selling dictionaries? What am I going to do with seventy-five dictionaries? What do I say? Nobody reads anymore. The ink comes off on my fingers.

Leon: Put in a few more hours tonight.

Jo: Why? I am stuck in the 718 area code. I'll be lost there forever. Searching for depleted vocabularies in the wilds of Astoria. Whitestone. Little Neck. (JO *pretends to use the telephone.*) Hello? My name is Josephine. I represent the New World Large Print Dictionary Company. Our word for today is *Pitchfork*.

Leon: *(Also on the phone.)* 'Scuse me?

Jo: Pitchfork. Noun. Agricultural instrument used in bailing hay—

Leon: Oh.

Jo: Now. Wouldn't our latest *New World Large Print Dictionary* be a tremendous asset to the young student trying to improve his or her reading and writing skills. Your son or daughter certainly. . . .

Leon: I ain't got no kids.

Jo: I know your wife would be delighted to add this genuine simulated snakeskin soft to the touch hardcover text to your library. . . .

Leon: I'm divorced.

Jo: Perhaps your elderly relative would greatly appreciate our large print text. Easier on the eyes you know.

Leon: Mama's passed.

Jo: Pardon?

Leon: Dead. Dead.

Jo: . . . And you, sir, when that word is just on the tip of your tongue. When you're puzzling over your favorite crossword? How convenient it would be to reach for this deluxe edition of the *New World Large Print Dictionary*. We accept all major credit cards, Master-Card, American Express, money orders and, of course, cash on delivery. How many orders may I put you down for?

Leon: I'm blind. If the books don't talk I ain't interested.

Jo: Christ!

LEON: Poor baby. . . .

JO: It was easier once. I was younger, only a child but for a time, all I needed to do was smile and money would fall from the sky. Into my lap. Quarters, nickels, dimes, even the occasional silver dollars. They were bigger in my hand.

LEON: You took them.

JO: No. But I wanted to. I pretended the coins were payment for the work I was doing. For a year, my face was everywhere, on billboards, the sides of buses, sugar packets. Pictures of me standing with my crutches, or sitting in a wheelchair. People gave more money if I surrounded myself with the appropriate equipment. I wore braces on my legs. It was for a good cause, I was told. I was part of the cause. Money for Crippled Children. Organizations existing solely to help Crippled Children. This was before the days when we were called Disabled. Everyone said Crippled without wincing. You should have seen. Pink-cheeked and smooth. Stare straight into the camera and smile until my jaws locked.

LEON: The Marigold Queen.

JO: Queen of the Marigolds. A banner pinned to my dress, a rhinestone tiara in my hair. With a prince at my side, he was only there for decorative purposes. I said, "Hello. My name is Josephine. I am eight years old and I'm a victim of cerebral palsy. Let me spell it for you. C-E-R-E-B-R-A-L, Cerebral, P-A-L-S-Y, Palsy. Won't you find it in your hearts to donate just a little bit of money for crippled kids like me? Your generous donation will go a long way to send a kid to camp, or buying a wheelchair, or even, with your help, to find a cure." Once, I gave a speech perched on a man's shoulder. God Bless us, every one. He was a football player, a real quarterback. During that whole year of television appearances, parades and bilingual speeches, I remember loving that height. It made me dizzy, I could hardly catch my breath. And the poor guy, I held on to his hair to keep my balance. I smiled down at the crowd. Nobody could touch me.

LEON: You were a bona fide star.

JO: People waved at me from their cars. Looked at me as if they knew my name. I was the most well-known complete unknown I knew. What am I now? I'm a cripple in a hurry. I'm a handicapped person with a disability who is physically challenged and out of a job. How could I look like a homeless person in a soft gray suit? Leon? What happens when the poster child grows up? Christ.

LEON: Jo. . . .

JO: I hope He hears me!

LEON: He provides.

JO: I hope He showers us with back rent.

LEON: Pick a card.

JO: Not now, Leon.

LEON: Pick a card or I'll sick Deuteronomy on you.

JO: It's been a long day.

LEON: Pick a god damn JESUS MAY HE BURN IN HELL CARD! (JO *picks a card.* LEON *steps back.*) Remember it. Got it? Good. Now toss it back.

JO: What?

LEON: I said toss it back. Throw it at me. (JO *tosses the card.* LEON *catches it.*) Good. Three of spades? Catch. (LEON *tosses it.*)

JO: You're not supposed to look at my card—

LEON: Look at your hand. (JO *looks.*) What do you see?

JO: A five dollar bill.

LEON: Ain't that something. Wonder where that card went to. Let's see. . . . What's this behind your ear? My. It's something all folded up. Blow on it.

JO: Leon. . . .

LEON: . . . And they took the fruit of the land in their hands and brought it down unto us. . . . (JO *blows on his hand.*) What do we have here? Why, it's another five dollar bill. 'Lot of good that'll do us. (LEON *drops the bill.*) Where is that card? Well, it might be tucked nice and tidy in your ear. Let me just. . . . Look! Another piece of something folded. . . . Blow. . . . (She *blows.*) Twenty dollars! Girl, your head is plain stuffed with money. I don't know, Jo. I do hate to crack a fresh pack of cards for want of a three of spades. . . . You better check my pants. (*He stands in front of her and raises his arms to give her room. She checks his pockets.*) Not my pockets. Inside my pants. (*She reaches inside his pants.*) Careful now, careful. (JO *brings out a handful of bills. She stares at the money. She lets the money fall.*) Guess the card ain't in there. . . . (*He lifts his leg.*) Shoe. . . . (JO *unties the laces, and pulls off the shoe. She waves it above her head. Paper and coins cascade. She peels off his sock and empties it. She does the same with his other foot. He throws cards and money. They laugh. He dances around her. He grabs the wheelchair and spins* JO *around. He tips the chair back until the handlebars rest on the floor. He covers her with money.*)

JO: How much?

LEON: Four hundred and thirty-five dollars. And change.

JO: Liar.

LEON: Four hundred and thirty-four dollars. I spent five quarters to take a bus ride home.

JO: When?

LEON: Today! Today! Every bit of it. Set up at eight-thirty. Cart it home by four. I waited for you. Think of it, Jo. A couple of days like this and we won't owe the landlord squat.

JO: I don't believe—

LEON: We'll have enough money left over to go out to dinner. I'll take you out to dinner every night for a week. We'll try one of those fancy places where the waiters pretend to speak a foreign language and we'll pretend to understand. Use napkins that stand like party hats. (*Pause.*) Wish for something.

JO: We can pay the rent.

LEON: No, I mean don't you want soft, Italian custom-made boots? In five different colors and in the two weeks it takes for you to wear them through more will be made to your precise specifications?

JO: Boots?

LEON: Or let's get out of the city. A sand and sea vacation. Heck, we'll buy an island and sail on pea green water. I'll build a boat.

I'm good with my hands. Don't you want anything fanciful? Make a wish with me.

Jo: *(Struggling.)* I want. I—

LEON: Yes?

Jo: I don't know. I don't know.

LEON: Say it.

Jo: I want a fan. A ceiling fan. No, I mean an air conditioner. I want a big, huge air conditioner.

LEON: You dream of a big old noisy metal box hanging out of your only window?

Jo: I want a house made mostly of windows. Windows on the roof, windows in the basement. Windows instead of doors. Windows, windows, windows. And in each window an air conditioner. All my busy boxes roaring at the same time. My house will sound like a god damn airport but it'll feel very, very cool. . . .

LEON: A castle with gators in the moat. An R.V. to travel cross—I'll build an air conditioned ark. I'll live to be ancient, braid myself a beard and become Noah. . . .

Jo: I want to pay rent. I want to be able to pay my rent.

LEON: Well, Miss Josie, now you can pay back rent. Let the Baby cry as loud as she pleases.

Jo: Seventy-three dollars. Since I've known you. Your best day since I've known you was seventy-three dollars. . . .

LEON: Look what I went out and bought today. Did it first thing. *(LEON shows her a tool box.)* This one is to tighten the spokes, this one to put the screws in right. . . .

Jo: Tell me how you did it, Leon.

LEON: This one to reattach the missing rim, and here is the most important tool . . . tightens the brakes. . . .

Jo: Seventy-odd dollars. You carried them in your hat and counted them on my floor. *(JO tries to get out of the wheelchair but she is unable. LEON pulls the chair upright.)*

LEON: You won't need to walk to the restaurant. I'll fix Baby up pretty and she'll roll like a chariot. You can wear your softest new shoes since your feet won't be needing the ground.

JO: The Baby can't go outside.

LEON: She will when I'm finished with her, fix her to be strong and sturdy again. A four-wheeled chariot.

JO: She can't take the road anymore, Leon. She's old and loose and past her better days. Tell me about four hundred and thirty-four dollars!

LEON: A miracle you might call it.

JO: I'm tired, Leon. Through my bones, I'm tired.

LEON: Walk to me.

JO: No.

LEON: Gotta do your exercises. Improve your balance. Refine your hand-eye whatsitcalled. Today, it's your balance.

JO: I have no balance.

LEON: Walk to me.

JO: I'll fall.

LEON: Not with me standing right here you won't. I won't tell you about a dime of that money with you sitting easy like that.

JO: The word for today is *pitchfork*.

LEON: Get up. (*He stands before* JO *holding both arms out. He keeps his arms rigid as she pulls herself up. He talks as* JO *concentrates on steadying herself, preparing.*) I walked to Museum Mile early this morning. Find my place by the steps. I borrowed Baby—

JO: Thief.

LEON: I borrowed Baby, put her arms back on, loaded the tricks and pushed it on over. I don't know why I never thought of it before. (LEON *turns his hands so that his palms are up.* JO *rests her hands on his.*) Ready?

JO: No.

LEON: No one was paying attention. They liked the juggling and all but my hat stayed near empty while folks walking by were stuffing hot dogs down their throats—

JO: Ready. *(LEON fully extends his arms and steps back. JO still rests her hands on his palms. Slowly, LEON lowers one hand as she does the same. Pause.)*

LEON: One . . . two . . . three. *(On "three" LEON quickly pulls back his other arm. He does not extend his arms as she walks toward him. She sways slightly before taking her first step. Her walk is awkward and uneven. She manages to take four steps before losing her balance. LEON waits a moment too long before reaching for her. He catches her in time. JO is breathless.)*

LEON: I got you. You're all right. I got you.

JO: *(From "You're all right.")* Don't let go. Don't let go. Don't let go. Don't let go.

LEON: There now. You took three more steps than last time. Imagine. Three more steps.

JO: How many?

LEON: Well, it was four steps all told. That's three more than last week. More than double. And looking at you, I'd say that your hands held the air a full ten seconds. You did fine, Miss Josephine.

JO: I felt the air holding me. As if someone's hands were pressing on my back.

LEON: Weren't my hands I can guarantee you that. These hands hung here next to my knees waiting for something big to happen.

JO: Leon?

LEON: Yes, Jo.

JO: I've never taken that many steps before in my life.

LEON: Ain't it something.

JO: How am I supposed to get back?

LEON: Where you wanna go?

JO: Back to the Baby.

LEON: Crutches. . . .

JO: Behind you. (*LEON spots the crutches. Still holding* JO, *he makes an exaggerated attempt to reach for them.*)

LEON: We might stand here until our bodies turn to stone. . . .

JO: Tell me about the money.

LEON: . . . Or we might perform unspeakable acts with one or the two of us standing up.

JO: How did you make the money? (*LEON hesitates. He kisses her. He lifts* JO *and carries her back to the wheelchair.* JO *suddenly feels afraid. He walks away. During the following monologue he distracts himself by arranging props and practicing some tricks.*)

LEON: I tried all morning to get something going with the crowd but they just weren't buying it. So after a while, I took two bits from the hat and bought myself a hot dog. I dumped all of the stuff out of the Baby and sat there watching the crowd pass me by. I sat to think a few things through but nothing passed into my head. It was too hot to think and I was too hungry. The only thing I could come up with was the list of three activities my father considered sinful. Playing cards, dancing, and listening to what he called fornicatious music.

JO: What?

LEON: Anything with rhythm, dear. Mama's favorite joke. She liked to whisper it to me whenever he mentioned fornicatious music, which he did regularly in those sermons. But there I was, not in my daddy's church, or my mama's house, but on the street in the Baby, with no magic happening between my hands. It came to me how Baby felt soft in just the right places. How unlikely it would be for me to move again seeing the hole in my hat wasn't about to be patched with dollars. And the heat. This heat wasn't rising. I picked up some pins, still sitting in the Baby, I flipped them slow trying to wake these hands. A pin fell. It rolled along the sidewalk but I felt no urge to retrieve it. This lady, a little old lady, said, "Let me get that for you, dearheart." Dearheart. . . . She stopped the pin from rolling in the gutter, wiped off the dirt and handed it over to me. I thanked her. And in my tall black silk hat she folded a ten dollar bill. Ten whole dollars. As fresh as you please. "God bless" she said. "Yes, ma'am. And bless you." That was the beginning. The folks kept coming 'round. I spun the pins, made fire in the middle of the air, pulled cards. Did every trick I knew and some I didn't. My hat was full. My pockets. I stuffed money in my pants, my socks, my shoes. People I didn't know kept saying, "Bless you," or "Courage" or "Believe in yourself!" Bless You. Bless You. Bless me. Doing my tricks, I picked one man out of the crowd and I followed his eyes. They led me past my own hands. He was staring at my belly. His eyes were roaming around my legs and down by my feet back to my belly and on up. And then it came to me. It wasn't the sum of my parts that held his interest. It was the fact that I was sitting in the Baby. Using the Baby. The Blue Baby. I just happened to be sitting there. Comfortable. Crippled. His face told me how amazing he thought it was that a man all crippled up could be doing such fine tricks with his hands. "Bless you, bless you," they all said and I took it all. I took whatever they gave me. I been keeping the money warm for you, Josephine. I blessed them. I thanked God. I took the money and I waited to welcome you home. *(JO and LEON stay perfectly still. Then JO steers the wheelchair straight into him. LEON is knocked over. Anger pulls her out of the chair. She falls on top of him, looking to hurt him. Hitting him. At first her words are unintelligible. Soon she says:)*

JO: Taking what doesn't belong to you! Taking what doesn't belong to you! God damn cripple lover! Goddammit! Tell me how long! How long?!

LEON: Four weeks. Five.

JO: Where? The same place? Always the same?

LEON: No.

JO: I can't hear you.

LEON: NO! I went along Museum Mile. I did a couple of them. Two or three. Three.

JO: Let me guess. The Metropolitan, the Guggenheim . . . and did you try the churches? Primed after a morning service when the congregations are still feeling warm all over after emptying their wallets into the collection plates. A real charitable institution like St. Patrick's or—

LEON: I didn't go to no churches.

Jo: I understand. Afraid your daddy's gonna come a chasin' you bearing a cross, carrying the Good Book. Daddy gonna send you straight to—

Leon: I didn't go to church! *(Pause.)*

Jo: How much?

Leon: I don't know. Say fifteen hundred.

Jo: Liar!

Leon: Four thousand dollars. Even. *(JO laughs.)*

Jo: You're a regular one man band. It must be quite a performance. A thousand dollars a week. Tax free. Where'd you stash it?

Leon: It's in the bank.

Jo: Are you certain, Leon? Check under the floorboards. Under the mattress. Any more change rattling in your shoes? Let me do a strip search.

Leon: That's all there is. I swear.

Jo: *(Picks up a handful of money.)* Where did this come from?

Leon: I had a good day today.

Jo: Yes. Yes, you did. Clean it up. *(LEON begins to gather the money. JO pulls herself to her wheelchair. JO locks the chair, pulls herself to her feet and pivots in order to sit. LEON moves to help her but she keeps him away. There is no break in the dialogue.)*

Leon: What'll I do with it?

Jo: Take it out of the bank. Give it to the homeless. Give it to the church.

Leon: We'll be out on the street.

Jo: There are other ways.

Leon: My daddy who doesn't want to know my name. Your mama's poorer than we are. . . .

Jo: She sends what she can.

Leon: It ain't enough.

Jo: I'll find more work.

LEON: How long you been trying? Twelve months. Eighteen. How many shoes you gonna put holes into before you find something else to do? It ain't enough. If you could see their faces, Jo, when they smile at me, hoping to look me in the eye. When that old lady puts money in my hat, she walks away feeling happy knowing that she's done something good. Giving means something special to her. The tricks are all tricks she's seen before but she'll remember them because of the Baby.

JO: I've seen their faces. Every day of my life. People look at me and for a second, for a moment they feel pity. But for the grace of God go I, they tell me. They say that to me. And then you know what happens? They feel guilty. Guilty. Why are they, the lucky ones? How come what happened to me didn't happen to them? And you know what gets me Leon? What really gets me? It's that no matter how smart, or how strong, or how pretty I am, the pity still flickers in the faces, only for a moment. I've seen it. And when that little old lady puts money in your hat. It's guilt money. She puts the money down and says now I don't need to think about this poor suffering cripple because I've done all I can to relieve what she thinks is your suffering. You are not suffering.

LEON: No, you can't call it that. Suffering ain't the word. I wake up nights smelling food I only dream about. I worry about landlords who don't turn the heat on in the winter without jacking up the rent. What am I good for but doing somebody else's dishes or turning a cheap sleight of hand? What's the harm in hoping? The money that folks gave me says "I hope this will make you feel better." It's a small thing to do to give a dollar, but it's a way of sharing hope.

JO: It's a lie.

LEON: My Daddy puts his hands on a man in a wheelchair, tells him to rise and when he's on his feet, folks know that God is doing his work. They are witness to His power. The man don't need the wheelchair, maybe he never did, but the hurt shoulder he came into church with is all healed up. The wheelchair reminds people that their lives aren't as bad as all that. It ain't the important thing. In the end, everybody goes home feeling better. It's faith what lets us hold on long enough for something else to happen.

Jo: Misdirection. Isn't that what you call it? Keep my attention on one hand while the other hand is busy. What a magician does best? It's a lie.

Leon: A lie is what makes your voice sweet on the telephone to sell books nobody reads. Dictionaries with half the words spelled wrong. Dictionaries with missing covers, with blank spaces where the words should be.

Jo: I don't play the fool. I don't coerce anyone into buying anything.

Leon: Like hell you don't. Spin the sugar in your voice. Or they like the way you laugh, they warm to the pleasant conversation used to sweeten the transaction. Chances are you wouldn't sell any books if it had to be done face to face. You couldn't bring yourself to tell a flat out lie in the form of a dummy book. Would you sell a lie? *(Pause.)*

Jo: No.

Leon: I can't hear you.

Jo: NO!

Leon: Seems to me the only difference between us is that folks see me while they can only hear you. Nobody would've given any money that they didn't want to give.

Jo: Leon, it isn't the amount of money. I don't care about how many hats you fill. It is the ease with which the money is given. They do not think about what they are doing. They don't think about what the giving means.

Leon: I work for what they give. My magic is a service. I entertain the folks. For a minute as they pass by I show them something different in the routine of their lives.

Jo: Yes, you entertain them. But I know you work as hard sitting in the Baby as you do standing up. The crowd doesn't expect you to work that hard. They don't give a damn about the service you provide. They say, "How brave he is. Crippled but still able to spin his magic."

Leon: A little flight of fancy could get us out of here. Just for a little while. Me and the Baby want to make life easier, is all. Just for a short time.

Jo: Don't put me back there, Leon. I don't want to see pictures of my face on the sides of buses. When you sit in the Baby and people hand you money for it, you're putting me right back there. I don't know how to smile on command anymore. Please get rid of the money.

Leon: I can't.

Jo: Please!

Leon: It's gone. I spent it.

Jo: What? You spent it? You spent it.

Leon: We got a couple of hundred dollars left. Money enough for a couple of fancy meals in fancy restaurants. Maybe some new shoes. I could get you a fan for the ceiling.

Jo: I don't want anything.

Leon: So help me Jo. I spent it for you. So help me.

Jo: It doesn't matter anymore. I don't want to know.

Leon: Don't you dare give up on me! You hear? I ain't come this far for you to lie down now. I worked too hard! *(LEON walks to the window.)*

Jo: Where are you going? Don't leave me in here. *(LEON goes out on to the fire escape. He returns carrying a new wheelchair. It is a state-of-the-art racing wheelchair, built to be used out of doors. The wheelchair is blue.* JO *stands to stare at the chair.* LEON *places it in the middle of the room.)*

Leon: Look, Josephine. It's a state-of-the-art racing wheelchair. A wheelchair athletes like to use. Marathoners. Look at it, Josephine. Tilted wheels with bicycle tires. Low back, low armrests, leather seats. I've never seen a finer vehicle. Lighter than air, Jo. I can lift it with one hand. And you know what I love best about it? It comes apart, each piece. I can take it apart and put it back together. I'll maintain it for you. I won't let her grow old. Not this baby. She's beautiful ain't she? I've never seen anything finer. *(LEON waits for her to come forward and sit.* JO *does not move.)* Come on, Jo. She's waiting for you. Our baby's all grown up.

Jo: She's got arms.

LEON: I'll take them off.

Jo: Take her arms off.

LEON: They're gone. . . . (JO *does not move.*) Come on, Jo, come on. She's waiting. All you gotta do is sit.

Jo: I can't. . . .

LEON: Yes, you can. Ain't she clean and pretty. Yes, you can. It's easy, Josephine.

Jo: No. (LEON *locks the wheelchair. He walks over to* JO *and picks her up and carries her to the chair.*) No! No! No! NO! NO! NO! NO! (LEON *puts her in the chair.*)

LEON: Put your hands on the wheels.

Jo: No.

LEON: She rides like the wind.

Jo: I want to get out.

LEON: Put your hands on the wheels. (JO *tries to spring out of the chair.* LEON *blocks her.*)

Jo: Please let me get out. (LEON *forcibly pushes her arms until her hands are on the wheels. At first* JO *does not move but gradually she lets herself feel the tires and then she cautiously pushes the chair, enjoying the feeling. She knows it is a beautiful machine and it is perfect for her.* LEON *approaches. He kneels by the chair.*)

LEON: Ain't it just what you wanted?

Jo: It's perfect.

LEON: Ain't it just what you wanted?

Jo: Yes. It's just what I need.

LEON: I knew it. I knew it.

Jo: Yes.

LEON: I feel it in my hands. The magic. The power. I knew it was still there. The power. It was always there. Between my hands. In my hands.

Jo: The power. . . .

LEON: The power of God. In Jesus' name. His power is everywhere. He is inside me.

Jo: Yes.

LEON: Listen to me! I know this to be true. The power. How else can you explain it?

Jo: Explain what?

LEON: The money. A thousand dollars a week. I ain't never smelled money like that before. It just kept coming, Jo. God was talking through my hands. He was talking to the crowd. He helped to keep me going. Me and Baby were working together. God was working through us because He knew what we were working for. . . .

Jo: Haven't you heard me? Haven't you listened to a single word?

LEON: . . . We were doing it for you. Raising the money to get you just what you wanted. A new wheelchair. A new Blue Baby to do the old baby proud. But I want to fix the old baby. Keep her around as a spare. No, Josephine. I'll fix her and we'll give her away to someone who needs her more.

Jo: Why are you here? I know. I know. You're a god damn God-fearing cripple-lover. That's it. Christ. Does it make you feel special sleeping with damaged goods? Huh? Tell me different. Pry my spastic knees apart. Come on. Do my scars excite you? God damn God-fearing cripple lover. I know you. Be nice to me and earn your points for your place in heaven.

LEON: Shut your mouth, Josephine.

Jo: What is it your daddy would say? Crippled folks should stay at home where their families can keep an eye on them? Leon?

LEON: I don't care what my daddy would say.

Jo: And now look at me, Leon. Drooling all over the streets. Screwing my brains out. My God, Leon, I may even make more crippled babies.

LEON: You're not like one of them. Those droolers.

Jo: Why? Because my body doesn't twist or shake in ways that make you want to look away? Because my tongue allows me to speak in ways that you understand?

Leon: Exactly.

Jo: *(Getting out of the wheelchair to the floor.)* Leon. I am just like the rest of them. I am one of them.

Leon: You are not— You are not—

Jo: Say it! *(LEON tries to respond but cannot.)* Leon, you see all of me. You massage my feet when my toes cramp. You pick me up off the floor when I fall—

Leon: Me and the Baby that's all we want to do. We want to make life easier for you.

Jo: How?

Leon: With the power in my hands.

Jo: You're a magician.

Leon: The power in my hands is a gift from the Almighty.

Jo: A rabbit from the hat, man.

Leon: Don't turn away from the power of the Lord. He is every-where. Can't you feel it in the air?

Jo: I feel nothing.

Leon: I know that He is here with us.

Jo: I feel nothing.

Leon: Let me try.

Jo: Why? Do you want to make me straighter? Would you love me more if I had straight legs? Do you want to draw all of my spasticity out of my body? So I could spread my legs further apart? Would you love me more if I could run into your arms? If we could make love acrobatically?

Leon: YES! (JO *is deeply hurt. She knocks over the wheelchair. She tries to take it apart.*)

Jo: It is not a chariot. It is not a vessel of God. It isn't a symbol of suffering. It isn't a baby. It is a wheelchair. A chair with wheels.

A chair with wheels. A chair with wheels. It's only a chair with wheels. . . . I don't want to fight anymore, Leon.

LEON: You took four steps to me today, Jo. Four whole steps. That's three more than ever before. It's a sign, Josephine. It's another sign. Can't you see that? Don't you see? *(LEON scoops her off the floor. She does not protest. She is drained. Somehow, she is without spirit.)* The Baby's waiting for you. We're waiting on a miracle. *(LEON puts her in the Blue Baby. During the following scene JO does nothing to help or hinder LEON. She does nothing to protest or change what is about to take place. While it is important that the healing scene seem authentic, effects should be added to enhance the sense of "witnessing" in church. LEON raises his hands above his head.)* Lord. Hear me, Lord. We are humble Lord, humble before your power. Humble because I have witnessed your glory. I have seen your love work inside your flock. Your flock who is lame, who is poor, who is weak, who is suffering. Only when we believe in you do we have the power to make a miracle happen. Lord, I have witnessed your power and your love. I have felt your love. I am your servant, Lord. Jesus. I place myself before you like the humble servant you know I am. The gift of my hands stays with me, Lord, through you and the healing I have done. I raise my hands to your love, Lord. I need my healing hands, Lord. Use my hands to do your work. In Jesus' name. I raise my hands in Jesus' name. Lord, you have healed so many. Help me heal one of the flock. Help me heal Josephine. Her body is hurting but her spirit is strong. Take her crippled legs and let her stand straight and tall. In Jesus' name. Josephine, do you believe in the power? Do you believe that it is only through His love that your legs can be made whole again? Do you believe in His power to heal all living things? Josephine?

JO: Yes.

LEON: His is the power to heal the weak and the lame. Do you believe?

JO: *(Louder, with more conviction.)* YES!

LEON: *(Shouting.)* JOSEPHINE?

JO: YES! YES! *(Interspersed throughout this next speech LEON speaks in tongues. This is an improvised series of "words" of no recognizable language. The words are spoken rapidly in a stream of sound. For LEON, the effect is trance-like. He has no control as to when he speaks in tongues. He can alternate easily from one language to another.)*

LEON: Praise the Lord. In Jesus' name. Josephine commits her body and her spirit to you. Heal a member of your flock who greatly needs your power now. In Jesus' name. She is ready for your healing love. Show us your power. Lord. In Jesus' name. In Jesus' name. Yes! Yes! In Jesus' name! Yes! In Jesus' name! *(As he speaks, LEON has pulled Josephine to her feet. He keeps one hand on her forehead. When he pulls his hand away Josephine takes one step forward, sways and falls straight back. She makes no attempt to break the fall. There is a brief pause. JO is motionless on the floor. LEON kneels by her on the floor.)* GET UP. GET UP. GET UP. GET UP. GET UP. WHY DON'T YOU GET UP? GET UP. PLEASE GET UP. PLEASE GET UP. PLEASE. PLEASE. OH GOD. PLEASE GOD. PLEASE. GET UP. GOD. PLEASE. *(He shakes her. They are crying. He grows more desperate.)*

JO: *(From "Oh God.")* I can't. I can't. I can't. I can't. I can't. I can't. . . . *(LEON finally surrenders. As he cries, JO sits up and slowly moves toward him. She cradles him. Making comforting sounds as he gradually calms down.)*

LEON: . . . I almost didn't notice at first. My hands hardly spoke. But then, the animals started coming. Little breathing, living things, birds. I don't know, dogs with pains in their bellies so bad they couldn't come right up. Oh but they tried. They did. Crawling and crying. And they stopped when I put my hands on them. I knew their pain was gone. Soon, the people came and I was touching limbs all crippled up with pain, swollen joints, legs that weren't more than dead weight. I saw the look in people's eyes, Jo. The look of peace when the pain rolls away. My hands heard their pain.

JO: I know.

LEON: And I went to my daddy and I showed him my great gift. "Look what the Lord has bestowed upon me. Look, Daddy!" And I asked to preach the word of God. My daddy and me side by side. But he didn't want to hear. He didn't want to see the evidence of His power in my hands. He sent me away.

JO: Baby. . . .

LEON: I didn't want to go.

JO: Poor baby. . . .

LEON: And when I sat in the wheelchair on the street, I saw the same quiet moment in their eyes. *(Pause)* I swear. No more healing. No more laying on of hands. I'll never do that to you again. I promise.

JO: *(As she speaks she begins to put the new wheelchair together. Eventually* LEON *joins her.)* Yes. Yes you will. You'll plan carefully. Hoping I won't notice. You'll try because in your heart it's what you truly believe.

LEON: Why am I here?

JO: You help to imagine something different for myself. You know how to dream.

LEON: Is that enough?

JO: Yes.

LEON: I believed I could heal you. I believed. I knew it. I felt it!

JO: Help me up. *(The new wheelchair is reassembled. Without armrests.* LEON *stands behind* JO.*)*

LEON AND JO: One . . . two . . . three. . . . *(On three,* LEON *lifts* JO *to her feet.* LEON *carries her and puts her in the new wheelchair. As the lights dim, he sits on her lap.)*

Mishuganismo

SUSAN NUSSBAUM

Mishuganismo was first performed in 1991 at the Remains Theatre in Chicago, directed by Mike Nussbaum, and later at the Matrix Theatre in Los Angeles under the direction of Mark Travis. It was performed with a simple set consisting primarily of a table, leaving the actor free to roam the rest of the stage in her wheelchair.

There are snatches of music within and connecting the scenes. Musical cues are indicated in the script.

SCENE ONE

Music: The Gipsy Kings

MIGUEL

I gotta bad case of mishuganismo. That's when a Jewish woman goes crazy for a latin guy. Or when a Jewish man loses it for a latina. Or when a latin gets weak for a Jew. Hetero, homo, whatever. Anyway, I'm suffering. The other day I started planning the menu for my wedding. Tacos stuffed with chopped liver. And maybe a Babs Streisand piñata filled with little butterscotch Che Guevaras. This is strictly fantasy. I'm not getting married. I barely know the guy. But I'm torching so bad over Miguel Montoya, I can barely sleep.

One day, he comes into my dressing room just as I'm putting on my coat for dinner break. He asks me what I'm doing for dinner. I'm putting on my coat, with the usual degree of difficulty cuzza the wheelchair, and he starts to help me without asking if I wanted help. And he took the collar and adjusted it around my neck and he took my hair and untucked it from the coat, and this whole time my heart is about to shoot straight out of my chest, but all I could think of to say was, "*Chinese* food, there's no good Chinese places around here, what're you crazy?" Mishuganismo.

I don't know how or when my mishuganismo first gripped me. But it's not just the individual *people*, you know, it's the whole culture. It's *being* in those countries. Like Nicaragua, before Reagan destroyed it with the contra war. Or Chile, after the CIA murdered Allende and the people fought back and we started hearing the word "disappeared." And Argentina, don't cry for me. And São Paulo, Ayacucho, Cayenne, Tucumán, Santo Domingo . . .

You can have Paraguay.

I wonder if my political beliefs get mixed up with my personal fantasies. Like is it in bad political taste to go to Nicaragua to do disability support work, and wind up in a clinch with a Sandinista who bears a striking resemblance to Edward James Olmos? Is this a kind of complex racism on my part? Is my mishuganismo related to the sick legacy of southern plantation owners who got off by paying regular nocturnal visits to the slave quarters?

Oh, absolutely not. While George Washington was busy being the unwed father of our country, my people were occupied fleeing from cossacks. I am the descendent of a nomadic and tortured tribe, with a dreadful cuisine, long memory, and a good head for numbers. Miguel is the descendent of Spanish conquistadores, escaped African slaves, and native American Indians. A people with an ability to see ghosts everywhere, unbe*liev*able rhythm, and an addiction to poetry.

You hafta admit, it's a perfect match.

One day, we're called to rehearsal and first the director is giving notes, so all the actors are sitting around listening. I've completely lost all touch with reality, so I decided I'd bring a banana to rehearsal and eat it in front of Miguel during notes. I actually planned this whole banana seduction thing—I felt like United Fruit Company about to fuck the Third World—so I unpeel the thing and start sucking on it, all the time aiming these smoldering glances over at Miguel. Who didn't seem too impressed. But I'm sucking away, when suddenly I realize this guy in the cast named Ivan is catching every slurp, and has a ridiculous grin on his face, apparently thinking the banana routine was strictly for his benefit. This always happens to me. Ivan is a real nice guy, but he plays the *accordian*, like one good polka and he's off, so please. So I just ate the banana up real quick, and rationalized it this way: potassium-wise, I was set for the rest of the day.

I've already envisioned the inevitable desolation and black void existence I will lead after Miguel breaks my heart. That is, if we ever do get together. That is the mishugana part. Imagining how miserable you're gonna be before you even get to the part where you're actually happy.

SCENE TWO

COMRADE SISTER FRANCES

Of course, the tragic beauty of my syndrome is how my Jew guilt dovetails with U.S. military adventures down South. Like this whole thing in Nicaragua, which was my fave revolution of all time, and the U.S. goes in and hooks up a giant cattle prod to the whole country.

So I joined this group called the Pledge of Resistance, and we decided to stage like a sit-in thing at the office of Alan Dixon, this Senator who I always hated, way before he voted in favor of contra aid, that slime.

In his office, we plaster the walls with stickers that say "Contra Free Zone," and people are singing something, sounds painfully '60s, but that's just me, and Dixon's staff is getting more fried out by the second. His chief guy is hollering at us, and he didn't look so good, very red in the face, and we're chanting "no contra aid" and this one nun, Frances, says to me, "hey, why don't you block the door with your wheelchair and put on the brakes and then the police won't be able to get in!" I thought, Yeah! I'll block the door! They wouldn't hurt me. I'm a cripple!

"No contra aid! No contra aid!"

And the chief guy is screaming, "you're all a bunch of fucking communists, get out!" Then he sticks his face in my face and yells, "get this woman out of here! I don't want this woman to get hurt!" and I said, "it's a little late for that" and Frances laughed. The sisters think I'm a real caution.

Then suddenly the place is crawling with cops. That's the last time I ever follow a nun into a charge. You know, for them they figure if things get outta hand they can go to heaven, but I know *I* am *fucked*. Frances didn't even blink when these two hairless federal dicks with ears start yanking on my technology. And I'm trying to be "*brave*," right, so I won't take the brakes off, and the cops' eyes start spinning around in their sockets like pinwheels, and meanwhile, all of my earnest comrades, *all* able-bodied, *ignore* me as the cops jerk my wheelchair back and start dragging me into the hall. Then they say to each other:

COP 1: Sure would be a shame if this thing fell.

COP 2: Sure would.

COP 1: Wonder what would happen if it just dropped.

I swear! My stomach twisted up and my mouth went dry. I said, are you threatening me?

COP 1: No, we're not threatening you.

ME: You're threatening to drop me, don't tell me you're not threatening me.

Then there's lots of beeping, on their radios, and they all pile into the elevators. Pfft. Gone. So I got out of there as fast as I could. And later I found out no one got arrested, just dragged out. But I was shaken up for hours after that.

Not that bravery is a real *quality*, like brown hair. It's not in the *DNA*, I don't think, but some people get a real jolt from danger, they get a charge, whereas I just get nauseous. And people use getting arrested as a *tactic*, they say, "people will see us on TV getting arrested, they'll see how much we're willing to give up for this cause, and then they will agree with us." But I wonder about that because sometimes I see the arrests on TV, and I just feel numb, nothing. I don't think, "yeah, they're brave, I will agree with them." And if I see a bunch of right-to-lifers getting dragged off, I don't then *agree* with them. I still think they're repellent. I get pissed cause they usurped the tactics of the Left! Who the hell are they to pretend they're not a part of the system? So I just wonder about what good it does to get arrested. Does it *win people over to your side?* I don't know . . .

I'm still struggling in the dark trying to figure out how I fit in to all this . . . how can I be effective . . . how do you keep from being paralyzed by fear and despair? I hope I'm never tested.

Music: "Sitting Here in Limbo"—Jimmy Cliff

SCENE THREE

LIPS. PLEASE.

Miguel thinks I'm brave. That's a common error made by most people about crips. Disabled people aren't brave to wanna live their lives, they're just sick of holding that tin cup out all the time. But Miguel thinks I'm brave.

Maybe I can exploit that.

Total mishuganismo.

I made the gigantic mistake of mentioning my passion to a friend, and she right away started suggesting I read those idiotic co-dependency books, like mishuganismo is some sick result of a childhood trauma or something. As if mishuganismo can be dealt with by a how-to book. As if any amount of analysis, drugs, twelve-step programs, electroshock therapy, frontal lobotomy, war, drought, plague or religious enlightenment will ever exorcise Miguel Montoya from my heart and soul.

I was always attracted to dark men. Except when I'm attracted to dark women. But anyway.

One day, I showed Miguel my pictures from my trip to Cuba. Because of course not only is he Puerto Rican, but we have heavy-duty political unity, we're both socialists, so let's face it—lower the lifeboats, abandon ship. I don't wanna think about it. Luckily, I already know life sucks and there's no justice, so I'm prepared.

On opening night, I picked out a picture of Fidel that had particularly struck him and on the back I wrote, "For Miguel on Opening Night, Love, Susan." It took me about twelve hours to figure out that message. I'm lying in bed the night before thinking, should I put "love" or "your friend" or "su compañera" . . .

When we are onstage together, I always look straight at him. Even though in the play I'm supposed to be in love with this other guy. I can't bear not to look at him every moment.

He said, "You're more latina than most of the latinas I know." (Gawd only knows I am not submerging my natural Hebraic tendencies. At dinner one night I *told* him I was from a different planet than him. Plus I told him I was an atheist. Bad move.)

       Music: "Sonho Meu"—Beleza Tropical
(blissfully transported) I'm so Latina. I'm so Latina.
Miguel does not like his name.
But I do. Miguel Montoya. Miguel Montoya.
Knows who Shining Path is.
Knows about the FALN.
Except he called it the FLAN—terrorist dessert of choice.
Lips.
Please.
Accent.
Stop. I'm dying.
Writes poetry.
They all do.

SCENE FOUR

STEEPLECHASE

Maybe I presume too much to say Miguel is a socialist. But I don't think so. My thing is, the world is like a gigantic trap. Like one time right after I broke my neck, I'm in the hospital, and I'm thinking they could have a fundraiser with all the patients, they could have a steeplechase thing, and the patients would compete by disability category. The wheelchair people would race through a big oil slick, or the people with pacemakers would have to race through the microwave pit. This has a metaphorical ring to me . . . sometimes. See, I don't get—I simply can't comprehend how anyone living in the world as I see it, could be anything but a socialist. Not the kinda socialism where you march in line behind some maniac chanting "Pol Pot Hits the Spot." Because socialism is an *attempt* to live humanely.

Socialism is, "if I get there first, I'll wait." Capitalism is, "if I get there first, it's mine. If you got there first, it's also mine." Capitalism is, "bend over and don't make a sound." Socialism is, "do you have protection?"

So that's why I work in solidarity with progressive movements in Latin countries. Which means I hang out with people who hate the U.S. government and try to stop it from doing nauseating things. Clearly, we haven't enjoyed gigantic success.

Music: "Viva Cepeda"—Cal Tjader

One night, this was '86 or '87, I'm at a fundraiser dance sponsored by Central America Medical Aid. And I like to meet people. If they have good politics and taste in music. So that night is when I connected with The Two Henrys.

Los Dos Enriques.

SCENE FIVE

THE TWO HENRYS

Okay, so neither of the Henrys was Latin. Love is unpredictable! But both Henrys were involved in projects to get the U.S. out of Central America. This is an impeccable Love Connection reference in my book. Actually, I won Henry *Numero Uno* in a raffle. No, but he had just returned from Nicaragua, and the idea was, a prize dinner with someone fresh off Aero Nica.

And my friend Mary fixed the raffle so I would win. The raffle guy calls my name, I thought, *damn*, I hope I don't have to produce the winning ticket, cuz I didn't even *buy* one. But Henry was real great. I thought to myself, he doesn't have to act that pleased, it's okay. But I didn't say that because I don't like to put myself down. In public. It's a bad strategy and it's been done.

You know, the Left doesn't just have *dances*. I mean, our dances are different. Like I can't remember a dance that didn't start and end with a speech about Mozambique or Guatemala or the West Bank. And there's tables set up everywhere, not with food, well, some of the tables have food, usually there's about two table-loads of three-bean salads at every dance, but most of the tables are filled with books, pamphlets, buttons . . . *end*less tables covered with commie literature and sign-up sheets and big coffee cans used as cash registers.

So at this *same* dance, I meet Henry *Numero Dos* at the VVAW lit table. VVAW is Vietnam Veterans Against the War. We're talking about fundraising for a video that VVAW wanted to make during their Nicaragua trip. So I say, yeah, I'll help. We set a meeting time, he looked into my eyes real deep for a few seconds . . . I thought, "oh! I get it!" and then I went home.

Music: "Two Lovers"—Mary Wells

Enrique Numero Uno is a mathematician. He's forty-five. I like that. We finally set a night to fulfill our raffle obligations, and although I had privately admitted to myself he would make a squeeze *par excellence*, I never imagined he'd be interested. So I dressed for rejection in my ugliest sweater. He showed up with flowers, all dressed up, I was totally unprepared. And my chair was sort of broken and kept making a clunking sound every time the left wheel rotated. At the restaurant, I couldn't fit under the table, so I had to sit mostly sideways. It was the worst-case scenario. All I needed was to start choking on my food.

Later on, we were sitting in my living room, and he asked me if I was seeing anyone. I figured he meant, was I seeing a psychiatrist. Anyway, I said no. So later that week he called me and we made plans to go out. I was be*side* myself. This was above and beyond the raffle requirements.

Meanwhile, Enrique Numero *Dos* started to move in. So we went out a couple times. Henry #2 was in the Navy, and spent a year in Vietnam. He was kicked out with five other guys for their anti-war activities. So the day Henry Numero Dos leaves for Nica with the VVAW delegation, is the *very* same day as my second big date with Henry Numero *Uno*. This time I put on my nice shirt, some makeup . . . I looked real good. We went to a Chinese place, sat in a dark corner, ate some wonderful garlic thing and made out all during dinner. So since that night we've been seeing each other not *con*stantly but *reg*ularly. We made out in Mexican restaurants, Cuban, Thai . . . all the major cuisines.

When the other Henry touched down from Central America, the Chinese restaurant Henry left for ten days to do some lectures and see his kids. It was like *(waving s.l.)* "Bye, Henry, have a good trip!" *(waving s.r.)* "Hi Henry, how was your trip?"

I like this juggling thing, I've never had that before. Two squeezes. And *good* squeezes, men I picked.

(*Sing:* two *a cappella* lines from "*Two Lovers*")

And when I got the part in the Goodman Theatre play, Henry Numero Uno brought flowers and wine, and he didn't even know I had been cast yet. It was just something he did for no reason and then I was happy. That was happiness. To have something to celebrate, and then someone to celebrate *with*, and wine and flowers.

That was the first big post-wheelchair part I had. The show I'm in with Miguel, I have a relatively small part. I play a repressed wife. I say stuff like, "Isn't that the doorbell?" about three or four times. If the doorbell cue doesn't work, I say, "Didn't I just hear someone at the door?"

Whenever possible, I hang out with Miguel backstage. Most of the time, I am too desperately choked with love to think of anything cogent to say. So I sit there and whistle. Miguel told me that was bad luck one night just as the show was gonna start and I told him that was pure superstition. I'm not superstitious because that doesn't fit with my world view.

Then I went onstage and my skirt which was very long, my costume, got caught in the front wheel of my wheelchair and started rolling up in there like the way Isadora Duncan got killed, although of course my skirt wasn't around my neck but still I couldn't move suddenly and everyone onstage pretended that this was a *nat*ural thing, and the guy playing my husband comes over and says, "what should I do dear," and I said, "just pull it out of the *wheel*, Thomas dear" (it was a period piece) and so we finally got the skirt out after about thirty seconds of total Actor's Nightmare misery. After that, I stopped whistling backstage. Lenin calls this, The Law of Uneven Development.

SCENE SIX

CUBA

Let's face it. There's the wheelchair, a fact, and if you can, you will figure out a way to use it to your advantage. Which is how I wound up in Cuba. It's illegal to visit Cuba without a special visa. You can only get the visa by being a journalist or a professional in your field, doing research. So I *am* a professional disabled person. Me and my crip friend Simon decided to form a Disabled Delegation to Cuba, and pretty soon we were flying into the José Marti airport.

Music: "Caprichosos de la Habana"—Arturo Sandoval

Me and Simon hung out with the Organization of Disabled Revolutionaries in Nicaragua together, so we are real tight. It was Simon who finessed that great tenet of Marxist-Leninist doctrine, "Imperialism is the highest stage of Capitalism," by pointing out that "Quadriplegia is the highest stage of Disability." Cuz there's like a hierarchy of cripdom. There's wheelchair users and there's *wheelchair* users. As far as most quads are concerned, any crip who has full use of his arms and hands is practically faking it.

Simon started a list about five years ago called "20,000 Advantages to Quadriplegia." Some of the things are: your shoes need replacing very infrequently. Ummm. Smoking pot provides excellent relief from muscle spasticity and could theoretically be claimed as a medical expense under current tax law. Also, you get lots of cloth napkins for free. At least I do, cuz when I'm in a nice restaurant, after I get home and take off my coat and toss my purse on the couch I realize my napkin is still in my lap. Because when you don't stand up to leave, it's very easy to forget about. So over the years, you can imagine. They don't match though. And they need ironing so forget it. Another thing on the list is you don't have to worry about getting in a terrible accident and becoming a paraplegic. It's a short list.

Anyhow, we wind up in Cuba right before Christmas, which is perfect timing from my perspective cuz Christmas in the States is, to me, like the celebration of the birth of the Credit Card, and in Cuba, the whole thing is pretty low profile. Opiate of the people and all that. We hook up with the Cuban crips. They have a group called ACLIFIM—*Asociación Cubana de Limitados Físicos Motores.* There's this quad guy named José Luis Silva, he looks just like Pablo Picasso, and he tells us all the stuff we're gonna be doing. This is like 8:00 in the morning, we're sitting around the Habana Libre sipping mojitas, I'm thinking two things: 1. I'm incredibly happy. 2. I hope there's an accessible bathroom nearby.

They take us to these sheltered workshop places. We go in and all the workers stand and applaud us. There's blind people, deaf people, amputees, the whole shot. They shower us with presents. We get shell earrings, shell ashtrays, shell sculptures. As we leave, I pass out crip rights buttons from home as gifts. Secretly I'm thinking, this is fucked up. It's a dead end. Even though the Cubes insist the sheltered workshop deal is temporary, just a pass-through thing on the way to employment in a regular factory or office, it sounds fishy. Okay. I'm confused. I'm making a major mental note about this when my friend Eleanor who lives in Nicaragua starts criticizing the macho Cuban men to our tour guide Lilia. Lilia's a member of the Communist Party. She says Eleanor is a feminist extremist and they've practically eliminated sexism in Cuba, and Eleanor says no, unh-unh, sexism is alive and well in Cubetown for a fact. And Lilia says, where else in the world is there a law requiring that men do half the housework? And Eleanor says, yeah, they passed the law, but everybody knows the women still do 100% of the housework. And then she demonstrates for Lilia the chorus of sounds that accompany women down the street every day. *"Ven aquí, mamacita, mira como camina! chiquita, chiquitita, aya!"* Pant, pant. And Lilia has to laugh at this thing which she knows is true. And I ask Lilia when do we get to meet Fidel. She says write him a letter. We're both kidding but suddenly I'm thinking about what to say in this letter to Fidel.

One night we're invited to a party. I go up to this guy, his name is Noel and he says "are you a romantic?" and I say "si." He recites a poem he's written about this woman he loves but she won't take him seriously because his body is twisted. He tells me there are two kinds of people in this world. The first kind *(Cuban accent)* sing a love song with their full heart and soul, the second kind sing the love song but their full heart's not in it . . .

You can take the revolutionary out of Tony Orlando, but you can't take the Tony Orlando, well, you know. Then I tell him that in the U.S., disabled people take mean words used against us and use them with each other almost as endearments. Like we say "that guy's a good crip" or something. I ask him if there's an equivalent in Cuba. He says *"cojo."* We formed the Cojo Club.

This one guy, Joselito, was disabled fighting in Angola. I try to describe to him how in the U.S. there's a cult of independence. Not just affecting disabled people, but everyone, a worship of the individual, a shamefulness attached to being on welfare, or aging, or even weighing too much, implying a lack of inner resources. And disabled people must "overcome" shit, or remain children forever, Jerry's kids, because a disabled child with needs is adorable, but a disabled *adult* with needs, *any* adult with needs, is un-American. He tells me they don't deal with that here. That disabled Cubans live in the context of a collectivism that is stressed throughout society. So it's not shameful to need help, or rely on the family, because it's part of a socialist perspective.

Well, that fits. Socialism creates different priorities, different values. I'm feeling much better now, like "yeah, I get it." I'm feeling downright cubified.

Except the part about relying on the family for critical things like getting dressed. That sounded fishy. It's one thing to get help up a curb, but if you gotta rely on Cousin Rosalita for the *real* help, the cojo always ends up getting the help on the terms of the *helper*, when they feel like it or have time, like a favor. Wouldn't it be better if all the cojos who needed help had control over the process? A person they could hire and supervise? See, the Cubes kept insisting that the family doesn't *mind* dealing with the care and feeding of the cojos. And is this what it all comes down to? I mean, where in Marxist/Leninist thought do they talk about who takes the cojo to the toilet?

Meanwhile, Eleanor has written this love letter to Fidel. Is this an American thing, this needing to meet the star of the revolution, or what? Then we spend the whole afternoon tooling around a hospital in Havana, talking to patients, checking out the technology which is a combination of state of the art and whatever works. They have a factory there where they make prosthetic limbs, and the workers are all busy at workbenches or on these Dawn of the Industrial Rev machines from Bulgaria or something and I ask, "how many of these limbs can you turn out in a month?" And the tour guy says, "Compañera, we're not into turning out a certain number. We just want to make limbs that fit people. We don't expect to make money in health care." Boy, these Cubes are square.

Later on we check out this prison where Fidel was kept after the attack on the Moncada garrison. This prison is now a museum, and there's a blue-eyed Cuban on hand who tells you all about the place. I'm getting this creepy déjà vu feeling, but I *know* I've never been to this place before but it reminds me of something and the blue-eyed Cuban is talking about how this prison was designed in the U.S. and suddenly I remember it looks just like Stateville Penitentiary! Which I've been to a lot because I used to counsel disabled prisoners there. Me and these two other activists would drive to Joliet about once a month, because an inmate in a chair called our office one day. He said, "please come, I don't know what happened to my body, can you come?" *(outraged)* He was shot by the police, which is how he was in a chair. *(an afterthought)* He was robbing a bank.

And when we met him, he looked at my legs and asked me how come they weren't all thin like his, because his legs had atrophied, and I said, "well, I have fat legs." And he said, "can I still have sex?" (Number One question asked by all gimps after regaining consciousness.) *Can I Still Have Sex?* So I said, "Yes! Absolutely! Just not with me."

It was a very scary place. There was a huge woman guard with a red beehive who would search inside my shoes and inside my seat cushion and frisk me like crazy, looking for contraband, we'd go through like five checkpoints, with metal detectors and stuff, then they'd let us into the infirmary where they kept the disabled guys. It was a filthy, stinking place, and there were lots of crips there. This one kid, he was twenty, he had a terrible pressure sore, and for treatment, the night nurse put a leaf from a tree on it. An oak tree or something. We knew that kid was gonna die. And there was a big painting on the wall of Jackie Kennedy. A painting by an inmate. Jackie looking down on Camelot.

"Compañera! Compañera! Necesita ayuda?" And I look up and realize the Blue-Eyed Cuban is smiling into my eyes, like man to woman as opposed to guide to tourist, so I decide to pay closer attention to this lecture. After about an hour we have to leave, and I look out the window of the bus and there are the blue eyes staring, and I think, nice tour. Mishuganismo.

In Lenin Park, I'm feeling kinda smashed up in my chest. It doesn't hurt but it's not going away. But I'm sure that it will. But I have to admit that something is wrong with me, like I can't breathe, and I'm in Cuba, and unless some miracle happens real quick I'm about to experience socialized medicine up close and personal. And I am one game cojo if ever there was one except for this one eensy little phobia which is hospitals. Visions of health care professionals wielding scalpels and chattering in Cubish are racing through my head. In the emergency room, the doctor is a calm, collected type woman who diagnoses an asthma attack, and I end up in a hospital room, an i.v. stuck into my hand.

And I thought about how when I was thirteen, I taped this big poster of Che to the wall right over my bed. Che had asthma really bad. I remembered a book my brother gave me when I was in high school, and on the inside cover was this quote from Che. "Let me say, at the risk of seeming ridiculous, that the true revolutionary is guided by great feelings of love."

And as the medicine started to work and I felt better, I noticed that nobody treated me like a curiosity. And nobody asked me to fill out forms, or show an insurance card. I found I even felt secure communicating in Spanish, like they'd take the time to listen. They never do that at home, even in English.

In the morning the doctor says I can leave and everybody says I look *mucho mejor*. I pass out crip rights buttons to the whole staff, give the official Cojo Club salute *(Susan flails hand limply)* and they hug me and Eleanor takes pictures. Hellos and goodbyes in Latin countries require more of a flourish than in El Norte.

Back at the hotel, I stack some pillows up on a table and crash my head down cripstyle and sleep for the first time since the bus in Lenin Park. And then Eleanor is saying, "Susan, wake up, it's happening." And it hurts so bad to wake up but did she say it's happening?

"It's happening?" I say.

And then we're in a room way high up in the hotel and there is our whole group and everyone is smiling and way down the hall a man in a green uniform and gray beard is walking toward us.

And God, Fidel can talk. We got onto this thing about how each hemisphere has produced certain things, like rice or cocoa. He wondered where alcohol was first produced. He told us a story from the Bible. About Noah, after the deluge. Noah came out of the ark, and planted grapes, and from the grapes, he made wine. One day, he had too much wine and got drunk, and one of Noah's sons laughed at him. To punish the son, God said all of his children would be Black. *"Increíble,"* Fidel said. He said it sounded like Noah lived in the U.S. or South Africa. He said, if the Bible plants racist ideas, and says women are sinners, and work is a punishment from God, then maybe the Bible scholars around the world needed to make some revisions. He said, if Marxism-Leninism is being revised today, why not the Bible?

And everyone laughed. Swapping Bible stories with Fi. But I never liked the Noah story. Two giraffes, two zebras, then God stuffs everybody else down the toilet and flushes hard. I'd rather avoid those apocalyptic visions of fixing the world. I want Fidel to do what he said, to rethink Marxism-Leninism. But I know he won't. And this Flood that's happening now, it will cleanse nothing, and spare only generals and TV evangelists. Fidel will be swept away by this Flood.

There was a time when Fidel stood for self-determination. For liberation. Well, that was a long time ago. For me, he will always be fantasy and history crashing into each other.

Music: "La Vie Dansante"—The Neville Brothers

SCENE SEVEN

THE SPONGE

Back in the U.S., patriotism is spreading like peanut butter. Number nine on the list of 20,000 Advantages to Quadriplegia: You never have to stand for the National Anthem.

One weekend was a big deal for all the Vietnam vets because the government decides to have a "welcome home" parade twenty years after the war is over. Henry Numero Dos has been dreading this for a while because it is such an incredible bunch of bullshit. This is one of the reasons I love him, because he has good politics. He's also expert at fixing broken wheelchairs. In many ways, Henry Numero Dos is my dream man.

But I'm still seeing Henry Numero Uno. For birth control, I'm using the sponge. Of course, there have been condoms for a very long time, but women always are the ones to take responsibility for birth control, I'm sorry but that's a fact. So to take the burden on fully, women never want to say, "hon, here's the condom. Put it on." We'd much rather preserve the mystique that we have magically swallowed or surgically implanted or stuck up us some sperm-busting agent, before the deed, cuz it's so romantic that way.

But meantime I'm hearing, sponge . . . wonderful thing . . . just stick it up there . . . okay . . . I can do that . . . except then you have to get it *out.* Friends tell me stories about how they couldn't find the little string up there, and their cousin had to go to the emergency room where teams of highly trained professionals work to extract the sponge, which by this time must be kinda the worse for wear.

So what am I gonna do? Like I'm really gonna be able to find some little slimy string up there with my gimpy hand. So this is how my disability makes my life so ab*surd,* cuz I have to ask my personal assistant—the person who helps me get dressed in the morning—to root around up there. This is now part of her *job* description. I have no privacy! Most people can at least get laid without having to ask *by*standers to yank out their birth control. Cuz I'm too shy to ask the man to do it. I'm not too shy to be fucked within an inch of my life, but then suddenly I get freaked about asking the man to stick around and . . . pull out the thing.

And then all the stories are true. It's impossible to get the sponge out, it's attached itself, like barnacles, to my insides, we have to hitch the little string up to a twenty-mule team to pull it out. So forget that shyness thing, cuz that's it. I'm a rubber girl now.

The thing about disability rights work is—it's not abstract. These are our issues: Who's gonna pull out the sponge? Can I get into the bathroom? Can I figure out a way to stay out of the nursing home? Can I figure out a way to *get* out of the nursing home once I'm there? Will public aid buy the new wheelchair when the one I'm in only works as a can opener? For disabled people, it's just day to day survival stuff.

Music: "My Blood"—The Neville Brothers

SCENE EIGHT

ATLANTA

It was disabled activists who were responsible for the Americans
with Disabilities Act, a piece of civil rights legislation signed by
Bush in '90, in a display of hypocrisy and photo opportunism that
would make Jerry's Telethon look like Masterpiece Theatre. Anyway, before the Act was signed, disabled people fought for years
to get on the bus. In '88, we went to Atlanta for a confrontation
with the men in suits and women with nice neck scarves. The
enemy. They are having their convention there and somewhere
on their agenda is the thing about the cripples who wanna ride
the buses and trains with the real people. The Suits and Scarves
tell Congress it's too expensive for the crips to ride the buses. So
this is where the battle is joined. We want to, *have* to ride. The
enemy, typically, fights the inevitable, so we come to Atlanta to
crash their convention.

I'm on the plane. I just tossed back one of those little airplane
bottles of cognac, cause the pilot announced: "Ladies and Gentlemen, sorry for the delay but it's due to our differently-abled
passenger." Please. Differently-abled. It's like calling Black people
"Afrorific." Anyway, booze goes straight to my head, so I'm feeling
extremely philosophical and deep-like. And I started thinking
about how underneath everything, I was really scared to go to this

demo. Because the fight has really escalated over the past couple years, these crips have adopted a very militant approach, and at some point I'm gonna find myself face to face with one or more officers of the law, and the whole idea makes me sick with panic. What if I'm handcuffed? What if they're putting me in the paddy wagon and I lose my balance and fall? But on the other hand, what if I'm a coward? If I don't get arrested, will it mean I'm not tough enough to do what I know is right? I'm so afraid. I'm good at talking about fighting back, but really, I'd much rather be safe at home.

Atlanta is funny. They've done a lotta construction since *Gone With the Wind*. Next to our hotel is this restaurant called "Tokyo Shapiro." Jewpanese cuisine. The hotel is already swarming with crips, it looks like an Oral Roberts recruitment center.

At 7:30, I go to the big planning meeting. I could only just sit in the doorway actually, because the place was jammed full. Must've been about three hundred people. I've been in places with tons of disabled people before, but these people were *really* disabled. Verrrry gimpy. There's spozed ta be actions for three days, culminating with a big blockade of the Federal Building.

Now if there's one thing that's guaranteed to bend a cop right out of shape, it's a blockade. The lead crips said if at least forty people got arrested, the police wouldn't be able to handle the crip-to-cop ratio, and everyone would therefore be released and not have to sleep in jail. Oy.

Most of the gimps were men. Mosta the ones who talked were men. Lots of the people were from Denver, which is mission control for militant crips, and they had long hair and bandanna type headbands. Mostly everyone was poor. There were lots of people with cerebral palsy, and it took a lot of time to understand what they were trying to say, because their tongues are so spazzed out. Anyway, it got late, and I was wiped out. Went upstairs, got into bed, thought about Enrique Número Uno for a while, and finally drifted off.

Next morning, we're supposed to gather at 8:30, so I figured, by gimp time, the show wouldn't get on the road till at least 10:00. It was 8:45, plenny a time for breakfast.

The lobby was already crowded with my disabled sisses and bros. I asked someone when the vans were leaving and they said, they left. What? But I haven't had my coffee. When will they be back? They won't be back. People like you can go in your chair. Okay. Okay, I say. How far is this place. Two miles, they say. By now I'm getting the idea that these are either some seriously dedicated, or seriously brain-damaged, gimps. But hey, I got the spirit. I came to Atlanta for a demo, and dammit, I'm gonna go to a demo. A line of electric wheelchairs, sounding like a swarm of mosquitos, heads out of the hotel, and into the street. I fall in.

Outside, it's cold. In the '30s, and all I'm wearing is a sweatshirt. With wind chill, 80 below. No matter. I can't feel my legs in any weather, so what the fuck. I won't think about it. None of the people in my little group of travelers is saying anything. They're cold, too. Every now and then a car passes and the people check us out. They just look. We don't care. We're used to it. They don't exist. Too goddam cold. Finally, we get to the place, and it's just a big parking lot. Crips as far as the eye can see. Meanwhile, about half a dozen cop cars pull up and watch. There were a few chants, like "We Will Ride," then this quad guy in the leadership, who has very long braids, says, "Okay, now we're all gonna march to the Westin Hotel, and have a big rally!" I'm thinking, great, oh boy, we're starting. Then I find out the Westin Hotel is exactly two miles back in the direction we just came from, and then another mile. My attitude's beginning to wear pretty thin. They must've had the learning disabled committee plan the route.

So okay, we get in another line, and start the march. By now, there are easily twenty squad cars with us. There were a couple casualties along the way. Two people needed stitches when they pitched forward outta their chairs going down steep curb cuts. Me, I'm just in a "let's get there" mode. We're about a block from the Westin when suddenly my chair just said "fuck it" and stopped moving. Some other crips stopped to take a look, somebody flagged down a van, and I got in. And you know what? The van was heated. This guy from Alaska fixed my chair. They gave me coffee. I figured this must be how crack feels.

We spent the next day picketing in the drizzle. This time I had on two sweatshirts, cuz I bought an extra in the hotel store. It had pictures of peaches dancing and laughing on it. Everything is

peaches with these Georgians. So we're picketing, and the trans-
portation people couldn't've cared less. Helen Keller could've
been out there, FDR, José Feliciano, it wouldn't have moved them.

Helen Keller was a socialist. She's one of my heroes.

So me and my friends split from the picket. We had seen a restaurant, not too far off, looked accessible, looked good, thought
we'd check it out. The second we get out of the car, the rain gets
real intense, and I'm headed for the spot I saw with no curb. But
suddenly there's a car parked right on it. Shit. I'm soaked. I holler
at some patrons, "can you please just give me a boost up this little
curb here?" Antoinette is with me. Antoinette has cerebral palsy
and her feet jut out to one side. This guy helps us up. I'm inside.
"Can I talk to the manager? Yeah. You're the manager? Hi, look,
someone parked right over the curb cut, my friends and me are
getting drenched, could you have that car moved? No? Wh—? It's
your car. Mmm hmm, I see." On the way to our table, some man
comes up to us and says, "Don't you girls have nurses?" I just
said, "No."

No, we don't.

And I think, I'm Me. I'm me and I have a life. I'm a writer, I read
books, I fall in love with the wrong people, I tell jokes, I'm Me.
Then I had to use the bathroom, but the bathroom was inacces-
sible. That was okay. I went outside, and emptied my leg bag all
over the manager's car.

Music: "Hallelujah"—Handel's Messiah

The next day. The last day. Federal Building Blockade. I always
prepare in the same way: 1. no earrings—cops like to grab onto
them. 2. no glasses—you could get broken glass in your eyes.
3. one piece of i.d., carry nothing else of value. It's still raining,
so I cut a hole for my head in a Hefty bag and join the group,
which by this time has swelled to over 400 people. At the Federal
Building, everyone goes inside and people split up into teams to
block the doors. No business as usual will go on this day. We'd
let people out, but we allowed no one in. And people got angry.
They called us names . . . some of them said we were freaks. But
some people said good luck, be strong, we're on your side.

So the hours pass. The police had the idea that if they just left us alone, we'd get bored and go away. The demo organizers send someone out for food and everybody gets a sandwich and some pop. I was stationed at a door with a guy named Marcus who had cerebral palsy, and I ended up feeding him.

And it gets dark, and the cops are looking desperate, cuz they have to get us outta there, but meanwhile the press has arrived. Now the crips with chains and locks weave the chains through the revolving doors and lock themselves by the neck to these doors. People who can walk, like deaf people and stuff, are chaining themselves to people in chairs. The police announce "if you don't leave the building now, you will be arrested." So the people who don't want to get arrested go outside and chant. And I have to decide . . . I'm not sure . . . I look at the paddy wagons . . . I'm thinking how many cops it'll take to lift me in there. And then, fuck it. I wedge my chair deeper into the doorway, and put on my brakes.

The arrests begin. I see the cops trying to shove people's chairs out of doors. But every time they dislodge one of us and start on someone else, the dislodged crip rushes back into the void. The disabled folks outside move up to the building and they start screaming and pounding on the windows, and it's like something out of a Fellini movie, the sound of people pounding on the glass walls is like thunder. "The People! United! Will Never Be Defeated!" The cops are bugging out. "The People! United! Will Never Be Defeated!" It's serve and protect time, with a vengeance. They bring in *chain*saws and try to get the people out of the revolving doors. A woman has a seizure and the cops drag her away from the fray and let her lie there in the rain, seizuring. Several cops grab me, my heart is pounding in my head, and everything's in slow motion like when you're in shock. And I say "yeah, that's right I'm not moving," and they try to jam and pull me out of the door. Cop grabs the control of my chair and sends me flying forward at full speed, he won't let go and I'm losing my balance, I careen into another demonstrator, smashing her footrest in as her chair is thrown back. And there's lotsa screaming and I see Marcus, the guy I had to feed his lunch to, he throws himself out of his chair and lands right at the threshhold, and then some cop grabs Marcus and yanks him out of the door, and he's laying on the wet sidewalk, angry and struggling still, and then two cops pick him up and dump him in the back of the paddy wagon. And Marcus's wheelchair just sat empty in the rain, like expensive abstract sculpture.

Pause.

My friend Antoinette got caught in the crossfire. She kept telling the cops she didn't want to be arrested, that she was trying to move out of the way, but they were way past listening. She was so freaked, her legs kept jerking out more than ever, so the cops took a rope and tied her legs to her chair. I hope she got in one good stiff kick to the pig who tied her down. And many people were arrested, but not me. The one time I actually *wanted* to go to jail, and the police ignore me. Yeah, well, the gimp world is a crazy place to live.

Music: "Many Rivers to Cross"—Jimmy Cliff

SCENE NINE

EIGHT BALL

One night, I asked Miguel if he'd ever been arrested. He said, just the usual stuff. Like he'd be hanging out with friends in his neighborhood and a police car would drive up and a cop would yell, "Hey, you! Over here!" And they'd frisk him and bat him around a little bit, then drive off. When he told me this, I wanted to kiss him for a million years.

I asked the Eight Ball if Miguel and I would become lovers, and it answered, *It Is Certain*. Then I asked it, will we be happy. It said, *Outlook Not So Good*.

And I hafta say, when a person is torching, the person goes out of his way to be with the person. And I see more and more that Miguel is not going out of his way. So I don't go out of *my* way in return, to see if he notices. And I have to say, after much thought, he doesn't seem to notice that I'm not going out of my way. But wait. Maybe he sees I'm not going out of my way, and loses confidence. But wait. I don't think so. But it's altogether too soon to jump to conclusions. Mishuganismo takes great patience, and is an enemy of logic. Normal rules do not apply. And I am beautiful, a beautiful-faced woman. Can't forget that.

And less and less am I able to look straight at him onstage. Other women can flirt with him. It's easy for them cuz they don't have the Syndrome. I watch them and I think how wonderful it must be to be free to go right up to him and just touch him like they do—one woman kissed his neck and he laughed and said, "oh no, not my neck," and I wanted to be the one doing that.

Then one day we have a long dinner break between shows. I'm in the lobby calling my answering machine and in he walks, with a bag of chinese carry-out. So I say, what're you doing, come into my dressing room, you can eat and we'll sit around and talk.

Music: "Love and Passion"—Sarah Vaughan and Milton Nascimento

And I said, What? You've never been in love? You're thirty years old and you've never been in love?

"No, never."

Cuz we were telling each other what heaven would be like (don't ask, I was goin' with the flow), even though there's no such thing, I said.

In heaven there would be an eternal smorgasbord, and anyone could eat whatever they wanted, and you would be in love all the time, with lots of sex, and there would be good bands playing in different places. And he said, he didn't care much about the food, but sex was the most important thing. But then he changed his mind and said, first love, then sex. (I'm thinking, but you said you've never been in love.)

And he said, I'm a cold guy. What, you don't believe me. And I said, no, I believe you. If you say you're cold, I believe you. (And this woman in the cast had left her little pink panty things on the dressing table, right by where he set his eggroll, and more and more I'm sitting there feeling like Elephant Man.)

And he said, if I want a woman, I will do anything to get her. Anything. And I said, who do you want? And he said, no one, now. And my face was burning up, from the fact that he was killing me.

And then he left and I thought about this, and decided to get over it. Then about five hundred years later, the stage manager says places, and I go out in the wings and he says, why don't you look at me onstage anymore. I want you to look at me. And I said, the other women will look at you. And he said, that's okay, you should still look. And I thought, cold guy.

And I didn't look.

Pretty much. Mishuganismo.

SCENE TEN

THE LEFT

Maybe mishuganismo is that duality thing. Love and politics. Cruelty and nobility. Embracing atheism but being sure not to whistle backstage.

I have become more alienated from the so-called Left than ever in my pathetic political history. I am *embarrassed* to defend my comrades' behavior to the uninitiated. Not that there is any visible behavior, because aside from burning the occasional flag on the Capitol steps there is absolutely no-fucking-thing going on. The Sandinistas lost in Nicaragua. The CIA and the contras made them an offer they couldn't refuse. "Say Uncle Sam or die." What the West refers to as the Communist Experiment is dead and buried. Lenin is twirling around in his tomb like a dreidel. Yesterday, I heard that a guy who used to be in my committee actually *bit off the ear* of a fellow worker—then ground it into the earth with his foot as two guys tried to restrain him. WHAT THE FUCK IS GOING ON? Is the Left just another religious cult for lost souls like me who can't fit in at health clubs and tanning salons? If there wasn't a Left, I worry that half the people I work with would be just as comfortable in the Moonies or 700 Club. They need a structure, a set of ideas to hold on to. I absolutely can't stand it one more minute. I'm sick to death of polarizing tactics, sectarianism, ultra-leftism and empty and useless political gestures which nobody ever hears about anyway so what's the use?

Well. I'm over-reacting. *One* guy bit *one* earlobe off. And some of the back part. But I'm making this too big a thing. Like my friend Antoinette who didn't want to get arrested at the Atlanta demo? She's one of our best organizers now. That experience really turned her into a leader. So this proves there *is* a point to being arrested. It politicizes people.

Socialists have to take a big bite of reality sandwich and just say, look, we're in a time of transition and things are unclear. We know the classic Marx-Lenin thing isn't gonna cover all the bases, and we know the capitalists have nothing to offer but designer jeans and despair. We have to be able, at least, to *imagine* a sane world.

"Let me say, at the risk of seeming ridiculous, that the true revolutionary is guided by great feelings of love."

I don't wanna be cynical anymore. It would be nice, not to be cynical.

Music: "Cruel, Crazy, Beautiful World"—Johnny Clegg and Savuka

Contributors

JOAN ALESHIRE received a BA from Harvard/Radcliffe and an MFA in writing from Goddard College. She has published two poetry collections, *Cloud Train* (Texas Tech, 1982) and *This Far* (*Quarterly Review of Literature*, 1987), and is writing a memoir. She teaches in the Warren Wilson MFA program.

TOM ANDREWS's first full-length collection of poems, *The Brother's Country*, was selected for the National Poetry Series in 1989. He is the editor of *On William Stafford: What the River Says*. His second collection of poems, *The Hemophiliac's Motorcycle*, recipient of the Iowa Poetry Prize, was published by the University of Iowa Press in 1994. He is an associate professor at Purdue University and is writing a book on hemophilia, for Little, Brown, and Company, that grew out of his last poem in *The Hemophiliac's Motorcycle*.

VICTORIA ANN-LEWIS is the founder and director of Other Voices, a program dedicated to new voices in the American theater, at Los Angeles's Mark Taper Forum. In June 1995, she organized *Chautauqua '95: A Writing Seminar* as a follow-up to 1994's *A Contemporary Chautauqua: Performance and Disability*, a new model for the development of community-based art. Her documentary plays include two television specials for Norman Lear's Embassy Television, *Tell Them I'm a Mermaid* (1983) and *Who Parks in Those Spaces* (1985); *P.H.*reaks: The Hidden History of People with Disabilities* (1993); *The Greatest Stories Never Told* (1987) for the AFL-CIO; and *Teenage Ninja Mothers* (1991), with African-American and Latina teen mothers. She is also a professional actress with an extensive list of stage and TV credits.

DORIS BAIZLEY is a founding member of LA Theatre Works and was resident playwright for the Mark Taper Forum's Improvisational Theater Project for seven years. Her plays *Mrs. California* (CBS/Dramatists Guild Award), *Tears of Rage, Catholic Girls* (L.A. Dramalogue Award), *Daniel in Babylon,* and *Guns* have been produced in regional theaters, including the Mark Taper Forum, A Contemporary Theatre in Seattle, the Cleveland Playhouse, Capital Rep, the National Theatre for the Deaf, and the Divadlo Na Zabradli in Prague.

JOHNSON CHEU has cerebral palsy. His work has appeared in *The Bridge, The Progressive,* and *A Revolutionary Blueprint Anthology,* among others. He has held lecture appointments at Guizhou Normal University in Guizhou Province, China, and Oakland University in Michigan. He currently lives in Columbus, Ohio.

ELIZABETH CLARE, originally from Oregon, is a poet, essayist, and activist living in Michigan. Her poems and essays have appeared in a variety of periodicals and anthologies, including *Sojourner: The Women's Forum, Sinister Wisdom, Lesbian Ethics, The Disability Rag, Hanging Loose,* and *The Arc of Love.* She holds an MFA in Creative Writing from Goddard College.

MARCIA CLAY was born in 1953 and has had cerebral palsy since birth. "Wolf" is her first "official" publication and is excerpted from her novel, *Cats Don't Fly.* A resident of San Francisco, she teaches writing at the University of San Francisco and is a single mother.

TIM DLUGOS was the first editor of Ralph Nader's *Citizen's Alert* newsletter in Washington, D.C. His books include *Entre Nous* (Little Caesar Press), *A Fast Life* (Sherwood Press), and *Powerless: Selected Poems* (High Risk Books/Serpent's Tail). His poems have appeared in *The Paris Review, BOMB, Washington Review,* and the anthologies *Poets for Life* (Persea), *The Name of Love* (St. Martin's Press), and *A Year in Poetry* (Crown). He was pursuing a master's degree at Yale Divinity School when he died of AIDS in December 1990, at the age of forty.

ANDRE DUBUS is the author of *Dancing After Hours* (Knopf, 1996), for which he received the Rea Award for the Short Story, and eight other books of fiction, as well as *Broken Vessels,* a collection of essays. He has received the PEN/Malamud Award, the Jean Stein Award from the American Academy of Arts and Letters, the *Boston Globe*'s first annual Lawrence L. Winship Award, and fellowships from the Guggenheim and MacArthur foundations. He lives in Haverhill, Massachusetts.

LARRY EIGNER's first collection of ten poems was proposed by Robert Creeley, who then published it in *Mallorca* in 1953 when Eigner was twenty-six. Thirty-five others have appeared since (plus solo numbers of seven magazines), mostly booklets like the first one and the latest, *A Count of Some Things* (Score Publications, 1991). In 1984, he received half of the San Francisco State University Poetry Center's prize for his 1983 collection *Waters/Places/A Time* (Black Sparrow Press). Larry Eigner died in February 1996.

STANLEY ELKIN's last novel, *Mrs. Ted Bliss*, received the National Book Critics Circle Award. The author of numerous works of fiction, he received the National Book Award for *George Mills*. Mr. Elkin was the Merle King Professor of Modern Letters at Washington University in St. Louis, and received fellowships and awards from the Guggenheim and Rockefeller foundations, and was a member of the American Academy and Institute of Arts and Letters. He died in 1995.

MIKE ERVIN, a graduate of Southern Illinois University journalism school, used to write obituaries. Fortunately, things have gotten better. He has written hundreds of newspaper and magazine pieces on disability. His previously published short stories are "Man Versus Wood" and "The Antelope," and he cowrote two plays on disability, *The Plunky and Spunky Show* and *Activities of Daily Living*.

ANNE FINGER is the author of the novel *Bone Truth* (Coffee House Press, 1994), the short story collection *Basic Skills* (University of Missouri Press, 1988), and an autobiographical essay, *Past Due: A Story of Disability, Pregnancy and Birth* (Seal Press, 1990). She has received grants and awards, including the D. H. Lawrence Fellowship and the Louisiana State University/*Southern Review* award for short fiction. She lives in Detroit with her son, Max, and teaches creative writing at Wayne State University.

KENNY FRIES is the author of *Body, Remember: A Memoir* (Dutton), *Anesthesia: Poems* (The Advocado Press), and the play *A Human Equation*, which premiered at LaMama E.T.C. in New York City. He received the Gregory Kolovakos Award for AIDS Writing and a Lambda Literary Award nomination for *The Healing Notebooks* (Open Books, 1990). He has received a Ludwig Vogelstein Foundation grant and residencies at The MacDowell Colony and Yaddo. He teaches in the MFA in Writing Program at Goddard College and lives with the painter Kevin Wolff in Northampton, Massachusetts.

TERRY GALLOWAY is a deaf writer, performer, and Texan who lives in the part of Florida that is not Miami Beach. In the early eighties she began presenting her one-woman shows at W.O.W., Limbo Lounge, P.S. 122, the Women's Project, and American Place Theater. Her shows have since been produced all over the United States, England, Canada, and Mexico.

LUCY GREALY is an award-winning poet who attended the University of Iowa Writers Workshop. She was a fellow at the Bunting Institute at Radcliffe and at the Fine Arts Work Center in Provincetown, and has had residencies at Yaddo and The MacDowell Colony. Her article "Mirrorings," on which her book *Autobiography of a Face* is based, won the 1994 National Magazine Award for essay writing in *Harper's*, and was selected for the 1994 Best American Essays. Grealy was born in Ireland, grew up in Rockland County, N.Y., and currently resides in New York City.

MARILYN HACKER is the author of eight books of poetry, including *Presentation Piece*, which was a Lamont Poetry Selection of the Academy of American Poets and received the National Book Award in 1975; *Going Back to the River*, which received a Lambda Literary Award in 1991; and *Winter Numbers*, which received the Lenore Marshall/*The Nation* Prize in 1995. "Cancer Winter" received the John Masefield Memorial Award of the Poetry Society of America and the B. F. Connors Award from *The Paris Review*. She lives in New York and Paris.

DAVID MANUEL HERNÁNDEZ grew up in Whittier, California. He formerly worked at a national Latino nonprofit organization in the San Francisco Bay Area and is currently a graduate student in American Studies at the University of New Mexico. His work has appeared in *Liberty Hill Poetry Review*, *onTarget*, and *Revista Parallax*.

JOHN HOCKENBERRY is a two-time Peabody Award winner who spent more than a decade with National Public Radio as a general assignment reporter, Middle East correspondent, and program host. He has received an Emmy for the ABC news magazine show *Day One*, for which he is a correspondent. His memoir, *Moving Violations: War Zones, Wheelchairs, and Declarations of Independence*, was nominated for a National Book Critics Circle Award.

LEONARD KRIEGEL is the author of six books, including *Falling into life*, *On Men and Manhood*, and *Quitting Time*. His work has appeared in *The New York Times Magazine*, *The Nation*, and *American Scholar*. His essay

"Falling into life" was chosen for Best American Essays of 1989. He is professor of literature at City College of New York.

STEPHEN KUUSISTO is a graduate of the University of Iowa Writers Workshop. His poems and translations have appeared in numerous journals, including *Antioch Review*, *Partisan Review*, *Poetry*, *Poetry East*, and *Seneca Review*. His memoir, *The Planet of the Blind*, is forthcoming from The Dial Press. He is Director of Alumni Relations and Volunteer Services at Guiding Eyes for the Blind, one of the nation's premier guide dog training schools, in Yorktown Heights, New York.

RAYMOND LUCZAK lost much of his hearing due to double pneumonia at seven months. After graduating from Gallaudet University in Washington, D.C., he moved to New York. His essay "Notes of a Deaf Gay Writer" was featured in *Christopher Street*. A playwright, he has edited *Eyes of Desire: A Deaf Gay and Lesbian Reader* (Alyson Publications, 1993) and has written *St. Michael's Fall* (Deaf Life Press, 1995). Stories from his forthcoming novel, *Loud Hands*, have appeared in various anthologies, including this one.

NANCY MAIRS is the author of *Ordinary Time* and *Carnal Acts*, both named New York Times Notable Books of the Year. She has taught writing and English at the University of Arizona, and her many reviews have appeared in the *New York Times*, *Los Angeles Times*, *San Francisco Chronicle*, and *Chicago Tribune*. Her other books include *Remembering the Bone House*, *Voice Lessons: On Becoming a (Woman) Writer* (Beacon, 1994), and *Waist High in the World* (Beacon, 1996).

LYNN MANNING adapted the Cornerstone Theater's Watts-based production of Brecht's *Caucasian Chalk Circle*. A former member of the writing group Blacksmyths, he is currently a participant in the Mark Taper Forum's mentor program. He received a 1995–96 Playwright Fellowship from the California Arts Council, a 1994 Brody Arts Fellowship, and a 1993 Dramalogue award for *On the Blink*. A former Blind Heavyweight Judo Champion of the World, in 1992 he won a silver medal representing the United States at the Para-Olympic games in Barcelona.

VED MEHTA has been on the staff of *The New Yorker* since 1961. He is the author of nineteen books to date and is at work on a memoir about his years at *The New Yorker*.

DAVID MIX lives and works year-round in northern Michigan.

EMMA MORGAN is the author of two collections of poetry: *Gooseflesh* (Clothespin Fever Press, 1993) and *A Stillness Built of Motion: Living with Tourette's* (Hummingwoman Press, 1995). She lives and writes in Northampton, Massachusetts.

KATINKA NEUHOF received an MFA in Fiction Writing from Columbia University. She recently was invited to participate in the Other Voices Seminar at the Mark Taper Forum. She works with adults with developmental disabilities and continues to write plays. She lives in New York City.

EDWARD NOBLES was born in Arlington, Massachusetts, in 1954. Due to an early childhood illness, he lost total hearing in his left ear. As the vestibular nerve was also damaged, he periodically suffers from extreme vertigo. His poetry has appeared in numerous magazines, including *Boulevard, Denver Quarterly, Paris Review, VOLT,* and *Witness. Through One Tear* will be published by Persea Press in 1997.

SUSAN NUSSBAUM is the author of five plays, all of which have been produced in her native Chicago and around the country. Her first play, *Staring Back,* produced at Chicago's Second City, won a Jefferson Award for playwrighting. She is an ensemble member of the Remains Theatre, where she first performed *Mishuganismo.* She has worked as an actor in many Chicago theaters, and directs and teaches, as well. A longtime disability rights activist, she has traveled to Nicaragua and Cuba to build ties with disabled people in both countries.

MARK O'BRIEN was born in Boston in 1949. In 1955, he became paralyzed by polio. He graduated from the University of California, Berkeley, in 1982. His writing has appeared in *Whole Earth Review, The Fessenden Review, The Sun, Margin, Saint Andrew's Review,* and *Tight.* His chapbook, *Breathing,* was published in 1990. *Breathing Lessons: The Life and Work of Mark O'Brien,* a film about him and his work, won the 1997 Academy Award for Best Short Documentary. He lives in Berkeley, California.

ADRIENNE RICH has published more than fifteen volumes of poetry and four prose works. Her most recent books are *What Is Found There: Notebooks on Poetry and Politics* (1993) and *Dark Fields of the Republic: Poems 1991–1995.* Among the many honors paid her during her distinguished career is a MacArthur Fellowship in 1994. Since 1984 she has lived in California.

MARGARET ROBISON's books are *The Naked Bear* (Lynx House Press/ Panache Books, 1977) and *Red Creek* (Amherst Writers and Artists, 1992). She has published in anthologies and journals including *Sojourner*, *The Disability Rag*, and *Yankee Magazine*. Since partial recovery from a stroke, she has led creative writing workshops for women with disabilities.

BARBARA ROSENBLUM, a creative sociologist, taught at Stanford University and Vermont College, and was widely published during her life in anthologies, journals, and magazines ranging from the *American Journal of Sociology* to the *San Francisco Chronicle* to *Sinister Wisdom*. Her book *Photographers at Work* (Holmes and Meier, 1978) was an early entry in the emerging field of the sociology of aesthetics. *Cancer in Two Voices*, which she wrote with Sandra Butler, was published by Spinsters Ink. She died of breast cancer at age forty-four.

TOM SAVAGE has published six books. His latest, *Political Conditions/ Physical States*, was published by United Artists Books in 1993. In 1990, Coffee House Press published *Processed Words*. His work has been anthologized in *Out of This World* (Crown, 1991) and *Nice to See You* (Coffee House Press, 1991). His work has appeared in *The World*, *Oblek*, *New American Writing*, *Talisman*, and *Tyuonyi*.

NANCY SCOTT has had poems and articles appear in *Byline*, *Cat Magazine*, *Dialogue Magazine*, *The Disability Rag*, *Feelings*, *Hikane*, *Lifeprints*, *The Lucid Stone*, *Newsreel*, and *Slate & Style*, and in the anthologies *The Ragged Edge*, *Sisters*, and *Voice of the Diabetic*. Her disability is blindness.

JEAN STEWART is the author of the novel *The Body's Memory* (St. Martin's Press, 1989). Her poems and essays appear in *With Wings: An Anthology of Literature by and about Women with Disabilities* (Feminist Press, 1987), *Beyond Crisis: Confronting Health Care in the United States* (Penguin, 1994), and other collections. She is nationally recognized for her pioneering work with disabled prisoners. She lives in Richmond, California.

JOAN TOLLIFSON is the author of *Bare Bones Meditation: Waking Up from the Story of My Life* (Bell Tower, 1996). She lives in Oakland, California.

Credits

Acknowledgments

〜◎ ◎〜

Editing *Staring Back* could not have been done without the assistance and support of many individuals and organizations. Thanks to Joan Larkin and Lesléa Newman for anthologizing advice; to Kim Addonizio, Andre Dubus, Jocelyn Lieu, Lorenzo Wilson Milam, and Chuck Wachtel for leading me to writers whose work I did not yet know; to Paula Elliott at Forbes Library in Northampton for her assistance in tracking down books I couldn't locate on my own; to David Pfieffer for research information that assisted me with my initial proposal; to Raymond Luczak for his understanding of deaf culture; to Paul K. Longmore in the History Department of San Francisco State University for his astute disability studies perspective; to Other Voices at the Mark Taper Forum in Los Angeles, whose *A Contemporary Chautauqua: Performance and Disability* gave me the initial idea for the book; to Fred Morris of Jed Mattes, Inc., and Alex Swenson and Alexandra Babanskyj at Dutton for answering my countless phone calls and questions, and for providing the information and support I needed; to Jed Mattes for his instant support for this project and guidance along the way; to Carole DeSanti, one of the best editors around, for her insight, trust, and willingness to forge into uncharted territory; to Ann-Ellen Lesser at the Millay Colony for the Arts, who is building without barriers so we can have a place to write; to the Blue Mountain Center, the Djerassi Foundation Resident Artist Program, The MacDowell Colony, the Ragdale Foundation, the Virginia Center for the Creative Arts, and Yaddo for residencies during which much work editing this anthology took place.

To Kevin Wolff for his patience, love, understanding, and willingness to read and reread much of the work I considered.

To Victoria Ann-Lewis, director of Other Voices, writer, actress, activist, and friend, for her forethought, insight, and inspiration—and for giving a stage to the voices of disabled writers before anyone else. To Elizabeth Clare, who was the first to make me realize I was a teacher. To Gene Chelberg, fellow traveler and disability rights leader, for being more than a sounding board. To Susan Nussbaum for her humor, friendship, and perspective, as well as for the anthology's title, which is borrowed from one of her plays. To Katinka Neuhof for her inimitable buoyancy and spirit. And to Anne Finger, writer and friend, whose artistic and political wisdom served as support and counterpoint every step of the way.

DUTTON **PLUME**

ON FRIENDS AND FAMILIES

☐ **BETWEEN MOTHERS AND SONS** *The Making of Vital and Loving Men* **by Evelyn S. Bassoff.** With great clarity and sensitivity, this groundbreaking book from an acclaimed psychologist explains how mothers can remain nurturing presences in their sons' lives. It offers an invaluable perspective on what mothers can do to insure that their sons become vital, loving men. "An extraordinary, poignant book."—*Washington Post Book World* (274621—$12.95)

☐ **ORIGINAL KIN** *The Search for Connection Among Adult Sisters and Brothers* **by Marian Sandmaier.** Drawing on the latest research and compelling interviews with eighty men and women, the author explores the complex array of influences that create and maintain adult sibling relationships, particularly the profound and hidden influence of gender. "A moving and pragmatic guide to healing a crucial set of relationships."—*Philadelphia City Paper* (273773—$11.95)

☐ **GIRLFRIEND TO GIRLFRIEND** *Everyday Wisdom and Affirmations from the Sister Circle* **by Julia A. Boyd.** An experienced therapist and her supportive group of sisters are role models for *real* women who face real challenges every day. Together, they remind us to laugh, to love and care for ourselves as much as we do for others, and to celebrate who we are every day. (93958X—$15.95)

☐ **IN THE COMPANY OF MY SISTERS** *Black Women and Self-Esteem* **by Julia Boyd.** Sassy, intimate, and full of wisdom and practical insights, this book takes a hard and honest look at the realities and issues of Black women's lives. Drawing from the wealth of experience of the Black women's support group, her "sister circle" that meets monthly to "shoot the breeze . . . and talk about everything from the political to the personal," Julia Boyd presents a new vision for healing, self-renewal, and growth. (937080—$19.95)

☐ **THE LOSS THAT IS FOREVER** *The Lifelong Impact of the Early Death of a Mother or Father* **by Maxine Harris, Ph.D.** For anyone who has survived the early loss of a parent, as well as for those with a spouse, friend, or lover who has lost a parent in childhood, this powerful book explores all aspects of this life-defining event and shows how the human spirit can survive and even master the ultimate loss. (938699—$23.95)

Prices slightly higher in Canada.
